BEST
EUROPEAN
FICTION
2014

Praise for
BEST EUROPEAN FICTION

"The collection's diverse range of styles includes more experimental works than a typical American anthology might . . . [Mr. Hemon's] only criteria were to include the best works from as many countries as possible."—*Wall Street Journal*

"This is a precious opportunity to understand more deeply the obsessions, hopes and fears of each nation's literary psyche—a sort of international show-and-tell of the soul."—*The Guardian*

"Readers for whom the expression 'foreign literature' means the work of Canada's Alice Munro stand to have their eyes opened wide and their reading exposure exploded as they encounter works from places such as Croatia, Bulgaria, and Macedonia (and, yes, from more familiar terrain, such as Spain, the UK, and Russia)." —*Booklist* Starred Review

"We can be thankful to have so many talented new voices to discover."—*Library Journal*

"What the reader takes from them are not only the usual pleasures of fiction—the twists and turns of plot, chance to inhabit other lives, other ways of being—but new ways of thinking about how to tell a story."
—Christopher Merrill, PRI'S "The World" Holiday Pick

"The English-language reading world, 'wherever it may be,' is grateful."—*The Believer*

"The best of the stories here are finely attuned to the coincidence of lightness and pathos in things, and there is not one that is not worth reading."—*Times Literary Supplement*

"The book tilts toward unconventional storytelling techniques. And while we've heard complaints about this before—why only translate the most difficult work coming out of Europe?—it makes sense here. The book isn't testing the boundaries, it's opening them up."—*Time Out Chicago*

BEST EUROPEAN FICTION 2014

Preface by
DRAGO JANČAR

DALKEY ARCHIVE PRESS
CHAMPAIGN / LONDON / DUBLIN

ISBN 978-1-56478-898-6
ISSN 2152-6672

www.dalkeyarchive.com

Funded in part by the Illinois Arts Council, a state agency

Please see Acknowledgments on page 313 for additional
information on the support received for this volume

Printed on permanent/durable acid-free paper
and bound in the United States of America

Cover: design by Gail Doobinin
composition by Mikhail Iliatov

Contents

Preface

In recent years, a number of European institutions and journal editors have asked if I would write about whether such a thing as European literature exists. Ever since East and West shook hands across the debris of the Berlin Wall and began living together politically and economically—and particularly since the last tragic experience of Europe's twentieth century, the wars in the former Yugoslavia—some people apparently have assumed that the all-encompassing European idea of international coexistence and maximum tolerance must of necessity also lead to an all-encompassing European literary aesthetic. I believe that Europe, just as the rest of the world, needs these values in order to live and survive, but should it be the job of literature to build and promote them? I'm doubtful, because that would mean we view literature as a pseudo-religion. And what sort of aesthetic would that have? Would it need to combine—as I read somewhere—the "profundity" of German, the "artistry" of French, the "humor" of English, and the "suffering" of Russian literature and of the so-called Russian soul? I'd say a few ingredients are missing from this mess of clichés—for instance, the Švejkism of Czech and the intense longing of Slovene literature. And what would the Poles, Irish, Serbs, Estonians, or Catalunyans have to add to this literary melting pot? All in all, not a good sign for attempts to define European literature in questionnaire format, most of which seem to be stuck at the superficial level of "What ten books would you want to have with you on a desert island?"

The question becomes less amusing if we look around and consider the environment that literature actually inhabits today. A few snide jokes at the expense of clichés aren't going to make what is so obviously taking place in every European literary market go away; to wit, the erosion of well-defined aesthetic criteria and a flood of literary commercialization that demands and rewards superficiality, easy reading, and bestsellerdom. Even in the eyes of a growing number of publishers' manuscript readers, these qualities have apparently replaced the elitism, challenge, and tedium of Great and Profound literature. It's apparent that not only publishers, but even authors and critics have come to equate quality with commercial success, just as culture has given way to the "culture industry." The confusion is considerable, especially in the eastern reaches of the European literary continent, where the collapse of dictatorships was accompanied by a collapse of that tension between literature and society that paradoxically kept writers at the center of readers' attention. These countries witnessed a sudden flood of mediocrity engineered by the publishing market. Hugely disparate ideas about literature and its functions inhabit this part of Europe, jostling and undermining each other—from former literary and cultural eschatologies that still eke out a living, to postmodernist scholasticism, to the kind of writing that mistakes the aesthetics of screenwriting and genre for literature and would like nothing more than to sate the publishing industry's hunger for enormous and immediate success. To the regret of most of these authors, who have developed a characteristic way of poking fun at Great and Profound literature, their dreams of bestsellerdom have for the most part had only a limited trajectory. While it's true that amid the countless new literary soap operas that keep getting produced, and more recently the countless new detective stories with a human face, plumbing the depths of the seven deadly sins and weaving countless new criminal, political, and even historical plots for us, occasionally some refreshingly distinctive heroes and original stories do shine through, publishers and even quite a few talented writers have interpreted their successes in this mode as proof of some imperative to go on following the trend. Of course, the publishers, for their part, have long since figured out what's at stake and what has to be sacrificed in order to win it: domestic or foreign literature (in translation or otherwise) that requires exertion on the part of the reader, literature featuring any kind of linguistic experimentation or thematic "depth"—in a word, the "tedium" that only a hopelessly small minority of bookworms can afford as a luxury.

In Eastern Europe, there is no shortage of disappointment in this brave new world. Many writers who once thought that democracy and the new, relaxed atmosphere it lent society would validate the deep longing for freedom that was present in their works and that once brought them renown, now look upon the general apathy of their societies in despair. Others, who were convinced that their literature spoke from out of the depths of the nation's spirit and expressed an authentic *genius loci*, look at the literary kitsch everywhere around them in disgust. And still other writers, who joined in on the easy minting of generic entertainment, which in their case was supposedly *still* literature despite all, are discovering to their amazement that democracy is in fact a very majoritarian affair, well-suited to mediocrity, and always happy to welcome in even more superficiality, even more facile tricks than their *still literature* could ever accommodate. And with it, even bigger sales figures.

The problem is that art isn't democratic, much less capitalistic. In the century of democracy's great rise, Witold Gombrowicz understood this early on and wrote that art loves grandeur, hierarchies, feudalism, and absolutism, while democracy wants equality, tolerance, openness, and fraternity.

Back in 1984, when I visited America for the first time, on my very first day I noticed to my surprise that, try as I might, I wasn't going to find a section labeled *Culture* in any of the newspapers. Exhibits, plays, even literary readings were all listed under *Entertainment*. I actually found it amusing that as sacred a European word as "Culture"was practically nowhere to be found, and that the next most sacred European word "Literature" only appeared in the supplements of a very few, major newspapers, and that even there its meaning was broadened to admit reviews of books from disparate disciplines—psychology and history, for instance. This amusing misunderstanding continued in my course on creative writing, where to my misfortune I had to teach students who were curious and hungry for literature and who already knew perfectly well how they would have to write their first sentences—those fateful first sentences that are supposed to grab the reader's attention—when they became writers. My students' questions kept coming back to one of the few European authors who was being read in America at the time, Milan Kundera. Reading Kundera is *entertaining*, but why does the author make fun of optimism? The trigger event in Kundera's novel *The Joke* is a sentence that the protagonist writes on a picture postcard: "Optimism is the opiate of the people!" What's wrong with optimism? I didn't want to start lecturing about Marx in a creative writing class, so I tried to explain that in Central Europe literature often contains a kind of anxious laughter that's neither funny nor entertaining, but rather the expression of a sense of humor that's by turns ironic, sarcastic, or just plain hard to figure out, which writers from Kafka on have recorded in rather darkly comedic tones, because they know that great optimistic ideas often culminate in the crowning idea of a concentration camp filled with political minorities and sometimes entire nations. We weren't getting through to each other. I see your point, one student said, but optimism is part of the spirit of individualism itself, it's at the heart of American democracy. I see *your* point, I said, but it's also at the heart of the collective spirit of Soviet communism, including its literature, in which writers were referred to as "engineers of human souls" and they all knew that their job was to write interesting, entertaining books to make people optimistic. Although our conversation was polite, and it was all very *entertaining*, the gulf in understanding between us remained unbridged.

Aleksandar Hemon will appreciate that little story.

But even in Europe, despite the economic crisis—which is leading many people to wonder anxiously, what's next? will life tomorrow be as good as today?—a spirit of optimism still prevails. Why, with the exception of a few eccentric Euroskeptics and frightened nationalists, do all of us cling so tightly to the idea of a united Europe? Often because we want to escape our own provincialism, the suffocating national self-satisfaction and the interpersonal nastiness that this sort of environment generates. And escape our own history, as well. In twentieth-century Slovenia, a person could have spent his whole life in some mountain village and still have seen the uniforms of numerous armies, dealt with tax collectors and policemen from various countries, and listened to religious, nationalist, or social evangelists who kept promising him the best of all possible worlds—and each time, he would have been disappointed. Instances of courage and nobility aside, in the process of loading themselves down with history during that century, so many Europeans, and especially those from the so-called East, also took on burdens of brutality and, in a variety of countries and systems, burdens of foul deeds great and small. This is why for the majority of people the European idea is so redemptive and new, and possibly their last great hope. But literature carries within it the memory and experience of Europe's insane century as it was lived by fragile, frightened, and vulnerable human beings, who often had to salvage their dignity and sanity not just with the balm of melancholy, but also with laughter, skepticism, irony, and black humor. I suspect that the stories in this and the previous *Best European Fiction* anthologies offer individual, unique human experiences that are more European than tirades about European solidarity, tolerance, and cooperation. In Mr. Hemon's past selections, for example, I can see distant reflections of his life and writing, his understanding of Europe and America, the convulsions of his complex Bosnian microcosm and the ease of the so-called wider world, but above all the open landscapes of the literary imagination.

Perhaps it's presumptuous to say that this anthology and the poetics of its authors are giving birth to something that in the future might, without any clichés or qualifications, be referred to as "European literature." Not just because European literature is quite simply everything that's written in Europe's various languages and out of its various traditions and experiences, both historical and personal. No, because an ongoing awareness of the individual aesthetics emerging in various languages leads to an interpenetration and merging of their content and the linguistic and stylistic solutions they bring to bear. Perhaps it's odd for this sort of understanding of European literature to emerge thanks to translations into English, and this at a time when none of us has any intention of abandoning the beauty and linguistic power of our individual European languages. Just as Latin was the language of European intellectuals in the Middle Ages, so indisputably is English the European *lingua franca* today. Younger authors, especially, use it not only to communicate with each other, but thanks to the creative force and assistance of translators, our literary brethren, they read each other in it. This is not to say that we're moving in the direction of linguistic unity, and much less that we're giving up creating in our own languages: phenomena like Beckett, Conrad, Makine—and

Hemon—who have taught themselves to write in a second language, are rare. It does mean, however, that precisely with the help of these anthologies we can at least provide some information to each other, as well as to readers—if only in the form of short stories, whether fragments, sketches, impressions, or even the hints of novels—about the diversity of our authorial quests and methods. In fact, these anthologies provide us with a surprising view into Europe's enormous writing workshop. In them we experience human distress and misunderstandings as we travel through the labyrinths of the world of the present and the past and the mazes of the human spirit and mind. This is an awareness of writing that is emerging *now*, in Europe's capitals and its provincial backwaters, of writing that is in the process of being shaped by its authors. These are no national literary canons that we're getting to know fifty years after the fact (if at all). This is, instead, the live ferment of creative diversity. The awareness of literature in Europe today that these anthologies offer has not been dictated by publishers' marketing departments, but by a selection made, to the best of their abilities, by people who have devoted their lives to as beautiful and useless a thing, as Oscar Wilde might have said, as art. A continually new world emerges with the stories that come to us out of this big creative workshop, a world that isn't necessarily the author's homeland or region or city or history, but is most assuredly a personal experience, individual and unique, connected to a specific milieu. In previous editions of *Best European Fiction*, as in this one, one can observe the authors, with few exceptions, moving away from the so-called great themes and immersing themselves in decidedly personal and, at first glance, minute literary explorations. It's obvious that these stories shy away from the more and more powerful unification of European and global space that new communications technologies are facilitating at tremendous speed, and instead seek creative meaning in markedly personal worlds, in tiny interpersonal plots or simply—bewilderment. The world is present in the details. The more unified it is in its Europeanizing and globalizing tendencies, the more individually focused, atomized, and fragmented it is in this literature. While the absence of so-called great themes may not necessarily align with my own perception of literary art, these stories' intensity, the tension between their forms and subjects, give them, if we read them carefully, the power of a significant existential response to the individual's place in the world today.

In contrast to the superficial storytelling that the publishing industry would like to force on us, in this and previous *Best European Fiction* anthologies, we encounter a taut authorial relationship to the world and to language. Mathematicians use the term "congruence," which in this instance would refer to an unshakable harmony of content and language. This kind of harmony grows out of the inner tension of a literary organism, not out of the mass production of detective stories or screenplays. And although these are small, though never marginal stories and fragments, they have the confidence of Gombrowicz's textual absolutism. These are stories that grow out of humanity's restlessness, this is literature that expresses humanity's restlessness, but also the restlessness of this era of European history and the consequences of its past, which have precipitated out into our unseen experiences. The tension in all writing is also the tension springing from the dissatisfaction that we all feel in recognizing the social or historical sediment underlying our experiences, or even just the contours and rhythm of one human life. It's precisely that restlessness which creates the taut congruence of plot and language whose fascinating and awkward merits necessarily surpass the limits of "mere" entertainment and mechanical storytelling. Literature as an organism with its own internal dynamics, literature that serves nothing else, yet is by itself, and in and of itself, something more.

But, a word of caution. We must be very careful whenever we say that we want something more of literature, more than entertainment, more than barely dressed plots, more than glorified film treatments—we have to be very careful, and attentive too. Because wherever there's *something more*, there's also the "search for meaning," there are also those spiritual domains that the "hollow man of today" is supposedly seeking out: the lowest possible form of literary entertainment, whose flaccid phrases and transcendent surrogates are gulped down by readers hungry for meaning and which the hyper-productive publishing industry loves to shovel down their throats like so much new-age fast food. Because in "today's materialistic world," our hollowed-out, hungry souls want more and more and always more of that spiritual stuff in particular, which, as distinct from the modest *policier*, barely has anything to do with literature at all.

Literature, at least as I see it, is a modest thing. It feels at home on the margins of history and of today's grand visions of the fate of Europe and the world—whether it's dealing with the so-called great historical and social themes or just with bits of a single human life. It's at home wherever the fragile, vulnerable, finite human being is, enmeshed in misunderstandings with others, with the world, and with itself. And through this prism of multiple but individual human lives, it tells of human uncertainty, fear and courage, nobility and betrayal, joy and sorrow. Or else, certainly, it can be a lot more full of itself, offering no answers, just asking questions. Indeed, sometimes it asks in an innocent voice: Just where are the margins, anyway, and where is the center?

DRAGO JANČAR

BEST
EUROPEAN
FICTION
2014

VLADIMIR KOZLOV

Politics

I come out of the dorm in black jeans, a leather jacket, and a white, red, and white-striped scarf around my neck. Today is the protest against Lukashenko.* I'm going alone—my roommates won't be showing up. They're just lying on their beds and spitting at the ceiling because they don't have any money for vodka. Fuckers.

In the street, I pass a bunch of dull, beat-to-shit people. They don't have any interest in politics or anything else. All they want to do is buy some sausage, stuff their faces, and then sit all night in front of the television, watching some asinine series or other. Not that I hold it against them, though.

The group is gathering in Yakub Kolas Square. From a distance I can see the crowd and a white, red, and white-striped

---

Translator's Note: Anti-Lukashenko protest rallies like the one in this story were frequent in Belarus between 1995 and 1998, but violent arrests and university expulsions effectively suppressed the popularity of the opposition movement. Still president of Belarus, Lukashenko is often referred to in the West as "Europe's last dictator." He is notorious for rigging elections and suppressing opposition with brutal force and political maneuvering. However, he enjoys immense popularity with a less educated portion of the Belarusian population, who believe he brought "stability" to the country. This story was inspired by opposition rallies in Minsk in the late nineties that Kozlov covered as the editor of Belarus's only English-language newspaper. He told me that, as independent media, he had to be careful to avoid arrest at the rallies, since any non-state media was considered part of the opposition. While the story is set in the mid-nineties, there was a surge in similar protest activity in the wake of the December 2010 presidential election, in which Lukashenko was reelected. However, the authorities' brutal crackdown on the protesters once again suppressed the scale of the street protests.

3

flag. I recognize some guys from the International Relations department at the university, say hello. We stand around, smoke, wait, then move up with the other people. Somebody takes charge in front and we move forward again. We walk along the pavement to the opera house—that's the designated area where we're allowed to stage a protest. The main thoroughfare is out— the riot police are lined up along the pavement, waiting, so they can beat back anybody from our group. But the real danger, God forbid, is that they might drag one of us off the street and into a courtyard for some real police brutality.

So there are some guys from other departments in the group, but I don't see anybody from mine. We yell in Belarusian, "Disgrace!" "Lukashenko Belongs Behind Bars!" and "Long Live Belarus!" Passersby glare at us—we're keeping them from going about their petty business, they have to press themselves against the walls of the apartment buildings to let us pass.

Attendance is weak at the demonstration—a thousand at most. There are still some people coming straight over to join our group, but not very many. A group this size doesn't generate much of a buzz. If we could get ten or fifteen thousand together, neither the riot police nor the regular cops could do a thing about it. Then we could stage a rally at the presidential administration building itself.

We walk up to the opera house. There are hundreds of us with flags and "Long Live Belarus" signs, but there are even more cops and riot police. Where did they all come from? They never do anything for all the businesses that have to pay protection money to the mafia, but when it comes time to stifle the opposition, here they all are. And there are even more riot police on a bus over there. Sitting, waiting, playing cards, looking out the windows at us.

The protest starts. A journalist is running along beside us— she was at our last protest, and I've seen her a couple times on

TV screaming about democracy and free speech. She's about thirty years old, sharply dressed.

Two cops, a sergeant and an officer, are watching the journalist. The sergeant says in Russian:

"Look, it's that one again. Fucking whore. How she gets any work done between sucking cocks I'll never know. Every time she just waits around for her chance to fuck with us. That bitch thinks we won't touch her since she writes for some fucking rag. One time we pulled her on the bus, smacked her around. But then she made such a stink—free speech this, free press that, blah blah blah. You know, she actually almost got us in trouble that time!"

"Is she married?"

"How could she be married? She's divorced. There's not a man alive who could live with that kind of a bitch."

"You don't say."

The journalist comes up to me.

"Good day. Svetlana Ryabova, *Minsk Courier*. May I ask you a few questions?"

"Sure, of course."

She takes a dictaphone out of her bag, sticks it under my nose, presses the button.

"Introduce yourself first. What is your name, where do you study or work?"

"Antonovich, Sergei. I'm in my third year at Belarus State University in the psychology department."

"So tell me, why did you come to today's demonstration?"

"Well, we're here to express our dissent against the politics of the ruling regime. They're the reason our country is so impoverished and our economy is in decline. Also the reason our state officials have managed to line their pockets so nicely."

"In your opinion, how effective can a street demonstration like this be in fighting the regime?"

"Not very effective, because not many people come. If more would come, then the authorities would be afraid of us and would have to do something about it. But when it's like this, they can send cops and riot police rather than listening to what we have to say."

"And what do you think about the state of political activism in today's youth, in students? How would you describe it?"

"Well, people aren't much interested in politics right now. Some quick cash and a good time, that's all that's on the mind of the majority of today's youth. As far as politics is concerned, it's like they just don't, well, don't give a damn."

"So they don't see a connection between our country's political situation and their quality of life?"

"They probably don't. I don't know."

"Okay, thanks." She turns off the dictaphone and leaves. Everything I said was right, sort of. It'll all be okay if she edits me a bit in the article. But what if the dean comes across the piece? A year ago they expelled three guys from International Relations because of a protest, so now they're studying in Prague. They got invited over there for free. Lucky bastards. Some guys from their department told me they were still in touch with them—they're still there, the guys said, and they get a stipend. It's even enough for beer.

The protest ends. The leaders of the political opposition make their way out to one side of the crowd and sit in their cars so they can speed off in case anything dangerous starts up. A bunch of the demonstrators start to head off too, except the very active ones, including us, the students. Somebody suggests we walk down the street to Independence Square, and we start walking. Some of us are kind of freaked out—we're not allowed to walk on the street, which means that now we're giving the cops the right to detain everybody. Or if they don't detain us right away, they'll wait, and then, when we disperse, they'll pick us up one by one. But, fuck it. We keep walking anyway.

There are about two hundred of us left. We hold hands so the cops can't grab any one person, and then walk down the street.

Cops are walking behind us and on both sides of us, but they're quiet and they haven't laid a finger on anyone yet. This means they're still waiting for orders. Not far from us are that same sergeant and officer. Ryabova appears from somewhere, catches up to the sergeant.

"Good day. Svetlana Ryabova, *Minsk Courier*. May I ask you a few questions?"

"Get out of here. I don't talk to people like you."

"Why should I get out of here? Why can't you talk to me? What does that even mean, 'people like me'? Let me guess: first of all, women, second of all, journalists. Am I right? You, sir, are a complete jackass!"

A few people in our group stop to see what will happen. Me too. We move up closer. Some others in our group come to a halt, turn their heads.

"You better get out of here right now, or else we'll take you back to the bus—then you'll find out what happens when you fuck with us."

"You know what you are?" asks the journalist. "You're a freak of nature. A total scumbag. And you know what? A loser like you can never get laid. Not with an actual woman, anyway."

The sergeant raises his fist. I run up and kick him in the balls. He doubles over, and the rest of the cops pile onto us. We've got nothing to defend ourselves with—no sticks, not even anything we can dismantle, like a fence or some concrete. We dash into a nearby courtyard. Riot police with clubs are already charging out of their bus—at last it's their hour. They've just been sitting there, bored, and now they can wave their clubs around and break a few ribs.

On the run I see two cops grabbing Ryabova and dragging her

to the bus. She flails her arms and legs, trying to hit somebody. Tough luck. But it won't be a big deal for her—they'll keep her for half an hour and then let her go. But if they corner *me*, it'll mean my ass: They'll club me in the gut and give me five days for "participation in an unsanctioned protest" and "defying authority." I run through an archway. A courtyard with cars, garages. Behind me are a few more from our group, and behind them the riot police. I hide behind a garage. I'm all alone and helpless in here, and I feel like I'm going to shit myself from fear. In fact, there are already two piles of dried up shit on the ground behind the garage. I pick a place where I won't step in them and pull down my pants. It would, of course, be hilarious if the riot police took a look behind the garage and caught me in such a state. I hear a noise, some screams, from around the wall. Somebody's getting nailed. Steam rises up from my pile of shit. I take a piece of paper out of my pocket. It says, "We belong in Europe's class, Lukashenko can kiss my ass!" I got it from Sakovich, who's a fifth-year. We'd scattered them all around in the auditorium. Good thing I have about ten sheets left. I wipe my ass with the piece of paper, pull up my pants, and quietly peek out from behind the garage. Two riot police are taking down a bald guy in glasses with a leather bag on his shoulder, clubbing him in the gut. The guy screams bloody murder. The bag slides slowly off his shoulder and onto the ground. The riot police drag the man away.

There's nobody else in the courtyard. I wait around for about five more minutes and then come out from behind the garage. It's getting dark. I go over to the bag, look down. There are two bottles of vodka in there. That's all. No documents or papers, nothing. Maybe I should gather them up and take them to the guys in my dorm.

I guess this means we won! Lukashenko can kiss my ass!

TRANSLATED FROM RUSSIAN BY ANDREA GREGOVICH

[BELGIUM: FRENCH]

THIERRY HORGUELIN

The Man in the Yellow Parka

Only after a few episodes did I notice him. He was trying to force the door to a rundown house at the corner of a derelict street. He was too far away to pick out his features, but his yellow parka made a blot on the background. In the foreground, Marion and Detective Burns were discussing their current case, without paying him the slightest mind. Vapor escaped their mouths. Winters are cold in Cleveland.

I forget the plots of movies quickly, but I have a good memory for visual details. Don't ask me to summarize *Intimidation* or *Out of the Night*. But I do know that in the former there's a bridging shot in which Clive Owen passes a pretty brunette with short hair who pauses for a moment in the background to scratch her shoulder, a charmingly offhand gesture (I'd bet my shirt the director picked that take for the kernel of truth in it), and that in *Out of the Night*, on the wall of the seedy diner where the fugitive criminal couple hides out at dawn, there's a Hopperesque chromo that seems to echo the lovers' loneliness. To cut to the chase, I was sure I'd seen the man in the parka in an earlier episode of *Simple Cops*.

I'd come across the series by accident during one of my nights of insomnia. My prescriptions at the time left me muddled all day and then overstimulated till the wee hours. Then, too tired to read but too wound up to sleep, I'd collapse in front of the small screen and let myself drift into its Bermuda Triangle, the watery grave of shipwrecked shows that have been exiled to the hours after midnight. Nodding off before a nature documentary, I'd doze my way through an Australian soap from the '80s only to wake up in the middle of the nth rerun of *Derrick* or *Cash in the Attic*. This image salad would extend into drafts of dreams, and I'd wind up asleep on the sofa, surfacing only at dawn with heavy head and aching back, while onscreen a dapper weatherwoman would be announcing a day of rain ahead with a radiant smile.

So, one night, the voice of Detective Burns roused me from half-slumber. He was clearly not happy. I opened one eye, my radar on alert. Cops. A local precinct. We were in the chief's glass-walled office. The blinds were drawn against prying eyes. It was one of those classic scenes where the experienced "I know the streets" detective gets chewed out by his "rules are rules" superior. With a parting shot, the detective opens the door and makes to leave. Ten to one the chief will call him back for a final retort. "Burns?" Bingo. Burns—that's his name—turns and raises an eyebrow. The chief softens up and hints he'll cover for him, but tells Burns to be careful. Fade to black. Next comes a sequence set in the city where two officers, alerted by the neighbors, find the body of an old lady in her easy chair, already dead for a few days. Wide-awake now, I followed the episode with some interest. It wasn't that bad. Totally watchable, even. A nice change of pace.

A TV weekly I bought the day after informed me of the title of this particular program, and I was surprised to find myself eagerly awaiting the next episode—Tuesday at 2:30 a.m.—as if the burly Burns and his colleagues were beckoning me from the other side of the screen. I was lonely and depressed; it had gotten to the point where I would kill time checking off the name of every film I'd ever seen in my copy of *Maltin's Movie Guide*. I was looking for a diversion, a buoy to cling to, anything at all. So *Simple Cops* seemed to fit the bill nicely.

Off the top of my head, I'd have said the series was from the beginning of the '80s. It was a sort of poor man's *Hill Street Blues* or *NYPD Blue*, a respectable if standard police serial, neither brilliant nor embarrassing. I suspected its creators of having launched it to capitalize on the success of Steven Bochco's work, which had just renovated the genre from top to bottom. *Simple Cops* (yeesh, what a terrible title) purported to be a chronicle of everyday life at a particular precinct. The cast consisted of a dozen policemen who formed a representative sampling of the so-called American melting pot. Their work was always interfering with their private lives, and their personal problems—one's alcoholism, another's marital woes—were the subject of many a subplot. Each episode took place over the course of a day and depicted two, sometimes three parallel investigations that often turned out to be related along the way. Few spectacular crimes; the series tried for realism and offered up a mosaic of prosaic urban violence, all the while highlighting police routine and internal conflicts among the precinct cops, in their hierarchy, between their team and the various attorneys that became involved. Never wildly original, the writers still demonstrated a certain savvy, albeit within the limits of some pretty worn-out dramatic situations. This soothing feeling of déjà-vu was not unpleasant in and of itself; after a few episodes, as is often the case, I wound up growing fond of the characters, or more precisely, the appealing efforts of the actors—all those dependable workhorses of TV who'd lacked the dash of charisma that launches a larger career—to make their roles believable.

The only truly original aspect of the series lay in its setting. It took place not in New York or San Francisco, nor Miami or Los Angeles, but in a town rarely featured onscreen. Cleveland, as viewers came to know it, was a strange, ghostly city, all endless thoroughfares and vast, oddly deserted plazas. The parks, the headlands, the abandoned neighborhoods, the harbor on Lake Erie, well mined by excellent location scouts, offered a wide variety of settings on which the clearly low production values conferred an almost documentary feel. At heart, the city was the series' main character. And as in many cop shows, exploring it over the course of investigations that involved every level of society was as a pretext for an x-ray of American social ills: community tensions, deindustrialization, widespread unemployment, and massive poverty—the term "The Poorest City in America" recurred in the dialogue like a leitmotif, sometimes tinged with resignation, and other times with deliberate self-deprecation, like a joke between locals on the corner.

And now there was the man in the yellow parka.

That the same extra, in the same loud jacket, had ambled through two episodes of a single series was already unusual. Was the production really that broke? But when I saw him again the next week, I really thought I was losing it. Still, there he was, sitting on a bench in the background of a public square, bringing a bottle in a brown paper bag to his lips. What did it mean?

The shot had only lasted a few seconds, just long enough to establish the setting. The POV was already tightening— in medium shot—on Detective Atkinson, deep in discreet conversation with a stoolie. Truth be told, their exchange barely held my interest, and I watched the rest of the episode distractedly, my mind on the man in the yellow parka. What could his furtive presence signify? Nothing seemed to justify it. He had no part in the action, and the main characters didn't even seem to notice him. Burns hadn't spared him a glance the week before, no more than Atkinson did now. Was he a minor character whose entrance the writers were readying on the sly, a pawn surreptitiously advanced on a narrative chessboard? Why not? Except that his appearances were so subliminal that this seemed especially unlikely. Or perhaps his presence was an in-joke among the directors, like in Chabrol's heyday, when you were sure to catch Attal and Zardi in small roles or hear a henchman humming "Fascination"? Or even—but, frankly, this seemed pretty doubtful—a constraint gratuitously imposed by a nutcase producer who loved Oulipo? Was it possible the man in the parka figured in *every* episode of *Simple Cops*?

While waiting for the next episode, I set about some basic research in my books and online. Which led to the discovery that *Simple Cops* hadn't exactly left an enduring impression in the memories of telephiles. Martin Winkler and Christophe Petit made no mention of it in their useful dictionary of TV shows. A single lukewarm review on IMDb, which criticized the series for being a drab carbon copy of *NYPD Blue*—a not completely misguided point of view. Specialized American websites listed it among a hundred other such shows with full credits and a brief blurb more or less recycled from one site to the next, with few variations. The "Anecdotes," "Trivia," or "Production Secrets" sections, where one might hope to find some mention of the man in the parka, were empty. Information was sparse all around. Still, I learned in passing that the show had only had a very brief life. It had been canceled in the middle of its second season, no doubt because of low ratings. For that same reason, it hadn't been released on DVD—or I would have rushed to order it. All the same, sifting stubbornly through the several pages of links the search engine had disgorged so undiscerningly, I finally found a more complete source of information on an Australian site, including an episode guide with short synopses. This codex would prove useful in finding my footing, since the series, relegated to nightly spackle for programming gaps on a local affiliate, was clearly being broadcast all out of order.

From that point on, I systematically recorded the episodes while continuing to watch them as they were broadcast. I'd come to enjoy my Tuesday date in the silence of the night: feeling the city asleep around me strengthened my privileged connection to Cleveland's cops. Notebook in hand, I also began watching the series with a new eye, no longer caring at all about following the cases (rather repetitive in the long run), or finding out if Burns would reconcile with his delinquent son; if Atkinson would wed the adorable Marion Sanders, whom he hit on with touching awkwardness; if Morales would beat his cancer and Resnick divorce his wife who cheated on him left and right. Instead, I attentively scrutinized the edges of each shot, keeping an eye out for the mysterious extra's next appearance. And, to my great astonishment, my wildest hypothesis was confirmed. The man in the yellow parka figured in each and every episode—at least in the dozen I saw, since I'd started midseason. He never left the background, played no role in the plot. And yet, as I fit the puzzle pieces together, a certain coherence eventually emerged from his successive appearances. They seemed to trace a parallel story, as though in dotted outline: the career of a poor guy going to seed.

- In Season 1, Episode 3 (the earliest one I caught), he was crossing the street with a halting step, casting worried looks all around.
- In S01E05, you can see him coming out of the store next door to where Sanders and Colson are investigating an armed robbery, and, almost immediately, entering the next store down.
- In S01E06, he's going through the revolving door to the courthouse while Bauer gets told off by the DA in the foreground, on the front steps.
- S01E07 was the one where I noticed him for the first time, trying to enter an abandoned house.
- In S01E09, he feeds pigeons in a park.

- In S01E10, he emerges at the end of a hallway in the precinct and makes a beeline for a locked closet door, rattling it violently (the guy seems really obsessed with doors).
- S01E12 is the one where he's boozing it up at the far end of the square where Atkinson is meeting with the stoolie.
- For the first and only time, he makes two appearances in a single episode: S01E13. First we see him panhandling on a sidewalk, while Colson and Thaddeus proceed to arrest a dealer in the foreground. A bit later on, he slips between two loose slats in a fence around a construction site.
- In S02E01, he's negotiating on a doorstep with a retiree who then slams the door in his face.
- I almost missed him in S02E02 . . . yet there he was, lying around with other homeless people in an industrial squat that Burns and Morales visit in search of a vanished witness.
- It's in S02E05 that we get the best look at him. Bauer and Resnick are on a stakeout in a van under an overpass. Bums warm themselves around a fire in an oil drum. Among them is the man in the yellow parka (not that yellow anymore; in fact, more dirty gray)—poorly shaven, features gaunt, gaze vacant.

It's strange to watch a film or series while focusing on the backgrounds and edges of the frame. You develop a curious attentional walleye, and realize that most of the time you don't really *watch* movies. On one hand, you keep following the unfolding plot despite yourself. You register names, facts; you sense a twist coming up; you figure out who's guilty. On the other, you find that even the most conventional fiction is full of bizarre, surprising, incongruous, or simply poignant details, sometimes deliberately arranged by the director—whose reasons aren't always clear—sometimes recorded unbeknownst to him by the camera, like the short-haired girl in *Intimidation*: fleeting, fragile moments, gestures all the more precious for being involuntary, forever imprisoned in the frame . . . Aren't these, at heart, our most secret reason for loving movies? I noticed several such details in *Simple Cops*. Monica, the pretty precinct receptionist, had an inexhaustible collection of sweaters. She wore a new one every episode. Thaddeus, Bauer, and Mentell were all left-handed—three southpaws on the same show? And what to make of the excessive proliferation of watches, wall clocks, clock radios, sometimes shot in close-up, if called for to ratchet up suspense, but more often in the background or the edges of the frame, like the sign of a furtive, barely hinted-at obsession? And how to take all that graffiti in the form of cries for help—"Help!" "Get me out of this!"—which showed up at regular intervals in exterior shots, spray-painted on walls or scribbled hastily in phone booths?

This wild goose chase lasted three months. One Tuesday, I settled into the sofa, remote in hand, ready to start recording. At 2:33, after the gauntlet of commercials, two uniformed strangers suddenly appeared instead of the familiar titles—a beanpole of a blonde and a well-built black man, getting out of a NYPD car. Goddammit! They'd stopped showing *Simple Cops* without warning! And replaced it with another old stopgap of a show. I was furious.

Over the next few days, I met with another disappointment. Trying to re-watch the episodes, I found out that—unbeknownst to me—my old VCR was on its last legs (like most everyone I knew who still had VCRs, I recorded lots of things only to set them aside till months later). The picture was warped, snowy, unwatchable. It was impossible to see a thing in that soup. I'd taped a whole bunch of movies during the same period, and they were unwatchable too. I thought of my old friend Bernard, a fanatical cinephile who always checked to see that the film he'd set the VCR to tape the night before had been properly recorded. He was right to be so uptight about it. I could've kicked myself.

Simple Cops had come to occupy such a place in my aimless life that I might've sunken into very real doldrums just then, if I hadn't gotten a call two days later about a job with a cultural delegation to Germany that I'd applied for but never really thought I'd get. I was one of four people who made it to the final round. The interview was held a few days later and went unbelievably well, maybe because I hadn't entertained any false hopes. My German came back all on its own, so easily it amazed me. A week later, they called to say that despite my having been a very competitive candidate—blah blah blah—they'd decided to go with someone else. But a second job that needed urgent filling had unexpectedly opened up in Berlin, and they'd thought of me. Of course the responsibilities weren't the same, and the salary was lower as a result. Perhaps I might even be overqualified for the posting? The man on the other end of the line seemed apologetic. I pretended to think for a moment before accepting, not letting on that no solution could have suited me more. I've never liked having, as he put it, "responsibilities." I had to pack, fill out a pile of paperwork, find a subletter. My days were suddenly very full.

I liked Berlin right from the start. I felt like I'd just emerged from a long hibernation. There was a great deal of work; office hours often spilled over into evenings and weekends, but it didn't bother me. From time to time, I remembered the man in the yellow parka. I even brought him up with a few close coworkers, but none of them knew the series and my comments were met with polite, skeptical silence. This was a bit before TV's big boom in popularity: most people who worked in the culture sector just weren't interested in those kinds of stories, which they condescendingly considered by-products of mass culture, and so beneath them. Since I was already thought of as the department joker, I didn't insist, and steered the conversation toward a book or an exhibit.

The first six months went by like a dream. Then, one fall morning, checking the movie listings in the paper, I saw an ad for a new American release, *The Cleveland Ultimatum*. I didn't recognize the director's name but, remembering all the hours I'd spent in that city in the company of Detective Burns and his teammates, I went to see the movie the next Saturday afternoon. It was a big, fairly leaden thriller with endless shoot-outs, a conspiracy whose mastermind was of course some CIA bigwig, and the insufferable kind of editing one can't seem to escape, these days, where the angles change every three seconds to give the film the illusion of rhythm and mask the fact that the director doesn't know where to put the camera. If it hadn't taken place in Cleveland, I'd have left after twenty minutes. But I was happy to catch a glimpse, however briefly, of the Terminal Tower again, and Erie Harbor, and the arches of the Detroit-Superior Bridge.

The shot went by so fast I thought I was seeing things. But that little yellow spot in the background—wasn't that the man in the yellow parka? Valiantly I endured the avalanche of inept incidents till the end of the film and stayed for the next showing. When the sequence in question came up again, I had no more doubts. Many years had gone by between *Simple Cops* and the shooting of *The Cleveland Ultimatum*. His beard had grayed. His hair had thinned. But it was him, in his old yellow parka, that I saw on a street corner, with two other vagrants. I was flabbergasted.

On my way out of the theatre, I was assailed by all manner of thoughts. Quite banal ones, really. I thought that while my life had just taken a turn for the better, other lives had remained inexorably stuck at an impasse. A bit like when you go back to the neighborhood where you grew up and find the same lady at the bakery's still there behind the counter. The man in the yellow parka was just like her. While the world turned, he'd continued his nomadic existence for all these years without being able to leave Cleveland; or—the phrase took shape of its own accord in my mind, and so quickly I was dumbfounded at myself—without being able to leave *the image of Cleveland*.

Sometimes chance moves things along in strange ways. The next week I was sent on an assignment to Cologne. At the evening's end, I went back to my hotel exhausted, collapsed on the bed, turned on the TV while noisily kicking my shoes off, and started channel surfing. I stopped on Eurosport, where there was a game of snooker underway that I watched till the end, trying to remember the rules, a red ball then a colored ball—I've always been fascinated by that game. After which I started surfing again, flipping quickly through five or six channels, then back: I'd just spotted big ol' Burns. It was an episode of *Simple Cops*, one I'd never seen before. I turned up the sound. Naturally, the series was dubbed in German, which highlighted the strangeness of stumbling across it by chance here, of all places, in a hotel room, although still late at night. The plot also proceeded at a different pace, with something awkward about it, as if the writers hadn't found their rhythm yet. It seemed to be endless exposition where the characters were introduced in turn, and several storylines whose resolutions I already knew were being set up. After fifteen minutes, I realized I was watching the pilot.

So I waited, hoping the appearance of the man in the parka—his first appearance—hadn't gone by yet. And soon I saw him, lying on a park bench around which various people were walking about, among them loving couples, mothers with strollers, and finally Burns and Atkinson crossing the frame to sit down a bit farther off. The two cops weren't on duty or discussing the current case, but rather their personal problems. The sequence ended as it had begun, with a long shot of the park. The man in the parka was still sleeping on his bench.

And as the episode went on and sleep overtook me, I caught a glimpse of what had happened that day, as they were shooting *Simple Cops*. It was a scene with lots of extras, a ballet of passersby that must have taken a lot of rehearsal to get right. The second AD had asked the extra in the yellow parka to just lie down on a bench and play a sleeping homeless man. They'd rehearsed, fine-tuned a few details—you, lady with the stroller, walk faster; loving couple, you go slower—done five or six takes. Lying in the sun, the man in the parka had wound up falling asleep for real. When the director was satisfied, the AD had sent the extras home while the crew packed up. They'd paid no further mind to the man in yellow lying on his bench. When he'd woken up an hour later, the park was empty.

How had he realized that he'd slipped into another plane of reality? Quite naturally, he must've wanted to go home to his wife and kids, but that was no longer possible, since his house hadn't been filmed. So he'd spent days and even weeks going around in circles through a virtual Cleveland that expanded as the production of *Simple Cops* consumed new locations. When he ran out of money, he'd started begging to get by, sleeping where he could, making friends with other homeless people. Maybe sometimes he let loose and told his story to his comrades in misery. The guys would laugh without malice, taking him for a harmless, sweet-natured nutcase, and pass him the bottle again. And all the while, he'd be looking desperately for an exit, a way back to the other side, the right side of the set. He'd go everywhere, try every door, but utterly in vain. In a warehouse where he'd squatted, he found old cans of spray-paint he used to graffiti SOS on the wall. One day—who knew?—someone might notice his presence? But ten years later, when *The Cleveland Ultimatum* was shot, he was still a prisoner of that strange parallel world, only visible to cameras. Perhaps at this very moment he is wandering from street to street, door to door, in hopes of someday finding a way out of the screen.

TRANSLATED FROM FRENCH BY EDWARD GAUVIN

ELVIS HADZIC

The Curious Case of Benjamin Zec

Once upon a time, not long ago, in the mountainous Balkans, a land of peasants, lived a boy. His name was Benjamin Zec and, some would say, he was just an ordinary boy.

Benjamin swung through the branches of chestnut trees like Tarzan. There was no tree around his little town that he hadn't climbed. He was the best marble-shooter on his street and an excellent second in the school's kilometer dash. The other boys in class respected him, as he was the best goal scorer on the soccer field, but the girls kept their eye on him, giggling, because Benjamin did not hesitate to pinch bottoms or stick out his hand, as if yawning, to grab a barely formed breast. Perhaps this is why he often bore proud bruises under his big green eyes.

Benjamin, the little devil, used to return from recess cradling to his chest a T-shirt full of early cherries. Then he would eat them during class and throw pits at the teacher's pets sitting up front. He never liked school much, nor what they taught him there. Benjamin loved the smell of the woods and the earthy primrose buds more than any science lesson. Once, he even challenged the physics teacher with the extremely rude and bold statement that Newton had in fact been defecating under that famous tree, and that no apple had fallen on his head, but that he, Newton, was actually inspired by seeing his own shit succumb to the force of gravity! Benjamin went on saying that the legend about the apple tree was an obvious fabrication anyhow: apples don't just fall off trees like that. Besides, he added, the best ideas always come from relieving oneself in nature! The whole class laughed, and Benjamin, of course, got a D in physics.

Benjamin Zec did not like science, but he loved to read books. *The Literary Reader* was his favorite textbook and Serbo-Croatian language class the only class that he ever looked forward to. Classrooms were just suffocating walls and the soporific monotone of the teacher—but in the countryside, surrounded by the thick shade of spruce and pine, he was free to make himself the hero of every adventure he read.

Yes, indeed, some would say that Benjamin Zec was just an ordinary boy.

And he might have remained so, until, that is, he decided to become a ladybug . . .

One time, as he fell off the branch of a cherry tree, he lay spread out, one freckled cheek on the wet ground. His eyes were caught by the frosted grass through which a ladybug was slowly pacing. A ladybug is a marvelous thing, he thought: it's never in a hurry. Acrobating nonchalantly from one blade of grass to another, as if surprised that its own tiny weight is still sufficient to bend the tip of a blade of grass. Strange, he thought, how ladybugs seem to make their decisions at the spur of the moment, and suddenly, stretch out their wings from under their black-spotted armor and fly off who knows where, taking your good luck with them.

The palm of his hand was turned toward the sky and the ladybug jumped onto his life line.

He'd always wanted to become an actor, to star in action movies or play a major role on that famous American Broadway . . . whatever that meant . . . But now it seemed to him that becoming a ladybug would suffice. To be able to turn into one of these insects, like this one here, which was so delightfully walking over his palm—to grow wings and disappear, well, that would be something . . . *Ladybug, ladybug, show me the way,* he whispered the children's wish-song.

At that very moment, a bang burst through the back of his head, while the whole cosmos buzzed through his ears, and a cold silence poured down over his forehead. And then, Benjamin Zec was gone. Only a monotonous beep was left behind, brash and piercing, bouncing off the trees in the forest. The sound wandered for a while through the neighboring villages and then was reduced to a faint echo, only noticed by birds, until it was lost forever.

That hot summer day was the last anyone heard from the boy. Some kids from the neighborhood alleged that Benjamin had grown wings, no really, that he did in fact turn into a ladybug and had flown away. Others, however, kept faith in the prospect of his eventual return, believing that he would come back one day and organize nothing less than the most spectacular soccer tournament imaginable. Others, again, were completely indifferent, saying that even if Benjamin did miraculously rematerialize in the bazaar, everyone would get tired of him in three days time, and who knows, maybe he's here already, maybe he walks among us and is getting a good laugh out of the whole town wondering where he got to. There seemed no rational explanation, or at least none that could be reached by mere mortals. And yet, who cared? So another difficult kid had vanished. It was neither the first nor the last time someone like Benjamin disappeared, evaporated, just like that . . . It happens, right? In fact, maybe Benjamin just got a little lost, wandering the surface of our little planet, and when he realized he'd escaped his warders, just seized the opportunity and ran like hell. People had bigger problems to worry about. So no one troubled themselves about Benjamin Zec for very long. What was he good for but watching movies anyway? He didn't fit in. He couldn't play along. No great loss, that one.

Years later, and did anyone still care about the mystery of Benjamin Zec? Perhaps only his swaybacked mother, who still kept watch over the canopy of wild chestnut trees, and with her bare hands dug up primroses . . .

Time dripped into gutters of oblivion. Tick-tock, tick-tock, tick . . . Drop by drop, Benjamin's mother drank rainwater from the gutters and sadly chewed cherries every late July . . .

The curious case of Benjamin Zec eventually became folklore. A fairy tale. And even though most people had forgotten the real boy behind the story, there were those to whom the question did occur, every now and again. They would conjure up their memories of him, if only for a moment or two—a freckled boy with green eyes who used to pinch the girls and holler like Tarzan while climbing trees—and so he became the ghost of the town, a myth to be recounted around shifting candlelight, a legend that was flying around on the black spots of ladybugs, a fathomless public secret that no line of inquiry could penetrate, a surreal remnant of a forgotten past. The only evidence of the boy's actual existence was a black and white photograph: he, Benjamin Zec, in pants torn at the knees and a threadbare sweatshirt, squinting at the sun from underneath an unkempt head of hair, with marbles in his hand. His mother kept that photo close to her heart, walking the wide world to pull this memento out of her brassiere from time to time and shove into the face of oblivion a disheveled Benjamin Zec.

People prayed to him for a good harvest and begged for forgiveness when a drought hit their fields, as if worshiping some ancient pagan deity. When they told their children the story, they always began like so: Once upon a time, there was a boy . . .

It's been said that Benjamin Zec was sighted in America; that he hadn't become a fairy tale at all but a religious fanatic who blew up thirty-three people at a fish market along with himself. Whereas some said, no, he hadn't done himself in; he was in a loony bin now, though happily everyone agreed on the number of people he'd killed. And then, another theory: he'd joined the US Marines in penance and was working as a landmine clearer in Iraq. And another still: certain people were claiming that Benjamin had become a Wahhabi, had let his beard grow, had taken to wearing a turban, and had married a woman with dark and mysterious eyes.

But there was only one grain of truth to the whole story: that Benjamin Zec *did* end up in America. But, to complicate matters, Benjamin himself had no idea how or when he'd arrived. He didn't remember a thing. All he knew was this: he'd simply appeared one day, on a stage, in a theater, in the middle of a Shakespeare play, and in the spotlight to boot, wondering:

"To be or not to be?"

And he was . . .

He was on stage, on Broadway, and the audience was on its feet. They applauded Mr. Benjamin Zec for so long that he thought he would die of old age standing there, adored by his audience.

"Bravo! Bravooo!" the amazed masses shouted, throwing flowers at him.

No one knew that Benjamin didn't know how he'd come to be there. He didn't even know who or what he'd been before his arrival. But he was game, as ever, and soon had readily accepted his role.

While enthusiastic crowds continued to cheer his name, Benjamin was ushered toward a dressing room. On the way, he signed three autographs and absentmindedly nodded at a pushy pitch for a movie role as a Serbian war criminal. How did they learn his name, he wondered. Benjamin said nothing but simply glided through the crowd. There, in the wardrobe mirror, he stared at his freckled face. He stripped himself of Hamlet and rediscovered Benjamin Zec. He wondered how old this familiar yet unknown figure could be. *Not more than twenty-five*, he thought, pleased. *Twenty-five!*

Oh, Benjamin Zec was very satisfied with the body he'd found himself in possession of. Proud of his manly facial features, strong chin, and piercing green eyes—whoever he was, he certainly deserved this new life of his. No question about that. It felt good to be grown-up and successful. He decided to go along with this adventure, to ignore the past he didn't remember anyway, to be whomever he had to be, for the situation *was* already whatever it was . . .

After the show, a limo driver called out to him in a familiar way and Benjamin understood that this was his personal chauffeur. He treated Benjamin like an old friend, politely inquiring whether the opening was as successful as the year before. He drove Benjamin to a beautiful house, grandiose with its Greek columns and Gothic arches, facing the Atlantic Ocean.

Inside, the servants had already kindled a fire in the fireplace. They referred to him as "Mister Benjamin," and he replied in perfect English, though something told him that it wasn't his first language. He could feel his tongue twisting and straining, and words tumbling around in his mouth in a strange accent.

Benjamin decided to go through his house, look through his own stuff, and hopefully find some clues as to his past life. It was out of the question for him to ask his own servants where he'd come from and how long he'd lived here! He didn't want them to think that he had lost his mind somewhere between slipping into and out of Mr. Hamlet's skin. Benjamin thought that they must have known him very well, as they treated him with respect, but also a kind of intimacy.

The house was his, of course, because he found he knew

exactly where every little thing was located, but he didn't have conscious memory of any of these apparently familiar objects. Any emotional understanding of the things around him was distant and unfathomable. Even his portraits and photo albums were no help: all of them showed a recent Benjamin, in the here and now, with the same dark hair, the same spots around the eyes, and the matchless youth of his face. It seemed that he had never been younger than he was now. As if he had been born just like this, twenty-five years old, and now was meeting himself for the first time. But how was it possible that he didn't remember anything? How was it possible that there was nothing from his past that he could grab hold of? How did it come to be that he was playing Hamlet on Broadway, just like that? Did he have any friends or family? A father? Mother? Where had he been born? When was his birthday? Benjamin knew nothing. It was as though someone had just made him up, whole-cloth.

He looked at the photographs on the walls. The pictures were unflattering, he thought—they showed an arrogant man, struggling to smile. Cold eyes followed his every move. And why did he have so many photographs hung around the house anyway? And they all seemed as if they'd been taken yesterday. Even his painted portraits appeared to have been completed just the day before, as if the oils had managed to dry overnight. Was he trying to tell himself something?

Well, yes, he realized almost immediately: *I do not age!*

Oh, how confused Mr. Benjamin Zec was just then . . . He had the face of eternal youth, like that Dorian Gray fellow! And that was another thing. The same way he'd known *Hamlet* by heart, the same way every line had somehow been etched into his gestures, now this "Dorian Gray" raced into his consciousness— equally inexplicable.

And that was nothing compared to the next miracle.

Remembering Dorian Gray, Benjamin ran into the bedroom.

The room was upstairs, the first on the left, and in the night-table drawer was a book—he knew it. So he opened the drawer. The book that he found in there had a cracked, fragile cover and yellowing pages. And it wasn't in English. But Benjamin knew how to read it, and the cover said:

Oscar Wilde

The Picture of Dorian Gray

Benjamin opened to the first page and began to read. He understood every word; they rushed inside him, first ingratiatingly, warm, pleasant, and familiar, but then painfully, as though this strange language was piercing deep into his soul. Every breath Benjamin tried to take caught in his chest; he felt as though something was sawing his lungs in half, as though his ribs were closing in on his innards. He was going to faint. Pictures of his well-mannered smiles spun around him and his pupils rolled under his fluttering eyelids. A deafening bang forced its way into the back of his head, and all the silence in there escaped out of his forehead.

Benjamin lost his balance and fell to the ground.

Bright light soon swallowed the darkness and he found himself back on stage ...

"To be or not to be?" The audience applauded, he bowed. He saw his face in the dressing-room mirror. He wondered who he was and why he was there. His limo driver knocked on the door, identified himself as Benjamin's chauffeur, and asked if he was ready to go home. Benjamin had a beautiful house with Greek columns and Gothic arches. All the walls were decorated with his portraits and photos. Benjamin looked at himself in the mirror and realized he wasn't aging. Just like Dorian Gray! In the bedroom, he found a book by Oscar Wilde, opened to the first page ... and fainted.

When he next opened his eyes he found himself once again under the glaring spotlight. To be or not to be, again, oblivious to the nature of his predicament. Another standing ovation. He became reacquainted with his face in the dressing room. The figure in the mirror was somewhat familiar. His chauffeur drove him home, a grandiose house overlooking the Atlantic Ocean. Benjamin looked at his reflection and realized that he didn't age, just like the main character in a book. *The Picture of Dorian Gray*! He ran to his bedroom. Panting, he opened his night-table drawer and found a book by Oscar Wilde. He opened to the first page . . . and was quickly comatose.

When he came to again, he saw the spotlight, the stage, he spoke Shakespeare's famous words, the crowd was shouting his name, and it all happened as it did the first time, and the second, and who knows how many other times . . . It always started with him waking up on the stage and ended when he opened to the first page of *The Picture of Dorian Gray*. Then, unconsciousness, and begin again. Benjamin Zec was like a skipping LP, trapped at one point of his revolution, in a vicious circle of time. And he would have stayed there, in this parallel world, forever, if there hadn't, finally, been a slight variation in his routine—hurrying upstairs, he stumbled and something spilled out of his pocket: a marble.

The next time Benjamin Zec ran through his usual loop, when he dashed upstairs to seek out *Dorian Gray*, he slipped on that marble and fell. And . . . time skipped ahead of time, just like a stuck record player might finally break out of its rut only to skip the refrain and jump right to the third verse. Benjamin did fall into his usual oblivion, but the light that welcomed him when he awoke this time wasn't from a spotlight, but from a summer sun . . .

He saw a vast green meadow and in it a single cherry tree. The fruit of the tree had the dark red color of blood, and its sweet flesh hung heavy with juice. Cherries that have no worms are no good, Benjamin thought. The tree was bursting with life, and its fragile branches swayed easily in the wind. Hints of cherry scent played across Benjamin's lips. He licked them so as to carry off even the least trace of sugary stimulus.

Some people were digging close by the lone tree.

Benjamin wanted to pick some cherries. He extended his hand, but just at the moment his fingers plucked a fruit from its branch, the ground beneath his bare feet went as dry and loose as the interior of an hourglass. He fell. The soil pulled him down, devouring him in a single bite. He tried to hold on to the cherry tree, but, to his surprise, he dragged it with him into the abyss.

The terror of being buried alive shut his eyes fast.

When his consciousness got hold of a little light at last, Benjamin found himself on a pile of bones and grinning skulls, disfigured and broken: skeletons hugging each other in a heap. Benjamin held firmly to the cherry tree, which was now just a root attached to a tiny skeleton in the fetal position, like an umbilical cord . . . The shrunken bones were the bones of a boy, Benjamin knew. The skeleton's skull had a hole in the back and an even bigger one in the front, and between its teeth was gripped the seed from which the roots of the wild cherry tree sprang.

And then, oh, only then did Benjamin Zec realize it was his own skull. His teeth . . . His bones . . . His life . . . His death . . . His restless soul that wandered around like a gypsy song.

Benjamin looked around and found that he wasn't alone. Many other souls were down there, looking for their bones. He recognized some of the kids from school . . . There were also people from the neighboring village . . . And his physics teacher . . . And Benjamin's father too! And one of the neighbors . . . And then another . . . And many, many others . . . Many that he didn't even know . . . They were all there for their bones. Quietly, obediently, they searched through this shrine-abyss filled with skeletons.

The dead were coming for their bones while the living above

them were exhuming a mass grave.

Skeletons were placed side by side and numbered. Benjamin Zec was number 25 . . .

And, there he was: a little boy again. He was eating cherries when one of the soldiers violently yanked him down off the lowest branch of the cherry tree. As he fell to the ground, he felt a marble slipping out of his pocket; it got lost in the deep grass. The smell of grass wafted around him. The soil was still wet. It calmed him down. He didn't want to think about his fear; he completely ignored the agony of the moment. He watched the carefree ladybug whose tiny feet crossed his life line. As the Kalashnikov barrel was pointed at the back of his head, he thought . . . he thought of Dorian Gray and his never-ending youth . . . He wanted to be an actor on Broadway, to have a personal driver and a house with great Greek columns, Gothic arches, and a view of the ocean . . . Or if he could at least . . . if he could at least transform into this beautiful insect . . . and fly away . . . *Ladybug, ladybug, show me the way*, he hummed . . .

At that moment, the ladybug spread its transparent wings and flew out of his open palm to fulfill the wish of Benjamin Zec.

To the victims of the Srebrenica massacre . . . in remembrance, with love.

TRANSLATED FROM BOSNIAN BY THE AUTHOR

KATYA ATANASOVA

Fear of Ankles

The first time, I was fourteen. I remember it clearly. It was August, we were at the seaside, and I still have this thing about the sea, so I remember everything I experienced there, starting with the ever-surprising fragility of seashells, the amazement at seeing the sand flowing through your fingers like time, somewhere in the late afternoon, say around six, in the loneliness of the empty beach, and the swimming further and further in, and finishing with the endless noisy parties in Southern and Northern bars— as ecstatic at night as sad at dawn. It was also the first time that I spent several evenings with friends, without all the advice, reproach and prohibition that parental presence inevitably implies. The most important thing, however, happened on an unabashedly ordinary sleepy afternoon.

I was walking slowly with my father (I loved this time of the day), we met some chance acquaintances of his and the woman—remarkably, the woman—suddenly and somehow sharply (perhaps it was just her natural voice?) and very earnestly, said, "What lovely legs your daughter has."

My puberty-ridden brain didn't perceive this cheap civil remark of the fading middle-aged lady in the way you might suppose—as a stimulant for my otherwise missing confidence of beauty.

I actually thought I was on the chubby side, my face was un-remarkable and the boys were dying to confide in me about the girls they had a crush on; basically, everything people said about me had been in the semantic vicinity of *cool, streetwise, pretty smart* (the greatest weapon against the beautiful "bimbos") and *weird*—I especially valued the latter and tried to keep the legend alive and even enhance it by sitting on the floor at parties, three to four hours at a time, staring at nothing and keeping quiet. The very epitome of thought and weirdness, if you will. Thus, among the qualities which made me famous, there wasn't a single one resembling beauty. Ordinary beauty we pretended to despise: eyes, lips, hair and body—"body" meaning "legs." Mine were far from long (the necessary requirement for anything beauti-ful); what's more, they were frankly short-ish and chubby-ish (the *ish* a feeble effort to evade self-loathing by a sickly sweet diminution).

Until that afternoon at the seaside and the stupid civility of the middle-aged lady, the facts were well-known—but dormant on the fringe of my teenage consciousness, unable to activate the complexes everyone has, at least at this age. Anyway, I didn't lack attention, safely barricaded behind *coolness, streetwise,* and *pretty smart.* I had a good life, but the middle-aged lady broke through my defences—they might have been fragile to start with, I don't know, but what happened was like a bullet in the head. The bun-ker of my defence exploded, leaving me naked and alone.

After that, the horror started. I spent the whole day look-ing at myself in the mirror, measuring the circumference of my thighs, calves and ankles, following insane diets (there was one which included drinking four litres of champagne and eating a kilo of grapes every day; I'm still fond of champagne, with grapes on the side), and working out with abandon. The results were paltry, at least in the body section I was interested in. Beauty equalled legs and thus I was forever deprived of it. No point in ever-more or less cool images I had designed for myself in the eyes of the world (i.e., boys). Because sooner or later they would inevitably look at me below the waist—straight to my shame, to my ugly legs, and this would be enough for them to forget everything else about me. In this moment, they would see me for what I was.

I abandoned skirts and dresses and took to wearing trousers. Not shorts. In this way I was hiding what should not be seen. I started acting even more weird than usual and initiated long conversations, hiding in the blur offered by evenings and darkness.

But I couldn't hide my ankles. No matter how long the trousers were, the damned things were still visible. I kept my hands over them when I was sitting (I was still in the habit of sitting on the floor and keeping as silent as possible, because otherwise it was time for talking—a never-ending effort to demonstrate the number of books one has read, easily hopping from Hemingway—my "trick" was to dislike him—to Steinbeck or Vonnegut, a particular favorite of my friends and myself, the very best experience was to find the person of your "karas," you might recall it, sitting on the floor and touching your feet; then on to the monumental artists of Mexico, and, of course, Sartre and Camus), and I stared at them when I was standing up. I couldn't keep my eyes off them. So it is with ugliness. It attracts attention, just like beauty. I realized that everyone saw them, my damned fat ankles, and this horrified me.

And then, on cue, came the second time. I chanced at a party (the usual Sunday bridge was off, though we usually played partly to enhance our intellectual prowess, partly to attain the familiar sensation of safety and mysterious, mystical conspiracy among the players, born from the realization that you know something other people don't), I only knew one of the girls—fatter than me—and an acne-ridden boy from school, I happened to sit on

a chair (the floor already occupied by several of my kind), opposite a boy with long hair. This is important, otherwise I wouldn't
remember it, because boys with long hair were a rare catch these
days, almost non-existent, and thus were considered a valuable
score. Even if you don't like him that much, the mere effect of
him appearing by your side was enough to compensate for the
sacrifices made in the name of the absolute bliss caused by the
envy of girlfriends, schoolmates and women of all shapes and
sizes. Why delude ourselves, envy is a great boost for our ego (I
don't have the time to check what Freud has to say on this but
you can accept it as a truth based on experience, I think that's
what we used to say on such occasions). I, for one, used envy in
all its boosting capacity wherever I could, because few things are
more insecure than the ego of a young girl with fat ankles. The
boy's name was Paul. I don't recall the words that were said, I
don't think they were many; I can't formulate clearly the meaning of the looks that were exchanged, though they must have
been more. As I already admitted, I was pretty methodical in
my impression-making tactics. However, in a dark, late and very
drunk hour Paul suddenly said,

"You have gorgeous ankles."

No, really. He said it. He even put his fingers around and
caressed the chubby proof of the absurdity of what he'd just said.
This was the turning point. He chased me like a madman for
months; I was not satisfied with avoiding him, no, at the end
I hated him so much that I tortured the boy in every way imaginable, including the most mean way I could then (and even
now) think of—by hitting on noted jerks in front of him and, of
course, sadistically introducing them to him. I forgot to say that
he was throwing knives. He did it as a hobby, had an impres-
sive collection of knives and, when drunk, insisted on throwing
knives at the wall, usually above the head of a girl he fancied.
You can guess which was the girl on most evenings. Finally

Paul surrendered and stopped calling me. I did not forget him, however, and kept thinking about his incidental homage to the most unattractive part of my body. The fact that someone had loved my ankles and desired their obvious roundness did not save them from my own contempt. I kept trying to put my fingers around them, I couldn't and this drove me insane. I stared at the legs of every woman on the street and, in horror of my own imperfection, found out that even the most slovenly, fat, old and otherwise not eye-pleasing women have better ankles than me. They all had the beatific, elongated, smooth line from the delicacy of the ankle to the round, healthy firmness of the calf. I had a couple of bony lumps, topped almost directly by what I called "centurion" calves.

The third time was at the hospital. I lay in the dark, pinned to the bed by the tubes which fed my weak body life in the form of nauseatingly red (because it was someone else's) blood and clear, hopelessly slow-dripping glucose, and someone was lying next to me. I don't know if it was a he or a she, the face was covered by a sheet, as was the body. I could only see the feet—blue and white, huge, with crooked toes and delicate ankles. They shone, lumunescent in the dark, and in their own terrible way made me look at them. Later they took the body out (much later, probably at dawn) and only then I moved my eyes. The effort of staring left me drained and I fell asleep. The dream was white. Light-white, to be precise. I saw myself in the hospital bed, in my short pyjamas, with my feet showing below like two lonely reeds, and above them—my beautiful ankles. There was even a thin silver bracelet on one (I'm certain because I know silver everywhere), gently hugging it, and the soft shimmer of the silver merged with my shining ankle. My infinitely thin, elongated and amazingly beautiful ankle.

When I woke up, they moved me to another wing. The nurses there knew me (I had been with them about a year ago) and changed my pyjamas every day. I always had a short one and my ankles kept showing, fiercely alive. They were thin and I liked them. I walked them around the hospital corridors, full of open bellies with tubes hanging out. I planned to buy a short skirt as soon as I got out. So that my legs show. My pretty legs, with my thin ankles.

When they let me go, I took a shower. I hadn't taken a shower for a week. Then they gave me an injection that hurt. And I didn't buy a short skirt.

TRANSLATED FROM BULGARIAN BY BOGDAN RUSEV

[Croatia]

OLJA SAVIČEVIĆ IVANČEVIĆ

Adios Cowboy

The summer of 200X came early. A nasty heat had already built up in May and frazzled the early-summer roses in the city's parks and flowerbeds.

At the end of July I packed all my things, left the rented apartment where I'd lived a few wasted years, and traveled home.

My sister was waiting for me in the kitchen of our old house with her suitcase, ready to leave. In the hour and a half we sat together she got up from the table four times—once to pour me some more milk and three times to go to the bathroom. Finally she returned with her lips painted bright pink, which surprised me, though I didn't say anything. She never used to like that color of lipstick. She sent a few SMS messages and talked with me on the side, then got up, straightened her skirt, and went down the long hall and the stairs. Ma was lying in the downstairs room channel surfing.

They said hello briefly as she left, I heard their voices, and from the balcony I saw my sister vanish around the street corner, behind the baker's. For an instant she was an unreal apparition on a real stage, a simulation. I sipped the cold coffee from her cup with the print of a pink rose.

Before leaving she told me how she'd got on with Ma over

the last month.

Their daily ritual was clear-cut: they got up early, always at the same time, and sat with their coffee for at least twenty minutes; then, before the sun got too hot, they'd set off on foot, one after the other, along the main road to the cemetery. The thin roadside strip, just wide enough for two feet, turns to a fine dust on summer days. This imaginary path leads between the road on one side and the blackberry bushes, ragwort, and unplastered houses on the other; the dust swirls up into your eyes and throat and creeps into your sandals, between your toes.

"Did you know that some people eat soil?" my sister asked Ma as they walked through the dust along the road. "It's called geophagia."

But Ma was off on a completely different tack: "Dust to dust . . . It's better to be buried in the ground than walled up in concrete."

"I don't give a damn about death," my sister cut in. "Stupid fucking death! People can get used to anything, I guess."

"It's normal that you don't give a damn," Ma said, but clearly offended. She shook the dust out of her wooden-soled sandals and went on, chin raised, with the dignity of the dead-to-be, a step ahead of my sister.

After washing "our" grave and weeding out the dead flowers they'd go down to the beach with a livelier step.

"Dead quiet, like in a microwave," my sister commented as they were passing through backyards and drought-stricken orchards—well, she liked to speak her mind.

At the beach Ma took bruised pears and bananas out of a paper bag that was in a plastic bag that was in a Tupperware container in her bag . . . and plied my sister with fruit, accompanied by her famous Hollywood grin, which would make any *normal* person feel better, my sister remarked. But Ma seemed to take that mien of hers out of a filing cabinet or out of the straw carry bag she lugged around with her, day in day out. That smile was an ace from the sleeve of soap-operatic gestures that Ma sometimes pulled out at the wrong time, my sister thought.

Their togetherness would end when they returned home, after lunch, when my sister withdrew into her upstairs room; she stayed there until evening and tried to get on with her work, although she was on summer vacation—she was a schoolteacher. Ma would then feed our ginger cat Jill, get into position in front of the TV, and announce: "My show's starting."

Minerva, Aaron, and Isadora resolved to find out the real identity of Vasiona Morales—a treacherous siren, and rescue Juan from her.

All telenovelas and serials are important for Ma, without distinction.

She'd fall asleep in front of the TV bundled up from head to toe, although on those days the temperature didn't drop below thirty, even at night.

My sister was worried that Ma might overdo it with the sleeping pills, one of these days—she didn't move beneath the sheet or even breathe—just farted every now and then in her sleep.

"She's horrible," Ma said about my sister once she'd gone. "She says terrible things. I don't understand, Dada."

That's my name—Dada. My parents gave it to me.

When I took Ma to the main road, the heat was already rising up out of the ground: At seven it's up to your ankles. On a dry Monday morning just after midday the heat begins to scorch down. The city is worst around five: The salty air becomes sultry, everything that moves has to plow through the afternoon molasses, and the symphony of a million sounds blurs to a monotonous electric hum. Intoxicating.

Ma is ramrod-straight when she's sitting or standing, but when she walks she sways over the edge of the road. Several centimeters of her shoulder vie with the gas tankers and ice-trucks with fish. Perhaps there's no room for anyone other than motorists anymore, I thought to myself.

"Those idiots ought to be shut away in pedestrian gulags, they don't know when they're taking their lives in their hands!" my sister snapped. I think it was when we were driving to Danijel's funeral in her former husband's turbo jeep and a few boys darted across the road.

"You have to love pedestrians. They created the world. And when everything was ready, cars came along," I said. Everyone looked at me as if I wasn't all there. "I read that in a book."

I was sitting in the back seat on the sticky synthetic leather among wreaths of palm branches that pricked my bare arms, between a chrysanthemum arrangement and a bouquet of blooming roses with a big black bow. The wreaths were wrapped in violet ribbon with names written on in gold magic marker.

"So that everyone knows who's in mourning," my sister commented, which was considered inappropriate.

"How primitive we are," she snorted and rolled up the window after flicking out a lit cigarette butt the color of blood. "You can see it in things like that. Love is always put on the scales. A bigger obituary, bigger announcement in the paper, marble, a golden cross, more dough, more love. It's about throwing money around. The more luxurious the vacuum cleaner for the newlyweds the greater the love, it's the same thing. There's no such thing as a poor relative—he's just a miser who couldn't give a shit about you," she ranted at me over her shoulder.

I sat there dumbfounded between the prickly wreaths, trying not to crush the flowers, and watched the people picking cherries by the cement factory. They were in caps and blue aprons and up on ladders. They looked content—diligent digital proletarians. I wondered if cement dust fell on them when they used hooks to pull down the branches. The dust was like a soft carpet, a pleasant memory.

I didn't answer my sister, and that spurred her to reload; her words whizzed by me like projectiles. I wasn't really there.

"Come on, calm down just a bit!" mumbled her former husband, an insipid, peaceable sort of guy, soft and numb.

Now in the distance my mother had shrunk to a mole beside the *Jesus Loves You* placard of the pastoral center, then to an extinguished shooting star next to the Kuna Komerc store, and to a little minus beneath the giant, faded poster of General Gotovina, as she shuffled along in the dust by the road, past the gas station, on the path just wide enough for two feet. The speed limit here is sixty, but people drive at least eighty; the four-lane motorway begins a bit further down and drivers lose their sense of relative velocity. And then a farmer on his tractor comes out from an unsealed track or side road and completely clogs traffic.

You could even find horse manure on the main road until recently, but not anymore. It's too dangerous to go by horse and cart now. I think there's just one person in the whole city who still owns a horse; it's illegal to keep horses in the city, but he's an old smith, so they're waiting for him to pass away, if what Ma says is true. I wondered what would happen to the horse when the old man died. He used to run a smithy in Staro Naselje—down in the port where the restaurant La Vida Loca is. But it was closed down the same year that Danijel was born. I remember the sound of the horses being shod, their neighing, I remember the dark and the fire. I was very small and just saw things from the distance in the summer light that hurts your eyes when you look into the open dark of an old building. I was very small, and the clatter of hooves on the worn cobbles filled our street, an unreal sound, as unreal as that of the Ledo ice-cream truck jingling during my afternoon nap. Willy Wonka comes to your town too!

But there are no fresh horse-droppings on the streets anymore. Only dog shit that no one clears away, just like no one did with the horse manure. But at least no one will chuck dog shit at you. Anyway, it would surprise me if someone did.

When Ma's image in the distance had become a little dash—the mirage on the road squeezed her horizontally into a minus sign rather than a vertical line, as you might have expected—I turned and rushed home, up the concrete stream beside the new buildings built to house war invalids. Once you could find everything you wanted, vile and useful, in it; spring would send it gushing into the sea over a weir of trash. Since it's been cleaned up and concrete-bedded I've noticed a line of slime that oozes along the bottom, drying to green caked mud in summer.

"How about you go to the cemetery by yourself tomorrow?" I suggested to Ma yesterday, my second day back. "I've got some things to attend to in town, they're fairly important," I lied.

That made Ma laugh, just like my sister said—she got out her Hollywood grin at the wrong time. She had nice teeth, with a golden incisor at the bottom. Sometimes she'd tap her fingernails against her teeth to check that they were firm and healthy.

"Ma looks like a smiley on acid," I told my sister on the phone.

"What did I tell you," she replied, blowing smoke into the receiver.

I found Xanax, Prozac, Normabel, Praxiten, Sarafem, and Apaurin on the floor under the kitchen cabinet in a candy tin together with Band-Aids, aspirins, and throat lozenges. She didn't even try to hide them like my sister thought she would—or maybe

Ma knows that one of the best ways to hide things is not to hide them at all. And yet, last winter she threw everything out; I saw it happen.

"How on earth does she get the stuff?" my sister fumed.

It's not terribly hard, I thought to myself. Half the student dorm was on vodka or wine and Valium, other sedatives, and other substances you could allegedly only get on prescription. It was cheaper than candy. A Rasta from the second floor had a plastic bag; the principle was "reach in, and whatever comes out is yours," my roommate told me.

"The problem is that every jerk who doesn't want to wash his hair thinks he's a Rasta," I remember saying.

"Leave her Lorisan so she can sleep," my sister advised. "Whatever else you find can go down the toilet." I flushed several times; a blue Prozac tablet kept bobbing back up. Finally it too disappeared.

I'm swinging on the balcony and can see over the roofs. Neighbors greet me from the street and I wave back.

When she came from the west—first a minus, then a mole— and finally appeared from behind the baker's, I waved to her too. The moment she came through the door I said, "Ma, I've decided to stay a while. Can you take Danijel's things out of my closet?"

She stood in the bathroom in front of the washbasin, scrubbing her hands with soap under a stream of hot water.

"All right," she answered, turning off the faucet and wiping her hands on the coarse old terry towel.

"No point watering the plants, they'll scorch in a jiffy on a day like this," she added, absorbed in her own thoughts.

I saw it clearly—everything changed faster and more fundamentally than me. I spent the last few years treading water while everything else sped along and grew. I only rarely got to go home; whenever I went downtown, to the western part of the city where my sister lives, I'd get stuck at the sparkling showroom, the garish exterior of a smashed and stolen world. Entering that city is a digital adventure; around familiar corners there lurk gangs of conspicuous, siliconed Barbies. Wafts of adrenaline penetrate and corrode my lungs.

I visit the big concrete beaches with their deck chairs and cocktail bars, the marinas with moored Russian yachts bigger than the houses in our street, and the hotel complexes with their barriers and security; a sea of rubble and broken glass, excavators and trucks; steel skeletons and smooth prisms of black opaque glass, whose metallic flash on a hot day makes you envy the blind. I pity the birds, dolphins, and flying fish—such sights must horrify them when they launch out of the sea or come down from the sky.

The city's east is an industrial zone. The east is one hulking shipwreck. The shipyard with its tall green cranes, warehouses, the cement factory, and the neglected ironworks, and behind that huge junkyard, at the edge of the peninsula, the faded façades of Staro Naselje with its post office and church and the murky mire of the polluted port—a laughable little town beneath the distant high-rise blocks that blink down to us at night . . .

. . . to me and Ma sitting on the balcony drinking lukewarm beer from plastic bottles, or eating melon, with the fan on the balcony railing pretending to be wind. Neighbors who don't have air-conditioning sleep on fold-out sofa beds out on their terraces, whole families. They take position and start watching TV as soon as the *Dnevnik* current-affairs program begins. Nothing has changed here, nothing has moved on. Perhaps this is the only speck of the world that I know, my home base, my sanctuary, my snail shell. Despair plus asylum, a little island of happiness in the tepid, bitter liquid—25% More, Free!—with maybe a puff of air from the sea, but not what you'd call a breeze.

The oleanders, capers, and bougainvillea in the courtyards are in flower. And ginger Jill has a streetlamp like a star in each eye.

On evenings like this, the world and the city are not divided into east and west, but, like in the primordial brain of an animal, into north and south. *Urbi et orbi.* That is the message of the moss, the compasses and wind roses, the migratory birds, the rhythms to which people rise and dance, the kinetics of language divided into hemispheres, the eels and smelts so engrossed in fucking that you can walk right past them as they writhe and thrash in the shallows, the migratory birds, *mapa mundi*, the Luna and the North Star, and the line in the hills that the Spanish broom grows up to . . .

Then everything can seem okay, and sometimes that's the same as if it really is.

"When the pension rebate comes I'll do up the grave," Ma said, cutting the melon with a blunt knife.

She'd also sold some shares and was going to deposit the money into my bank account.

"It might help you finish university one day."

"Okay, but I'll keep it for when I'm retired," I said. "Then I'll be able to go to the moon, though I imagine your shares won't be enough to cover more than a few minutes of moonwalk, at the going rate . . ."

"At least you'll be able to go there," she concluded. Preoccupied and nodding, she took her slippers out from behind the green curtain that separated the kitchen from the improvised catch-all space, a kind of dining room cum living room that we call a *tinel*.

"That old baby!" my sister complained one day, meaning Ma.

"Have you noticed how her cheeks have started drooping? Like a basset!"

"Cate Blanchett thinks wrinkles are good," I said. "They give you character."

"*Cate Blanchett thinks* . . . Jeezus, Dada, what's that got to do with it?" she huffed, taking a sip of her coffee, and then delicately wiping a stray brown ground from the corner of her bright pink mouth.

"You're hungry," the green curtain called. "But there's no fresh bread. Albano closed early and I didn't manage to get any. Just a sec, I'll make you some French toast."

I don't like French toast, why can't you remember that—I was *about* to say. But then I changed my mind: "Oh, yes please!"

The clang of metal plates, the breaking of eggs, and the gurgle of milk came from behind the curtain.

"Did you know that swallow fish molt when they return from the north to the south? Their feathers fall off, and they grow scales and fins so they can swim again."

Sometimes I tell her nonsense like that just for fun.

"After Chernobyl anything is possible," she answered as she whisked the yolks, milk, and sugar. "Miškovica from Donja štrada has just had a child from three fathers."

I know every rathole, shelter, and emergency exit.

All of us have that knowledge—in our legs more than our heads. Like the foreign language hiding like a stowaway in our middle ears, and we grafted its temperamental Romanic melody onto the trunk of our own, relatively staid Slavic. The boys from the new housing projects across the railroad track who came to stay with us in the summers—our cousins, the Iroquois Brothers, and some other "outskirters," always with freshly shaven heads— wanted to be like us, so they soon talked like we did, different to their sweet, fat mamas and disheveled fathers whose vowels stuck in their throats; whenever the men absolutely needed to talk, they brought out nothing but strangled bellows, as I recall.

We knocked together our tongue from what we learned at home from our parents and from the anonymous translators of subtitles and dubbed cartoons. That Croat-American mishmash picked up off the street, cribbed from the *Dnevnik* anchorman and stolen from Dylan Dog, Grunf, Sammy Jo Carrington, and Zane Grey was our gangsta rap, our *lingua franca* from the west and center of the city, via Staro Naselje, and up to the railroad track—wherever there were kids who yakked and yelled. We followed each other around and lived like hobos; there was nothing else for us to do, but that was all we wanted, as I recall.

There were endless combinations and permutations to our games of hide-and-seek. Or when we played group hide-and-seek. Back entrances led through unlocked courtyards or through the kitchens of pastry shops and ice-cream parlors with their pots of pudding and vats of gelato, through dark, arched alleys that led down to even darker basements. Cellars became narrow lanes between the houses, pipes led into bare courtyards with sheets drying high above, stairwells that ended in the sky, attics with rotten beams, roofs we jumped over to get to the old castlet, where we scaled its seaward side, edged along the top of its walls, and slid down into the park beneath the twisted ships in the dry dock.

That's where we found Danijel when he got lost the first time; he was hiding under a boat and singing to himself to keep up his courage. Later he ran away often, and each time he was gone for longer because he wasn't frightened anymore, he said.

I bet everything we did there, all our games and wars, were more exciting than the childhood of a savage who goes by the beeches in the forest or the cocoa trees in the jungle—which they have in Baranya, too—or by the cactuses and the sun in the prairie.

The prairie is up in the foothills, above the cemetery where my father and brother are buried, but most of it has given way to a sprawl of dilapidated houses with strutting chickens.

Once I fought a battle in the lunar landscape behind the cement factory and the old saltworks, between the street and the prairie, and there I won my true name, Ruddska, after my reddish skin. That day I fell three times for justice and freedom, was braver than Boudicca, and even today I still call myself by that name—Ruddska.

During a volunteer exchange in the mid 1990s, immediately after the war, we had a precocious freshman from Heidelberg here. He interviewed us for their student radio station about the postwar life of young people in Croatia.

"You live in a multicultural country . . ." he began.

"I don't!" I declared into the tape recorder like a speaker in some televized debate.

"Yeah, but I know what he means," my sister butted in. "There are various ethnic groups here, on our street there are at least two in every house, but it's all the same culture—shitty culture, if you ask me. Only the Chinese can save us from boredom."

In her own way, she embodied the spirit of internationalism.

Soon British and Dutch, Belgians and French began moving into our narrow alleyways. I guess the Chinese don't find poverty all that romantic. It was fascinating to watch old dwellings rudely fashioned from stone, cement, and guano—their beams alive with maggots and nesting mice—transform into quaint picture-book cottages. Beauty for those with time and money to spare.

All the Chinese I've ever met live in high-rise blocks, I thought. But some people prefer durability—people from suburbs like ours the world over.

"Hey," my sister said to the guy from Heidelberg, giving him a friendly whack on the shoulder, "when we played war games with the tourist kids before the war, the little Germans and Italians played the Germans and Italians. One of them even cried, for Christ's sake!"

"But what about during the war? And afterward?" he cleared his throat and pointed the tape recorder at me.

"I dunno. No one played the Balkan wars, if that's what you mean. Everyone wanted to be Croats, for fuck's sake."

"Yep," my sister confirmed.

"That's why we played cowboys and Indians."

"With the outskirters."

"*Against* the outskirters. There always has to be someone to fight, you know? Cowboys and Indians."

TRANSLATED FROM CROATIAN BY WILL FIRTH

TÕNU ÕNNEPALU

Interpretation

She rose from her armchair, where she had been waiting for me. I was running slightly late, because I had misjudged the distance, thinking it shorter than it was, as always happens in Paris (I somehow always manage to reduce the city's dimensions to the scale of Tallinn and Tartu); I was out of breath from my quick pace, even emphasizing it somewhat so that she would see I had hurried all the same. With her first words, she was able to erase the embarrassment of my excuses without further ado; to create a kind of natural, almost comradely atmosphere. I was in seventh heaven. I was certain she knew who I was, because in any case, Denis S. had told her about me. I quietly hoped that perhaps she had even seen my films, and perhaps they had left an impression on her. If so, she would then be the first person I'd met in Paris who had seen them. I've generally gotten used to the idea there that all of the people shuffling around me have never seen *The Railway Watchman's House*, nor do they want to see it, and if it were shown to them by force, then they would give it a shrug at best. I've once again become accustomed to being a nobody. Liz Franz was able to rise from her armchair and walk up to me, was the first to extend her small hand in such a way, with such an expression, that all at once I became *someone* again—all of my suppressed vanity and self-awareness came back in a rush.

I don't remember what we talked about. We waited there for a *Le Monde* journalist, Nicole Zand (that was her pseudonym), who was supposed to do an interview with Liz Franz for which I was meant to act as interpreter. She was running late herself, so quite a heart-to-heart took shape between Liz Franz and I right there in the hotel foyer. She seemed so simple and natural to me. I gazed upon that short woman with bobbed hair, who had risen from her low armchair so gracefully and nimbly, and had walked toward me—it was as though I had known her for years. Which, in a certain sense, was indeed the case. Naturally, I didn't come right out and tell her about how I would cry and masturbate while listening to her record at the age of fourteen. And I still haven't told her that, in all honesty. Still, I think she could surmise it. Somehow. And immediately.

Interpreting (*interprète*) turned out to be very easy. After exchanging the first polite formalities, it became clear that Nicole Zand spoke quite decent Russian, and the two women continued speaking without my assistance; I was only able to help Madame Zand on a couple of occasions, when she couldn't remember some expression and had to search for it via French. Liz Franz spoke Russian with a very heavy accent; I was amazed how purely she pronounced every word when singing. Apparently, it was a question of will, of style.

Madame Zand was an older Jewish lady with dyed red hair, quite lively and nervous. Her husband had worked for years as the *Le Monde* Moscow correspondent. They had been to Tallinn, too. It was during the sixties or seventies. She had been astonished by the old, prewar European/German aura there. All of those little ladies wearing hats and sitting in cafés, eating cream pies. She wanted to know whether Estonia was still like that, now that it was becoming free again.

I noticed that Liz Franz replied quite tersely and stalely, but Nicole Zand liked her answers and burst out laughing several times. Liz Franz was apparently used to giving interviews and knew what would have an effect, what would go into the article and what there was no point talking about. She never went into details, never dwelled on nuances, and always replied directly and without mincing words, although perhaps not entirely honestly (when I think back to it now). I was enthralled by her "performance." At the end, she suggested to Nicole Zand that she also speak with "our young, renowned cineaste," by which she meant me. Nicole Zand cast me a quick glance sizing me up, and gave me her business card, even writing her direct number on it, asking that I get in touch. (Once, that business card actually did turn out to be very helpful.)

When Madame Zand had left, Liz Franz made an effortless proposal for us to go to a café somewhere and have a bite to eat—she was dreadfully hungry, apparently. No-no, I shouldn't worry, she made a gesture of refusal—her record label would pick up the tab, even for me; that was their agreement. Truly—from the very beginning, Liz Franz showed exceptional discretion and skill at disguising her charity. She asked me to be her guide: apparently, while she had indeed been to Paris once before (I now know that it was with Umberto; back then, I didn't know about Umberto yet, or really anything about Liz Franz's life at all—all I knew was that she lived in Rome), she had a poor knowledge of the city. So, I played the expert and took her to Place de la Contrescarpe, in order to show her the picturesque rue Mouffetard Market. Contrescarpe's cafés were incredibly chic, in my opinion—on cold, gray days, I dreamed of sitting there in the warmth behind the glass and eating this or that, the entire square smelling of it, while drinking a hot, fatty *café crème*.

Even so, I didn't dare to order anything other than a chicken salad: the names of many items on the menu were completely unfamiliar to me. Luckily, Liz Franz didn't demand that I translate the menu, but instead ordered a salad Niçoise right after me—a salad that, by the way, she only picked at; so much for her ravenous appetite. I, in any case, cleaned my plate entirely. We also drank red wine at Liz Franz's suggestion: a toast to our acquaintance. I don't remember any part of our conversation, only that we talked nonstop; evening had already descended long ago, we had ordered more wine, and she hadn't picked up on the fact that I was quite drunk. All of a sudden, however, she looked at her watch and shouted, horrified, that it was imperative for her to go—the head of her record label was apparently already waiting back at her hotel. Which didn't mean that we picked up the pace on the way back. Liz Franz never ran anywhere.

• • •

All in all, my obligations as Liz Franz's interpreter in late January 1991 were quite easy to fulfill. As I had hoped, I was able to sit next to her at lunches and gorge. A true interpreter doesn't eat, but interprets; however, Liz Franz spoke with her label head in Italian (true, in a rather stiff Italian), in even stiffer German with some new tablemate (but Liz Franz was never ashamed of her linguistic deficiency—she spoke as she spoke), and, naturally, in Russian with some Russian *comtesse*, who was as shriveled as a dried plum and decked out in gold, with shining eyes. For some reason, there was always a Russian *comtesse* or *princesse*, a countess or a duchess, at the table. Liz's label head apparently had some particular weakness for them.

He was a unique old gentleman, that Monsieur Mieroslawski. More than anything, he loved antiques and odd objects brought from distant lands. On the street, he routinely dragged us in front of the display window of some antique store, if not *into* the store, for us to gape with him at a lamp stand made of large seashells (probably a decadent fin-de-siècle work). Or at a little Chinese chest guarded by a golden dragon: when the chest is opened, the dragon spurts fire and smoke, as Monsieur Mieroslawski explained to us in French (because I didn't understand Italian), and as I then had to translate to Liz Franz, who was bored but feigning great interest. The ignition mechanism wasn't working at the moment, but it was apparently possible to fix.

M. Mieroslawski's apartment on a quiet cul-de-sac near the dome of Les Invalides (with a view, if you parted the heavy velvet curtains, of the golden cupola of Les Invalides, and down onto the square) was a genuine exhibition of ancient junk. The curtains kept away the daylight, so that M. Mieroslawski's mise-en-scène could have a better effect on the viewer. An African mask grinned beneath a spotlight, while in another corner a Japanese aquarium sparkled with its green plants and red and white fish. All of the furniture was heavy and antique; the ashtrays, dishes—nothing originated from this century or from the part of the world called Europe. We visited M. Mieroslawski at his home for a good-bye dinner before Liz Franz's announced departure (she didn't actually fly out that day, although she even had herself transported to the airport). That "dinner at home," which was served by a butler, was excruciating. I felt awful sitting there in my shabby clothes. Everyone else was decked out like bohemians—a well-known TV journalist and cultural commentator, a music critic, a professional musician, and a then-fashionable columnist for *Le Nouvel Observateur*—but I soon saw that those bohemian, open-minded pants, jackets, and shirts were very, very expensive.

I also felt slightly demeaned because I was the only interpreter present. The label owner's wife did ask me, out of politeness, what I did in my native country, but she took no notice of my reply, because while I was formulating it, the entire table had managed to burst out laughing at the TV anchor's joke, which went over my head (as did most of their jokes), because it involved references to some inner circle and targeted, as far as I could understand, the highest strata—all the way up to President Mitterrand. I had to translate those jokes for Liz Franz.

To my relief, no one seemed to be all that interested in her, even though she was the dinner party's guest of honor, because no one could be bothered to converse via an interpreter, and, furthermore, they had quite enough of their own Paris affairs to discuss, each one wanting to be in the spotlight at least once during the course of the evening. I also noticed that after each guest's departure, the remaining diners began backbiting mercilessly, although it was all somehow done in a way that left a friendly, private impression. Nowadays, having somewhat greater experience with Paris's cultural circles, I know that it was an ordinary, even normative scenario for an evening. I've also learned to take part in such conversations and understand the jokes. The only thing I haven't acquired is a knack for *producing* these jokes. I'm too slow and am never able to seize upon whatever infinitesimal slit in the fabric of the conversation into which I might jab my own poisonous allusion.

Naturally, at that dinner, no one said a word about yesterday's concert (aside from a couple of polite statements dropped during the appetizers), at which a couple of the guests *had*, however, been present; nor of Liz Franz's recent album release. In my naïveté, I had imagined that Liz Franz would be asked to perform one or two of her prettier songs for the guests (I now know that she wouldn't have done so anyway). Liz Franz was dressed in black again, from head to toe, just as on stage; but this time, it was a pantsuit. I had liked the previous evening's black velvet dress more, of course, but I also saw that it would have been out of place at that "bohemian" dinner. All the same, I would have been perfectly happy to see that striking sight as often as possible: Liz Franz, during her last song—her hit, "Prayer," which was popular in the Baltic States' freedom movement—on a dark, black stage, kneeling right at the edge, in a spotlight, her head slightly lowered, the microphone held between her hands, seemingly pressing it against her chest; just like the white rose on her concert poster. The silver microphone *looked* like a white rose in her hands, at that moment. Then, the fading of the last notes, and several more seconds of tense silence, Liz Franz frozen in the same pose, barely moving; then, the storm of applause, people rising to their feet, shouting "bravo," whistling; everyone had the feeling that they had been present (*assister*) at something very special—as Nicole Zand wrote the next day in *Le Monde*, probably summarizing the feelings of many: "the few chosen ones who had the fortune to make it into that concert partook of a powerful and, at the same time, inexplicable common experience, which can be summarized in a few words: the birth of freedom."

Truly—upon reading those words in the newspaper, even I felt that Nicole Zand was absolutely right. I was very proud that I had been able to share in that moment. And, overall, I was euphoric. Even *I* was free once more—I had money again.

The thing was that the very next morning after the concert, I had to do quite a lot of work. Liz Franz was attacked by an entire horde of radio- and newspaper journalists (she had gone on television without me), and this time I really did have to translate. Following that tense media session, a small meeting was held at the record company, during which a rundown of the coming record launch was made; a contract was likewise signed for the release of another record, for which Liz Franz was supposed to receive quite a nice (for me, anyway, back then) advance. I have to admit that the album was never released, and it probably won't ever be, given the fact that the Paon record label was dismantled as well, meaning that M. Mieroslawski can now dedicate himself entirely to his true passion, which is the collection of old and odd items. He was apparently able to net a pretty sum for himself from the sale of Paon.

Translating Liz Franz's contract in Paon's small office that afternoon (luckily, M. Mieroslawski didn't realize that I couldn't actually understand the contract's legal terminology in the least), my mouth went dry and my head began to buzz. When the meeting was over, M. Mieroslawski invited the two of us into his office (I had picked up on the fact that M. Mieroslawski had taken a peculiar liking to me), where he led us to his window, making a sweeping gesture and asking us to marvel at the view.

Presumably, the view was one of the pearls of M. Mieroslawski's collection. Outside the window was a small monastery courtyard—a garden, absolutely invisible from the street. It contained a couple of ancient, pruned trees, a few oddly shaped hedges, a grassy square, a small pond with greenish water, and a moss-covered fish statue on the pond's stony bank, from the mouth of which water gurgled. Truly, gurgled. The effect when M. Mieroslawski opened the window was, overall, one of genuine tranquility—unbelievable for the *septième arrondissement*. A black thrush sang quietly, but somehow passionately, reminding that winter would soon turn into spring. Then, M. Mieroslawski closed the window again, went over to his large, empty desk, took an envelope out of its main drawer, and handed it to Liz Franz. Cash, I supposed. Then, he said a couple words more about the (then) upcoming dinner (something to the effect of expecting both of our presences), after which—as if he'd recalled something else at the last second—he turned neither toward me, directly, nor toward Liz Franz, but somewhere in between, with a question, or more like a statement of opinion, saying that an interpreter is also entitled to his fee. I had initially counted on perhaps a couple hundred francs, but in the meantime, I'd also come to terms with the likelihood of being forgotten about completely.

M. Mieroslawski paused a moment after his words, for

suspense, as if expecting me to name my price. After that, he stuck his hand into the breast pocket of his moss-green cashmere jacket, pulled out two banknotes (it suddenly seemed to me that all of his drawers and pockets were full of cash), and handed me two five-hundred-franc bills.

"Will this be sufficient?" he asked politely.

I was only capable of nodding dumbly. "This" exceeded all of my expectations. "This" was a moment of enlightenment, during the course of which I realized what money really is. Money isn't, of course, those rubles with which I had managed the majority of my life. Nor was money the one thousand Finnish marks that I received from Helsinki for screening my film, because, in my opinion, even for one movie, that wasn't exactly generous. Nor was money the nearly four thousand francs earned for breaking my back on a cru, one thousand of which was spent right there on food. It wasn't much for an entire month's worth of very hard work. No, *money*, I realized, standing at that moment in that quiet office with its view of a monastery garden, is when M. Mieroslawski takes with an absentminded and almost indifferent gesture two five-hundred-franc notes out of the breast pocket of his green cashmere coat, and hands them to you, asking if it's enough. Is it enough for walking around the city with Liz Franz, and for the numerous café sessions, which Liz Franz insisted upon again and again, and during which she always treated me, and to which I had quickly become accustomed? Is it enough for the several luxury (Thai or Japanese style, in the private rooms of the most expensive restaurants) lunches, at which immigrant Russian *comtesses* and *princesses* jingled their gold?

Truly—is it enough? It's never enough, but it's bearable if you get it just the same, and for nothing to boot. *Then* and only then it is money. Otherwise, it's a salary, wages, or who-knows-what. According to the laws of economics, added value is created during the course of work. You receive a part, often only a trifling part, of that added value as remuneration. As such, you basically *give* money for working—you don't receive it. You make money for others, and money is exactly that: whatever is in those other hands. Money is the rain that falls upon a rich field, but doesn't fall on a poor one. Money is freedom.

I, for example, felt exceptionally free thanks to the two five-hundred-franc notes that appeared out of M. Mieroslawski's coat pocket. I was no longer dependent upon my Estonian acquaintance outside of Paris, or on his Citroën, lying on its belly in his driveway, for transport. I could buy a bus ticket and travel back to my homeland all on my own. But I wasn't in any hurry, initially. At that point, it still seemed as though Paris had many more interesting things in store for me than did wintery and poor Tallinn, where there was nothing available *at all* anymore, as the rare tourists who arrived from there reported to us where we usually gathered in Paris—goods were apparently only available with ration coupons. Moreover, I was in no hurry because Liz Franz remained in Paris at first. Specifically, she used the freedom contained in that rather fat little envelope handed to her by M. Mieroslawski as follows: she didn't bother to use her return ticket to Rome, which M. Mieroslawski had purchased. She did indeed have herself driven to the airport, but upon arriving, before checking her baggage, she shook off her escorts and waited a little while, then took a taxi back to the city. She had informed me of her plans beforehand, saying that she wanted to "stroll around" Paris for a few more days without having any bothersome obligations and escorts (but I wasn't a *bothersome* escort—that much I realized immediately); new obligations would be awaiting her again in Rome, one way or the other.

She took a new hotel room as far away as possible from the old one (and likewise as far away as possible from M. Mieroslawski's stomping grounds), on rue de Courcelles, on the *Rive droite*, in the *XVIIème arrondissement*. Interestingly, it's quite near to my current apartment and I pass it often; however, it's been ages since I've felt anything when looking at that hotel's facade, even though I do think back—again and again—to that decisive (if it *was* decisive) evening with Liz Franz, there in that very building. From time to time I've thought of stepping in to see whether that same receptionist is still at the front desk—a boy with a dreamful face, who watched us just a bit too sharply that time, and who I ineptly tried to make eyes at. But even if the same receptionist is there, he'd be a middle-aged man by now—no longer a boy. Just like me, really. Not that I'm reconciled to that, just yet. Looking at shorts yesterday in the Tartu Department Store—taking into account the fact that, according to a gay friend of mine, people in New York walk around in shorts all the time, unlike in Paris, where only American tourists wear them—rummaging through those overly athletic and boyish shorts there at the department store, not finding anything at all that could possibly look youthful, sufficiently chic, and solid all at once, I suddenly realized that I *am* already an old man, or will be becoming one very soon, in any case. That I'm no longer a boy. The realization hit me very hard. Life, which has always seemed dreadfully long, suddenly appeared incredibly short. Youth has passed, and there's been nothing . . . nothing of what I dreamed about throughout my youth, and which I'll probably keep on dreaming about as an old, pathetic youngster manqué, ridiculous in his pubertal implacability. (Three pimples appeared on my nose after my fever: I looked at them, like—see? Puberty *again! Another* one!) Really, there's nothing left for me to look forward to. What's been has been, and I even thought with a certain sense of satisfaction that the plane *might* actually crash into the ocean or something like that; I may not want to die, especially, but there wouldn't be anything especially tragic about it if you look at it rationally: it would simply be cutting my agony back to a reasonable length. For the agony already began long ago, maybe so much as eleven years ago, when I knocked on the door of Liz Franz's hotel room on rue de Courcelles at the prearranged time—four knocks, likewise prearranged (so she wouldn't have to open it for the maids, etc.). I was twenty-eight years old then—it already felt as though my life was ending, although I was actually very young; furthermore, I looked young for my age. Actually, one day at the gym, recently, when paying my fee, I was asked rather stridently whether I wasn't a student. Yes, I'm a student—Liz Franz's eternal, moronic student; but I don't get any kinds of discounts for it when taking the bus or going to the gym.

TRANSLATED FROM ESTONIAN BY ADAM CULLEN

MOX MÄKELÄ

Night Shift

I'm going to end it, because they're at me all the time. I'll mess them up bad, even though it isn't right, in fact it's completely wrong. Everything's wrong, that's the whole problem, it was wrong right from the start.

The old guy's dim as a jug of rotgut even if he doesn't drink anymore, and so's the old lady, but she's drunk on the Word. She keeps harping on about higher-ups even though they never pay her a visit, not the earthly ones or the heavenly ones. Everybody keeps their distance from us and sneers at us. Stuck in this same rut ever since I was little, but back then I didn't know how bad things could get when they really set their minds to it.

The old man makes sure we're always working. Even if it's just smashing rocks with a hammer for no reason, the sound of damns and hells should be audible, and him complaining about the pain in his back and hips and butt, and the old lady adding to the chorus with her pious songs, which are supposed to calm the restless spirit and soothe the weary laborer. I often go out, run along the beach, spit and curses running out of my mouth all the way down the trail, which is the best world there is for me. I curse these demons that I live with, that I'm trying to get away from.

I can see the shore, and the opposite shore, as I pace back and forth puffing smoke. I know it's all there, on the other side, a place I can't get to. That's where my real home is, my nest in the dim depths of the forest, under a tall tree where a hawk sometimes rests in the highest branches.

There are wadded up cartons and broken glass on the beach—groups of kids toss them down off the rocks. Sometimes there are gun nuts on the rocks, too, shooting shooting shooting, and the birds flounder in their own blood after those battles and I gather up the spent shells along the rocks and sometimes I shout for the birds' sake, as if I could get them back up into the sky, the blood back circulating in their veins.

When I go out among people the demons always get into me and I can't get along with them. I can't stand them because I can't understand them. I can't stand to be anyplace where people are in heat—the hell, the spread of it. I trudge past the church and the church comes after me and tries to drive me down to the market, but I'm too clever, I swerve under the lip of a tarp at a construction site. It's muddy and the wind blows, but I'm safe. The church doesn't like it and stays behind to spy on the other sinners over in the park.

I go to the hardware store to buy some string and I hear whispers like they're going to murder me there in their backroom, the storage area. At the bakery at least no one stares all that much. The baker doesn't sneer, since he knows how to at least be somebody, to be himself.

I go across the spoiled beach. It wasn't a sin to put shit in the lake back then, and it still isn't. I say unto you, birds, forgive us. I don't know what gets into me sometimes when I ask for forgiveness, and they sit like that with their heads tilted and ask me what for.

I keep going and now the soft, shadowy path is like freedom again. I could stay here overnight and sometimes I do, but then I get cold and go back to hell. I open the door and the old lady's eyes are like slits and she squawks that somebody's been somewhere slacking off, daydreaming. She's a body, she's been killed. I let myself be in other worlds. But then there's that hymn again, yowling because the cassette's old and the tape's wearing out. A sheep bleating about salvation. But the old man has his own word he's preaching, about how he's been digging a hole all day long, yelling at me to fill it up tomorrow, saying I've got worker's hands even if I do go around with my head stuck in ants' nests and other daydreams.

None of it matters, but he's a working man and keeps that uppermost in his mind and the old lady says that the mighty shall serve the low and if you'd just look at the stories in the bible it's all very simple. I don't really understand that, since I've never seen anyone serving her, and anyway the stuff you get from books is just a confusing mess.

This is all a nest of something I don't want to let inside me and when I'm in it myself I try to act like I'm swimming in piss, all my bodily orifices closed, not letting any of the juices in even if the old lady does talk like it's all as clear as water. A person might even believe it if you forced them into a corner. Or maybe I'm the crazy one, I'm the filth, the worst of the bunch when I don't swim over to her saints' corner, not even a real person when I'm out dreaming in the forest.

This is the sustenance I'm given, I think, when the old man's fist hits me in the side. He says I'm a deaf, crazy cow who doesn't have a man. I run outside, feel the evening and the mist from the shore against my face. He doesn't strike in malice, only when appropriate.

I can see the hole he's dug. There's a stink of gasoline in the shed and soap in the sauna. Will I die if I eat the soap and pour gasoline over myself? If I eat nails and the chain from the chainsaw and drink lighter fluid and then run into the dark road and someone comes around the corner and runs over me? If I walk to the beach and try to stay underwater long enough? If I could just lose myself without having to try. I don't know how to do it. I don't know how to do it right.

I set traps for him in my mind every night when I got to bed. I think about these things all the time, about how I could be left alone. I don't have the courage to really do anything and he knows it, from the moment he wakes up in the morning.

A skinny little cat comes into the yard from the beach. It rubs up against my legs and tries to jump into my arms. I pet it, the sun warms us, and a seagull is calling. The old man is standing on the beach and he has that satanic grin on his face. I remember what he's said about cats that come into the yard. I know what he's about to say. I pick up a broken branch and strike. The cat jumps away but the blow gets its back. It cries out in pain and I cry out too. I run out of the yard and I hear the old man yelling that there might be a little spine in that slut if she didn't start bawling at the drop of a hat. I yell and run and everything's churning around in my stomach. When I get to the woods I yell some more and pray to god that the cat will forgive me. Why the hell did he send the cat into our yard?

Is this all I know how to do, amuse the old man, then complain that I've hurt myself, and hurt an innocent part of nature? Am I like the old lady, like my whole family—the whole family of humanity—a predator, a bully?

He says that they're going to put the old chemicals and oil from the garage at the bottom of the pit, it'll keep the ants out of the yard, and besides, an ordinary person can't begin to pay the exorbitant fees at the dump, not with a household to support. He says let the worthless girl fill up the hole since she seems to have nothing else to do. It'll make her forget her daydreaming for a minute.

I carry the bags to the edge of the pit and all the old man's poisons go flying in. I shovel dirt over them and I'll shovel him in too, like I do every night, put him under that pile of stuff, and this time he'll have something burning under his butt, why not since he's always complaining about his aches and pains anyway. He'll really have something to complain about now, from all these different bottles.

One of his old workmates came into the yard and asked him something, and he talked a lot of shit, running off at the mouth, explaining the hole so that I laughed a shit laugh into my sleeve and the old guy thought I was crazy, and I am.

The neighbor comes over, a little old man who's a real whiner. The old lady's at home, the old man's at a meeting in the village. The neighbor complains about me tearing his nets and tangling them up. I did it when I saw what a shit he was, rubbing his car in the yard with a little piece of cloth, subscribing to gun magazines. The old lady tells him I haven't done anything. He yells that he saw me and she says you saw wrong and then he leaves and she goes after him and says she prays for everybody and especially troublemakers and wrong-thinking people. When I hear those two crazies I laugh out loud with a voice that fills the beach and then I crouch down behind my old man's nets and piss on the waders he left thrown over them.

That night the old man rants about what he heard at the meeting and the old lady comes in now and then with passages from the bible. I'm lying down in my room. The door's open—it always is, since the doorframe droops, and you can't get it shut. The old man says the house is not falling down, that if anything's out of whack around here it's young lunatics like me, and maybe I'll do a little less playing with myself with the door open. He's the one who jerks off, and he used to go to cheap whores when he was still working. Me, I don't have the urge to satisfy myself anymore. I only do it once in a while. It's lonely sputtering at something that isn't there. The only thing is that I feel a little calmer afterward. I don't understand these things, even though there's sex and cooing on television and whores on the covers of magazines. In school the teacher used to talk about "sexual matters" and say that it's a beautiful thing that happens between married people when they're close to each other. I don't know anything about that. When I start to bleed I know there's no point in it for me. But my body wants to give birth. It's really despicable. It would even go for the old man.

I would close the door between us if I could, be alone and at peace and sleep better. I wouldn't have to listen to the old man snoring and farting, the old lady walking around at night, the sound of her going to pee, muttering prayers. I could nail a board over the door and use the window to come and go and have my own life, but that's not allowed in this house. I'm reading a book but I don't understand anything that's written in it. I quietly tell myself that it's the wrong book, that I'll look for a better book, one that's written in a different way.

They sing their songs and read their bible every so often. The old man's gone down to the beach and is banging around with the boat, pretending to do something. I was supposed to tighten the screws in the oarlocks and I didn't do it and now he's cursing me. A piece of crap plastic dinghy, not even a real boat. I sit on the stoop of the shed and wait for him to go somewhere else, to take the boat somewhere.

He doesn't leave, keeps hanging around. Waving a shovel around at the end of the dock and talking to himself. He doesn't know how to do anything right, but he talks like he's some kind of unusually knowledgeable person. He insists that I should be doing something all the time, even though he says women haven't got the hands or the brains for work. He was one of the first to get the boot from the factory, and it must have been because they didn't want to hear any more from the crew about how they could never find where the shithead was hiding on the job site. A head full of bullshit. He should have been a gentleman, so he could use that head of his, spin his wheels in bullshit to his heart's content.

My sister got out of this hell when she moved abroad. She sends Christmas cards and calls the old lady sometimes. She asks me to come to the phone, but I've told them if she asks I'm not home. She left me here alone, even though she ought to know.

When the migrating birds come in the spring, I start writing. I write like I'm writing to the birds, and I also write down what they answer. It's like real life, a life where I'm good, and they've noticed it too. The way they watch me is wonderful and awful. I'm separate, lower. So much more crippled than they are. That bright space that's constantly changing shape, that moves along inside their circle, their combined voices offering a real song in every direction. And what do they say when they answer me? They say "You one-feather, you one-feather, your night is dark and your day is black, one-feather, you fly alone from the rock, an arrow got you, one-feather."

They know, because I tell them, and only them.

I also write to the others who come with the spring growth. I speak to the wind directly, I don't write much about it, but sometimes about the things it makes happen. The wind's tricks make me smile. It tears at the hedges and sweeps and smooths things as it goes and tells me I can do things, even bad things. The wind is like my friend and family, all the parts of the weather, which are servants of nature and visitors in nature at the same time.

The person inside me is coming out. She would like to be with other people, to calm down. The thing that would remain in me when that person left would be pure like a lichen and I could be at peace. I don't know how to be a real person. I wouldn't know how regardless of what my old man was, even if the old lady had a brain. People are all the same. This kind of monster in our house, other kinds of monsters in other houses. I see it on television and in the paper all the time, although sometimes they're so attractive that I give in and make up dreams about them. They're always a disappointment.

I win a prize when I send my writing to a contest. It feels good, although the old man's sour about it. I go to meetings and I'm like other people for a little while, but it's all a dream. These friendly people come and touch me on the shoulder and I think they can see me. A fast talker wants to print my new writing in a book, hands me a business card, writes in pen on the back and says that it's his private number, says to get in touch with him anytime, and I promise to send some pages. He hugs me tight, holds me there against him and asks me to swear I'll send him the things I haven't shown anyone. He says that I'm unique, that he's completely sold.

Later I send the pages, but I use a pen name so that the prize and the fog of the party drinks aren't the main thing, the main thing is what's most important to me. I tell myself I don't care, but I'm nervous waiting for the mail. I think I'll get a response right away, but it doesn't come. I'm left waiting.

Many months go by and I get a letter. It's large and pure white. The old man and the old lady don't get a chance to see it and taunt me, because I get to the mailbox first, and I walk straight to the trail in the woods with the envelope folded under my shirt.

I sit on a rock. It's a special moment and I look to see if there are any birds. The sky is empty, no one. I open the envelope. There's a white paper inside that looks blank at first, but it's just the wrong side. I turn it over and read the letter, which says that the company thanks me for the trust I've shown in them, but the material I sent doesn't fit their list at this time. At the bottom is the name of the person on the business card in my room. Suddenly I feel horrified that the card is in my room, in the same box with my writing tablets. As I'm running I scrunch the paper up into a thin horn and twist it like I'm wringing out laundry.

The surface of the water is smooth. The wind is somewhere else now, and I don't see any birds. I haven't been fishing in a long time—I don't want to kill them anymore. In this calm you can see their lives clearly. I let the boat stay where it is and sit motionless. First the little fish come in a school, then the bigger ones. They're listening to voices from faraway seas, because they all live in the same pool. There's complete silence around me, but everything I've seen is shouting in my head and it can't get out and I can't get out, nothing that yells like that can get out even though I can see the fish listening to the same sound.

I'd like to touch a fish sometime, but that's impossible. Fish are smart, they run away from people.

I'm told to go look in the old man's pack when he comes home from hunting. Dead birds and a thermos. Get a whiff of that so you'll know its scent, girl, he says, so you can sniff out meat, the basis of life and everything. He's crazy as hell. The old lady's brought her own carrion back from her prayer circle, and is spreading it around. Another crazy. This is hell and this is what I was born into, and you can't win paradise as a prize when you're in hell, so I could be any way at all, and the way I exist and how that feels bounces from one wall to the other, sometimes stabbing, sometimes stinging.

Next to the house is the speed demons' road that leads to the summer cabins. Their cars are like glistening snot, and so are they. Sometimes they stop to ask something and you're supposed to act like a person around them, you can't just glare at them and pluck your banjo or stare into their eyes and not say anything.

One of them drives into a ditch and stands there wondering at it. He doesn't understand that a car can end up in a ditch if you drive fast on this little road. The brat neighbor comes to wonder at it, too, and moan over it, but I say that it's a simple law of physics that everybody's taught in grade school. The speed demon says that this isn't something for a country girl to get smart about, it's a serious matter and I say serious serious shit flyer and I leave and the brat shakes his head and I hear him say something about me to the guy and I think let the dried-up turd say whatever he wants.

I go back there when they've gone looking for a neighbor to tow the car out, and the nearest neighbor is far away. The car door is unlocked. Between the two front seats there's a cup holder with an unopened can of cola in it. I open it and pour about half of it on the driver's seat. I put the can back in the cup holder and close the door. Later on the guy comes into the yard making a racket and says he's going to send us a cleaning bill, but Ma and the old man tell him that he'd better have a witness if he's going to start making accusations. Then the old man gives me a real beating later on, but the cola-ass's anger is still a sweet memory.

The autumn land is soft and dim. A little wind blows through the yard. Red spreads out to cover the whole western sky.

I heat up the sauna. Some good memory of a lost time comes to mind as I sit on the sauna bench. The fire I built on the beach is still smoking. I watch it from the sauna window. I feel good, languorous. I don't know if it's evening or morning.

I wake up on the bunk in the outer room of the sauna. The heat has dissipated, it's a little cool, but I don't want to leave. I pull the towel from the nail on the wall over me and fall asleep again.

I hear a car pull into the yard. I can feel my heartbeat in my throat. Someone is talking to someone else, walking around the yard. They walk to the house and then back to the yard. Their steps are coming closer. The door opens and I open my eyes at the same moment and I can't see anything. They ask me questions and another car comes into the yard and more people and more questions.

I'm perfectly tranquil and I think it's good to be asked questions calmly, and listened to, and have someone look me in the eye. I could talk about anything, but they only have their own problem to discuss.

They're looking for them, because they've disappeared completely. They're not in the house anymore, and I don't know where they are. They might be in the woods or on their way to someplace of their own. I was out in the yard all day and then in the sauna and I've just been thinking my own thoughts and haven't noticed anything.

They leave for a moment and then come back. They ask me to come along and I'm happy to go with them, to leave this place.

TRANSLATED FROM FINNISH BY LOLA ROGERS

ERIC CHEVILLARD

Hippopotamus

Don't expect anything sensational out of him. His name could be Jules or Alphonse. His name could be Georges-Henri. He's just as French as a Sioux adorned with war paint is Sioux. He doesn't hate the rain in Brittany. He's a good guy, but quite frankly has no business going to Africa. It doesn't even cross his mind. Africa? He would be less surprised if he gave birth to eleven puppies.

He has been invited to live and write in a village in Mali, on the Niger.

Ridiculous. Guatemala or Suriname would seem less random, as destinations go. Mali is the name of a meteorite, that much is certain. Of course it had to fall right in his backyard. It had to go and fall right in his little backyard right at the moment when he himself was there. And what was he doing in his little garden? He was gardening. It fell right on top of him. He was trimming his rose bushes, he was hoeing his square of vegetables.

His name must be Jean-Léon.

Why in the world must one always leave? What if it were more adventurous to stay? Life is there, at any rate. He asks himself if those who leave might nurse the dream of going where life is not, without admitting as much. He develops a solid argument based on the beauty of habits. He raises his heavy philosopher's head. His eyes wander along the walls of his bedroom.

Oh! He won't go.

To Mali, not so fast. One hardly even knows where it is. Another one of those countries. He's quite happy enough on his native turf. He knows the area. Sometimes he nurses the idea of taking a trip to Prague, or to Portugal. We'll see. But Mali, what an idea. Not once has he ever concerned himself with Mali, either from close-up or far away, not even with Lima or with Bali, even, while he's at it.

He's not going to pretend all of a sudden that he has some reason to go there.

He has been invited to be a writer-in-residence in a village in Mali, on the Niger. As though he needed to be there in order to write. Let someone bring him a table, a chair, a pencil and some paper. Subject, we said, Africa. Easy. Such is his frame of mind that he thinks right away of the great animals of the savanna. His limited imagination instantly calls up the giraffe and the elephant.

Let's read.

When Albert Moindre lands in Africa, the first creature he encounters is a giraffe. He can hardly believe it. He questions the evidence of his senses. Could he perhaps have fallen victim to a hallucination? He wonders what this tall thing could be good for. Then he has a flash of illumination.

—There's nothing it could be except a hat rack.

But to use such a tall, beautiful, and rather sophisticated construction for such a prosaic purpose is admittedly out of the ordinary. Not to mention that great care has clearly been taken not to overload the image as a whole so as not to harm the equilibrium that assures its singular elegance, its blend of solidity and gentle grace, whether seated or soaring.

A Western man wouldn't have failed to multiply the number of pegs in order to make the object more cost-effective.

Albert Moindre contemplates the giraffe. What could you put on it? A baseball cap, or a melon.

If you have two hats, you need two giraffes.

So that's how herds are born, Albert Moindre realizes, slapping his hand to his forehead.

Albert Moindre thought he had finally made his way around the elephant. It had taken him at least fifteen years, without ever slowing his stride. But this time he arrived at the end of his circuit. Wasn't he starting to recognize things that he had already seen, people and places? Still, he pressed on. For as soon as he decided to stop and put down his bag, doubt crept in: what if these were only resemblances, providential similarities? And so he took off again. He was going to see what was around the bend.

Poor guy, he's still walking.

Has no one ever made it around an elephant? wondered Albert Moindre as he lengthened his stride.

Africa: there you have it. It's certainly enough. At least when you stay at a distance from a thing you can get a good view of it in its entirety. Why should he wander all the way there and risk never again being able to grasp more than the handful of dirt at his feet? And thus lose all contact with Africa? Moreover, he's not the type to go running around the globe. What does it get you? Can you ever really finish? There's always another island, a mountain, the steppes and the floes. The Pampa.

So he'll stay nicely and peacefully at home.

One begins to make out this moderately complex character. A certain talent for the rhetoric of justification and bad faith could have misled us. But no, we quickly saw through it. He's a coward. He can only breathe easy within his own lair, amid his own scent. Beyond his little redoubt extends the land of shadows, of malevolent spirits. From which no one has ever returned.

What a lot of fuss!

His intelligence torments him a bit nonetheless. He toys with being tempted by Africa. Not seriously. He won't go. But still, he starts talking about it with whomever happens to be around. He pretends to be hesitating. Perhaps I'll go to Africa at the beginning of next year, I don't know yet. I'm feeling it out. He leads people to believe that his life consists entirely of that— plans, departures, running zigzag across the planet.

Rest, never, but sometimes he lies down for a moment to nap beneath the forest canopy. Or, rather, his sofa.

Casually dropped in conversation, the information is fascinating. He manages to take on all the prestige of a traveler without moving an inch. Let's see about doing it next winter, he says, then adds, unless I'm in Africa. I'm thinking about popping over to Mali in January, he murmurs dreamily, as if to himself. Listen, I can't get too involved, it's not out of the question that I'll be in Africa by then.

Who does he think we are?

He won't go. But he's taking advantage of his position. The word is enough for him. The word Africa is his now. He has the right to use it. Doesn't deprive himself of it. Africa Africa. In his mouth, it's not such a blatant incongruity as it once was. He gazes at the horizon with the eyes of a landowner. He's at home out there. He has good reasons to articulate the word Africa.

When he talks about it now he even seems just the slightest bit blasé.

One would think he had already been to Africa. Think that he spends half his life there. Six months of every twelve. He's kind of had enough of Africa. He's going to take a break. A few months without Africa, that would be good for him, a change of scenery. He would take advantage of the break to read, to write, at last. He doesn't say it in so many words, but everything about his attitude, his allusions, and his silences suggests a weary adventurer who wouldn't mind granting himself a little break.

Oh! But only to bounce back even higher.

What a lark! This man who seems to think that nobody knew how to use paper before he gave them a demonstration, now he wants to pose as a man of action, and in order to do that, he wants the word Africa to resound as often as possible. Africa Africa. Sometimes he says Mali instead; it's more accurate.

Precision is one of the most acclaimed qualities of his style.

Indeed, he has been invited to Mali, to a village, on the banks of the Niger. He will decline. He won't give his real reasons. He won't say that it's because of cowardice, indifference, and because in the confines of his stunted spirit he feels so pleased with himself that he sees no reason whatsoever to modify his condition and prefers to let the marrow melt delectably under his tongue with his eyes turned inward.

An attentive ear would hear him snoring.

Great poems rise up in him:
Africa Red land of the black man
Land of the return to self when the dust settles
Here discipline and savagery are co-wives

Here you must dig a well in the crust to reach the fruit
Here you see and admire yourself in the shining ebony face
Etc.
People would believe it. Why bother actually going?

Africa Dry shore of the Milky Way
Moon of the moon without water or electricity
Without its astronaut boots the elephant won't go far
Here the weapons are coarse but the sun has been hit
Here is its great body outstretched on the earth
Etc.
Because he no longer believes in poetry, he no longer believes
in Africa, either.

Africa has never been more than a poetic creation to him, a territory peopled by the dream of chimerical animals, elephants
(elephants!), giraffes (giraffes!). Because poetry, exhausted, suddenly has no words left to name it, it must disappear. How long
has it been since a new pachyderm was evoked? Our pragmatism from here on out can do nothing with these childish fan-
cies. Africa is far behind us, ancient history.
It was nothing but a dream.

Naïve fiction of innocence preserved, of a prehistory that has
lasted into the present. So quick to marvel before the authenticity of the Fula and the Masai, the western traveler refused
to recognize or admit to his own—suddenly, curiously enough,
authenticity equals rusticity. Then he pretends to envy the Fula
and the Masai who haven't lost theirs and laments that he must
belong to a derailed civilization, incomprehensible and false.
But this rapture and this refusal and this pretense and this
lamentation characterize nothing other than the authentic
western traveler.

For he has theories that he doesn't hesitate to divulge in public. He considers himself an authority ever since he received the invitation from Africa. The western traveler, he says for example, has no fear of affirming, considers the Fula or the Masai as individuals who are essentially inhabitants of a place, typical, leading lives tightly structured by their customs, their rites, their traditions, and the western traveler broods over them, feasting his eyes on them, filled with tenderness.

Don't they live in truth?

The Fula is one hundred percent Fula. Fula from head to toe. Fula when he sleeps, too. Fula consenting prisoner of Fula. Fula like none other would know how to be Fula and especially not the Masai, far too Masai for that, Masai to the tips of his fingernails, Masai even when he thinks about something else, intractably and definitively Masai, in each of his gestures, in each of his actions, Masai.

Fula Fula and Masai Masai.

Fula inside and out, Fula in depth and on the surface, Fula with no other horizon than Fula, Fula in the Fula in the Fula in the Fula, Fula sewn up with Fula, stuffed with Fula, son Fula and father Fula, Fula as only the Fula, and especially not the Masai who is nothing but Masai, stuck in Masai, rooted in Masai, married to Masai, eating Masai, dancing Masai, singing Masai, dying the death of the Masai.

Masai Masai and Fula Fula.

As for him, the western traveler, he is endowed with a freedom not only physical, economical in nature, but also mental, psychological, which is precisely what permits him to travel, to understand all cultures immediately and perfectly, in any case that's what he seems to think, as if he weren't typical with his baseball cap and animated by reflexes acquired in his native land, made up of the same clay as any other, and where he'll remain as nothing more than an empty bowl on the potter's wheel.

Spirit without attachments or prejudices flying across the world offered up to his curiosity, to his limitless understanding, and which reserves for him its hidden beauties: this is how he sees himself.

Nonetheless, it's difficult to find a more determined, more predictable, more folkloric individual than the western tourist. It's not by chance that caricaturists sitting on their folding chairs wait for them in all the high places. Rigorously truthful portraitists who amuse their models by holding up mirrors to them. And the more the latter laugh, the more their traits swell, their nostrils flair, their noses lengthen.

And it's hardly worth noting that they have fat knees.

Not him. He won't go running headlong into it. But he's looking for information about the village. He feels he needs to flesh out his discourse with a few concrete details when serving it up to his fascinated and moving audience. He obtains the regional gazette, which informs him:

The waters of the river rose abruptly and flooded the banks up to the first houses of the village. A hippopotamus wreaked havoc among the sand tradesmen. Two of them have already died. Tiémoko Coulibaly lost his life on Monday following an attack by the animal. According to witnesses, Tiémoko and his companions had already finished loading their canoe with sand when they were attacked. Tiémoko fell into the water. His body was not found until the next day. The second victim was Hamadoun Touré. The angry hippopotamus stomped twice on the pirogue, which capsized. Hamadoun Touré sank like a stone.

Is that concrete enough?

At the same time, this lamentable news brief reinforces his incredulity (a hippopotamus!). Africa is improbable. He then remembers that they were planning to house him on the riverbank. The Niger lapping against the walls of the Residence. Never before had the threat of being stomped on by a hippopotamus made him shudder. Faced with this peril, he remained stoic.

But suddenly his courage wavers.

He's there quite comfortably in his imagination, in this distant country. The trip itself has proven utterly uninteresting, just the hassles of airport and visa, the chore of dealing with the baggage porter. As though his African adventure could accommodate such a trampling. *Mali* means *hippopotamus* in the Bambara language. All you have to do is know it and say it, and it's the same as having been there, as returning from there. I am expected in the Republic of the Hippopotamus, he says.

And you?

Little by little the trap closes on him. He can no longer back out. People wouldn't understand. Now he regrets that he didn't hold his tongue. He's just about to leave, he hears them whisper behind his back. They're chasing him out. They're banishing him. Here he is, forced into exile. His decision still unmade, people come from everywhere to say good-bye. Fine, fine, he'll go.

He will have been brave for once in his life, trembling in every limb.

He's going. He situates himself comfortably in the reclining seat, in position for takeoff. Through the clouds he makes out a Spanish scarf, he dips his toes in the Atlantic, he rakes the Saharan sand with his fingers. He passes through some turbulence, faints briefly, then the doctor removes his rubber glove, tosses the syringe in the trash, all set, you can put your shirt back on.

He needs no fewer than six vaccines to finally feel affected by Africa.

He's going to go. It's still the surest way to come back. Then he'll be mistaken for another man. A new man. Africa changed me completely. I used to be that, now I'm this. I was White and now I am Black. He already hears himself say: Life's not worth living without the harsh test of Africa. And: You think you understand Africa from the papers and the news, but no, not at all, don't make me laugh. You have to have been there.

You have to have lived there to know what Africa truly is.

He already hears himself say: Submit yourself to the harsh test of Africa. If you want to know yourself, my boy, go to Africa. Go search for your truth in Africa. Renounce your bourgeois habits, renounce your morbid, nauseating happiness, go to Africa. You who doubt, you who contemplate yourself in frivolous despair and bitterness, go instead to Africa. Take the risk of Africa.

And he will write *My Mali*.

He usually writes in pencil on loose-leaf paper. It's not ideal for travel. You have to be able to write on your knees. You have to be able write shoulder to shoulder with people in a crowd. You have to be able to write at night, by the light of a hurricane lamp or a match. And perched in a tree. Lying on the grass. In a trough of sand or dirt. He dreams of obtaining a little pocket notebook.

Black, covered by moleskin, with an elastic closure.

In the meantime, he's just received his passport. I had to have it renewed, he says. But it's clearly the first time he's ever had a passport. He grabs the flat object by a corner and dangles it in front of his face, then taps it with the palm of his left hand. With his fingertips he caresses the smooth and luminous cover, with its very fine grain. Until now he has only known such intense feelings when handling the cover of his checkbook.

And yet now it's the contrary. He's done with petty savings.

And long live exhausting your resources. Living without counting. Double or nothing every second, playing with fire. He strokes his brand new passport. He considers accelerating its aging process. Maybe if he ran it under water, or forgot it outside in the grass for a night? Should he cover it with dirt, or scour it against a rugged stone? Or would it be enough just to scratch it up a bit with his fingernail?

A passport isn't worthy of the name unless it has made it out of the lion's den.

And as for him, will he also expose himself to violent winds and storms to tan his own hide a little before he leaves? My God, he's so pink! The baby doesn't change! Skin unchangeably baby-soft, it makes you want to kiss him on the neck, caress his thighs. I'll have to have all that beaten out of me. No corns on his feet or calluses on his palms, this little cutie.

Where are his scars?

He's leaving, and that's final. He tells everyone, even when nobody asks. —And what is the purpose of your trip? —Humanitarian. —Really? —Yes. In this country devoid of shadows, mine will soon appear . . . At this point, one thing at least is certain: He won't come back any stupider. Why is he going, actually? What is he going to do in Africa? Simple enigma. As always, as everywhere, he is going to look for a book.

Did you think he was going to bring back the moon?

He's not going with the intention of pillaging the treasures of

African art, or of trafficking ivory, rhinoceros horn, and gorilla thumb. He won't stuff the cargo hold of the plane with baby wild animals or parakeets. He won't hide an ebony trunk in his intestines. But if he finds some bit of old mythology that's not too well-known here, if someone tells him a wonderful story that he could claim as his own with impunity . . .

Writing, for him: to raid.

For he's far too lucid in any case to keep a journal and try to persuade his reader that he's the first white man to land in Africa. You can't just talk about about your travels anymore, unless it happens that the telling itself becomes a catastrophe, that all his slides display backwards, and then one of these slipped in by mistake, there's a scandalous flash of nudity, with nothing to do with his adventure at all, and then the screen falls off the wall.

And then the projector catches fire.

His nights are troubled. The boat pitches from side to side. He dreams that Africa is an open hand that threatens to slap him and this hand does actually hit him, right cheek, left cheek, then crushes him against his bedroom wall like a bug. He wakes up hollering, his companion takes his hand, wipes his forehead, speaks softly to him. He breathes. He calms down. Little by little he relaxes. He falls back asleep, relieved.

Striking him like an axe, Africa splits him in two from top to bottom.

Where is he going with that wheelbarrow? To the pharmacy. He fills two whole travel bags with medications. Dying is now out of the question. He also buys whatever he needs to preemptively arm himself against specific dangers: sunscreen with SPF 100+, protective lip balm, mosquito repellent, antivenin, capsules to purify water. It reassures him, but it terrifies him too.

Could he, despite it all, just pretend that he'd lived in Africa?

Will he even be able to claim that he survived the harshness of Africa, so long as he has the protection of these sundry coverings? People will think he sent his grandmother instead of himself, or that he had expedited a smooth, cold photograph of himself across the land. And yet it's the skin that really travels, the skin alone. It's the skin that discovers America and both poles through its pores and nerves.

The eyelids learn of new realities much more quickly than the eyes.

And yet he's getting ready to go to Africa without it, without his skin, seeing as it's so thoroughly coated and saturated by protective lotions that it will no more experience Africa than if it was parting ways with him for a nice trip to Norway, or if he'd left it hanging in the soft shadows of his closet, alongside his winter clothes. But who said anything about feeling or touching? He wants only to take, and a gloved hand can do it as well as the bare.

Nonetheless, he prefers to cite the elephant as an example, tender heart and damp eyes under its muddy crust.

At the pharmacy, he also buys an aerosol bottle of herbal elixir. Two sprays in your mouth and your confidence will be renewed, serenity will return, love of self; your wise little, shrewd little nerves, like termites, will have nothing left to consume of your body's squishy interior, they'll stop their quivering, you'll feel good, peaceful, you will swim in euphoria.

He drafts his will.

Torn to shreds by a crocodile, he will no longer fear the fangs of degenerate farm dogs deep in Auvergne. He talks nonsense to himself to encourage himself. In front of others, he acts flippant. At times he even feigns impatience. I can't wait to be there, he says. Give me the African sun! But in reality, if he's counting the days, it's more as someone would if his doctor had just given him only a certain number of days to live.

Rhinoceros, my friend, shall we exchange shirts?

In January, no, impossible, I'll be in Africa. Might as well take full advantage of the prestige that this position grants him (he figures). Wait, wait, you said end of February? No, I won't be back from Africa yet. Yes, I take off like that from time to time. I have to leave, it's imperative, get away from all this. Sometimes I just can't take France anymore. God, just to get the hell out!

As a matter of fact, his plane ticket and visa arrived this morning.

It's a rude awakening. He never really believed it, of course. He won't actually go to Africa. It's a joke, a game. How could the airline company have taken him seriously? Even the consulate of Mali fell for it. Clearly nobody can take a joke anymore. It's a sad world when even humor's out of bounds.

One satisfaction: at the bookstore, he found a small black moleskin journal, with an elastic closure.

Truly a beautiful object. He looks at it sadly. He cries for the new shoes that one takes into the country, on the muddy paths, into the brambles. He has an entire collection of upholstered boxes, containers, cassettes, that he uses to protect his belongings. He has a little foam container for everything, or else a globe. He can even imagine himself quite easily in a wetsuit, like a deep-sea diver.

If such reckless creatures didn't go carelessly gallivanting through the heights and the depths.

It's the night before his departure for Africa, and he still has to protect himself from the rain. But instead, he throws his head back, opens his mouth, and drinks in the storm until the last drop, he refreshes himself as much as he can, he drenches his flesh, he fills his pipes and tubes, his bladder is a precious wineskin, a pear for his thirst.

He tries to sew the water into his pockets.

Winter will never allow such a frail creature to escape. Better to freeze such a magnificent specimen. Snow covers the airport. Traffic is slow, almost stopped. After waiting two and a half hours to check his luggage, he's finally at the gate. And so the hope for a better life persists in us, from one enclosure to the next. But for him, wouldn't it be a better life not to leave, to remain sheltered by winter?

Passengers traveling to Bamako are invited to board through door C.

It's a rude awakening. He gets onto the plane and sits down, miserable. His neighbor is a highly agitated young Malian who fidgets in his seat and nervously clutches his tray table. In mourning or withdrawal, he tells himself, thinking with the inward smile of a lexicographer that it's more or less the same thing. He offers his help but gets no response. At any rate he won't be able to revive the poor guy's father, or provide him with a fix. The plane still hasn't taken off.

They announce that there's ice on the runway.

Maybe they won't leave. There now, all is not lost. His confidence returns, even while his neighbor sobs compulsively and yanks on the tray table, mangling it. Then he curls up around his knees and rocks back and forth, moaning. It becomes more and more difficult to act as though everything is fine. Is something wrong? The other stands up suddenly, and he must stand up as well to let him pass.

He didn't see it coming. The fist flies and everything spins.

Decapitation in the guise of departure. This is what he gets for sticking his head into the unknown. They take him off the plane. He watches an air traffic controller work, leaning over him, as he stitches up his lip. He brings back a black mask from his little trip, which makes quite an impression. Women nurse those fierce invalids, home from hot countries.

His suitcases left without him. They'll tell him about Africa.

TRANSLATED FROM FRENCH BY KATINA ROGERS

GURAM DOCHANASHVILI

A Fellow Traveler

A little train is running from Bakuriani to Borjomi. There are only three men in one of the compartments, sitting facing one another. Two of them are younger than the third. The guys are wearing ski boots, tight trousers, and sweaters—one in red, another in light blue. The third man is actually somewhat old. He is playing with a cigarette holder, balanced on his knee, and looking out the window. The man is sitting with his back to the engine and his eyes seem to be following something out there. Whereas the young men's eyes are wide, as though welcoming something they see coming up. Of the three of them, though, it's the old man who seems most interested in what's going on outside the train. The guys are bored with Bakuriani, really. It was amazing at first, they were skiing, throwing snowballs at one another, just generally having fun, sliding down the slopes on their toboggans. They enjoyed their nighttime promenades, the snow crunching under their heavy boots. Dogs would bark just for the sake of barking, off in the distance, and sometimes the lights in this or that cabin would go off as they passed by, sleepy Bakuriani. As though to make up for it, the stars would light up in the sky . . . The guys were pleased with their entire trip, but those long strolls through virgin snow were their particular favorite. At some point, though, the guy in the blue sweater hurt his leg and had to be confined to bed. The holidays were over, then, all at once. Bakuriani saw off its visitors. The guy in the blue sweater would lie in bed, trapped, looking out the window of his room. And the guy in red stopped going out as well, except for food. This is what their fun got reduced to: looking out windows, one sitting, one lying down. Outside, the snow covered everything . . . Sometimes they would tell each other old stories to pass the time—they would begin in fits and starts, uneasily, then they would remember something or other that seemed especially pressing, and then they would pick up steam, proving a point, making a case for this or that. The more their subject was exhausted of enthusiasm, the more they would turn back, slowly and surely, to the window. Outside, the snow covered everything. The guys were already bored with the snow. They would turn their heads and look at the wall instead. The walls were pocked with spots of various sizes. Some of the spots had taken on various shapes: a bearded man, for example, or a bear, or whatnot. The guys would look to the wall for a little excitement.

And now they are sitting in front of the old man.

And the man is mainly looking out the window. One can see only snow and trees out there, nothing else. And the trees are welcoming our three men of various ages, standing (the trees) in pairs, or one by one, or in large groups. The old man is following the trees with his eyes, in pairs, or one by one, or in large groups. The younger men are soon bored with looking out of the window. They'd like to find something amusing to focus on; they're looking the ceiling over, they're looking over the floor. The ceiling, unfortunately, has received a recent coat of fresh white paint—now, try to find any fun up there . . . it's spotless and smooth. Whereas the hardwood floor has narrow channels running across it, between the planks, which at least has *some* potential, humor-wise.

I wish the skis would fall down, so I could stand them up again, the guy in the light blue sweater is thinking.

The guy in the red sweater would love to do a little singing, but he's bashful in front of the old man. Is he doomed to boredom? And if the old man weren't there, he'd talk to his friend, Temur, about Maia. He'd tell him what a caring soul she is. So caring that she even pities the hen they saw for sale at the market fair, hanging there upside down. Someone should cut it loose, she said. But, look—what can he say in the presence of this weird old man?

He's a real nuisance, the guy in the red sweater thinks, looking down at the old man's boots. Not that the fellow is doing anything wrong. No, he's just sitting quietly and looking out the window. His eyes taking in the sight of all those trees—in pairs, one by one, or in bunches . . .

The snow is losing its whiteness little by little, going gray. The lights have switched on in the carriage.

The guy in the red sweater wants to get a closer look at the old man's face. He knows, however, that if he steals a glance, the old man will notice. So he is gradually sneaking little looks, making a composite portrait. There's the cigarette holder, then the button on his shirt pocket. One peep more and . . .

What a long nose he has, the guy in the red sweater thinks.

The old man is still looking out of the window.

What a vacant expression he has, the guy in a red sweater thinks. The small train stops at Sakochao. The two guys look around out the window with renewed interest—maybe here they might catch sight of something funny. The platform is lit up. There is a bell hanging on a wall. A man is standing at the bell, so smothered in winter clothes that no one could have guessed whether he was thin or fat. The guys are staring out of the window with avid eyes, first it was only trees and snow and then, suddenly, there emerged this platform, its bell and man. This is new, or somewhat, and interesting, somehow. The muffled-up man feels the insistence in the guys' stare, and it bewilders him not a little. He doesn't want the guys to notice his bewilderment so steps aside and spits as nonchalantly as he can manage.

How I wish there were some spots on the ceiling . . .

The snow is now grayish. The snow is glittering in the place where the lights from the train touch the ground.

The two guys hear, distantly, the peal of the muffled-up man's bell. The muffled-up man has performed his duty and is now on his way—somewhere. He is still aware of the insistent stares coming from the train, following him, and is trying to walk as gracefully as possible. He swings his arms only moderately, and he finds himself lifting his knees a bit more than usual; well, there's a funny tension in his gait. The guy in the red sweater is smiling and turning his head toward his fellow travelers. Temur is smiling too. The man isn't playing with his cigarette holder anymore, but has rested it on his knee.

What a vacant expression . . . what a long nose . . .

The man is looking—somewhere.

I wonder what he sees out there?

But the man isn't actually looking at anything in particular. He is simply watching.

And now the little train is on its way again.

The man is toying with his cigarette holder again—or he's resting it on his knee, pointing this way or that, with the cigarette end forward, or with the mouthpiece, depending.

—Do you like it? Temur asks the man.

—What? The old man smiles, because he can't figure out what he's being asked.

—The snow . . . do you like it?

—Oh yes, the snow is great.

—You must really love snow, the guy in the red sweater says. You haven't looked away from the window the whole trip.

—Yeah, sorry . . . I do love snow, very much.

—Why? the guy in the red sweater asks, but his tone is so ingenuous that the irony behind the question is wholly inaudible.

—Well, I don't know . . . the man says. When I look at the snowy ground and the trees I feel peaceful. There's so much peace in the snow, an overwhelming amount of peace . . . can you call peace "overwhelming"?

—Sure, why not . . . anything can be overwhelming.

—All right, then. That's why I love snow.

—Because it feels peaceful? Temur asks.

—Yeah. Peacefulness is . . . peaceful. I look at the snow for as long as I can . . . then I start staring at some fir tree. And there's snow on the branches of the fir tree. And though they neither bend nor sway, I feel afraid on account of the fir tree, because it could always move in the wind, or get too weighed down, and then it would shake the snow from its shoulders . . . and the peace would be broken.

—Peace is a little too boring for me, the guy in the red sweater says.

—Yeah. You're young. You're not supposed to like too much peacefulness. If you love snow, no doubt it's because you love to ski, or throw snowballs.

—The guy in the red sweater doesn't like the man's answer much. He gets angry and is trying to find a way to show the old man up without his noticing.

—Excuse me, but you don't by any chance write poetry, do you?

—No. The man is smiling. Why?

—It's just that you described the winter landscape so sensitively . . .

—Ha! I guess I didn't do too badly at that. Still, the old man goes on, if I was really a poet, I'd have known whether or not you can call peace "overwhelming" . . .

The man is smoking a cigarette now, fumigating their compartment.

—Overwhelming, he says thoughtfully. A tremendous word.

—Tremendous how?

—I don't know how to explain it. It's just that . . . well, it seems to me that some words fit so beautifully, so particularly well with their respective definitions. I mean that the music of the word, its sound, happens to fit what it means. Take, for instance, "antiaircraft" . . . there's something so strong, so formidable in the sound of it. Or, like "bird" . . . when you say it, you can almost see a little, delicate, feeble . . . and, well, the sound of the word "overwhelming" too, I think fits its meaning. Do you follow me?

—Not entirely.

—Well, say "overwhelming."

—Overwhelming.

—Can't you feel it, something big, maybe too big?

—Nope.

—I think, Temur says . . . I think "lion" is a good one too.

—Lion? asks the guy in red. Not at all. I think "lion" is way too delicate. Effete, even.

—Yeah, said the old man. I don't think "lion" works at all. Think of it: a terrible beast on the one hand, and that little wisp of a word on the other: "lion."

—All right, all right—what about "moon"? (Temur is trying to play along.) I think that works very well. But not "sun." The sun should have been given some other name, something bigger . . . more euphonious . . .

—Yeah, exactly, the old man says, and feels happy that Temur understands him.

There's a lull in their conversation. The guy in the red sweater stands up.

—Where are you going Dato?

—I'm going to warm up a little. I feel cold.

—Why, it's not cold in here, boy, says the old man.

—Maybe not for you . . .

Dato starts shaking his hands to and fro, then he turns around a few times, sits down quickly, and stands up even quicker, Temur recollects his hurt leg.

—It's so good to be young, the old man says to Temur.

Without any particular reason, Dato feels awkward now and sits back down.

The train stops.

—Which station is it, I wonder? Temur asks, looking back to the window.

The snow is blue. It glitters only where direct light falls.

—Little Tsemi, the man replies and looks through the window as well. Yeah, it's Little Tsemi.

Dato stares at the old man, fuming. Why did he stop his calisthenics? Why does the man make him feel so awkward?

That big nose . . . that idiotic expression . . .

Again a bell rings. Again the small train moves on.

—It's actually getting colder in here . . . there must be a draft coming from somewhere, Temur says.

—Do you remember, Temur, how stuffy it was when we were at the sea, panting at the open window for even a little breeze. Do you remember?

—Sure I remember, Temur says.

—How awesome it was, the sea, Dato says, cheering up. Nothing beats the sea!

—We got bored with the sea too, eventually, as I recall.

—Not at all, I wasn't the least bit bored.

—Sure you were.

—Never! How could I get bored with the sea . . . ? Ah, the sea is so gorgeous . . . Just the pleasure of lazing around on the sand makes it worthwhile. No, you don't laze, you stretch out onto it, entrusting your body to the sun . . . The sun will burn you, will calm you, will take you over, till you can't think of anything, can't remember anything, you're just feeling the sun. Eventually you get up, and you're . . . can one say, "saturated" with sun?

—I'm not sure.

—Well, in any case . . . You're *saturated* with sun, and so you step into the cool, pleasant sea. The gorgeous sea! Now the sea, the sea really *is* overwhelming. The overwhelming sea . . . The word "overwhelming" actually fits the word "sea," I think, Dato says, looking at the old man.

The man is looking through the window. The snow is now dark blue.

What a foolish expression he has, Dato thinks, feeling compelled to engage the man in conversation nonetheless.

—Do you like the sea? he asks.

—Well, now, I don't really know . . .

—What? Have you never seen the sea, then?

—Yes, I have . . .

—How could you not love it, then? The sea is amazing, awe-inspiring . . . That's like saying you don't like sunsets. You've seen the sun set, right?

—Yes, certainly I've seen it . . . the man says uneasily, without taking his eyes from the window.

I was so sure that he'd love nature, Temur thinks.

—Well, didn't you like it? Sunsets too are awe-inspiring, Dato says, looking at the ceiling. It turns bluish-green and blue. A golden reddish disc emerges into the blue. The disc is leaving the blue space slowly, lingeringly, hiding in the bluish-green.

—Ah, the greatness of the sea, Dato says. How could anyone not love the sea?

—Perhaps it's not so rare as all that, the old man says.

—You only like peace, is that it? But isn't it peaceful at the seaside? Isn't it peaceful at the seaside during sunset? You know, I've often observed that when people go out to watch the sun go down over the ocean, they tend to whisper. They stand there and whisper! It's so tranquil, then they're so calm. They don't want to break the spell. They don't want to ruin the peacefulness of it all.

—You don't understand. What I like is . . . oblivion. To lose oneself in nothingness, you know? That's the kind of peace I enjoy.

—And the sea isn't good enough for you? Look, nothing obliterates the self like a raging sea! You haven't thought this through. How great is a raging sea, anyway?

The old man is nervously tapping his cigarette holder on his knee.

—How great it is to sit and watch the sea rage, Dato says, looking at nothing in particular. Think about it. The sea is preparing a wave. It gets a good running start. It shakes a little, then rocks back and forth, then it brings in other waves in clusters, then it swings them all around, and . . . you hear it roar, the waves all come crashing onto the shore, look at it roll those rocks around, the big ones too, and of course the little pebbles, and finally it's just clinging to the sand as it rolls back, it seems to me that a wave has fingers . . . Are you *sure* you don't like the sea?

The old man's muscles can be seen tensing up and relaxing again in his cheeks.

—Are you sure, Dato goes on, that you don't like the rough and powerful sea?

—Enough! the old man shouts. Why can't you leave me in peace?

The man is on his feet, glaring down at at Dato. He looks like he's ready to attack.

—Why, what did I say? Dato asks, astonished.

The old man sees that this surprise is genuine. He sits back down. Almost calm.

—Sorry, the man says, looking down.

But Dato is furious now. Why did he yell at me? What the hell did he have to yell about?

—You know, Dato says, if you were my age, I wouldn't let you get away with that. But, look, you're—what? My dad's age, probably. At least.

Silence is necessary and inevitable at such moments.

There are channels running between the planks that make up the coach's floor.

Dato wants to look at the man, but doesn't want to get caught doing it. He's a bit worried, frankly.

And the train continues on. And the train probably stopped at yet another station, in the meantime, at which yet another bell was rung, after which the train started up again, and is now continuing on.

Dato risks looking at the old man's boots. Then at his knees. Then at the button on his shirt pocket. Then at his face.

Which doesn't really have a big nose at all.

What a sad expression the old man has.

—Sorry, Dato says.

—No need to apologize, kid. You couldn't have known. Please excuse me for crying. I was crying because of the sea, the sea . . .

Silence again. The cigarette holder is tapping on the old man's knee again. First he taps it with the cigarette end, then with the mouthpiece, in turn.

Dato wants to console the man, or to say something pleasant to the man. He can't find the word.

The old man is looking back through the window. The snow is altogether black now. It looks black, anyway. But perhaps it's still white, somewhere.

—I love it very much, the man says. Yes, I see the sea, the raging sea . . . But when I'm looking at the snow, I forget everything. I just feel peacefulness. Sometimes I look at some of the fir trees too. There's so much snow on the branches of a fir tree, but the branches don't bend, they don't sway. Yet I worry that the tree might shake down the snow from its shoulders . . . If that happens, the silence will break, and the sight of the sea will come back to me, and I'll remember it . . . and I don't want to remember it. Peace, emptiness—those are better. The old man smiles sadly and says: overwhelming peace.

And back again he turns to the window. And, as ever, the little train is moving ahead.

Overwhelming, Dato thinks. Overwhelming is a real cool word.

TRANSLATED FROM GEORGIAN BY KHATUNA BERIDZE

ÓSKAR MAGNÚSSON

Dr. Amplatz

Guðjón was the first doctor in the long line of doctors who took
control of Ófeigur's life and the increasing number of afflictions
associated with it. Guðjón was the doctor at the health clinic
in the village, a highly educated surgeon who had seen more
than his share of blood and operating theaters. Consequently,
he was the only health clinician in that part of the countryside
and he dutifully attended to all its good, clean country folk. It
wasn't difficult to get an appointment with Guðjón; all anyone
had to do was show up at the clinic and wait a bit. Which is
how Ófeigur came to sit with the doctor a half hour after his
incident:

"I was having a conversation with the mayor in his office when
an odd sluggishness came over me and I just sat there in a daze.
It didn't last very long, maybe one or two minutes. I toughed it
out and I don't think the mayor ever noticed that anything was
wrong," said Ófeigur. Doctor Guðjón asked him to disrobe. The
first parts of the examination seemed innocent enough. He put
his stethoscope to his heart and then his back. Checked both
eyes; for color blindness too. Took his blood pressure. "Please
say the words, 'blood pressure monitor.'" Ófeigur pronounced
the words quickly and clearly. Everything appeared to be normal
and they went into the adjacent room to do an EKG. Everything

was still fine.

"TIA," said Guðjón. "Oh, certainly, I'd love some tea," said Ófeigur, who was raised to never admit that he was confused, and always look as though he was in control. "Perhaps something herbal—we wouldn't want any heart palpitations!" "Transient Ischemic Attack," said the doctor, ignoring Ófeigur's attempt at wit. "A momentary hypoxia, I think that's most likely."

Doctor Guðjón didn't think he could do anything else for his patient and recommended that Ófeigur travel to Reykjavik for a complete cardiac workup. He would make a few calls and get the process going. It sounded simple enough when the doctor was talking about it, but the next day things had already begun to snowball. Ófeigur's phone rang: "I'm calling on behalf of cardiologist Þorbjörn Guðmundsson. You have an appointment on Thursday at nine o'clock." The woman on the phone went on and offered three other possible dates, should this one be unacceptable, and also mentioned something about several necessary tests. There was no indication in her voice that she considered any of this negotiable as far as Ófeigur was concerned—after all, she worked for one of the country's most famous cardiologists, whose calendar was booked up a year in advance. Ófeigur took the first date offered. He didn't have the nerve to ask any questions. He'd learn more soon enough, he figured. "Our Guðjón has some pull in Reykjavik!" Ófeigur thought warmly. "He's already set things in motion. Not your run-of-the-mill country doctor at all."

Over the following weeks and months, Ófeigur found himself in the hands of various specialists in the capital city while under the care of Doctor Þorbjörn. He quickly lost track of all the tests he was subjected to; it boiled down to vivid memories of pedaling an exercise bike, half-naked, and jumping rope until he thought he would collapse. He went for X-rays as well as ultrasound and blood tests. EKGs were done after each stress test, and he became quite the expert at carrying urine-sample containers in his inside jacket pocket. He was lashed to a table for twenty-four hours just so that they could monitor his heartbeat. There was little chance to get any of his own work done while all these tests were going on, but Ófeigur always showed up to his various appointments in good spirits, trying to bear in mind that all of these things were being done for his benefit and that there was nothing for it but to be patient.

Close to dinnertime on a Friday six months later, Ófeigur's phone rang. The caller's number was blocked. "Hello, Ófeigur, this is cardiologist Þorbjörn." Ófeigur's heart jumped in response. "I'm a dead man," he thought. "The cardiologist calls me at seven o'clock on a Friday? This isn't good." "I felt it was best to call you and let you know before you start the weekend that I just got back the results from your latest tests, and it appears that there's nothing wrong with you," said Doctor Þorbjörn cheerfully. "But there's just one more test we'd like to run at State Hospital next month, and then I think that we'll be finished." Ófeigur had been trying very hard to avoid thinking about his health before the phone rang. He had been sitting outside by the grill with a beer. His main concern had been the piles of leaves on the lawn. Now he grabbed another beer to steady himself after this conversation and soon a third to celebrate that he was in good health.

After the final test at the State Hospital, Ófeigur went over to Þorbjörn's office—where, at this point, he almost felt at home. "We believe we know what happened to you in the spring," said Þorbjörn, leaning across his desk with a stern and professional expression. "It's not serious, mind you, but we have to determine what the right course of action will be." He told Ófeigur that they had found a very small hole in the wall between the valves of his heart. "Everyone is born with an opening on the septum—or wall—of the heart, but it immediately begins to close up and then vanishes completely over time. In your case, this didn't happen, and we believe your condition may be the result of a buildup of pressure, causing the blood flow to reverse; in such cases, an obstruction or clot can form that later causes oxygen depletion. We believe that's what happened to you—but we can't be absolutely certain." When Ófeigur asked what could be done, Þorbjörn told him that there were three options, in his experience: "First, do nothing at all. Second, we could put you on blood thinners in order to minimize the likelihood of another blood clot. Lastly, it's possible to perform a small surgical procedure to remove the clot, or else close up the offending hole."

Ófeigur didn't care for the first option. Blood thinners, he believed, were not a good solution. "Isn't it true that a person on blood thinners can bleed out in an instant if he cuts himself?" Þorbjörn told him that the surgery was relatively minor, it would be performed with a cardiac catheterization and wouldn't require opening the patient up; he would only have to be in the hospital for twenty-four hours. The doctor looked at the clock and proposed that Ófeigur think it over. Ófeigur didn't want to do that. "I want the surgery, without question," he said.

Þorbjörn said that he would have to consult with his friend and colleague, Hróar Heimisson, who had performed ninety procedures of this kind, all of them successfully. Hróar's office was in an apartment complex on the second floor of a two-story house. At street level was a pharmacy that had been opened there to prevent patients from taking their business anywhere else. "Maybe our health-care system isn't so different from the ones you hear about in other countries after all," thought Ófeigur. Hróar came out into the corridor to greet Ófeigur at exactly the appointed minute—something that had never ever happened to him before with any doctor. Doctors Hróar and Þorbjörn looked almost identical. Both of them were tall, with strong features and short-cropped, graying hair. They both wore white, unbuttoned smocks and jeans, possibly believing that the smock "doctored" up what would otherwise look like a rather casual ensemble. Hróar placed a chair at one corner of his desk and placed another at the next nearest corner. He sat his patient down and they went over the surgery in detail. The doctor put a sheet of graph paper that he ripped out of a spiral notebook onto his desk and began to draw a heart with a blue Bic rollerball pen. The pen leaked, two inkblots indicated a vein and heart valve, respectively. Hróar reached into his smock pocket and took out a short wire stalk encased in plastic and then began to rhapsodize about it as though he were a salesman showing a customer the beautiful inner lining of a well-made woman's coat.

"We call this procedure 'Amplatz surgery,' named after a certain Doctor Amplatz—a German. This occluder at the end, shaped like a plug, is, as you can see, made up of a densely woven assemblage of wire. We draw the wires together and insert it through this type of sheath." He handled the sheath and plug gently, rolling them between his fingers just like a mechanic might do with a screwdriver, and with as much of a sense that this was all a perfectly natural thing to do. "Once we've inserted it through the septum, we open it and then squeeze the plug in half, and the hole is closed for good. Tissue will grow over it, and you'll be a new man," said Doctor Hróar.

Hróar suggested a possible date for the surgery—in about two months—but said he wanted to do some tests of his own over the intervening time. Over those weeks, Ófeigur drove to the city for a few appointments, either to the doctor's office or to the hospital. He soon felt he was in very good hands, and got to know Hróar a bit over the course of these visits. "Hróar isn't just a good doctor," he said one night to his wife Lína, who had a growing interest in the procedure as the date drew nearer, "I really get the sense that he's a good person. His associates are capable and compassionate people, and when he speaks about his family, there's a touching quiver in his voice. And, you know, I've heard that he has, at a moment's notice, traveled to Boston, for example, on account of emergencies arising from infant heart disease. He always goes, despite whatever might be going on for him at work or at home. He's saved plenty of lives."

Ófeigur arrived at the reception desk in the basement of the State Hospital the day before his operation. The woman who checked him in was very inquisitive: "Do you have any allergies? Does diabetes run in your family? Is there any family history of heart disease? Have you been anaesthetized recently?" Ófeigur answered all the questions in the negative but recalled too late that he had indeed been anaesthetized nine years before. It didn't seem to matter. He was whisked into a room and blood was drawn and no one asked him any more questions.

After a short wait, he was directed to a small office, where the anesthesiologist sat waiting. She was a very tall, attractive, and energetic woman whom Ófeigur recognized from his university days. Her name was Hjörný Scheving. Ófeigur was grateful to run into someone he knew. Hjörný had always liked to talk, so their interview went long but interesting. Her oldest daughter played ice hockey on a school team in Canada. Hjörný asked Ófeigur if he had any allergies. She also wanted to know if he or any of his relatives had diabetes or heart disease. "Have you ever been anaesthetized?" she asked him at the end of their meeting.

The X-ray room was so far away from the anesthesiologist's office that someone had to escort Ófeigur through the long hospital corridors so he wouldn't get lost. He was shown into a small, cramped area and sat alongside a dreadful oil painting donated to the hospital by a grateful patient. Still, in the waiting room he was shielded from questions and looked through the available reading material: *How I Found Livingstone* as well as such classic tales as *Kit Carson* and *King Solomon's Mines*.

He then met with the physician's assistant, a young, beautiful woman. She was particularly interested in inspecting Ófeigur's toes. She finally couldn't refrain from asking him about allergies, diabetes, heart disease, and if he had ever been anaesthetized.

The final interview was with Hróar himself. Again he went over how the surgery would proceed, and then moved into restating, with a great deal of authority, all of the things that he had already discussed with his patient over the previous months. He was formal, but casual, and at the same time Ófeigur felt that he radiated a real kindness, a quality that had been there from the beginning. Hróar checked off items on a form while talking to himself: "No allergies, no heart disease, no diabetes, anaesthetized before."

In the early evening, a nurse arrived who said she wanted to shave Ófeigur's groin area so she wouldn't have to the next morning. While she worked, Ófeigur stared at the wall clock from the Milk Producers Association with its company motto: "Skim Milk / Every drop / Vitamin enhanced." Just before he was sent home, he had to track down another nurse to take the warm urine sample that he had been carrying in his jacket pocket all day long.

Ófeigur arrived at State Hospital at seven o'clock on the dot the next morning, and was immediately whisked off to be prepared for surgery. He was assigned a bed with a partition blocking the view from the corridor and was asked to remove his clothes behind it and to lie down in the bed. Minutes later, two nurses released the brakes on the bed and he was wheeled away. He could tell that they had just come on shift because their uniforms were stiff and crackly. A soothing and pleasant scent of perfume lingered over the bed on the journey through the long corridors. After they waited a while outside the operating room, a bearded man appeared in green scrubs and introduced himself to Ófeigur as Kjartan, the assistant anesthesiologist. "No and no and no and yes," Ófeigur said before the doctor could say anything else. Kjartan seemed satisfied with his answers and Ófeigur was moved onto the operating table.

In the operating room, there was a palpable atmosphere of professionalism. Two nurses, Þorbjörg and Hildur, prepared the room for surgery. They took out assorted apparatuses, instruments, and needles, and plugged in electrical cords. They removed tools from sterile, disinfected wrappings and placed them in precise places so that Doctor Hróar would only need to reach out his hand for them. Hildur hummed as she worked and made small talk with Þorbjörg. She turned toward a large stereo on a side table, couldn't find a radio station, and decided to slip in a CD instead. After that, beautiful music filled the operating room. "There's so much to keep track of . . ." Þorbjörg removed a long and narrow package, looked into the storage cabinet and talking to herself said: "Are we out of the sheaths?" She looked over at Ófeigur and asked: "Is everything all right?" "Yes," answered Ófeigur, "or it will be. That's why I am here." "See the screen over here?" and Þorbjörg pointed to six flat-screen TV monitors joined together and mounted on a metal armature directly over the operating table. "The doctor performs the surgery while looking at the screen, so that he can see what he's doing. We monitor what's happening with your heartbeat, pulse, breathing, and other vital signs on the other screens."

The number of bodies in the operating room was growing. Hjörný, the anesthesiologist, greeted him cheerfully. She was professional, deliberate, and very thoughtful. She placed her left hand on Ófeigur's chest and her right on the lower part of his body, and said to him after a second that she would be the one to put him under. The last person to come in, of course, was Doctor Hróar in his surgical scrubs. He felt along Ófeigur's groin and said to him calmly that this was the place where he intended to begin threading the sheath toward the heart and that they would then secure the hole in his heart with the plug at the end.

Incredibly simple.

"He's under," said Hjörný calmly. Hróar felt again for the pulse at the groin, made a small incision in the skin, and inserted the needle. "I have the artery pulse," he said contentedly and slipped the plastic sheath inside the vein and then the wire into the sheath. He never took his eyes off the screen that faced directly away from the patient. He saw the blood vessels and the sheath as it wound its way to the heart. On the other screen was the image of the spinal column. The doctor worked confidently and steadily and appeared to be as comfortable with the surgery as with cutting a loaf of bread in his kitchen.

• • •

"Ventilate him, does he have a pulse?" Anesthesiologist Hjörný's voice was calm but her tone was urgent. "Get a monitor right away, vitals have dropped to nil." She began chest compressions. "Give him oxygen and set up an IV line," she said quickly and continued with the compressions. "We've already called for the crash team," said the nurse Hildur as she set up the oxygen. "He's fibrillating, we need the paddles," said Hjörný. "Is he in sinus? Give him another zap." They kept at it; each had their defined roles. The exchanges were short and to the point and no one asked questions. The crash team had arrived on the scene: the department doctor on shift, an anesthesiologist, a general practitioner, two nurses, and one intern. The operating room was crowded. "I administered adrenaline," said the general practitioner, "no change in condition." "Find out if Þorbjörn Guðmundsson is in the building," said Hjörný and stopped her compressions as the department doctor took over. Things went on from there. Another electric shock, more adrenaline, oxygen, and constant CPR. Cardiologist Þorbjörn had long since arrived. A half hour passed, and then an hour, he was unresponsive.

"We've lost him," whispered Þorbjörn, his voice cracking, and he walked out of the operating room.

• • •

"The funeral for husband and father Hróar Heimisson, who died in the State Hospital on May 4, will depart from Langholt Church . . ." he couldn't read any more. He sat at the kitchen table: "You'll come with me, right?" he asked. "I didn't know the man at all," Lína replied, "but it's a different story for you, he saved your life." She was silent for a moment but then added: "How could something like this have happened in a hospital with the best equipment and specialists." She stood up and collected their coffee cups. "That's the thing," said Ófeigur. "The pathologist Guðlaugur told me that Hróar himself was living with an extremely rare heart condition. You're fine most of your life, but once it decides to give you trouble, you might as well have been shot in the head." Ófeigur ran his hands through his uncombed hair. "In fact, I heard later from cardiologist Þorbjörn that there was only one person in the entire country with the expertise and talent to treat to such a case, which is a little odd." Lína came back from washing the coffee cups and looked at her husband: "Odd, what's so odd about it since it was such a rare case?"

"Well, the only person who could have saved Hróar was Hróar himself."

TRANSLATED FROM ICELANDIC BY CHRISTOPHER BURAWA

INGA ZHOLUDE

Dirty Laundry

I'm walking. Past everything. Absurdly past. Some sort of apartment blocks. Who could live in these blocks? So I'm walking by these blocks, these gray buildings, and it's possible that I could be lost because these block buildings are all the same. Cemented squares with white seams, and someone lives in every one of them. But mainly cockroaches. Of course, my sister lives in one of them too. My mother lives in one of them. My father lives in one of them. Each in their own apartment block. Each in their own block. And both my grandmothers live in one too.

One of the balconies on that building beside the supermarket is not an ordinary balcony—it's painted orange, decorated with something that looks like yellow bananas. Extraordinarily unlike the other balconies in the block. Because the block building balconies have to be gray, or else white, freshly painted every twenty years, but certainly not orange.

I drag myself past these blocks. And I feel light-headed. I drag along, more and more light-headed. I see an orange cat in one of the windows, sitting very placidly. I look and look, and then I understand that it's a ceramic cat. In terrible taste. Then I look again. And I look again. Look all around.

"Hey, pervert! Yeah, you, you sicko. Nobody likes a Peeping Tom. Get lost before we call the cops."

You know, I meant no harm. I don't argue, because I really was staring. But that was because of you, to write a story for you.

I've been dragging past that gray block building for an hour already, an eternity, for kilometers. Or simply put, for the tenth time. And then that balcony! Eight pairs of pajamas are hanging on that balcony behind last year's dried-out vines. Ah, and such pajamas! Made from prehistoric flannel. Worn out and frayed on prehistoric behinds. All the family's pajamas. Generation after generation.

When I was a child, I always hated pajamas, because I didn't understand whether I had to wear panties under them or not. And if you didn't wear panties, then how often did you have to wash the pajamas? I remember especially one pair of despised pajamas, with red-white-red horizontal stripes. Even then I thought they made me look fat. Then I progressed, thank God, to nightgowns. Later to T-shirts, to negligees, to minimalism, to bias-cut silk, several in the same style, just different in color. Or, to be precise, three in that style—one black, one red, and a light blue one.

Now I lie in bed in the saddest of those colors. And I feel sadness and swollen veins throbbing in me, exhausted from the all-day torture of walking past the blocks. It's not so easy to write a short story, I console myself. And before going to sleep, the thought occurs to me that I should change the bedding, which smells strongly of hair, a head that has slept there for days and nights.

I've also slept nude, but I don't like it because I feel like a peeled orange, which, if not eaten immediately, dries up and gets hard. And there's a feeling that you'll dirty all the bedding with your nakedness. From childhood I've been raised to loathe specific parts of my body. Wash your hands after going to the toilet, phooey, yuck, kaka!

And if two sleep nude, side-by-side, flesh clings together with sweat, like glued paper.

I am, of course, very busy. Today, for example, I again have to go and walk through the labyrinths of apartment blocks. An exhaustive infiltration is required. This is my creative experiment. Previous creative experiments have included excursions to a psychiatric hospital, wandering through a market, resigning from work, going to the same bar every night for a week, starting a blog, a second life, a second-hand second life, and so on. But, before everything, I'll change the bed linen. I strip it off, fold it carefully, don't take out the bits of fluff inside the duvet-cover corners because I simply hate to do that; besides, when the cover comes out of the wash, they're no longer there anyway. I don't understand how often bed linen needs to be washed. It's not written down anywhere. In books intended for teenagers, for example, instructions are given on how often one must wash— girls twice a day, boys at least once. Mamma had a strict regime for changing bed linen, maybe each Saturday or every second Saturday, who can really remember now. But I do it irregularly. When the smell is overbearing, I change them. I fold the stripped bedclothes, place them in a pile, and take them to a laundry basket. I dump out the basket to separate the clothes, I dig and dive into the smell of dirty socks. Not of freshly dirtied ones, but of ones that have been left for a while, dried out, stiffened up. My separation strategy is as follows: bed linen is one load, clothes to wear in the immediate future is another; most-loved clothes go in one pile, socks in another, and panties, of course, are also their own pile, because you can't mix them with anything else. I'm doing the separating and suddenly I can't understand at all, what is that rag over there doing among my very fine dirty clothes. Some sort of cotton rag. I pick it up gingerly with two fingers. Something strange and smelly. I don't even know what to call it! A *whatchamacallit*. Well, you know, a pair of men's briefs. How have these *whatachamacallits* landed in my dirty laundry? I'm stunned, as if pinned to the floor, those *whatachamacallits* held between two fingers; suddenly I can't even throw them down on the floor, because it's my floor, my personal floor, and I can hardly soil it with some stranger's underwear. God only knows what kind of vile disease might be living in them! I go to the kitchen, find a plastic bag, shove the strange underpants in it, and then throw the bag out onto the balcony, so it won't foul the air inside.

The exterior walls have grown hot from the sun. Inside it's like a cellar, the air condenses and drips, centipedes crawl on the floor, there's the smell of vegetables that have been stored for half a year. How does your home smell?

In one of my neighbors' sun-heated and airless, glassed-in loggia, clothes have been hung out to dry and melt.

And the neighbors higher up are standing on their balcony half-nude, smoking. The whole family. The wife looking like she's on the fifth day of her hangover. Her old man, who hasn't been sober for almost three years now, by her side. And of course their offspring, such as they are. And all of them smoking. They spit worms of saliva off the balcony and toss their cigarette butts out into space.

My next-door neighbors of three years don't have curtains. If I wanted to, I could lean out from my balcony and find out everything I wanted about the anatomy of their intimate lives. Talking about anatomy, it seems the Discovery channel once showed a male and a female body being cut up into two-millimeter-thin slices, all of them then x-rayed, scanned, and so forth, all on behalf of science, of course. The two specimens were called Adam and Eve, of course.

I walk by the building's windows, listening in at the windows from which women with black eyes lean out into the street, crying; beyond which children beaten silly yell and then smother their sobs; outside of which, in the yard, teenagers get slapped by their fathers for having smoked their first cigarettes; next to which obscenities have been scribbled all over the walls; through which you're spat at with half-eaten chokeberries; near which you're told off for how you've tied up your garbage; near which people rummage through your garbage, leaving pairs of your worn-out, discarded underwear, which you'd thrown away and didn't want to see anymore, around the dumpsters like a table set for everyone, like your organs exposed on a white plate, so appetizing, like a Švankmajer film . . . and when all of this gets to be too much, I come home. I get into my bed fully dressed, because who cares, no one can see or chastise me anyway. I bury my head in my pillow, but find strange pajamas tucked under it. Suddenly my exhaustion vanishes. I don't know whose pajamas they are, what kind of fabric, what color, buttons, threads, what size, what smell, whose hairs are sticking to it, what microscopic particles of skin? What's happening? I examine them carefully, trying to recall in the minutest detail the last few days, trying to come up with an explanation. No one's been in my home, no electrician, no plumber. You know, there's this woman I know, who lives in this neighborhood, and is friends with a man who's a plumber, but who started out as an electrician, but finally settled into plumbing full time. And I think he's the one who got himself circumcised recently, I mean as an adult. Smell the pajamas. Nothing. Nothing I recognize. I don't know what to do. I put them back under the pillow. No, why bother? This is my home. No such old rags will litter my place. And yet, at this point, I start to have doubts as to whether this really is my place. I walk through the apartment. Yes, it's mine. I pull the pajamas out from under the pillow, stuff them into a bag, and throw them out onto the balcony next to the underwear.

I again lie down in bed fully dressed. Wait, I thought I saw . . . I jump up, run to the window, and sure enough, on the laundry line, pegged there with clothes pins, hang men's socks, black, two pairs. I look them over. One pair is dark blue. Still damp. I run to the washroom. Someone has used my detergent. Wait a minute—no, I've never ever kept detergent in the apartment, because I don't have a washing machine, I clean everything with regular soap in the sink, therefore it must be a stranger's detergent. On the washbasin rim is a single-use Bic razor—used. In the kitchen, breadcrumbs on the table and two empty beer cans. In the corridor, traces of sand from someone's gigantic footwear.

I immediately sit down at the computer and write all of this up in fine detail at my blog, which is at a site where many others record even greater absurdities: about their trips to the countryside after they've had arguments with their partners, about dumping their partners, about the experience of being dumped, about being underpaid, about aching teeth, about affairs. Banal love poems, lewd stories, all posted from the safety of their indecipherable pseudonyms.

The next thing I do is call out a disinfection brigade. Who knows

what sort of vile disease that person, thief, maniac has. A man in
blue overalls arrives with a sort of iron hose and questions me:

"Cockroaches?"

"No."

"Bedbugs?"

"No."

"Rats?"

"No."

Afraid he'll go on to list ants, lice, and every other insect he
knows, I decide to reveal that I need the place sprayed because I
think a strange man has been coming to my apartment.

"Well, lady," he laughs "I can't spray for that!"

"Never mind, spray the place with whatever the next best
thing would be."

"The next best thing to poisoning a human being?"

"Well . . . do your best."

I leave the room. I'm thinking that I should be writing a short
story, not preoccupying myself with some idiotic investigation
and disinfection. I also call in a locksmith to change my locks.
Done. Now I'm safe. I collect all the remaining things that have
mysteriously appeared, describe them in my notebook—perhaps
they'll be of use for some other story—and then put them in a
black garbage bag right there on the balcony, taking the socks off
the laundry line too, of course, so the neighbors have no reason
to let their imaginations run away with them.

In the evening, while my apartment is being aired, I go to the
grocery store. I dig through the tomato bin, looking for the most
beautiful tomatoes, finally taking two from the top. I buy freshly
salted trout slices whose best-before date is in three days, and
also milk, which has a shelf life rivalling the eternal flame. I pick
up some other items. I don't know why, but standing in line at

the cashier, I look over the labels of all the men's deodorants, compare them in terms of price and weight. I have the feeling that I'm being watched. By plainclothes security guards, for example. A disembodied eye glued to me. You know the feeling, that someone is sizing you up, picking out every one of your defects, every superfluous fold of skin, every broken nail, every bit of underwear showing, every stain on your outfit, each spot on your face, your yellowed eyeteeth, dark hair roots, the cracked skin on the soles of your feet, every awkward move and each embarrassing purchase.

I'm looking at the sweater of the girl standing in front of me. I can see the imprints of clothespins in the fabric. Freshly washed laundry.

I lug my purchases home. Half of them tumble out just outside the front door and a white bean can rolls down the stairs. I lock the door behind me. I unpack my purchases. But what the hell is this? Where did this come from? No, I didn't buy this—I just looked at it! I hold in my hands a blue Nivea deodorant. For sensitive skin. A stranger's sensitive skin. I start to doubt again—maybe I have kleptomania, maybe I stole it, I myself don't remember, or maybe somebody threw it into my shopping basket? I look at the receipt. I really did pay for it. Well, as long as I paid for it, I might as well give myself a spray, get a whiff. Not bad.

But the minute my apartment is clean again, the minute I've gotten all my new acquisitions shelved, can you guess what happens? I see a pair of underwear hanging on my laundry line—white briefs with that sort of what-do-you-call-it in front, through which you can pull out, you know what, and besides that a white undershirt. I grab both pieces of clothing. That's it. I've had enough! After a brief but thorough analysis, I conclude that it can only be my neighbor, whose balcony abuts mine. I ring his doorbell. He opens right up.

"You pig! You pervert! You, a family man! Who would have thought it! A cheat and a Peeping Tom! What the hell is this? What do you want from me?"

I throw the briefs in his face. I also throw the undershirt at him. I say that I'll be calling the police if he tries it again. I return to my apartment, sit down on my bed, my hands trembling, my insides boiling.

Even though Satan should now have been banished from my home, I have the feeling that someone is still hanging around. You know the feeling—when you're positive that there's no one there, but can nonetheless sense the presence of some sort of threatening mystical being that makes you freeze in your tracks, terrifies you, makes you turn on all the lights in all your rooms and walk through each of them carefully with a kitchen knife, just to conclude that, indeed, there's no one there, but you can't put the impossible threat out of your head, you keep thinking about it, perturbed, uncomfortable. But, actually, that's not quite what happens to me, because right from the start I head to the washroom and see nothing. But then I notice two black men's hairs in the sink. And I get angry. I get mad at the man who supposedly sprayed my flat, because he must have been the one who left them there. Or were they there before he came? Again I'm overcome with doubt. Am I actually in my own apartment? Really my own? Or has someone been here, has someone broken in, and for a moment I can't think about any sort of self-preservation instinct, but think instead about sex, about the perversity and sickness that this person has been guilty of in my home. I've always denied that spurious notion that a large percentage of women fantasize all the time about sex with a stranger or, what's even crazier, about being raped. But, in all honesty, this mess is, well, yes, somewhat jarring, but also arousing—just a bit, I mean an absolutely minimal amount of arousal. And I think about all those unbelievable, certainly exaggerated sex stories in *Confidential*, *True*, and *Private Lives* magazines, about women who seduce old men, millionaires, pensioners—I mean those women with their long legs fully exposed in net stockings, the ones with Chihuahuas. And I think about the people I know having sex, or I try to, anyway, because I can't really imagine any of them in bed with someone else, so I see them talking dirty, acting as people only do in private, undressing, maybe giving each other lapdances, or something, then washing up afterward, changing their sheets, frying up eggs for two.

I'm going to sit up all night on watch. Awake. I'll be prepared for anything. For the worst. For yet another unauthorized person sneaking into the wrong place at the wrong time. In my own personal wrong place and wrong time.

I watch old *Sex and the City* episodes. Laughable. I've always wondered what it was like for them to make the show, to be on camera, probably a big laugh. Tonight I smoke out on the balcony, leaning over the railing. Everyone else is sleeping, not a light is turned on out there, no windows are lit either above, or below, or beside me. The moon looks as though it was drawn in with a marker, placed like a period in the sky. All sorts of thoughts pop into my head. They just come. But these thoughts have nothing to do with this story. Totally off topic. I eat cold potatoes and minced meat, with a knife and fork, like in a restaurant, and I wonder why, I'm home alone after all and can make a pig of myself if I want, and I think about the embarrassment I felt when those men delivered my new sofa yesterday and couldn't get it through the corridor, so they had to remove a door. I think about what they must have thought. My nose had been running a lot, abnormally, really, so that probably about five liters of snot had dripped out of me in two days and the skin around my nose was like a scaly eczema, and the air-freshener in the WC was all used up. I couldn't smell anything while I had the head cold. The linden trees had come into bloom in the meantime, and I didn't smell a thing. The sofa still wouldn't fit through the corridor, though, so then they took off the doors of a built-in cupboard in the corridor and had to take out all its drawers because their handles were in the way. In the upper drawer was all sorts of junk. In the second drawer were stockings and tights in several colors, balled up. While in the lower drawer was all my underwear, nicely lined up brassieres with panties thrown in beside them, and when it was lifted out, one of the men said, "We get to see all the good stuff."

And I was so embarrassed. So embarrassed. But was it because my underwear was there for all to see, or because only *my* underwear was there, because there was no men's underwear in the drawer, or . . . because I live alone, or . . . because I had bought a new pull-out sofa, not a double bed? And a sofa that was made of cardboard with just one skimpy support plank and a "memory foam" pad, a sofa on which you couldn't ever have sex, because it would collapse beneath you, and they knew that full well. I wanted to sink into the ground. I wanted to be invisible. And I was invisible. And I also had an invisible man. Somewhere here. A skeleton in the closet. When I was little, I saw a black-and-white movie about an invisible man who was wrapped in bandages and made me very, very afraid.

I hear a car alarm sing under the balcony. I think about how to start and end my story, I think about the relationship between visible heroes and invisible villains. I think about *Birthday*

Letters. And all through this a bespectacled cat keeps looking at me from a magazine cover. My invisible man.

I water down my tea so I can fall asleep eventually, in the middle of the night, collapse right there on my new, hard sofa. And because of the tea I have to go to the bathroom all the time, and afterward I also have to go and have a smoke, because I've abandoned my computer, and been thrown off track anyway, and those thoughts, those thoughts are of no use for this story anyway. I go into the washroom and pee, and at first I can't understand what it is, maybe the cat has thrown up something white, because I see white foam in the sink. I look, then dip my finger in it, rub it between my fingers, taste it. It's shaving cream. Absolutely and for certain this is men's shaving cream. But it wasn't here when I first came in to pee, maybe about an hour ago. He's been here, without my noticing it, he snuck in and shaved. My weekend cotton panties are hanging from a string over the tub, light green with an unraveled band. And he saw them! I get nervous, go into the kitchen to have a cigarette, pour myself some more tea, which has been sitting in the teapot for so long that it's strong and bitter and has a skin on top. And I get even more nervous, because beside my cup sits another. The second one definitely wasn't there before. Everyone always helps themselves to my dishes, glasses, and cups, without asking . . . I mean, guests and other people. And then I notice that everything has changed, that I myself have changed everything, have brought pebbles from the seashore here and scattered them in every corner. I've borrowed all sorts of things, lately, and these are scattered around the apartment because there's no good place for them, I don't look for a permanent place for them because I know that they won't be with me for long. Lately I like things more than I like people.

Someone is sleeping under the blanket, I see a body, I see it, but when I throw back the covers, there are only empty, unlived-in, cold sheets. Cold. I feel them. I know what Freud would say about all this. Cold sheets you can warm up yourself, but who is this "you," your self? When I want to connect with someone, I log onto Facebook. Now I see something that makes me a bit paranoid—there's all these new links on my profile: where I live, work, study, etc., but also a particularly odd one: *Who's home when you're not home.* I immediately click on this, and I'm taken to a total stranger's profile. I look at his photo album. Nothing, I don't recognize anything. I look at his blog.

The first entry: I look at her sleeping in her light blue silk nightgown, one strap has slipped from her shoulder and is cutting into her skin, she doesn't feel it, her legs are spread out all over the bed, it's hot, she's kicked off that familiar thin sheet. I bend down to smell her, on the inside of her thigh I see tiny white hairs. She looks sad. The last few days she's been looking sad. Lonely, as if I don't love her.

The previous entry: She's lost her mind! Decided to get her whole apartment sprayed with who knows what! Such a stench, bad enough to gag you. And all that when we've never seen so much as a single bug here! Not a cockroach, not a red ant, not a bedbug or flea, fly, mosquito . . . not a one. Not even dustmites, which they say are indestructable anyhow.

The entry prior to that: I don't exist. She doesn't see me. I talk to her—she looks through me. Transparent. Invisible. A path in the fog. A horn in the mist.

One more entry before that: I, that is, she. She is her I. With a capital I. She sees only herself. Hears only herself. Senses only herself. Imagines her self. Why should she? I've already imagined her. Now we should simply be.

One more entry prior: blocked. The owner of the blog has not allowed public access to this entry. I click, click, click, click, and click. Then everything crashes. The entry is still denied to me. And suddenly something is crawling on my arm. Something is crawling. I jump. Frightened, I scream. It's a hair that has fallen on my arm, and it tickles. But no, something is crawling. Really crawling. My brain is crawling. Over my back and away. Like white worms that have infested rotting meat. Like pinworms in the first grade. Like lice in the second. Like that inflamed root canal in the third. Like the first bad report card from the teacher in the fourth. Like the first lies to my parents in the fifth. Like my first kiss in the sixth. Like my first cigarette in the seventh. Like my first period in the eighth. Like getting drunk for the first time in the ninth. Like feeling grown up for the first time in the tenth. Like now, when I want everything to be as it was, as it is for children, as it is for the little ones.

I must collect all the words that I've let drop so carelessly from my mouth. I must collect myself. Someone comes in and asks, "Do you see me?" And I think, what a stupid question. I wonder how to present myself on the outside, clean and believable. I wonder how to be here, not be -ing.

"I've been waiting for you. I'm doing the laundry. I'll be done soon. I bought you a new deodorant. Nivea. For sensitive skin. Can you hear me?"

TRANSLATED FROM LATVIAN BY
MARGITA GAILITIS AND VIJA KOSTOFF

JENS DITTMAR

His Cryptologists

As a freelance literary talent-seeker—nowadays known as a "scout"—Alexander Kraus (who since 1956 had adopted the name Aleph Kraus-Góngora) was able to devote himself to his dissertation on the Spanish melancholic, Luis de Góngora. He traveled frequently, pausing whenever possible in Barcelona— which, though far too expensive a home base for his studies, was an easy jaunt from Frankfurt via Strasbourg and Lyon. Only once did he make it as far as Cordoba, where Góngora had passed his "sodomitic, heretical" life. Góngora, whose coeval and nemesis, Francisco de Quevedo, would gladly have seen him consigned, for his offenses, to the stake.

Whenever he was back in Germany, he attended the meetings of the Cryptologists—a literary group whose members assembled each Monday in Wiesbaden. A white mouse dragging behind it a recumbent *A* served as the society's emblem. Their proceedings took place for the most part on the second floor of the *Altstadt*'s Hotel Bären, where a television set had recently been installed. Consequently, every now and then, when a football game was being broadcast, they'd have to wince off into the neighboring lounge. It was plain that the host had learned early on what it was that his customers expected: bread and circuses. And pleasant service. There at the bar, old Herr Bödeker would bore his punters with letters that Goethe had written in 1814 and 1815 to Christiane Vulpius, after taking the cure at this, the most popular guest- and bathhouse in Wiesbaden. And then, of course, not so long ago, the *Senior-Chef*, along with O. W. Fischer and Heinz Rühmann, had sipped their coffee here.

The bulk of each meeting was spent sniping at colleagues and their books, but occasionally there were genuine debates as well. Uwe Borowski—who they called the Polyglot—had been raised speaking multiple languages, and was now at home in sundry idioms. Thus he was fiendishly sensitive to the finest of terminological distinctions. In Polish he was another man; then he could even understand his father, whose German was every bit as good as his own, since he'd been brought to Gelsenkirchen as a child. By threading his stories with foreign expressions, he managed to achieve a sort of *moiré* effect. But if the talk turned to mimesis, he derided it as "rèpetitive art," with an *accent grave*, thereby bringing into play a whiff of the unsavory.

One day Borowski had brought with him the eight-point proclamation of poetic action that had been declaimed by H. C. Artmann at Vienna's Café Glory—according to which one could be a poet without, in fact, writing a word. Since then Borowski had repudiated any reproduction of poetic work whatever, whether by means of speech or script.

"Isn't that something for our Herbert?" they said. He, having yet to publish a line, was nevertheless considered a writer. Nobody knew precisely why. He prided himself on having once stolen five paperbacks at a go—it was his personal record: *White Fang* by Jack London, *This Gun for Hire* by Graham Greene, *1984* by George Orwell, *Darkness at Noon* by Arthur Koestler, and *The Diary of Anne Frank*. "It's a counterfeit, that," shouted Josef Silberbauer, who was attending one of the Cryptologists' meetings for the first time. Since nobody there knew the book, his assertion remained uncontested.

"Why are you always stealing things!" a literary critic from the *Sueddeutschen,* who was just passing through, added in disgust.

The Viennese paradigm was vigorously discussed among the circle of Cryptologists. Should they plan a poetic torchlight procession, a silent march with incense and Chinese lanterns, through the inner city? All of them chalk-painted, shrouded in black, squired along by a flutist, like the Pied Piper of Hamelin?

The idea was seconded by Andreas Schalk from Ansbach, who bristled at countenancing any rules whatsoever. He didn't believe in reason: for him the only thing that counted was wit, a sense of humor—the rest could come or go as it liked. Against the ground of this anarchist's agenda, anything was possible— including the absurd, the grotesque. With the undeniable drawback that his particular breed of waggishness would be understood by very few, since his wit generally called for a good deal of rubbing before it finally kindled. So that usually his poems elicited more perplexity than mirth. With a number of kindred spirits he later founded a satirical journal, which sank, however, without a sound—like the *Andrea Doria.*

"Are my texts incomprehensible?" Schalk asked. "Or is it rather that the reader has false expectations? Most of them want to hear something about the world, want facts, rather than taking any pleasure in the aesthetics of riddles."

"What does that mean, *to comprehend?*"

"If you can reiterate what I've said, I take it that you've comprehended me."

Upon which this little exchange of repartee fizzled out. Apparently not everyone was willing to share such pragmatism.

For Guenter Portmann from Bochum, also known as the Arab, the suggested poetic performance fell on fertile ground. He had no desire to conceal his sympathy for the Viennese

Actionists, and at every opportunity exclaimed: "The Essential is not my problem! Let someone else deal with it!"

And who would look after the widely neglected Inessential? Portmann, of course! He was at home on *terra incognita*, driving himself on toward those blank spots on the map, those thickets of negligibility—places where others, with their fixation on the Essential, would never set foot.

"Anyone can learn to write in the orthodox style," he said, "and teach it as well. Journalists have to write clearly, correctly. So that they'll be understood." But he, he had a weakness for arabesques. He relished the ornamentation that others considered a crime. And given the state of things, he was a willing criminal. "I write like a terrorist—someday they'll shoot me for it."

The Arab, who thought himself irresistible in his little canvas cap, made passes at the waitress, who didn't seem to shy from such advances. Fräulein Gerda was raising a kid on her own. Jochen's father had made a break for it. They heard that he'd rambled off to America, where everyone was going in those days. Gerda no longer believed he'd come back for the two of them, mother and child. So she had to take care of herself. A week before, the tyke had smashed a shopwindow, playing, and she had no idea how she was going to pay for it. The installment plan they'd arranged for her was very kind, all things considered, but still, she couldn't possibly afford to shell out eight marks a month.

Deviation from the canon of proper spelling brings with it a certain measure of subjectivity—for many, that's the classical definition of degeneration. But thinking that way betrayed a flawed understanding of the world. In which context Klaus Becker must be mentioned—Becker, who most of them called "The Engineer," or simply "Zuse," not least to avoid the danger of confusion: in Germany there were over 70,000 Beckers, and half of those are Klauses. He had renounced "message" in the conventional sense, and dreamed of sense-free poetry, crafted by means of computer. One day he wanted to develop a program that would write—using words selected from pre-established lists—not only poems, but whole stories and novels.

Not every hand is huge
Each bed is still.

And no one would realize, in scanning such lines, that a machine was behind them. For the time being, he confined himself, however, to a complicated permutational technique, so complicated that—thus far—he'd been able to generate only short texts.

Midway through the gathering, Kraus-Góngora left the Bären in order to go to the Roxy in Grabenstrasse and meet a character who had nothing to do with the Cryptologists, but wanted to deliver a manuscript to the editor of the Jonas-Wittling publishing house. They drank a warm beer standing up, and agreed to meet again the following Monday, same time, same place.

On the way back, Christa Reinig plucked him by the sleeve. She was on her way to Berlin, where she studied art history and archaeology; she bitched a bit about a colleague, who'd been awarded the Hessian Literature Prize. Kraus-Góngora closed his ears: he wanted nothing to do with that sort of thing; and definitely nothing to do with the dubious jury: amateurs across the board, and clearly half-blind. They had indeed—deliberately or not—overlooked the fact that their nominee hadn't fulfilled the criteria for the prize, since she hadn't published anything now in over a decade.

• • •

Dietmar Panskus had achieved astounding results with his

text-labyrinths, which shuffled numerals, letters, words, whole sentences. He arrived at such insights that everyone who held fast to standard language had trouble believing he'd come to them by his stated means.

"Have you already forgotten why you write?" he exclaimed. "Have you given up curling your hands into fists? We have to break the cross of common language—and we'll start with the teachers, those agents of power!"

Smoothness of style, he held, was nothing but a stratagem designed to thwart the writer. The more one aimed for comprehensive understanding, the more one found oneself entangled in cliché. (Thus, for him, a stammerer was always preferable to the most brilliant orator.) His goal was to defeat rhetoric and win his way to a natural poetry, in which things could simply be themselves. So he sympathized with the Viennese poet's social role-playing. The latter's poetic performance concealed many surprises, and paradoxically, the more they threw one off, the better the result.

"My wife has left me," he laughed. "She couldn't take my disorder. Jacket, hat, shoes—none of it orderly enough for her. My books, notes, scrap paper—she never looked through them. And when I spoke to her, she didn't understand me—because I heaped words up at random, allegedly. Her need for reason went unfulfilled, while I asked: *Which* reason? What *kind* of order? First she got a grip on herself, and then packed up her suitcase. We still phone, though, sometimes."

And that was what he called *true* interaction—forcing the audience to turn their thoughts away in shame. If literature is the expression of an idea, then something is expressed by the failure of that idea as well. An idea reflects a proper spiritual position—as does a paucity of ideas, or their utter absence.

"But literature has nothing to do with women."

Voluble protests from Heike Kuhn (the saucy Berliness, she

of the *Bilderraetseln*, also known as rebuses), Antonia Mikulov, and several others—men as well.

Panskus wanted to overturn Reason's reign of terror by means of pluralism, which in his opinion fostered tolerance.

"Look," he said, "if you find what I have to say boring, I can certainly leave."

"No, no! Please go on!"

So Panskus went on: "Naturally, everything's subjective—what else could it be? Maybe the thing in itself exists—I don't intend to deny it—but the moment I turn around, it disappears. That's Plato's problem." No wonder he got depressed and began to dream of unreason.

One was reminded by all these various positions of Dada, and of what the publisher Kurt Wolff (no relation to Gerhard Wolff, the Painter) had said: "Even before I became aware that what was performed and deformed in the name of Dada was utter drivel, the pedantry, tedium, and sheer dreariness of their [Tzara and Hülsenback's] correspondence had cured me of the delusion that they might be the source of any creative fun."

Gerhard Wolff—with a double *f*, like the Kurt just quoted—known as the Painter, hailed from Kassel. His "counterfeit love letters" with their fictitious, nonsensical system of writing, had brought him a certain celebrity. Though they certainly *looked* like letters, their calligraphy only simulated meaning. The suggestion of meaning, and its refusal, were the central themes of his work. Script and punctuation were aesthetic objects, gestural love letters, lacking a message—which meant that the message was evidently on a higher plane, inasmuch as it was the writing itself (rather than its contents) that signified.

As far as the audience for such a message, there is little to say aside from noting that they—if they existed—were the only intended recipients of these letters. *That* address wasn't feigned—but the letters themselves were only "as if." Hence

"counterfeit." And, indeed, collected under that same title—
Counterfeit Love Letters—they became an unexpected bestseller,
and because Gerhard Wolff had once had a beer with Arnold
Bode, he hoped to be able to show his love letters in the second
documenta exhibition in 1959.

Juergen Riesmann-Raab, the Cabbalist, wrote with an aba-
cus. His poems were math problems. From endless lines of num-
bers—prime or Fibonacci sequences—emerged cryptograms;
to decipher them, he supposedly called upon ancient, esoteric
Jewish doctrine. In doing so he accepted that he himself would
often be as confused as any of his readers, for he thought of himself as a medium, a printer's-devil to the Lord, like the mystic
Jakob Lorber before him.

A letter was even more than a convenient sign, as Kandinsky
claimed, it was a creative force, an alchemical game. This magical
sign brought the Logos into the world, but the code is foreign
to us. One would have to summon an angel from heaven, for
only the angels know the magic formulas, because they were
watching over God's shoulder when he created the alphabet.

"Every letter is powerful. And the powerful band themselves
together and form an army, called the alphabet. Their creative
strength has stood unbroken for a thousand years, because God
is on their side."

The Cabbalist—incidentally an eminent mathematician—
taught algebra at Frankfurt Polytechnic. He sat on the window
seat, swinging his legs and blowing his cigarette smoke out into
the open air. Because he'd studied in Paris, he was later known as
a companion of Isidore Isou, which established his connection
to the French student movement.

The Word is an ambiguous thing. Its alchemical being slips
perpetually from our grasp. Images in one's head are images of
the world. The brain has to distinguish between the hare and the
duck, and has learned to compare its various options with the

alphabet's aid.

"Or, as Einstein says: Theory helps, but brings us no closer to the secrets of the ancients."

And Roberto Altmann, the Letterman, added: "The ancients encrypted the book of nature using the rail-fence cipher. So that now we stand faced with their cryptography, clueless: DrAt a a uhdr Ntrmt dr Grezumt oevrclsete lehtds Bce auie atnan ehd eshusl."

He began, like the Dadaists, by using a vague, sympathetic force to smash words up, but unlike them, he believed in a deeper meaning, which it was necessary to extract from the wreckage. The goal wasn't senselessness, but *apeiros*, the infinite: that fount from which everything flows, and into which everything will return. Not capriciousness, but sympathy.

"I have concluded that Anaximander was a gentleman." The Letterman devoted himself to his family, his children, and the riddles of the world, which was difficult to coordinate, because Margarethe, his wife, suffered from terrible loneliness when little Claudine and Moritz went off to school. That is, every day. Apart from that, he put out a literary journal, which was called *Apeiros* and financed by his father. In all, only eight issues had appeared.

Altmann, like the Cabbalist, had lived in Paris, and had seen Debord's film *Howlings in Favor of de Sade* (*Hurlements en faveur de Sade*) back then; though in fact the howling had been in the theater itself, rather than on the screen, as the latter remained mostly black. The scratched film stock had made for an irritating flicker, and it was this that finally pushed the audience to riot.

And then there were a pair of Utopians, Heinrich Lorm and Antonia Mikulov, who performed in cabarets as finger artists. Using their finger-alphabets—meaning specific taps on various predetermined sections of their open hands—they were able to produce their texts almost as fast as with speech. For training purposes, they had developed a sort of glove marked with dots: tapping with the tip of the thumb = A; a quick slash at the middle of the palm with the index finger = B; tapping the wrist = C, and so on. Admittedly, it took about half an hour before the audience stopped laughing, and accustomed themselves to this twitching. Then they began to understand what was meant. Bearing in mind that the role of the accompanying facial expressions and gesticulations should not be underestimated.

The academic artists with their written drawings and text-pictures sought to shift the border between literature and the visual arts. Among this group were Maxim Henze, the Typographer, Boris Sokolov, known as the Falcon, and Alfred Zimmerman, the Objective.

Henze shrank from representing any sort of content, and refused to subordinate any one medium to another. For him, all were equally efficient, in terms of function. What interested him was pure form, the aesthetics of the typogram—be it on paper or canvas. With his *Typographical Fairy Tales* he had moved past painting, over and above it, into the public sphere.

Sokolov was a chirographer, and had originally trained as a typesetter, joining the Cryptologists in the course of his typographical experiments. His concern was the deformation of both type and content. Though outwardly playful, his procedures opened one's eyes in an unsettling manner to the relationship between form and content. In his youth he had written a single novel, and it would have seen print, too, if the prospective publisher hadn't abruptly filed for bankruptcy.

The texts of Zimmerman, the Objective, ultimately consisted of objects combined with arid words. Each of them was the size of a barn door. His publications, books one could walk into, were routinely found in galleries or exhibition spaces, and soon afterward disappeared again into warehouses. If Gerhard Wolff, the Painter, had distanced himself from literature with his

written paintings, Zimmerman, with his installations, had put it
definitively behind him. He was followed in this by Wolff, who
had marked the transition from the written and spoken word to
a gestural painting, one no longer legible in any sense.

One thing united the Cryptologists: the question of the
representation or production of certainty by verbal means. Two
positions emerged. On the one hand, the Realists, who held fast
to the sign and what it was originally meant to represent; and on
the other, the Objectivists, who turned away from conventional
signs, and allowed objects themselves to speak.

Thus, while the one side circled the essential difference
between literature and painting and pushed the dividing line
between them now to the right, now further to the left, the other
argued about political relevance. The formalists among them—
like the Mechanic—spurned relevance entirely. They weren't
interested in mimesis. They no longer trusted their medium. For
the functionalists—like the Polyglot—communication stood in
the foreground. They were pragmatists, for whom the artwork
was first and foremost the vehicle for a message. And when they
missed their target, then the vehicle had broken down.

In the gradual transition from traditional printed paper
books to text installations, some went so far as to fold public
spaces into their text landscapes.

It finally happened that fraction and schism struck the
Cryptologists, and the group split into two new organizations,
because, according to some functionalists, art must even
conquer the skies. The stormer of heaven, Helmuth Seidel, had
written his political messages in the firmament with a single-
prop airplane. He would later become famous enough that a
monument to him was erected in Stadt Kassel: a twenty-five
meter long steel pipe that stretched up at a sixty-three-degree
angle, upon which a male figure (Seidel himself?) was reaching
for the heavens. A female variant (Seidel's wife Ingeborg?) can

be seen in Strasbourg. He turned his back on the Cryptologists, and was received by professional visual artists with open arms.

Should literature invade public spaces? Are broadside posters a suitable medium for poetry? And what about *Poetry in Motion*, that is, poems on public transportation, buses, subway trains? Question after question.

"And what about copyright law?"

"Forget about that!" Vehement protests from all sides, even from the few women in the circle.

Dietmar Panskus's idiosyncratic answer rang out: "Literature isn't any more understandable if it's read by two hundred people or more." He'd studied Max Stirner's philosophy of individualism with great attention. And happily accepted all charges of elitism and hermeticism. Still others now demanded that they be able to protest against the Vietnam War, or the nuclear reactor in Garching, near Munich.

"Gentlemen, get ahold of yourselves!"

Vehement protest from the women.

Kraus-Góngora thought: Just look at these people: At first they clowned around, they played the smart-ass, and now the learned harangues go on and on. One of them works at the butcher's shop. Whence his concern with meat, with blood, decay—in sum, with death. And there's the one who's constantly scrounging around for a job, and fucks up every interview he's given. And again, there's one who brags about having dragged an old drunkard back to his room, a woman old enough to be his mother. But finally, instead of screwing her, he simply shoved her down the stairs.

TRANSLATED FROM GERMAN BY NATE LA MESHI

HERKUS KUNČIUS

Belovezh

Kalina Baluta slammed the door and left. He, a good-hearted
fatso, was tired of his wife's complaints that he was always in the
forest, that he was just a guest in his own home, a stranger.

But how else could it be—Kalina was a forest ranger. When
your work never ends, when your responsibilities are so wide-
ranging, you're hardly going to lounge at home in front of the
fireplace. But this was no excuse, as far as his wife went. She
wanted him to clean the well, then she wanted kids, then the
roof of the house was leaking, then the chimney was collapsing;
you never knew what she would want next. All Kalina ever
heard from her lips was a constant string of complaints—it was
hell, no kind of life. Anyone else would have gotten fed up long
ago, would have done himself in. But Kalina Baluta wasn't like
that—he was calm, gentle, and humble. Not a man, as people
say, but a doormat. The lowest of the low. All he had it in himself
to do was leave. Slam the door and leave. Like just now, heading
out to the forest, to his beloved Belovezh Forest.

Kalina felt rejuvenated in the forest. He chugged along.
He calmed down. It was here he could forget about his wife's
grumbling, the way she smelled. It was only in the forest that Baluta
ever felt good. It was there that he was in his element: he never got
lost, always finding the way home. In the forest, everything knew

him, and he in turn knew almost every living thing. Wild animals, trees, and birds were Kalina Baluta's best friends—they greeted him, spoke with him, and often consoled him.

Kalina Baluta was in no one's debt. He took care of his friends. It's no coincidence that the feeding trough he made was awarded a silver medal at the International Friends of the Forest Exhibition. His nesting boxes too received a special prize. And as much as the organizers of the exhibition tried to talk Kalina into selling his troughs, even offering huge sums of money, Baluta wasn't tempted. He kept repeating that he'd made them for his friends in the forest, which is why he wouldn't give them up to any strange animals he'd never met, not to speak of foreigners.

The troughs returned to the forest, as did the nesting boxes. Kalina Baluta never regretted it, though his wife grumbled that it would have been possible to buy a house in Minsk if he'd sold it all. No, Kalina Baluta would never move to the republic's capital. What would he do without the forest? He'd suffocate right on the asphalt.

And what pure air there was in the forest! All that oxygen! You want to breathe it all in, fill your chest, suck that freshness in.

Look, a squirrel galloping along the pine branches: his little tail twitching back and forth. And there Kalina could see moose tracks. Looks like the poor thing was limping, injured. Baluta wished he could take care of it—he felt sorry for the elk.

Everyone needs sympathy, love. If it wasn't for Baluta, there would be no wisents left for Europe to take pride in. Kalina fed the calves with his own hands, gave them milk, swaddled them, rocking them in his arms. Later they thanked him with their affection, following Kalina around as though he were their mother, never letting him go anywhere unaccompanied. They would stare down any strangers who approached. Kalina's wife was jealous again. And for no reason.

Kalina Baluta didn't like hunters, he didn't understand the morbid pleasure people took in killing animals, especially wisents. They were such trusting beasts. Baluta had never owned nor would ever buy a rifle. However, such was life: Hunters open fire at wild animals in the forest, claiming the animal population would skyrocket otherwise. Nonsense!

A badger ran off, thumping along . . . How adorable! Most likely going back to his family. And here's a little river, a beaver dam. Those crazy beavers, look how many trees they pulled down without showing the least remorse. Baluta will have to have a word with them.

He bent over, scooped up some water with his palms, and drank it greedily. Good-tasting water from the river—clean, pure, almost like bottled water.

Refreshed, Kalina Baluta stood up, wiped his thick mustache with the palm of his hand, and headed deeper into the forest.

It became darker and darker, harder and harder to force his way through the pine.

A hare bounded off, frightened. And this long-eared tailless wonder made good its escape.

Kalina smiled. He proceeded further. "What might be awaiting me?" he wondered. What is awaiting the marten, the forest polecat, the mink?

There was a problem with the wild boars. It was impossible to come to an agreement with them. Kalina tried one way to appease them, and then another, but no matter what he did, they still liked to make their way out of the forest, dig up the potatoes of this or that collective farmer, and leave tracks all over the fields. The collective farmers were angry, calling for revenge. Which was understandable—when there are no potatoes left, whole families go hungry. What can a forest ranger tell them (the people)? Nothing. Which is why he guiltily lowers his head, when they threaten to shoot all the wild boars.

Baluta was very angry, of course. The wild boars aren't to blame. The brown-nose fox, having killed his neighbors' hens, isn't guilty either, nor is the mad gray wolf that stalked and bit a bunch of students out mushroom hunting. All of whom died last fall. They should have been more careful. That's what nature is like; if you don't know how to deal with it, keep away. Don't go into the forest if you're afraid of ticks and snakes.

He couldn't imagine keeping away from nature himself. He loves it. Love, love is the only foundation for it all. As the forest ranger likes to say, nature tears down even the mightiest walls of distrust.

Baluta stood near a pine. He looked at its trunk. The bark was damaged, it's clear that a bear had sharpened its claws there. That disobedient bear—the forest ranger knows him well. A four-year-old male.

Kalina Baluta put his hand on the tree's wound. He caressed it. His fingers became smeared with resin. Kalina began to cry, together with the tree. He embraced it like a brother, like a beloved one. He comforted it. Baluta felt sorry for the tree, sorry for the broken branch, sorry for the trampled moss, the needle, the little dug-up lingonberry bush, the fallen leaf, the worm-ridden mushroom.

A cuckoo bird cuckooed somewhere nearby. Kalina Baluta listened. A nightingale sang in the depths of the forest. Another joined in. A third. A black grouse. The deafening chirping of this bird orchestra sounded sweet to Baluta's sensitive ear. Baluta would have liked to sit there and enjoy the concert, but he had to keep moving—there was work to do. Ever deeper.

It was already well past midday.

A small meadow opened up, as if there were no thick forest surrounding it. This was the territory of a regiment of timid partridges. Kalina Baluta, following them with his eyes, lay on the grass; he always did that. He looked at the sky. Not a cloud.

Blue. A jet was flying by, leaving a white tail behind. It dirtied the sky, which was annoying. A little beetle crawled onto Baluta's cheek. It tickled pleasantly. The forest ranger closed his eyes. The little beetle went along Kalina's forehead and stopped at his eyebrow. It waited. The forest ranger carefully reached for and picked up the little beetle. It flailed its legs, wanting to escape. A hawk circled in the sky. The freed beetle tripped, ran, and soon hid itself in the depths of the grass.

In Belovezh Forest.

Mushrooms. There are so many of them there: slippery jacks, gypsy mushrooms, red-capped scaber stalks, and yellow knights.

A beautiful little red-capped fly agaric mushroom met Kalina Baluta and saluted him. Baluta immediately repaid this honor and then marched ceremoniously toward a small spruce grove, raising his legs high. There was a plantation of chestnut boletus mushrooms under its delicate, scarf-like branches. Just take some if you're hungry, and aren't afraid of getting poisoned.

Kalina Baluta knew the mushrooms of his forest well. He doesn't eat them. He never has. He could eat one if he forced himself, but no, he will never put one in his mouth.

For Baluta, the forest mushrooms are works of art. Right there is the boletus, the king. And here are the others—his subjects, his courtiers. Kalina Baluta stepped carefully, trying not to touch any of them; heaven forbid he should injure them.

A good feeling. Calm.

"It's not far now, it's actually quite close," the forest ranger said to himself. Soon. There's the hundred-year-old larch, a pine with two trunks, an anthill. They, along with the forest, didn't seem so imposing anymore.

Kalina Baluta began to breathe deeper. His steps became faster and faster. The sweat of excitement covered his face. His hands began to shake, without his knowledge—and he saw a roe deer caught in a trap. The helpless creature, tangled in a noose, was laying on its side, not struggling anymore, dying. In her eyes—a dutiful resignation to fate.

"I made it just in time," Kalina Baluta thought. By a hair, he repeated as he listened closely to the weakening beating of the roe deer's heart.

Soon it will be dusk.

Still trembling terribly, forest ranger Kalina Baluta undid his belt, finding himself fighting a particularly uncooperative buckle.

He was nervous.

The roe deer was barely breathing.

It was time to save her.

Baluta deftly took off his pants and lay down half naked by the creature. For some time he didn't move, as if waiting for something, listening intently to something. Kalina waited.

Ready, he inhaled.

He tightened his buttock muscles.

He made the wailing sound of a roe deer male.

The threatening call of a deer buck echoed through the forest, frightening any and all nearby animals. You could hear them as they scattered in all directions.

Baluta pressed himself against the dying animal as though it were the Motherland itself—any closer would have been impossible. He placed one hand lightly on the warm fur of the roe deer, while the other grasped her tightly. A moment, and he's already . . . in her. At the beginning he moves very cautiously, slowly. Later, as his conscience clears, faster and faster, as if wanting to get somewhere, as if he was pursuing something, like a predator giving chase.

After some time, the forest ranger was stroking the fur of the roe deer with one hand, squeezing her hip with the fingers of his other, quietly lowing to himself under his breath, and panting.

The creature groaned.

Soaked with sweat, Kalina Baluta straightened his back.

He froze for a moment.

He'd burst inside her.

The roe deer, pierced through its side, winced. And yet, there was hope in her eyes.

The dew-covered forest ranger Kalina Baluta, having just freed the creature from that noose, slapped it on the back firmly with his palm, and leaned back. The roe deer jumped up on her legs as though awakening from some dreadful dream, then plunged into the forest. Free again.

Kalina Baluta, smiling mischievously, followed the beautiful little deer with a kind-hearted glance. He said good-bye in his thoughts. Would he meet her again in this life? Yes, they will see each other once more, he consoled himself, smelling the sweat of the doe, which had soaked into his body.

Satisfied, Baluta curled his mustache upward, and returned to the trap. He resets it for another creature.

It's as if nothing has happened in this forest protected by the state. The satisfied creatures got ready for bed, and the birds quieted down. Who will wind up in the trap next time, forest ranger Kalina Baluta wondered, making his way through the dark forest, heading home: a forest polecat, a lynx, or perhaps a very lost giraffe?

Once again full of energy, Kalina Baluta returned to his wife, and she was bawling. And our sensitive forest ranger had no reason to suspect that today, with just barely a year between himself and retirement, the largest country in the world, the USSR, had been erased from the map thanks to a few careless signatures in Belovezh.

Translated from Lithuanian by Jayde Will

[Macedonia]

VLADA UROŠEVIĆ

The Seventh Side of the Dice

The Secrets Around Us

All around us there are creatures we know so little about.

Have you noticed a new resident strolling Skopje's terraces and gardens or hanging around vine-covered streetlights on summer evenings—a tiny, translucent lizard called the gecko? It's not a native to these parts; it arrived from the Mediterranean some ten years ago and now clings to the walls above our heads, noshing on the midges attracted by the light and listening in on our conversations. How did it get here? All right, that's easy to answer. Let's say it arrived hidden in a crate of oranges or figs and immediately made itself at home. But for what purpose?

My neighbor, an electrician, told me that the rats in our attics have become remarkably intelligent: They gnaw away at the plastic coating of the electric wires, but never those with deadly current passing through them—only "zero phase" wires that pose no danger to them. How do the rats know which wire is live, whether they can bite into its insulation or not? What do they think about electric power in general, to what extent are they aware of our energy supply problems, and do they have a way of solving them?

Or at an even more basic level, take the behavior of houseflies. They all suffer from a form of compulsive behavior:

A huge percentage of them (eighty-seven percent, to be precise) have the habit of rubbing their forelegs together when they're about to dive down and land on the roast suckling pig, oozing scrumptious juices, that's just been taken out of the oven. Why do they make that movement, which at first glance has no visible justification? Is it perhaps a nervous reaction to our kind of diet, dissatisfaction with the fare on offer, or a feeling of guilt for succumbing to temptation? Could science please solve this riddle for us?

But for me I guess the key question is: What do these creatures that observe us every day think about our actions, our behavior, and our lifestyle? What are they planning in order to correct our mistakes?

DEMIURGE

The man came down to the beach every day. He'd sit on his reed mat and examine his surroundings attentively. The waves had cast some sizeable stones up onto the sand during the night; he bent over and returned them to the sea. Looking around, he was bothered by a protruding branch among the scraggly, yellow-flowering plants a little further back from the shore; he produced a pair of shears, pruned it back with several resolute strokes, and placed the cutting in his cloth bag. He couldn't stand mess, everything had to be in its place.

Sometimes he had his doubts: Did the bunch of seaweed washed up on the beach really contribute to the uniqueness of the site? As soon as he made up his mind, he got down to work. A few adept moves here and there: Ah, that's better now, he said to himself.

Several tussocks of spiky grass would look good on top of the neighboring hill against the backdrop of those trees, he felt; and the grass appeared. If the little path leading down the sandy hillside didn't have to wind around those thornbushes, it would certainly harmonize with the line of the mountains that rose in the background; and the thornbushes disappeared.

Briefly he had the idea that a kiosk selling donuts (with apricot-jam filling!) would go well at the end of the beach, as a kind of finishing touch, but as soon as it appeared and the children started whining and pestering the adults for money so they could go for a treat, he gave up the idea and erased the shop from the landscape—it hadn't been well thought out.

Every now and again he'd make a rock plunge into the sea and come up again a little farther away. Sometimes he made two rocks appear in a spot where no one had seen them. It was best that no other visitors to the beach see the changes as they were taking place. Besides, chances were they'd think him some sort of eccentric ecologist or absentminded esthete. But he was much, much more important.

When he saw that all the changes he'd made were good, he'd lie down on his reed mat for a rest. The world deserved to have its perfection consummated, and it was sometimes worth investing that little extra effort.

THE CLOUD SHIFTER

My job is a little unusual: I'm a cloud shifter.

Most of you aren't aware why a cloud that has loomed threateningly above the hills suddenly changes direction and drifts away toward the mountains instead of spilling its watery cargo over the plain. That's just how it turned out, you think, and it doesn't occur to you that a fellow sitting a little further along the shore of the lake, who seems to be looking inquiringly into the sky, is the cause of that change.

That man, whom you take for a casual sky-gazer but who is actually concentrating very hard, is me. I change the course of the clouds, and that obviously demands a certain effort.

The amount of effort depends on the task at hand: There

are clouds and there are clouds. Cirrus are the easiest—you can wipe them from the sky like a classroom monitor wipes away chalk scribbles on the blackboard with a wet sponge. It's hardest with cumulonimbus—the ones that look like a burgeoning cauliflower at the top and a pile of wet, dirty rags at the bottom. You really have to use force with them, sometimes! They don't give up easily, but I'm no quitter. However stubborn they are, in the end I always wrangle them away over the mountains.

Sometimes that saves a field of ready-to-harvest wheat from being flattened, other times I prevent rain from spoiling people's day down by the lake, and occasionally I help an ambitious amateur photographer (without his knowing!), whose shot of pine trees and rocks would look Photoshopped without that magnificent cloud towering above it. Shoved there by me, of course.

But it's not just about exercising a psycho-physical force; I also use some basic equipment. I have a rather loud whistle and two colored pennants: one yellow, one green with black stripes. These allow me to determine the direction and strength of the wind and then to contend with the clouds using that information. And while I'm doing this I toot away on my whistle—it helps, believe it or not.

People who observe me while I'm working think there's something's wrong with me. But their opinion doesn't concern me: I know I'm useful.

THE PEBBLE COLLECTOR

A woman goes down to the beach in the morning and is immediately drawn to the pebbles. She picks them for their shape, color, and pattern. There are whitish ones, whose slight milkiness seems to promise the transparence of crystal; there are ones with greenish-turquoise layers alternating with clear lines of regal black; some are a dignified gray but at the same time spangled with dark-blue leopard-like spots; there are pink, orange, and purple ones. Some pebbles bear the mark of a signet ring that made its solemn, rust-red imprint on their ivory-colored parchment; others have a bulging, dark eye that stares inward with Hesychastic persistence into its own mineral being; others again are covered with the secret calligraphy of a capricious geological pulse that beat in the molten magma eons ago as it lay cooling on the shore of an ancient sea. Rising up above the waves, moist and gleaming, the pebbles glint in the sun. The woman collects them from that wet line of sand at the edge of the sea where the waves cast them in the last hours of the night. There they have the sheen of fabulous riches scattered from a stolen chest by drunken bandits as they divided up the treasure on the run, soon to murder each other.

The collector washes the sand off her shiny gems and puts them covetously in her straw bag.

In the evening, back in her hotel room, she spreads out a piece of newspaper and tips a heap of gray, colorless stones onto it. Dried of the sea water that gave them their magic, they look nothing like the lovely baubles she collected during the day. She stands dismayed for a moment before these debased, devalued treasures—and then throws them noisily in the bin.

Later, when she watches television in the hotel foyer and hears in the news about the global economic crisis and the fall of share values, she smiles maliciously. She knows the reason why.

TRANSLATED FROM MACEDONIAN BY WILL FIRTH

[Moldova]

IOAN MÂNĂSCURTĂ

How I Was Going to Die on the Battlefield

I dedicate this story to my friend Nicolae Roșca,
with whom I used to go hunting for illusions

I am convinced—I feel it in the very marrow of my bones—that the spirit of self-sacrifice is the thing that best sums me up. Not just in a manner of speaking. It's the plain truth. For example, since my earliest childhood I've wanted to sacrifice my life on the battlefield. For the winning side, obviously, otherwise I wouldn't agree to the sacrifice and the war would seem a complete waste of time to me. It would have to be victory or death, or both the one and the other, if it was going to be interesting.

I could almost picture the columns of brave soldiers advancing into battle, with me in the vanguard. And then the enemy bullet hits me right in the heart. That bullet, for some unknown reason, and subject to hitherto unknown laws of physics, would first have had to orbit the battlefield and even the entire Earth, whizzing between weeds and soldiers, ricocheting off rocks and other solid matter before it finally swiveled and hit, precisely, me. The bullet would resemble a pudgy bumblebee or, perhaps more accurately, a mosquito.

The truth is that, also from earliest childhood, I've had a special relationship with those insolent creatures. If, for example, there were five guys sitting in a room and a single mosquito had been allocated to all five, the sole representative of that vile species would wander around until it found precisely me. I don't think the situation would be much different even if there were a thousand individuals of the same age, sex, and even eye color in the aforementioned torture chamber. Which clearly goes to show that you can't buck fate.

Well, this is more or less how the fatal bullet would set to work: After multiple, convoluted peregrinations, after scouting out the terrain, after sniffing out all the potential targets, it would identify me and then do me in.

Impatient as I was at that age, I had scripted my death as follows:

So, I've been identified. I've fallen and the bullet is lodged in my chest. My blood is streaming everywhere . . . In the twinkling of an eye, my comrades rally and give the enemy a sound thrashing. They give them a really good beating, whacking them back with anything they can get their hands on. The enemy, bloodied and perfidious, flee in terror, wiping away their tears with their pistols and anti-tank grenades. My comrades return to find me punctured. They wrap me in the flag and bury me with full honors. Some weep, some smoke cigarettes, others stand to attention. *C'est la guerre*, as they say. The main thing, as far as I was concerned, was that there should be plenty of salvoes from canons, rifles, and other firearms to mark my passage. Yes, the main thing would be that there should be as much noise as possible.

The finale would have to be stupendous: The supreme commander, having turned up from somewhere or other, gives a patriotic speech; the military brass band, conducted by a drum major, plays waltzes and rousing marches; fireworks light up the battlefield and the mound of earth beneath which I lie . . .

The only thing that upset me and even saddened me about all this was that I wouldn't be there to witness our victory. To tell the truth, at the time I couldn't really imagine what it was like not being able to see something. It seemed absurd to think that you'd have stopped seeing anything, forever, once you were dead. But the situation, on the whole, was even worse than that. And here's why. So, you've done everything you had to do, you've taken a bullet, ultimately you've sacrificed your life, and, if you please, it's others who get to enjoy the victory! Everybody is making merry, the sky is thundering with the army's cheers, the officers are clinking goblets of foaming champagne, the fireworks are turning night to day, and there I am, stock-still in my grave, because that's the proper way for a dead man to go about things, the valiant soldier who has fallen on the battlefield for the independence and freedom of his beloved motherland.

Yes, I swear, the fact that all of them would be having fun, carousing and smoking without having to hide from any teachers, while I lay in the damp earth, was something that upset me no end, despite the heroic death I'd scripted for myself. Many were the times when I wept on my own account, sorely bewailing my fate. And with good reason, as I think is obvious . . .

Nevertheless, because all the books said that it was a blessing to die for the motherland, I did my best to swallow this dreadful injustice.

It ought to be said that this idea of dying for the motherland didn't just pop into my head out of the blue. At school, we were taught that the great pioneers had all died long ago, winning great wars, seeing through wonderful collectivization campaigns, and in other—equally heroic—circumstances. And so it was obviously the done thing to die for something, or, best of all, perhaps: someone. Without question, each of us tended to imagine our own deaths as grandiosely as possible, without neglecting the appropriate sound effects or, of course, lighting.

A battlefield is a wonderful place for that kind of thing. I don't think they've ever beaten it. On a battlefield you can die in hundreds of different ways: ripped to shreds by an exploding grenade or shell, squashed under a tank, mowed down by machine-gun fire, bayoneted by a fearsome foe, put up against a wall and shot, marched into a gas chamber, and so on. I had chosen for myself, in all modesty, a commonplace—but consistent and reliable—bullet. And I have to tell you that this death seemed quite heroic enough to me.

But then, of course, I came to understand that for the motherland—if you have a motherland—you have to *live*, you're even duty bound to live. Thereafter I understood—and this was something even sadder, albeit magnificent—that it is not at all easy to live.

Well, that was much later. But back then children were taught to die, whatever the cost, for their motherland, as soon as they could stand upright. People were dying anyway, of course, all the time, children and the elderly, young women and men in the prime of life, but their deaths weren't really anything to cheer about. You might say they were tedious deaths, absolutely ordinary, no more festive than walking to school or visiting the dentist. For me, at least, after one or two experiences, I got so bored of these kinds of death that I would give all the funerals in the village a wide berth. Of course, it's another thing entirely when a head of state dies. Then there are all kinds of delegations, generals, honor guards, children bearing flowers. Everybody sighs and wonders who will be unanimously elected in place of the deceased and, as a result, when the next interesting state funeral will be.

Still, all told, nothing could really beat a soldier dying on the field of battle. What a pleasure it would be to behold!

Well then, thinking of myself as a good pioneer, I had made

a firm decision to sacrifice my tender young life for the beloved motherland. And this is why the motherland, as I understood it, had to resemble a very beautiful and kind woman. There was such a woman in our village. So, after I had died for her, the motherland would clasp me to her warm breast, as she had eagerly embraced so many others . . . not that I had these things in mind at the beginning of my career as a martyr, but I'll admit that the breast-clasping did come to occupy an important place in my fantasies later on.

You can see I had a lot of far-fetched ideas in my head, back then.

As there were plenty of men around the village who had been left cripples by the Great Patriotic War, I got it into my head that a *real* man had to have a minimum of one arm or one leg missing. And if all his limbs were still in place, he should at least have a limp. Less than that was out of the question.

Perhaps my hapless fellow villagers wouldn't have made such an impression. But I had happened to see a movie starring a particularly noble hero with a particularly fine limp. This brave and noble knight, or maybe he was a revolutionary, unless he was a pirate or some other kind of bandit, only had one eye, into the bargain, and I must say that he looked very good with that black patch of his, tied around his head diagonally. I had tried to gouge one of my eyes out, but the operation proved to be rather complicated and, above all, painful. Limping, though, was well within my power. I would go outside, and if I spotted someone coming, I would start dragging my leg, with a most solemn mien. And because limping is no simple task, I would hobble now on my right leg, now on my left, depending on the situation.

The noble hero in the film limped even when he had to run away. And the strange thing was how often he had to show off his prowess as a sprinter. His leg didn't bend at the knee and to see him run was highly comical. You would have thought it was a camp bed that had broken into a run, or maybe just a telegraph pole with a prop. Whenever I felt like playing the invalid, I had a mind to break into a run at the first opportunity. A hobbling run, obviously. Unfortunately, this ideal was to remain unfulfilled, like so many others. In the village there were plenty of smart alecks, who (precisely at the moment when I was limping in a more—how should I put it?—in a more *artistic* way, I suppose) would sneak up on me from behind and bawl something in my ear. The devil knows how, but the knee of my ailing leg would abruptly regain its flexibility, and, before I could realize it was all just a stupid prank, would surge forward, bearing me away as fast as the wind.

Anyway, I ought to acknowledge that limping brought me no spiritual or physical satisfactions and, shortly afterward, after certain tragic events (tragic for me, obviously) involving dogs and the sundry village pranksters, I gave up on this way of asserting my individuality. What used to happen with the dogs is a tale in itself, because almost all the mutts in the village knew me. Usually, when they saw me, and if I was walking normally, said curs used to greet me from a distance with a humble wag of their tails, or else they would desperately seek shelter under fences or in other out of the way spots. But a mutt is still a mutt. At exactly the moment when I had mustered all my inner resources and begun feigning a limp just like in the movies, the mangiest cur of all would pounce on me ferociously. It would make me a laughingstock, because the attack, inexplicably, would always take place in the presence of eyewitnesses. If there was no one around, I could limp for days on end without any fear, because on those days the dogs always had business elsewhere . . .

Well, much later, when I resumed this occupation, this time impelled, let's say, by a constitutional infirmity, I had to conclude that this limping business is neither romantic nor pleasant. Quite the opposite.

This is how the wheel of life revolves, allowing each individual to taste all things, sweet, bitter, or merely bitterish. One of the lessons life teaches us is never to precipitate events. Life and history have their own natural course. And if you're not lame for the time being, you ought to be thankful with all your heart, because it might just happen that the future will offer you the chance to experience the pleasure you formerly craved . . .

TRANSLATED FROM ROMANIAN BY ALISTAIR IAN BLYTH

LENA RUTH STEFANOVIĆ

The New Testament

It was Veseljko's first day at work, or rather his first night. Bedewed with sweat, he stood at his post in front of the premier's residence in his black boots and blue woolen police uniform, a size too big. The premier was in fact on annual leave and Veseljko had just been temporarily assigned to replace the regular security guards until his return. That morning he'd been to a meeting with the commander, who explained to him the significance of the position and the responsibility it involved. The commander also made it clear to him that he owed a debt of gratitude to his relative from the north of the country for recommending him in the first place. Veseljko now knew that he owed his relative a favor, while his relative owed one to the commander; that's how these things work.

So at ten in the evening Veseljko arrived at his new workplace for the night shift. He and the guard from the evening shift passed each other without exchanging a word, and Veseljko took up his post. He'd been given a short briefing about the setup there and told that the head of security would explain his duties to him in detail later.

The guard at the high-impact first checkpoint and the one at the rigorous second checkpoint considered Veseljko's duties at the third and last to be purely ceremonial; to date, no undesirables had ever made it past the tough guys at the first two checkpoints, so you could say that Veseljko was just at his post pro forma—a job for which he was indebted to his relative from the north after his poor marks in the final exams at police academy.

Veseljko was of medium height, chubby, with a belly that hung over his leather belt; his neck was short and thick, and his whole appearance, including his large, square head with bristly light brown hair, was reminiscent of a big, sluggish animal, perhaps a castrated old bull, for whom frisky heifers had long ceased to present any challenge, and for whom the proverbial waving of a red cape in his face would have been a minor and ignorable irritation at best. His big, bulging forehead seemed to overshadow his tiny, deep-set blue eyes. A prominent nose and full lips rounded off his figure, which the Almighty appeared not to have made too much effort on—possibly He had more important work to do, or maybe Veseljko's turn came right at the end of the working day, when it's a known fact that people and gods alike try to knock off as soon as possible and don't worry too much about the finer details.

Veseljko was born on the slopes of a gray mountain in the far north, the fifth of seven children; contraception was still not widespread in the Kingdom of Black Mountain last century, and the birthrate in those poverty-stricken regions was enviable. The same couldn't be said of the conditions in which the numerous children produced by this environment were raised, but they weren't acquainted with anything different or better, so they grew up as best they could, to the accompaniment of strange songs sung to the sawings of the one-stringed gusle. The closest elementary school was four kilometers from Veseljko's native village and his mother would chase him there with a stick every morning so he arrived for classes on time; she hoped he'd use books and knowledge to forge himself a path to a better reality than the one into which he was born.

It would be too much to say that there was anything interesting to tell about Veseljko's lot during his years at village elementary school or later during his training at police academy. Almost anyone's life is worth turning into a serialized novel when seen with sharp eyes and a healthy imagination, but our hero was uninspired and uninspiring in the extreme. Veseljko knew he had to get through the academy because otherwise even his influential northern relative wouldn't be able to find him a job in the city—and there were no jobs at all in his native village. The academy was tiring for him: most of the subjects were over his head, and the physical side of things fatigued him. But he found life at the student dormitory much cozier than at home and was pretty happy with the food at the canteen. He spent most of his free time sleeping or visiting his relatives who lived just a stone's throw away. Since it was a small town close to the capital, they counted as townsfolk and considered themselves somewhat higher on the ladder than Veseljko's immediate family, who were still just villagers. You couldn't say he was particularly fond of that branch of the family, nor, for their part, were they especially glad to see him, but he went there out of inertia and they let him in out of habit. They'd ask for politeness' sake how things were going at the academy, to which Veseljko replied *Good*, thus ending that part of the conversation. Then, with a substantial dose of malice, the family would recount private details of people Veseljko didn't know, to which stories he would cock no more than half an ear. Afterward he'd watch television with his relatives until it was almost bedtime and then say good-bye until next visit. In the summertime Veseljko would take a coach back to his home village for three months' holiday; a holiday by the sea would've been more to his liking, but his modest stipend meant that was out of reach, even though the coast wasn't far. And so his four years of training passed, and he followed the usual career path of applying to join the Ministry of the Interior, which he was accepted into thanks to his connections (a further relative owed his father a favor), and the new job entailed a move to the capital, Podgorica.

Like the majority of new policemen who hadn't yet started families of their own, Veseljko lived in the Bachelors' Hostel, a barracks adapted for this purpose. The building may have looked like a dump, but it represented a step up in the world compared to the small-town student dorm. Veseljko was assigned a bunk bed in a room shared with four other new colleagues, and the communal kitchen and bathroom were at the end of a long corridor that snaked its way from room to room toward the exit. Outside the front door of the barracks began a new world that was completely foreign to our hero—its café terraces, foreign music pounding from speakers, and scantily clad girls bewildered him. Until then, Veseljko had thought a world like that existed only on television, in some parallel reality that would never intersect with his. He wanted to be part of that colorful, cheerful world, although he knew he didn't belong to it. The snippets of conversation he heard in passing seemed to be in a strange language and he didn't understand what people were talking about. The shabby clothes he wore in his free time prevented him from fitting into this world, a fact of which he was painfully aware, but he couldn't afford new clothes on his paltry pay; he set aside most of his salary for his impoverished family in the harsh north—he did this out of inertia, again, because everyone did it. He spent his free day each week walking the streets of the capital, which was quite sufficient to fill him with dissatisfaction and the desire for a better life.

Veseljko hadn't figured out how to achieve his goal yet, but his determination to succeed knew no bounds. It was in this mood that he arrived at the residence of the absent premier beneath Gorica Hill that evening. It was Veseljko's first time in that salubrious suburb and along the way he saw sumptuous villas, chic women out with their pets, and flashy automobiles, all of which combined to give him his first real whiff of wealth and power; inhaling deeply, he concluded that this was exactly what he wanted. Although he still had no idea how to attain his dream, he was more determined to succeed than ever.

But the events that ensued took a most unexpected course. At three in the morning, a vehicle pulled up on the street where the premier lived; it wasn't a police patrol car but a most unusual chariot, and the three duty policemen there ascended in it to heaven; no one knows what happened to them up there, but after they came down, one policeman had lost his mind and another his religion, while Veseljko underwent a spiritual transformation and began preaching to the Montenegrins that their God was one, and all power rested in His hands; he rejected the false idols of political power and influence he'd previously bowed to and swiftly married an ex-prostitute, a former "fundfucker" who chanced to be nearby; when his colleagues objected and pointed out the woman's wanton past, Veseljko spoke to them, saying *Let he among you who is without sin cast the first stone at this once licentious, now demure woman*, and they withdrew their objections; although one among them, by the surname of Judaković, from the tribe of Iscariot, denounced Veseljko to the head of state security; Veseljko was wrongfully accused of spying for an infamous terrorist organization, court-martialed, and shot.

His body was laid in the chapel at Čepurci cemetery and closely guarded overnight by a special unit of the police because rumor of the righteous man and his death by treachery had begun to spread throughout the Kingdom of Black Mountain, and the head of state security had been warned that unrest was brewing. When the gate of the chapel was opened, under tight security, in the morning, Veseljko's body no longer lay on the catafalque; while in the old, downtown part of Podgorica a woman vouched that she'd not only seen Veseljko alive and well that morning but had even spoken with him while descending the stone stairs to the river; according to her account, Veseljko then graciously took leave of her, darted across the water as fleet as a gazelle, and disappeared from her view on the other side. Veseljko would later be represented in iconography as a tall man with long, graceful limbs, blond hair, regular features, and large eyes of deep blue; the special unit that had watched over the chapel in the city cemetery that night would develop into a military order that protected Veseljko's widow and child born after his martyrdom and legitimate canonization.

Until the end of his tragic life, the head of state security would suffer from unbearable migraines and curse his miserable fate; history would despise him as much as his associate, the informer Judaković of the tribe of Iscariot, who betrayed the righteous Veseljko. Veseljko's colleagues from night shift would compile his biography from memory, which over time became increasingly influential and increasingly fictional, having less and less to do with what really happened; they say that the former special unit, which evolved into a knightly order and began to support itself by loaning money on interest, owed its influence to the miraculous power of a relic—Veseljko's service belt, which in some mysterious way had ended up in its possession. Sometime later, the minister of the interior himself would accuse the knights of the special unit of being a notorious fifth column; he would have them insidiously tortured to coerce them into signing false confessions to fabricated crimes and then sentence them to death by firing squad. But that's a different story.

TRANSLATED FROM MONTENEGRIN BY WILL FIRTH

KJELL ASKILDSEN

My Sister's Face

Late one afternoon in November, on my way upstairs to my place on the second floor, I noticed a shadow silhouetted against my front door. At once I realized there had to be someone standing between the door and the lightbulb by the entrance to the attic, and I came to a halt. There had been a lot of break-ins in the area lately, some muggings too, probably due to widespread unemployment, and there was every reason to assume that the person standing motionless on the stairway up to the attic didn't want to be seen. So I turned and began walking back down; it's been my experience that you should avoid drawing attention to someone who wants to stay hidden. I had only made it a little way down when I heard footsteps behind me; I was frightened, until the moment I heard a voice say my name. It was Oskar, my older sister's husband, and even though I didn't much care for him, I breathed, quite literally, a sigh of relief.

I walked back, and realizing right away I couldn't avoid asking him in, I shook his hand. We hung up our coats on the hallstand, and then I went ahead of him into the living room and turned on the two freestanding lamps. He stood in the middle of the room looking around. He said he'd never been here before. No, I don't suppose you have, I said. He asked how long I'd been living here. Six years, I said. Yes, that would be about right, he said. He took off his glasses and rubbed one eye. I invited him to sit down, but he remained there standing, cleaning his glasses with a big handkerchief while squinting half-blindly at the room. Then he put his glasses back on. You do have a phone, he said. Yes, I said. But you're not in the telephone book, he said. No, I said. I sat down. He looked at me. I asked him if he'd like a cup of coffee. No thanks, he said, besides he had to be on his way soon. He sat down opposite me. He said my sister had sent him, she wanted me to visit her, she was at home with a sprained ankle and had something she wanted to discuss with me, he didn't know what, she hadn't said, actually yes, he said, apparently something to do with when you were kids, and when he told her she could easily write to me, she'd become hysterical, unscrewed the top of a tube of glue and emptied its contents over the carpet. A tube of glue? I said. Yes, he said, photo glue, she'd been gluing photographs back onto the pages of an old album. He took off his glasses again and rubbed his eye, then he took out his handkerchief again and cleaned the lenses. I'll call her, I said. Right, he said, then at least she'll know I've been here. Actually, he continued, if you give me your phone number, then she can ring you if anything comes up, then I'll be spared the journey halfway across town to call on you. I didn't want to give him my number, but so as not to insult him, I said I couldn't remember it. He studied me through his thick lenses, I was a bit uncomfortable, I usually only lie in self-defense, so perhaps it's possible to tell I'm lying just by looking at me, I felt that he could tell in any case, and I said I never used it, after all you don't call yourself very often. No, of course not, he said, and the way he said it annoyed me, I felt I'd been put in my place, and I went out and got some cigarettes from my coat pocket. I'm afraid I don't have much to offer you other than a cup of coffee, I said. He didn't reply. I sat down and lit a cigarette. You're lucky, you are, he said. Oh? I said. Living here all by yourself, he said. Oh, I don't know, I said, even though

I agreed. Sometimes I don't know what to do with myself, he said. I didn't reply. Right, I'll be off, he said, getting to his feet. I felt a little sorry for him, so I said: Things aren't great between you? No, he said. He walked toward the door. I followed. I held out his coat. He said: I'm sure if you call it'll make her happy. She says you're the only person who cares about her.

She must have been sitting within reach of the phone because she picked it up immediately. I said who I was. Oh Otto, she said, I'm so happy to hear from you. She seemed sincere and in no way tense, and the subsequent conversation progressed in a relaxed, friendly tone. After a while she invited me to her place, and I said yes. Then she said: Because you haven't forgotten us, have you? Forgotten you? I said. No, she said, us, you and me. No, I said. Are you coming tomorrow? she said. I hesitated. Yes, I said. Around one? she said. Yes, I said.

After I'd put down the receiver, I was in high spirits, excited almost, a feeling I often get when I've finished something difficult, and I celebrated by pouring myself a quarter glass of whiskey, something I wouldn't usually do at that time of the day. The feeling of elation endured, thanks now to the whiskey perhaps, and I treated myself to another glass. At almost half past seven, I locked the front door of the flat and went to the Bigwig, a dive that doesn't live up to its name, but where I have a beer or two now and again.

Karl Homann was sitting there, a man my own age who lives in the area, with whom I have a somewhat forced relationship with because he once saved my life. Fortunately he wasn't sitting on his own, so when he asked me to take a seat I felt I could take the liberty of finding a table to myself. I went to the very back of the premises. The fact that I had mustered the courage to refuse his invitation had me so flustered it was only after I sat down that I noticed Marion, a woman with whom I'd had a not entirely painless relationship. She was sitting three tables away. She was flicking through a newspaper and it was possible she hadn't seen me yet. I didn't necessarily have to have seen her either, so I ordered my beer and awaited developments. There was however something unbearable about the situation, and I tried to catch her eye. After a little while she glanced up from her paper and straight at me, and I knew then she'd spotted me ages ago. I smiled at her and raised my glass. She raised hers too, then folded her paper and came over to me. I got to my feet. Otto, she said and gave me a hug. Then she said: Can I join you? Of course, I said, but I'll be off soon, I'm on my way to my sister's. She brought her glass. She seemed to be in fine form. She said it was good to see me, and I said that it was good to see her. She said she often thought about me. I didn't reply, even though I'd also thought about her, albeit with mixed feelings, not least due to her sexual needs which I hadn't managed to satisfy and which on one occasion, the last, had led her to exclaim that sex was not a church service. To change the subject I asked how things were, and we chatted until I'd drained my glass and said I had to be off. Then she'd go too, she said. As we were getting to our feet, she said: If you hadn't been on your way to visit your sister, would you have come back to my place? I'd have been tempted, I said. Call me sometime, she said. Yes, I said.

She walked with me to the bus stop, and once there she pressed up against me and whispered some lewd, suggestive words which put my body in a quandary, and, well, if the bus hadn't come, but it did, and she said: Call. Yes, I said.

I got off at the next stop, and bucked by the self-esteem Marion's advances had stirred in me—she is a beautiful woman—I headed straight for the closest bar. But I only got as far as the door; when I opened it and saw the crowd of people and heard the noisy music, my nerve failed. It's a situation I'm well used to, the frightening sense of alienation in an unfamiliar place, and I closed the door and went home.

Later that night I was awoken by a dream no doubt influenced by said self-esteem. It was an intensely erotic dream, and unlike the typical sort, where the woman's face—or women's faces—are unknown or not even visible, this woman's features suddenly appeared, clearly, without diminishing my desire. It was my sister's face.

She opened the door before I had managed to ring the bell. She was leaning on two crutches. I saw you coming, she said. So I see, I said. She hugged me and lost one of the crutches doing so. I bent down to pick it up. Hold me up, can you? she said, putting her arm around my shoulder. I did, that is to say, she held herself up on me. She hobbled along beside me into the living room and sat herself down at the already-set coffee table. After I'd hung up my coat and gone back in, we ate sandwiches and talked about her foot. I took a furtive glance at the carpet, but couldn't see any trace of photo glue.

We'd been talking a while about this and that, when she said: You're more and more like Dad. I assumed she knew what kind of relationship I'd had with him, so I took slight exception to this, but I didn't say anything. I got up to look for an ashtray. What are you doing? She said. Looking for an ashtray, I said. She told me where I could find one, and I went to the kitchen. When I went back in, she said she'd been thinking about me a lot lately, about us, and how it was a pity we didn't see so much of each other, since we used to be so close. Well, I said, everyone's got their lives to live. Do you ever miss me? she said. Of course, I said. If you only knew how lonely I feel sometimes, she said. Yes, I said. You're lonely too, she said, I know you are, I know you. It's a long time since you knew me, I said. You haven't changed, she said. Yes, I have, I said. In what way? she said. I didn't reply. Then I said: You just said yourself that I'm getting more and more like Dad. What did you mean by that, by the way? There's something about the way you smile, she said, and you sway when you sit just like he did. Did he sway, I said, I don't remember that. That's strange, she said. I guess I didn't look at him as much as you did, I said. What do you mean? she said. What I said, I said. I didn't like looking at him. There was something unsavory about him. Oh Christ, she said. We sat in silence for a while; then I became aware I was swaying my torso and I straightened up and leaned back in the chair. Eventually she said: There's a bottle of sherry in the bottom corner cupboard, could you go and get it please. And two glasses, if you'd like some too. On the way to the cupboard I decided to only take one glass, but I changed my mind. I poured her a large one and myself a little one. You've never said that before, she said. No, I said, let's talk about something else. *Skål. Skål,* she said. I drained the glass. You didn't give yourself much, she said. I don't drink in the middle of the day, I said. Me neither, she said. I poured myself some more. I didn't know what we were going to say. I looked at my watch. Don't look at your watch, she said. Where's Oskar? I said. At his mother's. He's always at his mother's on Saturdays. He never gets home before five, so relax. I am relaxed, I said. Are you? She said. 'Course, I said. Good, she said, can you give me a little more sherry? I poured her some, but not as much as the last time. More, she said. I topped up her glass. *Skål,* she said. I drained my glass. Help yourself, she said. I remembered what she had said to Oskar, that I was the only person who cared about her, and with a sudden and almost triumphant feeling of freedom, I filled my glass up to the brim. She looked at me, her eyes were shining. You're staring at me, she said. Yes, I said. Do you remember how I called you my big brother? she said. I nodded. And you called me sister, she said. I took my glass and drank. She did the same. I remembered. Have you got a girlfriend at the moment? she said. No, I said. No one good enough for you? she said. Don't make fun of me, I said. I'm not making fun of you, she said. I prefer

living on my own, I said. You could still have a girlfriend, she
said. I didn't reply. After all, you're a man, she said. I didn't reply.
I got up and went to the toilet. I placed the plug in the sink and
turned on the cold tap. I put my hands into the water and held
them there until they hurt, then I dried them and went back into
the living room. I sat down and said what I had been thinking:
I prefer women who don't make any demands on me, but who
give, take, and go. She didn't say anything. I lit a cigarette. And
you say you're not lonely, she said, before adding: Big brother. I
looked at her; she was sitting with her face half-turned and her
lips parted; there wasn't a sound in the room and no sound from
outside; the silence lasted and lasted. What if, she said. What
if what, I said. No, she said. Yes, I said. But Otto, she said, you
don't know what I—what do you think I was thinking of? I was
just about to say; at that moment I almost had it in me. Instead I
said: No, how should I know. She took her glass and held it out
to me. It's empty, she said. Say when, I said. No, she said. I filled
the glass right up. We're drinking a lot for two people who don't
drink during the day, I said. There are exceptions, she said. Yes, I
said, there are exceptions to everything. Are there? she said. She
wasn't looking at me. Yes, I said. There was a sound of somebody
at the front door. Oh no, she said. I got to my feet. It was a
reflex action. Don't go, she said. I sat down. Oskar appeared in
the doorway; he was walking while supporting himself on my
sister's crutch. He halted. I could see by his face that he didn't
know I would be there. Hello, Oskar, I said. Hello, he said. He
looked at my sister and said: Your crutch was lying by the door.
I'm aware of that, she said. Sorry, he said and let the crutch fall
to the floor. Now what's the point of that? she said. He didn't
reply. He kicked the crutch against the wall with the tip of his
shoe, and then he walked into the kitchen. He closed the door
behind him. Don't go, please, she said. I'm going, I said. For
my sake, she said. I'm not up to it, I said. Oskar came from the

kitchen. He glanced at me. I didn't know you were here, he said. I'm just leaving, I said. Not on my account, he said. No, I said. He walked across the room and through a door. I looked at my sister; she stared straight at me and said: You're a coward, I'd forgotten what a coward you were. I got to my feet. Yes, just go, she said, just go. I went over to her. What did you say, I said. That you're a coward, she said. I hit her. Not hard. No, I don't think I hit her particularly hard. She cried out all the same. At almost exactly the same moment I heard Oskar open the door; he must have been standing right behind it listening. I didn't turn around. I didn't hear any steps. I looked at the wall. I only heard the sound of my own breathing. Then my sister said: Otto is just leaving. Oskar didn't reply. I heard the door being closed. I looked at my sister, met her gaze; there was something in it I didn't understand, something gentle. I saw she wanted to say something. I looked away. Forgive me, big brother, she said. I didn't reply. Go now, she said, but call me, won't you? Yes, I said. Then I turned and left.

TRANSLATED FROM NORWEGIAN BY SEÁN KINSELLA

KRYSTIAN PIWOWARSKI

Homo Polonicus

Once again, Prince Stanisławczyk was dreaming he was the King of Poland. He was prancing about in a carmine and ermined peignoir, a cerulean-blue caftan with large buttons and amaranth-purple culottes! His head bore aloft a twin-sided *cadenette* sprinkled with powdered sugar, upon which sat the Royal crown. Somehow his noggin managed to hold it all up. On either side of the palace enfilade, the terrified gentry from all across the province were beating the floor with their foreheads. Stanisławczyk walked along, beaming with glory and accepting tributes; upon some he granted favors, upon others he rained curses, and then all at once a nude African with a ring in his nose—as big as a firkin!—came leaping out from the-devil-knows-where, as if he'd emerged from the bowels of the earth. He held a black monkey on a chain and poked it with a stick.

"Why poke him thus?" asked a fuming Stanisławczyk, the noble King of Poland, for he thought it to be his gift from a Padishah in Brazil, and with all that poking his gift would surely get damaged. Suddenly he saw that the monkey on the chain was Niemczyk all shrunken up, and in his hairy palm he clutched a message bearing seals. Stanisławczyk understood that this message would be his undoing! Anon, he began shuffling his feet and waving his hands, he sought to flee post-haste, to hide from said undoing, from death, and thus he fled to the attic. On the way he lost his crown, and when he'd made it to the attic he caught sight of himself with neither crown nor powdered hair. On his head was his own hair, and it was aflame!

Then he launched himself from the uncharted depths of the dream, he came popping like a cork through the calm surface of the day. He awoke with bulging eyes.

"Dream scare us, Lord spare us!" he breathed, drenched in sweat. "How could I become the King of Poland? Why am I forever dreaming that I'm to become the King of Poland?"

He pawed at his head, groping to see if he'd grown any lumps or horns; he ran his fingers across his nightshirt. He grabbed the mirror from his dressing table and looked into it askance, fearfully. From the crystalline depths a rumpled face with a handlebar moustache, framed with ruddy mutton chops, leapt out to meet him; there was a birdlike stare in its dark, bulbous eyes—normally bright and penetrating, now filled with a mad terror—and predaciousness in the pointed nose, its shiny bridge, and the thin lips. All of this he touched, poking around here and there, and concluded that it was no one but himself.

"What kind of King of Poland am I?" he fumed. "And why all these dreams? If it's my destiny then let it come true; and if it's only a dream, then off with it, and let it haunt me no more."

Dejected, he set the mirror to one side and fixed the bedroom drapes with his gaze. The sun gently backlit the dun, torn, faded fabric.

"Better off a senator. Or a minister," he muttered. "Less of an honor, but at least nobody takes you for a madman."

He got up. He had another look in the mirror.

"Hmph!" he muttered again. "But a king's a king!" He went over to the window and pulled the broken string, parting the drapes.

As far as the eye could see, meadows fanned out, growing all about with clumps of hazel and the occasional tree. The green grain fields swayed back and forth like emerald water. It was still far from harvest time. Invisible skylarks tinkled from where they hung in the hot air, sparrows warbled in the violet lilac bushes outside the manor. High poplars guarded Stanisławczyk's land like sentries.

He leaned out of the window, knocking off a jagged shard of plaster and spooking the birds. They flapped off in a helter-skelter flock. A sound came from a cuckoo bird inhabiting the speckled iron tree trunk in the corner of the bedroom. Stanisławczyk counted the hours. It was broken; it cuckooed sixteen times, a spring twanged, and the cuckoo retired, content with its cuckooing.

"I've been had," he snorted. "Who ever heard of so many cuckoos? Italian craftsmanship, indeed!"

He propped his telescope up to one eye. Far off yonder, beyond the wall of poplars, stretched Sztorch's property. He lorded over his neighbors, he had no iron cuckoo, and he brought in a tutor to teach his children botany and the constellations. Closer, on his own haystack, the prince spotted a falcon drying its wings from the night's dew. His tongue felt for the gap in his teeth; one had fallen out as he'd gnawed a chicken bone the night previous. There was no predicting what could happen! The falcon flapped its wings and flew off. A cart of peasants armed with pitchforks and rakes arrived at the tilled meadow. The women hiked up their skirts. His men were good-for-nothing, unruly, and idle. He liked to punish the peasants, and severely at that. He put down the telescope and retired from the window. He spent a time studying the tooth on the table with a magnifying glass. The tooth was gray with brown and green flecks, and even a red one.

A servant knocked at the door.

"Who's there?"

"The Jew from town, my Lord!"

"Tell him to wait!"

Stanisławczyk threw on a Turkish robe and studied himself in the upright mirror. He assumed a commanding posture.

"Come in!"

A short, plump Jew in pince-nez appeared in the doorway.

"You called, my Prince?" he said with a bow.

Stanisławczyk pointed a finger at the table.

"Look good and hard, Grajcewer."

The Jew went to the table and inclined over the place indicated by the prince's finger.

"A tooth?" he asked uncertainly—for there were a thousand other things scattered on the table.

"*My* tooth."

"A marvelous tooth! Ay!" The Jew clapped his little, puffy hands. "A wisdom tooth. A rare tooth! An extraordinary specimen!"

"I wish to have it mounted. As a souvenir of a miserable youth. A souvenir of smothered hopes. What's your advice, Grajcewer? I thought a breastpin of some sort, what say you? For a shirtfront? Or a stickpin?"

"A most refined choice!"

"Becoming, wouldn't you say?" Stanisławczyk turned toward the mirror, pressing the tooth to his nightshirt.

Grajcewer scurried up on his little legs and stood behind the prince.

"A capital choice!" he cried.

The prince wound the tooth in a scrap of his robe that had torn off only the day before—as if the robe and tooth had been in cahoots—and gave it to Grajcewer. Then he went to the window and put the telescope to his eye.

"So be it. On a stickpin, correct?" he asked slyly.

"A breastpin, as the Good Prince suggested."

"You're a scoundrel, Grajcewer. A stickpin would come out cheaper."

"A breastpin is senatorial, my Good Prince."

"But the stickpin is cheaper!" the prince bellowed.

"A capital . . ."

"Cheaper! Tell me at once!" yelled the prince, jamming the telescope painfully to his eye, for the peasants were racing about the meadow. The farmhands were chasing the wenches. They never raced to work.

"Cheaper, my Good Prince," said the Jew with a hurt expression.

"You double-dealt me last time on that turquoise button, which was purportedly from the royal treasury!" Stanisławczyk turned his furious face to the Jew.

"It was, my Good Prince!" Grajcewer said, placing a hand over his heart. "Passed through the Dawłowiczes to the late Urszula Sieńczycka!"

"From one crook to another! Villain! I'll have you run out of town! It's as regal as you are honest! You want to reduce me to beggary! Suck my last drop of blood! You want to do a breastpin!" His bulging eyes bored into Grajcewer, as if seeking to plough through to his most deeply buried, infamous intentions.

Stanisławczyk, as usual, had decided that he would not be taken for a fool.

"You wound me, my Prince," the Jew dryly complained.

"As though I could wound one of your ilk! Whatever the case, you always come out on top! Your house burns down, all your livestock are slaughtered, and you turn the ashes to gold! You make me a stickpin, and make sure you count out every last gram! And that clock! What kind of clock did you sell me? Italian craftsmanship! How you praised it, boasted that it was just like the ones in the Warsaw salons—and it doesn't run properly! The cuckoo cuckooed sixteen times! It's preposterous!"

Grajcewer stared flustered at the clock, carved to resemble a trunk with a hollow. "I'll take it in for repairs. That Italian scoundrel."

"You're the scoundrel. And now look here!" the prince tapped a book lying on the table. "Here's a picture of a stickpin. Take the magnifying glass. Do you have a magnifying glass? Go, and get it right this time, lest I run you out of town. Indeed." Stanisławczyk sighed. "Did you bring me some baubles?" he asked, tossing a glance at the battered sack by the door.

"Allow me to show you!"

Grajcewer ran over to the sack, and plucked out a flat saffian box. This he opened and passed to Stanisławczyk.

"What's this?"

"The Chain of King Sigismund August."

"Why isn't it intact?" asked the disappointed prince, taking it into his hands. "It's only a piece of it. There's no clasp."

"Thus has it weathered the tides of history," explained Grajcewer, wiping the perspiration from his pince-nez.

"And how can you be sure it's from the Jagiellonian Dynasty?"

"Take the magnifying glass, your majesty, and study the medal. There it is: *Sigismundus Augustus Rex Poloniae.*"

The prince took the magnifying glass and the chain over to the window. He had a look and gave it some consideration. He muttered something under his breath.

"Where did you get it?"

"A Jew brought it to me."

"And where did he get it?"

Grajcewer raised his brows. He gave his head neither a nod nor a shake, as if to say: "How should I know? Why ask? One answer is as good as another."

"Crooks. Crooks, pure and simple," the prince muttered, turning the chain over in his hands.

"What kind of jewels are these?"

"Rubies and opals. Beautiful, pure. Rare."

"I don't know, I don't know. The chain isn't intact. How could I wear it? Haven't they noted in the public journal that you've stolen it?"

"Not a word! A widow found it in her deceased husband's cabinet!"

Grajcewer covered his mouth. He'd said too much, now the prince wouldn't let him get away with it.

"No respect from the widow. Not even for the deceased. What was this cabinet?"

"It had a secret drawer."

"Nothing else inside?"

"Nothing. Just bedbugs."

"Only bugs, you say. Who really knows? I won't be checking, will I? How much do you want?"

"The widow found it. She's a modern widow."

"The widow's a swine. Why did the man hide his fortune? She must have tormented him to death."

"A torment indeed," Grajcewer agreed. "A torment in her subtile ways. The husband of such a lady is sent packing to the next world all the quicker, by his wife's modern schooling."

The prince gave this some thought, for he too had a modern wife. He sighed. A wise man, this Grajcewer.

"How much do you want?"

"Ten rubles?"

"Not on your life!" bellowed Stanisławczyk, retreating a step.

The merchant spread his little hands.

"Let Your Lordship quote the price. You are the Lord, and I merely a foolish Jew, at your service."

"Take five, or I'll run you out of town! You and those sons of yours, and those daughters of yours . . . !"

The Jew nodded his head. He raised his hands and his eyes

toward the ceiling.

"Agreed! Agreed! Only God knows a Jew's pain. Will you have me replace the rest of the chain?"

"Replace it. What good is the thing without the rest? You must. I'll pay when it's all ready. And take the clock."

Grajcewer bowed and left, taking the tooth, the chain, and the clock with him.

"The crook," Stanisławczyk muttered. "The rogue."

He went back to watching the peasants load hayricks onto carts. There was too much laughter ringing out. But just enough of the girls' thighs flashing from under their hiked skirts. He felt hungry. Going to the mirror, he stared for a long time into the cracked, matte surface, as blue as ice on water. He opened his mouth, tilted his head, and studied the gap where his tooth had been. He pulled a gnawed toothpick from his robe pocket and poked it into the hole. It hurt.

"The crooks. No mercy."

He bared his teeth, counting those that remained.

"Plenty left," he muttered.

A soft knock sounded. He didn't respond at once. He crossed slowly to the window, ran his fingers over the telescope, and returned to the table. He brooded. His servants were good-for-nothing, dirty, and idle. Crooks, the lot of them. The artful widow had found a secret drawer in the cabinet. The prince felt ill at the thought that, after his demise, his wife too would find the secret drawer in his desk. Perhaps he should drill a hole in the table leg? But the leg was too skinny! What could he keep there? His children would have no respect, they'd find it and then drink, gamble, and carouse it all away! One man after another would come malingering round the widow, there'd be a widower too, and they'd pair up at his grave! But it didn't even have to be a widower! It could be a bachelor! Bachelors were the most despicable! There was never enough money for them! And if he could dance a jig or play the guitar, there was no widow in the world who could resist! And if he could slip a word or two of French into the conversation! If he said he'd spent some time in France, the son-of-a-bitch, at the cabarets!

The servant knocked for the second time.

"Come in!"

The prince had the kind of servants who helped deceive the husband.

A tall, barefoot girl entered the room. She had blonde hair, fulsome lips, and deep, twinkling eyes. The prince's ward. She was the only one who never deceived. She came in when she wanted, and left when she wanted. What kind of creature she was—this the prince did not know. She was carrying a letter on a dented tray. She tossed the tray onto the table. Then she moved as if to leave. But leave she did not.

"Hold on! What goes on in the village, eh?" the prince blurted out.

He breathed in the smell of feminine sweat, lye, and wood smoke. The scent of hay drifted in through the window. The prince ran his eyes over the girl's breasts, her hips, her bare arms. They came to rest on her dirty feet and broken toenails.

"Why aren't you off carting the hay, eh?" he asked, drawing nearer to the creature, placing a hand on her breast and squeezing. His fingers skimmed the stiffening nipple.

"I'm in the kitchen." She leaned her hip on the table and sloped her body forward.

"And what goes on in the kitchen? What's for lunch?" He ran his hand over her belly and quickly plunged it between her legs.

The girl seemed to have been waiting for this. She giggled. She pressed her thighs together, clasping the prince's hand. From this trap he could not escape! All was lost!

"Capon and dumplings," she purred.

"And soup?"

She nodded her head.

"And a golden sauce?"

"Golden," she replied, and stared at the prince with golden eyes.

And he pulled back his hand, but it would not come free! She gave a quiet laugh. At last, however, she had mercy on the poor thing and spread her legs enough for him to escape. The prince's round eyes glazed over.

"I am your captive," he moaned.

"You are only your own captive."

He hung his head, for he, too, was a humble servant of love.

The girl left with a smile that sent a shiver of both delight and dread through the prince! Only a goddess smiled thus, so that a mortal man dreamed of sweet death in her arms, as though it were not death at all, but salvation and eternal happiness.

"Come later," her lips breathed.

Stanisławczyk silently moved his own lips. Luckily a piece of plaster tore free and fell onto the window ledge, restoring the prince to his senses. He sat down to read the letter. Slupcyn was inviting him to town for a game of cards. What other matters concerned Slupcyn, indeed, apart from cards? Perhaps wine and women as well. The arch-scoundrel, the whoremonger, the son-of-a-bitch! He'd smash the desk to smithereens with an axe to find the secret drawer! He'd waste no time in figuring it out, in hunting down the hidden spring! He amused Stanisławczyk, because he could stick his mouth into a glass of wine, and drink like a hog while wiggling his ears. He was big, flabby, and hairy. Slupcyn was *somebody*—he had a great deal of power. His letter mentioned that he'd sent old Wypcza packing for his no-good son's political intrigues, and he asked if the prince wouldn't care to buy something for a pittance before the auction; Slupcyn would falsify some documents and spook Wypcza's distant relations.

Imbecile! How could he write such things in a letter? Just think who else might have opened it! The local gentry would find out! No breeding, no fear of God! The scoundrel sought to profiteer on human suffering! "Screw yourself, Pyotr Pyotrovich!" the prince thundered. He burned the letter in the oven. He burned all the letters from Slupcyn, replied to none of them, and sent back all his gifts. Slupcyn liked to laugh:

"You, Stanisław, are a flea. No one can see you, yet you cling to my collar, and there's no shaking you off."

"Up your ass!" muttered the prince, staring at the ashes.

He spit. He staved off all such unpleasant thoughts. And what were these gifts Slupcyn had sent? A square-shaped folding comb, toothpicks, a flute, a dried tiger's paw—but a small one, a cat's, seemingly—a ship in a bottle, some dirty illustrations and poems. He had a look at the drawings and read the poems, of course, then sent them back. None of it made much of an impression, though Slupcyn had raved: "They'll make you ram your head against the wall all night, until you bash a hole in it!" For a week he pondered how the ship might have been squeezed into the bottle. He took out the cork, prodded it with a finger, blew at the sails. He surmised the ship had been put in when it was the size of a seed; then it was watered, and grew like a pumpkin. And so he poured water into the bottle and waited to see if the ship would come bursting through the glass, it would grow gigantic and Stanisławczyk would cast it off to sea, sailing to Brazil; but everything just got wet, came unglued, fell apart. In a fury he corked it back up and sent it back to Slupcyn without so much as a word.

TRANSLATED FROM POLISH BY
SOREN A. GAUGER AND MARCIN PIEKOSZEWSKI

[Portugal]

RUI MANUEL AMARAL

Almost Ten Stories

With a Soul as Light
as a Butterfly's Shadow

Christoph Robbé lost all his teeth in a single day. It started in the morning and by the beginning of the afternoon there were none left in the top row. "In spite of all this," he thought, "it's not too serious, since I still have quite a few on the bottom." But just as soon as he thought this, another one fell out.

So he continued walking, as was his custom, down Bommel Avenue, and, stopping in front of a tobacco shop to read the newspaper headlines, another one went. Things were getting ugly. Christoph pulled out his handkerchief, blew his nose, and yet another one fell out. He picked it up and examined it between his fingers: it was the molar that had bothered him for years, and that the dentist had always maintained—in spite of all the evidence to the contrary—was healthy and thriving.

Meanwhile, his very own tongue had started to push on one of the incisors with the malicious intention of knocking it out of his mouth, which is exactly what happened around three in the afternoon. Christoph straightened his tie, ran his fingers through his hair, looked at the horizon with a dreamy expression, imagined poppy-covered meadows, took a few resolute steps, and seven of his teeth fell out at once. "Teeth have a very peculiar way of expressing themselves," he thought, philosophically. And he added out loud, but softly, to himself: "It's hard to ignore it—it just jumps right out at you." At that precise moment, his second-to-last tooth fell to the ground and bounced a couple of times in front of him.

Night fell, at last, but nothing good came with it. A single tooth remained. A sad, desolate, and solitary canine on the right side. All at once a radiant light appeared. And the tooth flew, with a soul as light as a butterfly's shadow, into the beyond.

THE LONG RED BEARD

When Zurbin Raimondi entered the café, everyone burst into laughter. He always had this affect on people. Wherever he showed up, everyone would soon start laughing and pointing fingers at him. He walked across the room and dropped down into the last chair, patiently waiting for the laughter to subside. As was his custom, he didn't exchange words with anyone. He wiped his neck, ears, and the curved end of his nose—all drenched in sweat—with his handkerchief. Afterward he drank a beer, paid, and left, in the midst of general laughter.

Zurbin Raimondi couldn't comprehend what it was about him that attracted so much attention and aroused such uncontrolled mirth in others. Especially because he hated to be seen: He spoke very little, and when he addressed people, even the sound of his own voice startled him. At night, closed up in his room, he gave in to tears and the most terrible hopelessness. "No, no, no!" he repeated to himself, tearing out his hair, his eyes rolling back in his head.

Then, suddenly, as a result of really focusing on the problem, he felt that he had come upon a way to put an end to all that. He grabbed a blade, held it above his neck, and set about cutting off the long red beard that had been his companion for years. So then, with a cleanly shaven chin, he went out into the street. And it indeed came to pass: Not a single smile confronted him, nor any suggestion of mockery. Instead, he saw serious expressions, worried and even hateful, in the office, on the bus, in the café, at every turn.

Over the following weeks he ceased to be the butt of jokes or a topic of amused conversation. No one noticed him anymore. Zurbin Raimondi was now treated like everyone else bogged down in the petty mire of life. As loud as he may have coughed or slapped his hand down on a table in the café, no one paid him the slightest attention.

So he made haste to let his sorcerous red beard grow out, so that fate could again reward him with some sort of humiliation. But nothing happened. Indifference had attached itself to him, and never let him go.

The Life and Almost Death of Arquimedes Trismegisto

In a few moments, three or four lines at most, someone will be murdered in this story. There are still a few seconds of reading left. Till then, we'll kill a little time. As is well known, the best way to kill time is to stab it with a ballpoint pen in the left shin.

"Ouch, hey, ugh, my heavens!" says time as I stab it in the right shin, which, I'll say in passing, is a beautiful shin.

"Not the right shin, you idiot, the left!" complains time with a loud howl.

Thanks for the help, I think, as I correct the error and stab my ballpoint in the proper shin.

I'll never understand why this is the only way to kill time. Why not use a pencil, a felt-tip pen, or a barbecue skewer? All right then, just for the sake of experiment and to contribute to further illumination on this subject, I decide to kill time by boxing its ears with a dictionary. But meanwhile I notice that time is already dead.

At this point, unfortunately, the number of lines has already surpassed the amount needed to pick up the story at the point where someone is murdered. And as one could expect from a second-class character, our victim, Arquimedes Trismegisto—or perhaps he went by another name altogether—snuck out through the back gate like a coward while we were busy killing time.

You can't trust anyone these days.

A LAMENTABLE EPISODE

Mardrus had lost a leg in the war. What a terrible thing! In its place he used a prosthetic leg. Now this leg had a very peculiar habit: At night, while Mardrus slept, it left the house and ran to the nearest bar to drink. One glass after another. It didn't stop until it was good and drunk, only returning home in the wee hours of the morning. Mardrus, for his part, had always favored a structured life. He was a serious and steadfast man, and nature had graced him with the noblest of sentiments. In short, virtue personified, a gentleman like no other. It's not surprising, then, that he had never suspected the despicable proclivities of his leg.

For a long time everything ran smoothly: The leg only headed out after its owner was already asleep and was always back before he awoke. But one night a horrible incident took place that shattered this tranquility and turned everything on its head, revealing the true character of that reckless prosthetic.

A violent conflagration broke out in the building where they lived* and spread rapidly throughout it, forcing Mardrus—that poor thing!—to hobble down the first flights of stairs and tumble** down the rest, stumbling amid the flames, his face a crimson red, his hair deplorably disheveled. A lamentable episode, doing irreparable damage to his reputation.

---

* Mardrus and the prosthetic leg lived in the garret of an old building in Baixa de Cedrinka.
** Bang! Crash!

All told, this is further proof, as if any were needed, that the wolf often presents itself in sheep's clothing, and that one can find the origin of the greatest tragedies in the least significant things (a prosthetic leg, for example).

Giovanni del Gobbo

On that morning, something in Giovanni del Gobbo's disposition changed. To be honest, I can't guarantee that this was his name, precisely. But I like Giovanni del Gobbo and I want to believe that this was his name. But let's get back to the story. Up to this point Giovanni had lived a quiet life in his little corner. He had long since given up any sort of ambition and had resigned himself to the most placid, simple, bucolic, and humble of existences, immersing himself in a pleasant and ineffable solitude: year after year, removed from all passion, desire, turmoil.

But on that morning, Giovanni del Gobbo awoke with an unusual desire to take some decisive actions. And, as a matter of fact, he undertook the most surprising of initiatives. He raised his head up about twenty centimeters, blew his nose thunderingly, positioned two pens behind his ear, caught a fly that had landed on the desk to gossip, poetically scratched the top of his head, let loose a fair number of "humphs," unleashed a piercing burst of laughter, which contained—it must be said—a note of malevolence quite unpleasant to the ear, and began to write: "On that morning, something in Giovanni del Gobbo's disposition changed . . ."

Dioptrics

There was once a man—let's call him Anke—who was extremely nearsighted. So nearsighted that if he stretched out his arms he could no longer see his hands. He had only a foggy memory of his feet. It had been quite a long time since he'd seen them. They had quite recently turned into two monstrous fish, and the man was completely unaware of this fact. The fish flailed their fins as he walked—plop, plop, plop—swinging to the right and to the left, trudging along with great difficulty. It was a spectacle quite difficult to describe.

Lacking any knowledge of his extraordinary "feet," Anke was a happy man. He lead as peaceful and comfortable an existence as his bulky lenses allowed. One fine day, however, his nearsightedness disappeared in the blink of an eye (that's how things go). And our man, full of hope, prepared to rediscover the bountiful shapes and forms of the world.

Just then, the infernal fish emerged out of the shadowy depths in all their splendorous horror. Anke didn't take a single step, didn't make a single gesture, didn't even move a muscle. The shock of it had frozen his voice and muscles. Oh, what a terrible sight! There they were, where they had always been, nervously flailing their tails—plop, plop, plop. It was difficult to imagine something that could be more offensive to good taste and decency.

He felt overcome by a very, very profound sense of despondence. His sadness and pallor were pitiable. He even thought more than once that he was going to die of sorrow. But he didn't.

Story of a Man Who Lost His Soul in a Café

As is his habit, José Augusto goes to the café after leaving work. He drinks a beer or two. What the hell, maybe three. So far, so good. He leafs through the newspaper and stares at the plump women as they pass by. Nothing particularly important. Afterward, he gets up, hands in his pockets, and whistles on his way home.

At home, he realizes that he left his soul at the café. José Augusto gets annoyed because he's already put on his slippers, and because his wife is giving him grief. His wife is convinced that the forgotten soul is nothing more than a pretext for him to spend the night out drinking beer and even, who knows, getting involved in something else entirely.

At any rate, José Augusto returns to the café. He looks for his soul on the table where he had been drinking. But both the table and chairs are empty. The employees say that if a soul had been left behind there, they would have noticed it. After all, it isn't easy for a soul to go unnoticed. Be that as it may, they don't fail to remind him that these days you can't trust anyone, and that it's possible that another customer made off with it to do who knows what. José Augusto is resigned to his bad luck and, with an abundance of sighs and groans, he heads back home without his soul.

All this took place some time ago. But even today José Augusto feels an extremely acute sort of pain in the spot where his soul ought to be. Especially during pheasant-hunting season. Or is it partridge? No, it's pheasant.

MIRRORS

There was once a man who had a very personal problem with mirrors.

Why?

Because every time he saw a mirror he discovered a new and unknown face on his body. In the morning the mirror would reproduce one face, at night another, and the following morning yet another, and so on, successively. Well, this made quite an impression on him (put yourself in his position). Furthermore, and as a result of this odd phenomenon, the man didn't even know what his true face looked like.

"This is absurd, absurd, absurd!" he exclaimed, stomping his feet on the ground. The man had traveled widely and peered into innumerable mirrors, in hope of finding one that would reveal his true nose, his true mouth, his true eyes, his true ears, to speak only of the nose, mouth, eyes, and ears. He had also tried many other things, devising schemes both exceptional and bold, visiting seers and saints. But with no success.

"Ah, what luck I have!" he wept.

The man spent his days downcast, pale, and desolate, dreaming of the day when he would be able to see his true face, if only for a second. Just thinking of this possibility made his heart pound vigorously and gave him shivers.

Finally, already a very old man, a brilliant idea flashed in his head. Hope was reborn in him. Oh, yes! Oh, yes! Oh, yes! Life is full of wonders like this: after so many years, he had found a solution.

"Finally!" he screamed, utterly thrilled.

Unfortunately, the solution wasn't very good and the idea, ultimately, wasn't all that brilliant, and the man remained as he had been from the start. That is to say: same old, same old.

The Man Who Had Two Hearts

There was once a man to whom nature had granted two hearts. Or rather, in whose chest beat two hearts. Or rather, who came into this world with two of those marvelous organs. All well and good.

One day, however, one of the hearts stopped. Nothing too serious, given that the man had the second one to fall back on. The problem is that the story wasn't that simple. I forgot to mention* that the two hearts bore an ancient, profound, and overwhelming passion for one another. As the saying goes, in the heart of those hearts burned the flame of pure love. So, when the first one stopped, the second dissolved into tears and stopped beating out of sorrow.

In conclusion, the man couldn't withstand it and died. Be that

---

* That's not true. I was very anxious to write this part. But I do try to be a competent narrator and, that being the case, I waited until just the right moment to make this significant revelation.

as it may, the death wasn't a result of these cardiac disturbances, as we'll call them. The man died in Arcadia as a result of a snakebite. And while death was no picnic, remember that life wasn't so easy for him either.

Orange Juice

A lizard is stricken with a life-threatening fever. In short time he transforms into a man. The lizard ambulance takes the man to the lizard hospital.* The lizard doctors provide their unusual patient with thoughtful care. Unfortunately, they determine that there is no treatment for his condition. They feel as though the ground has given out beneath their feet. This is the great trick that life plays on everyone.

The man continues to burn with fever. He starts to transform into a cow. No one knows what to do. The specialists run away out of fear that they'll get burned. It's an irresolvable case. A terrible blow to the scientific pride of the lizards. Centuries and centuries of research, work, struggle, and perseverance without end, all dashed to bits by the monster of impotence.

Their rigorous ethical code notwithstanding, the lizard doctors can't see any other option than just putting an end to it all. They give the elephant—meanwhile the cow had transformed into an elephant—a very peculiar orange juice to drink. The elephant dies in three seconds. The lizards breathe a sigh of relief, albeit with a trace of displeasure.

In conclusion, I saw all this with absolute clarity and I testify it before the world. But that's not all. After reading this, please do verify if there are any other similar cases.

TRANSLATED FROM PORTUGUESE BY RHETT McNEIL

---

* But does such a hospital exist? Yes, such a hospital does exist, to be sure.

NINA GABRIELYAN

Quiet Feasts

FIRST FEAST

Noiselessly he turned the key in the lock, stepped into the dark anteroom stealthily, and stopped, listening. They were already in—just as he feared! He waited a moment to let his face relax, then pretended he was Granddad and entered the dining room.

"At last!" said his wife seeing her husband's benign face.

"At last!" said his children seeing their father's grim face.

"Presents!" said the grandchildren, and he felt sorry for them because they had grown up and were finishing school this year, and who was to blame except his own children, especially the younger daughter, a divorcee who surely had plenty of lovers.

"Presents?" he asked and turned to the grandkids the face their parents had loved best when they were kids themselves: merry and mirthful. But he'd misjudged them. The grandkids didn't know that face, and failed to give the right response; they said, "Presents!" and prepared to cry. Again he felt sorry for them, especially the girl, because she was a big and robust child, and he generally disliked her.

"Leave Granddad alone," said his divorced daughter, smoothing out the blue cotton housecoat he'd bought for his wife the week before. "Hungry granddads don't like to be bothered."

He was about to glare, but thought better of it. What if

she had no lover at the moment and was out to prey on his emotional reserves? You'll get nothing, darling, only what I owe you according to the law! I'm not about to get all upset and give you more emotion than you're entitled to, according to the Code. He allowed himself an angry retort, however:

"Why are you wearing your mother's housecoat? Haven't I told you to bring your own when you're staying with us?"

The divorcee's hypothetical lover sank back into his chair and heaved a sigh of relief somewhere at the other end of the city.

"Want some soup, Dad?" his elder, married girl, whom he loved best, came to his rescue.

"Presents!" the grandchildren said again.

Alas, they had a point, and they knew it, especially the boy. Tiny and skinny—his girl cousin was a foot taller—he was to take up law after school, and knew the Code inside out. Now, he yelled, his voice trembling:

"Don't pretend you've forgotten it's the twenty-fifth Sunday of the year!"

Two crystal tears dropped into the soup from the abused idealist's eyes, and he cried out again:

"Article 14, paragraph 3, item 16!"

Alas, they were right—if not entirely so, however.

"Item what?" he asked in an encouraging tone.

"16," the boy repeated in a faltering voice that seemed to have wilted, its assurance draining away.

"16. Fine. Let me see . . ."

A pregnant silence fell. He waited a full minute before delivering his blow:

"Do you mean . . . 16*a*? 'Grandchildren staying with the parents of any of their parents are entitled to gifts from host grandparents every fifth and twenty-fifth Sunday of the year to stimulate psychological development.' Hope I have that right."

"I think so." Hope was still ringing in the boy's voice.

"That doesn't apply to you, boy. You aren't *staying* with us. You *live* here."

But the child was still pressing his point:

"I'm registered at Mom's place, not yours. Right, Mom?"

"Granddad's joking," said the divorced daughter.

She'd do better to keep quiet: It was her fault he hadn't bought anything for the kids. Three days ago, she told him over the phone she'd take the boy in for the holidays, and next Sunday her married sister's husband would take them all, both sisters and both kids, to the Psychotron for the ceremonial punishment of psychic energy vampires. As every schoolboy knew, the Code (Art. 14, par. 3, item 16 B) prohibited giving presents to children if they visited the Psychotron on the fifth or twenty-fifth Sunday of the year, and quite right too. The country had a limited amount of psychological energy and no one was allowed to get double stimulation. And here they were, the kids were left with no stimulation at all!

"Granddad's joking," the divorced daughter repeated, knowing she'd get away with it: Article 9, par. 7, item 5 prohibited anyone from accusing parents of pedagogical errors in the presence of children below a certain age. She knew her rights and now was calmly contemplating her father's angry face.

"You shouldn't make jokes like that, Daddy," the elder, married daughter cut in, addressing her father's kind face, which was turned to her. "You know item 16a allows for numerous interpretations; the grandparents may do as they see best, really. If the boy isn't registered as resident at your place, he may be regarded as guest."

"He may, and he may not."

"You want to spoil our holiday?" his wife chipped in looking incredulously at the face that was still in love with her. "Surely you know that next year they'll no longer be entitled to any gifts."

"Really?" With a tremendous effort of will, he forced himself to look astonished. All five of his family members now saw him wearing the expression of a forgetful geriatric patient, desperately embarrassed.

The boy was the first to get white as chalk, the divorced daughter next. Paleness spread around the room, and soon all were pale. At the sight of them he lost his self-control and was no longer a grandfather, father, and husband. He was a lop-eared primary school boy lost at the blackboard trying to recollect article 18 of the Code, paragraph 7, item 2. Again he was taking the silent oath never to play Lice-Hunt with the other kids before he did his homework. Again he stared with horror at the teacher's well-groomed hand as it put a bad mark by his name in the class register. He wept.

"O Lord!" his wife gasped. "What's all this?"

And then he ran.

He ran, waving his bony arms, and grew smaller and smaller as he fled from their startled faces, from the pain he was causing them. Tears streamed down his childish cheeks and fell into his soup. "Mummy, Mummy," he sobbed.

She rose, put her hands on his gray head, and pressed it to her bosom: "All right, darling, all right, now be a good boy." He fell into a grateful silence. He was happy now, he was a good boy, and the day before, the playschool teacher had praised him before the other kids for article 25 of the Code, paragraph 9, item 3b: In an emergency, children of preschool age shall receive a double portion of positive emotions from either of their parents.

Later, they lay in bed. He was fondling her gray head, which rested against his shoulder, as she whispered that he shouldn't take it to heart, the girls would come back: Article 6, paragraph 10, item 4 obliged everyone to visit his or her retired parents no less than five times a year, and their retirement age was near, five months to wait for him and three for her. They'd manage. She was rated as a good worker, and her office had recently awarded her two privilege coupons for extraordinary psychological stimulation, not at some shabby district Psychotron but at the Central House for Consumer Service Workers, where they would get the highest-degree stimulation possible by attending the execution of a psycho-energy rapist.

His mind dissolving in the soft music of her voice, he nodded and thought that everything would be okay.

Second Feast

"I want you to deflower me," she said, but he had no idea how to go about deflowering a woman who already had a son of fourteen. So he stayed silent and still.

She lowered her blue eyes, like a Madonna by some anonymous medieval painter.

"Darling," she whispered, blushing.

He looked at her with a mixture of admiration and hatred. What she was doing was downright criminal.

"Have a mercy on me, sir! Do not deprive a poor girl of her only treasure! You will break my dear mother's heart!" Provocative notes sounded in her little voice.

He felt like an idiot. A noise from the kitchen rescued him.

"The kettle's boiling!" he cried as he beat a hasty retreat.

When he came back to offer her tea, she was sitting in an outrageous position, right leg resting on her bared left shoulder, her miniskirt revealing pink lace panties.

"Gimme a cigarette," she said in a hoarse voice. "And a glass of porter."

Again, a wave of admiration and hatred swept over him.

"No? You cheap bastard!" She flapped hands at him dismissively, her dark eyes turning green. Her big predatory mouth compressed into a small and sensual one, which then blew five smoke rings at once, and said coquettishly, "How tedious you are! You make me want to sleep with you."

He pretended to take her literally, and started making the bed.

"What's this, sir? Shame on you! Abuse of office, that's what it is," she said, now austere and refined, in an ankle-length black skirt and immaculate white blouse.

He was losing his temper. This was a criminal offense she was involving him in, after all. This latest "sir" was the last straw.

"Don't you *sir* me!" he bellowed. "I've got a name!"

"I'm sorry," she warbled as she reassumed her own appearance and sprang up to nestle on the chandelier. "So you don't want to deflower me," she sighed as she swung to and fro.

"Stop making so much noise," he implored. "The people next door will squeal on us."

The chandelier was swinging violently.

"So you don't like me?" she said from up there.

His intuition told him that this time he was hearing her real voice. He was a gentleman after all, and he didn't want to be rude to the woman he was going to sleep with.

"The very idea!" he protested.

"Even a little bit?" she went on, still swinging.

"Little bit of what?"

"You don't like me even a little bit?"

She was really rather sharp, all in all.

"I like you psychologically," he said, honestly.

"And my body?"

He'd never thought a chandelier could squeak so loudly!

"You're good company," he said.

"How about my looks?"

"You're a very interesting person."

"But as a woman?"

"Get down, please, before the neighbors hear."

"What if they do? They'll never understand, they've never

swung on a chandelier, I bet. They'll think we're having a fight. Morons, all of them. Plus, there's no law against it!"

"Against *this*? No, you're right." He gave her a meaningful glance.

"Listen," she whispered, landing on the sofa softly. "If you like, I can be a big, heavily made-up blonde. Only, I don't know what sort of clothes they wear. You never tell me what you'd like me to wear."

He couldn't believe his ears! Whatever she'd been doing up to this moment was already grave offence, but this new idea of hers was the worst crime you could think of. He remembered both of the appropriate articles in the Code. The first began: "Deliberate change of appearance through psychic effort within the limits of appearance potentially corresponding to the psychological type of the offender . . ." etc., etc.—five years' hard labor. The other one was about "appearance potentially contradicting the psychological type of the offender . . ." He couldn't bear to think of the consequences! But then, the punishment fit the crime. The first offence threatened mere social micro-destabilization. The second, according to the Experts, could undermine the System itself, should it be allowed to become common.

He wasn't so naïve as to believe the Experts, and he wasn't really so cowardly as to be afraid of the comparatively mild punishment he would receive as her accomplice, but he still had enough common sense to disapprove of her constant pranks. After all, he wished her well, she really was good company and an interesting person, and very good in bed. As a gentleman, he didn't want the woman he occasionally slept with to run such risks. And for no good reason.

"What's the point?" he asked.

"You said you liked blondes."

Still, he didn't understand.

"Large blondes with lots of make-up," she went on.

"But the Code—" and he stopped short. He had never seen her looking at him like this before. Again, he intuited that this was her real look, her very own.

"I love you," she said softly, and started growing larger.

He wanted to shout, "Don't!" He was about to say that big blondes weren't his type at all, and they'd never had any interest in him either. Too late. Her dark curls were turning into straight straw-colored tresses. Her face was contorting. It was so unlike her previous transformations, careless and playful, that he buried his face in his palms in terror. Agonizingly, she was becoming someone who would never love him.

Many fists were banging on the front door, and many voices shouting on the landing. The man from upstairs was the loudest: "I was the first to catch the scent, it deviated half a degree from the norm! I've a good nose for this sort of thing."

When the Psychological Security officers were leading them out of the apartment, the man slowed down and did something he'd never done before. He put his hand around her shoulders tenderly, and hugged her.

THIRD FEAST

"Haaa! A-ha-ha-ha-ha!"

They were laughing till it hurt.

"Ooooh!" they roared.

"That was a nice one!"

She looked in consternation at the family writhing with laughter on the huge divan, then asked in a faltering voice:

"Are you crazy, or what?"

"Oooh!" they roared in a new fit of laughter. Her grandson was kicking his tennis-shoed legs high in the air, lost in ecstasy.

"Silly boy," she said.

The child slid from the divan and beat his feet against the floor issuing short blasts of laughter to the family's approval.

"Get off the floor or you'll have to wash your trousers yourself," she said.

Another guffaw and they all looked back at the television.

"What did I say that was so funny?" she wondered a minute later.

"Shut up," they said in chorus.

"Why do you always have to make such a fool of me?"

"Stop it. You'll miss this scene too, with all your talking, and then you'll be begging us to tell who killed whom."

"So he's already done her in?"

"He who?" Six pairs of mocking eyes stared back at her.

"The bearded guy. The musician."

"Aaah! I'll be damned! She means the detective!" her grandson bellowed.

"I don't know what on earth goes on inside that head of yours," her daughter winced. "What on earth made you think he was a musician? And there's been no murder as yet. Just sit quietly and watch if you want to know what's going on. It's impossible to watch thrillers with you around!"

"Tea!" said her grandson.

"Oh yes, how about our tea?" asked her husband.

She was silent.

"A cup of tea would be just what the doctor ordered," said her daughter.

"Make it yourselves," she said.

"What?" they all cried.

"Make it yourselves if you want tea."

"Who, us?"

"Yes. All of you."

They sat in silence for a while, thinking it over.

"Hmm, a well-grounded proposal," her grandson brought out at last.

"Appears so at first sight. But when you give it some

thought . . ." her daughter joined in.

"When you give it some thought, it's very thin indeed," the father summed up.

It would be best not to serve them any tea. But then, she would have no other excuse for talking to them till supper. She shuffled to the kitchen.

Stifled sobs reached the sitting room.

"Crying," said the daughter.

"Serves her right. After all this is for her own good," said the father, frowning.

"Shall I check on her?" asked the daughter.

"No!" said the father, an angry vertical fold climbing his forehead. "If you do, you'll just be giving her another chance to over-communicate."

"Dad, are you really so sure the Experts were right?"

"They're always right. Don't you see she's over-communicative?"

"She gave me the fifth degree yesterday about my astronomy lessons—as if she could tell an asteroid from a telescope!" her grandson complained.

"Asked me if I was going to remarry," her daughter giggled.

"Asked me how I was doing with the new boss," her husband whispered. "And that's not all. The day before yesterday, our ground-floor neighbor said she'd been inquiring after his wife's health and how his grandchildren were doing at school. See how far she's gone! I did my best to explain our predicament. He was understanding, though—sympathetic."

"The other day, she . . ." her daughter started.

"But now she's doing something that by all rights is your responsibility," the father cut in sharply. "The Experts told us to do something about her communicability, but they never said she was supposed to make your tea."

"What about yours?" the daughter asked nastily.

"What do you mean?"

"Did the Experts say anything about her making your tea?"

"Stop quarreling, now. Please."

They all jumped. She was standing in the doorway, smiling, holding the tea tray. Such amazing reserves of meekness in this old woman! They smiled back, but became serious just in time, as decent people should.

"Thanks," they all said. Each took a cup and turned back to the television.

"Is it good?"

"As usual," they all said in chorus.

"But recipe number two might still be better, no?" she asked.

"Sure," they said, in chorus.

She sighed, and made another try.

"How many classes do you have tomorrow?" she asked her grandson.

"Bang!" the grandson shouted.

"What?" she gasped.

"Now that was a great punch! Straight from the shoulder!"

She looked at the screen, then at her husband and daughter. She knew better than to look at her grandson. The boy was so pretty, with his flushed cheeks, bright eyes, and disheveled locks! She knew her hand would reach out against her will and stroke him on the head. It was Monday, and her grandson hated to be fondled out of weekly schedule.

FOURTH FEAST

They order him to take off THE THING. He pretends to misunderstand and hastily unlaces his shoes. "Don't act like an idiot," they shout. And what does he think he's doing undoing his necktie? He knows they mean something else entirely. And what is he unzipping his trousers for? They don't care what he has in them. Maybe that woman might be interested. They giggle. Yes, that one. She might very well be interested. And don't you pretend to be astonished. You know who we mean. We know all about her, and here's material evidence. They show him a red pomegranate with cracked skin. The sight of it gives him a splitting headache. They click their tongues sympathetically and say that to stop it he ought to take off THE THING. After he does, he'll never have another headache again. If he isn't brave enough to do it himself, they can help him. They are approaching. He makes a desperate attempt to disappear. The tension makes his ears ring. It grows into a roar, and with a sigh of relief, he emerges in another dream. He still has a headache and, to stop it, he must put his head into his mother's lap. Not the mother who celebrated her sixtieth birthday the other day, but the woman she was thirty years ago, when he was a child. He strains desperately to recollect how she looked then . . . and wakes up from the effort.

His headache is still with him, and he doesn't realize at once that this is no longer a dream. Then, he becomes aware that he's awake. Next, he's not so sure again. Then the final realization comes and with it panic. The men in his dream must have been right. Otherwise, why did they show him the pomegranate? Come on! He breaks into a triumphant laugh. That pomegranate was painted! What unbelievable idiots. He chuckles. They show him a real pomegranate instead of a picture and call it material evidence! The asses! They'd do better on a variety show than working for the Psychological Security Service. What did the goddamn fruit have to do with it anyway? Did they have a written complaint from the victim? Impossible. She never for a moment thought she'd been assaulted. On the contrary, she'd asked for it! He laughs and laughs . . . and wakes himself up with the noise.

He switches on his bedside lamp, gets up, takes the Code from the shelf, and leafs through it—a stupid thing to do, he knows. Without a complaint from her, they can't arrest him. And that's out of the question. She won't file a complaint because she wanted him to do what he did! As to the Code, well, he's leafing through it out of sheer curiosity.

The stool was gray and moldy, with sprawling crooked legs. It was obscene the way this ancient piece of furniture had positioned its legs. Even more obscene was the pomegranate lying on the stool and grinning with all its shiny crimson seeds through the cracks in its skin.

The silence was getting awkward, so he asked the ginger-haired woman artist if the picture had a title.

"Self-Portrait."

"Self-Portrait?"

She came up to the sofa on which he was sitting and, narrowing her beady blue eyes to slits, asked what was so strange about that.

"Oh, it's all right," he said. He couldn't admit to her that he was embarrassed by the look of that obscenely decrepit stool and that insolently grinning fruit. A minute later, he saw that the pomegranate had nothing to be so cheerful about: The stool was actually devouring it! There it was, a barely discernible crack across the seat, sucking in its juice. But for the moment, he hadn't noticed it yet. In the meantime, all he saw was the fruit smiling with all its seeds, and the slit-eyed ginger-haired woman waiting for his reply.

"That's all right," he said again.

She moved aside and asked in an unexpectedly timid voice:

"Want to see more?"

"Yes, please."

Another canvas appeared on the paint-stained table. She lowered her eyes. His nerves were on edge thanks to her sudden transition from arrogance to timidity, even submission. He looked away from her dirty skirt, the hem of which needed a stitch or two, and saw the new picture.

It was an iron, not the streamlined electrical appliance everybody uses now, but one of those heavy cast-iron things he remembered from childhood. It stood in the center of a snow-covered field, and huge mosquitoes with fat snouts and protruding yellow eyes were perched on its handle and sides.

"Another self-portrait?" he asked jocularly.

"No, I call it *Noah's Ark.*"

Her voice was again frosty, like the field in her picture. It was her only canvas featuring the color white, and even this was not quite white, given the touch of gray in it. Gray must have been the favorite color of this woman in her stained skirt and with that sparse, carroty bun on her nape! Gray filled all her pictures. Her work always seemed to be covered in dust, through which shone an occasional red or yellow spot.

"*Solitude,*" she said, and he felt a pang of compassion.

"*Solitude,*" she repeated and held up the next picture at a different angle.

It was an iron bedstead with a gray sheet on it. On this sheet, writhing in agony or passion was a woman's washed-out nightshirt, with her flabby breasts and stomach, as well as her knees, spread wide, all barely discernible inside the threadbare garment. Its short sleeves were stretched upward to either embrace or fend off an invisible presence.

"Magnificent!" he said with a pitying look. She threw him a glance, sharp as a needle—prick—or was he mistaken? He must be. The next moment, she was focused on her little fingers, which were engaged in a strange dance, now intertwined in a passionate clasp, now spread apart in helpless wonder.

"Thank you," she hissed.

Sure, he was mistaken.

He turned another page, and found what he was looking for. Article 59: Psycho-energy Rape. "It is a criminal offence to look one's partner in the eyes without his/her consent during intercourse." This was hardly applicable to him, though of course he did look her in the eyes, sometimes—just without intercourse. Catch him sleeping with that scarecrow! The next item, which banned talking with one's partner without his/her consent during intercourse, was no business of his either. So the men from his first dream had no reason to demand that he take off THE THING. The thought made him shiver. He thrust his hand under his shirt and felt his chest—not to check if THE THING was where it should be: He knew it would be there, but it was still reassuring to feel it, and he heaved a sigh of relief. Neurotic anxiety, that's all it was! It was an open question who had raped whom, anyway. True, he'd told her about his childhood. But what of it? Did the Code say a word about childhood reminiscences? But, wait a minute. Why the hell had he mentioned his complex about being short? There it was, item 7a: "It is a criminal offence to describe one's psychological complexes and thus compel one's interlocutor to show compassion." But then, he spoke so matter-of-factly. It couldn't have taken him more than half a minute to say it out. A minute and a half, at most. And, besides, she was hardly innocent on that score herself. Didn't she try to move him to compassion when she babbled about her fear of insects, especially roaches? He listened quietly to all the nauseating details of her childhood adventure, when her big brother dropped a roach inside her collar, and it ran up and down her spine, tickling her. She got it out, at last, but only when it had been squeezed to death. Since that day, the sight of insects was associated with death in her mind. Well, he did complain about his morning heartburn to her. But so what if he did? What was his heartburn against her detailed account of her school years, how her classmates tormented her because she refused to go lice-hunting with them? She was afraid to tell the headmistress, because her class was exemplary-experimental and trusted with self-regulation. So, really, who was the victim in their little encounter? It was him! Didn't his heart ache with pity as she rounded off her story? She turned pink with pleasure as she saw tears in his eyes. Yes, she blushed, he could swear she was glowing with masochistic pleasure! She even became a bit pretty, believe it or not. And having become pretty, she made him complain of feeling lonely. What do you mean, "made him"? Well, she kind of hinted he was free to complain. How did she hint? With a look. So there was no rape. And how many minutes did he complain of his loneliness, once he gave in? Or hours, rather? Look, let's get it down in black and white: He spent several hours complaining to her of his loneliness, making her compassionate. And don't try to convince us she wanted it. She might have liked it for the first five minutes—ten, at most. But to stand it for hours on end! Are you kidding? Here's the Experts' commentary on the law: "Compassionate attention to any person's confession shall be regarded as voluntary for no longer than ten minutes. Violation of this limit by the confessant, even in cases where the listener offers no clear resistance, shall be qualified as psycho-energy rape and punishable by the Supreme Measure." You know what that is, right? And stop groping around inside your T-shirt all the time! You're not a child, and you know no one will take off your protective screen here. Never seen a criminal executed? They do it at the Central Psychotron, with lots of people watching. The condemned is placed in the center of the stage, and his screen is removed during a solemn ceremony, after which he's left eye-to-eye with the audience, exposed. No one can say how soon the audience will use up his psychic energy. It all depends. He may be lucky and die instantaneously. Hey, stop that screaming. You're not at the Psychotron yet. You're at home! What's going on? Why are they here again? He must be dreaming. He'd fallen

asleep again without noticing it. All right, they believe he's telling the truth when he claims he's wide awake and that they can't
be a dream. Oh, don't be so nervous. If you're awake, you can't be
dreaming them. Fine, they're not here, and they have no statement from his victim. And she's no victim, for that matter. All's
well. It's okay. Okay, we said.

FIFTH FEAST

OR

THE ADVENTURE

"Rat-a-tat-a-rat-a-tat," the wheels beat on the rails in the dark
tunnel.

"Rush-shur-rush," newspapers rustled in the passengers'
hands.

"Hero Square. Next stop, Hero Square," the silvery voice
sang over the train PA.

He leaned back on his velvet seat and smiled happily. The
boyish face reflected in the opposite window—his own—smiled
back in silence. He winked at it, and the face winked back. He
winked again. The prim gentleman sitting opposite thought the
wink was addressed to him, took a paper out of his briefcase, and
angrily unfolded it like a screen. The boyish face over this man's
left shoulder disappeared. The winker could lean left to see his
reflection over the gentleman's right shoulder, but he didn't do
so, lest he could be misunderstood.

The wheels were beating their merry tattoo.

He listened to them and sighed as he tried to recover his joy,
but all in vain. Something had clicked up there in the celestial
spheres that defied his understanding, and he could no longer
tune his joy to the vigorous wheel beat and drew on its vigor. It
was a feeble little joy now, ready to die at any moment.

The papers rustled in the passengers' hands, hiding their
faces.

His joy was waning, so he tried to feed it with the announcer's voice, which merrily sang that they were approaching Hero Square. Ageless and sexless, it was an ideal voice synthesized out of thousands of individual voices, a meta-voice that defied all emotional contact. He had to refer to his pocket reference book. He thrust his hand into the back pocket of his blue jeans, took out the little book in its brightly colored binding, and opened it. The title page had large, beautiful lettering: A GUIDE TO EMOTIONS. He found the chapter on joy and concentrated on the subheadings: The Impact of Joy on Digestion, Joys Desirable and Undesirable, Unexpected Joy: Regulation Of, Unmotivated Joy: Positive and Negative Results Of. But none of this had to do with his own particular joy. He turned some more pages. Ah, there it was! Independent Joy Intensification. Now, how did it go? "In case you need to intensify your joy, and Method Three is not available (e.g., in the absence of a person willing and able to collaborate on said method), you ought to resort to Method Five, self-service. Establish contact with your reflection in the mirror . . ."

He shut the book. Nothing new there! He'd like to see the author try to establish contact with his reflection when there was a newspaper between him and the nearest reflective surface.

The gentleman opposite him folded his paper, and it disappeared back into his case. The train emerged from the dark into the floodlit Hero Square station.

"Next stop, Affluence Avenue," the silvery voice rang, and the train was back in the dark tunnel.

The wheels' rhythm got quicker. He smiled and contacted his reflection. Again, it was smiling back from the window, triumphant at its liberation from the void into which the gentleman's huge newspaper had cast it. The book's author was right after all: Half a minute after he established contact, his joy was twice as strong as before, and fell in with the wheels' merry rat-a-tat. It grew and grew, and was four times greater by the time the train reached Human Rights station, and had trebled by the time it stopped at Founding Fathers.

At Festival Square, a little old lady entered. She gave him a sweet smile and sat opposite him. His reflection was gone, but not quite, because she was so tiny. An ear and part of a cheek were visible above her shoulder. And yet, not enough for joy contact. He went on smiling angrily, simply out of inertia. The woman's wrinkled face smiled back not only with its thin pale lips but also with its merry blue eyes in their nests of crow's-feet. She smoothed out her faded headscarf. His joy must at this point have grown large enough to withstand all external influence, as he found himself smiling from ear to ear against his will. The old lady's smile grew even more endearing as he scrutinized her, trying to figure out what she reminded him of. It dawned on him at last: the joy thief from an old story he had read at school! The original joy thief. He wondered why he hadn't seen it from the start. It wasn't her shabby clothes—many passengers were poorly dressed—and not the absence of a newspaper in her hands—many weren't reading. But then, everyone who wasn't reading was contacting his or her reflection. Some smiled to intensify their joy, others frowned to work off their negative emotion with a bit of facial exercise, while this old woman was smiling directly at him, the only one in the car paying any attention to his or her fellow-travellers! Didn't the old dear see her efforts were pointless now that psycho-protective screens were no longer a luxury item that only the well to do could afford, and everyone had one on him to fend off psycho-energy thieves? She must have had bats in her belfry. She looked lonely, looked like she'd stumbled out of an old movie. What an adventure he was having! Pity he couldn't tell anyone about it at school. No one would believe him. The elderly no longer had any problems with communication. They received psycho-stimulation coupons once a month or even once a fortnight. But what if ... ? The idea was so funny he couldn't fight back a splutter. What if she was smiling for no reason at all? Her little face became radiant. The smile meant for him revealed pink toothless gums. Now he knew! He felt a pang of shame. Here it was, the only plausible explanation of the old lady's behavior. She'd lost her stimulation coupons for the month, poor dear. He sat thinking for a long time—a whole minute—then resolutely thrust his hand under his jacket, felt the screen under his fluffy sweater, and switched it off. Now his brain was emanating fluids of joy, first in tiny drops, then in a trickle. All of a sudden, joy flooded from his entire being. Unable to withstand it, he laughed, and the other passengers looked out from under their newspaper screens in shock.

TRANSLATED FROM RUSSIAN BY NATHALIE ROY

VLADIMÍR HAVRILLA

The Teacher and the Parchment

A young high-school teacher (31) falls in love with a dapper student boy (17) and, when they find themselves alone, when everyone else has left the classroom, they lunge at each other and kiss wildly. They also often end up in the basement, where they grope each other hungrily and partly disrobe. Over time, their affair begins to affect their minds, to the point where they actually hold hands for a moment while leaving school.

The boy suggests they slip away together for at least a week, that there's no point hiding like this, and he found a cheap ticket to Tunisia. He'll pay for their holiday so they'll have a free week, a week to themselves.

But they'd been seen in the basement, from time to time, and word gets back to the boy's father.

He immediately calls the teacher, demanding an explanation, insisting they meet at the Crimea restaurant, where he intends to give her a piece of his mind. And this happens. And the father, as dapper as his son, and in his forties, is initially quite severe at their table, but when the teacher tells him she likes jazz and often goes to the Jazz Café, he softens up a bit and makes a clean breast of his affection for the music of Gerry Mulligan. When the teacher invites him back to her studio flat in Petržalka, for a quick coffee, she tells him that she also plays tenor saxophone and will play something for him if he goes with her.

And again, this happens. In the morning they have another coffee together, this time she doesn't play her sax, but turns on a Lester Young CD. She's charmingly tousled, considerably confused, and says that only now does she know what it's like to be in the arms of a real man.

They enjoy more than one jam session. Father proposes—he's divorced, you see. She agrees.

On the day of the wedding, the teacher goes to visit the father's house. The son greets her, looks at her sadly, and says Dad isn't home, and that he actually did go ahead and book that trip to Tunisia for the teacher and himself, and that he doesn't want anything more from life than to have her accompany him.

"My silly little thing," the teacher exclaims and presses him to her bosom. The boy immediately covers her with kisses.

"And when would we go? Show me the tickets!" She looks. May 24th. "Are you kidding me?"

"Are you coming or not?"

The organ plays in the wedding hall. Today is May 24th. There are clusters of people milling around. We can't help but notice the father milling too.

The pleasant voice of a stewardess announces that the plane is now cruising at ten thousand meters. The teacher and her high-school beau sit back in their seats and drink with two straws from one glass, probably champagne.

"I'll miss a week of class. Will that be all right?" the student asks with concern.

"We'll work on it together and you'll catch up. I'll be teaching you . . . day and night."

"I don't mind, so long as it's in the moonlight . . ."

The teacher puts on headphones, adjusts the volume, and nods to the boy to do the same. They listen to Dizzy Gillespie's

"A Night in Tunisia."

The hallway of an average hotel. Two figures stand in the doorway of room 6853, a seventeen-year-old boy and a young woman around thirty. The boy turns the key, opens the door, and they both enter the room. The woman immediately walks to the window, opens it wide, and takes a breath of fresh air. "Look darling, we have the view of the sea."

The boy approaches her, grabs her by the shoulders, and covers her with a thousand kisses. He kisses her lips, eyelids, ears, neck, tears off her clothes, and rolls her onto the bed.

"Slow down, slow down, don't be impatient," the teacher murmurs, softly but resolutely pushing away the boy's eager hands. She holds his head in both hands, holds him close and says, "First I have to tell you a story about me. You should know who you're dealing with." The boy keeps kissing her hair, chest, shoulder, and hands, but she begins to tell her story:

"You know, little one, it's not so long ago that *I* was seventeen. I was what you'd call an ugly duckling. Very ordinary. And there were always these boys in front of our apartment block revving their motorcycles. One of them gave me a ride and I fell in love, like an idiot. You know how it goes. I wasn't ready yet. But he kept demanding that we go all the way, and I was so crazy that I gave in. Maybe I should have held out a little longer, then he might have appreciated it more. Anyway, that's behind me. So, what I'm saying is that I've had several nasty experiences, but I never knew any better than to give my all each and every time. I've been hurt pretty badly—I'm one big bruise, after all my adventures. If you want to heal me, darling, then by all means do it. If not, then leave now. It's up to you, you fruitcake."

Tired from the trip, the teacher is napping. The boy adjusts her blanket, kisses her forehead and tiptoes out to the hallway.

He closes the door behind him and takes the elevator down to reception.

When the elevator door opens, he sees his father, sitting in a chair and sucking on a huge cigar.

"Dad, I'm glad you came. The teacher is really getting on my nerves. She gave me a sermon, even. I almost fell out of bed."

"Son, there are some problems that can only be solved with a glass of whiskey. You're underage, but nobody will ID us here and I can tell you need a little first aid. Waiter!" He snapped his fingers.

All this took place in the hotel lobby, near a bar built into a niche in the reception area.

The father pulled out two plane tickets. "Tomorrow we'll look around town, check out the market, and leave in the evening."

"I'm really looking forward to being back in Bratislava, at good old General Štefánik Airport and the 83 bus home," the boy says.

The teacher wakes from her nap; someone's knocking on the door. "Come in, I think it's open," she says in English.

The door opens slowly and a waiter comes in. He's older, slim and quite elegant. He pushes a serving cart with refreshments ahead of him.

"Madam, I'm sorry to interrupt your sleep, but someone ordered salmon sandwiches and white Chateau d'Avignon."

"Oh yes, my little boy is so attentive," she says, first to herself and then aloud. "No matter, what's done is done . . . how long have I slept, anyway?"

"Sleep is always beneficial, madam," the waiter says vaguely, "Madam, please allow me a personal word here. I've been observing you ever since you arrived. I've taken a real interest in you, and, in fact, why should I prolong this agony—I love you. I'm particularly in love with your hair. It was I who came up with this refreshments idea. I ordered this food at my own expense. I joined the marines when I was young, made some money, gambled in casinos and was lucky—won a considerable amount. I bought a villa in the Caribbean on Abocada Island. But I was bored being there alone, so I began wandering, and at some point I came here.

"I've always liked big women, and since today's fashions have made such proclivities almost impossible to indulge, I never settled down with anyone. But when I saw you, your curvy body, I couldn't look away. Please don't let me down!"

The teacher is surprised from the get-go, but sympathizes with the older man, moved by his sincerity, and says quite frankly, "Well, not *all* my body parts are chubby, but perhaps those might be improved, in time. Right now I don't have much on, would you like to test me out?"

"If you don't expect visitors."

"Not in the next half hour, anyway."

"I've often watched sumo wrestling on Eurosport—that is the ideal to which I hope my wife would aspire. Me, I'm way too thin. Perhaps that's why I've always wanted a chubby woman. Would my thinness be a problem for you? If not, perhaps I would work at losing even more weight while you work on moving your beautiful hips—but really all your parts—in the opposite direction."

"I like crazy ideas. When do we leave?"

"This week. And now—may I close the blinds?"

A white, chubby hand gestures from under the cover.

"It's the wide strap."

The blind gently slides down.

The father sits by an old reel-to-reel tape recorder trying to thread a reel between the rollers. He grabs a cigarette from the ashtray, takes a puff, and sets it back down, still fighting with the machine. In the end, he tosses the tape into the corner of the couch in disgust, puts his cigarette back in his mouth, and reaches down into a cabinet full of records.

He puts a version of "What Is This Thing Called Love?" on the turntable and sets the needle. This is where we definitively say good-bye to the father. Schopenhauer recommends listening to music in hopeless situations, which are pretty much all of them.

You got what you wanted, you old lecher. Ciao.

The high-school student embraces his classmate, Bunny, near the now familiar metal lockers. He's breathing hard and his lips have little bite marks on them.

"Bunny, c'mon, someone might see us," he wheezes.

"Where did you learn to kiss like this? I'm sure I'm not your first."

"Hmmmm . . ." he says and wants to add, "I had a good teacher," but remains silent.

Bunny wears a pink T-shirt, pink pleated skirt, white sneakers, and short white socks. A pink plastic flower is pinned in her hair. Today she was training for a march as a majorette and hasn't had time to change. Her T-shirt has been pulled up more than halfway, and she's breathing heavily.

"I'm really sorry you're not the first," the boy says at last. "I was crazy about this one chick, but that's behind me. Bunny, with you I feel . . . I want to say, I feel like it's the real thing."

"Darling!"

"I'd like to marry you."

"All right, but we first need to finish school."

On a small island in the Caribbean, *something* walks out of a small house, a shack, really. Yet, despite the size of the building, the door is nearly two meters wide. Yes, some pink round substance has stuffed itself through the door and is moving down small steps to the nearby beach. Someone tossed a banana peel on the fourth step, however, and this aspic slips and rolls down to the beach. A pale blue bikini is apparent within the folds of this jelly substance. There is only a small fishermen's jetty on the beach and on it a large sheet of parchment stretched over some bones. Looking at the jetty from back at the shack, which is rather far away, you might almost think that there was somebody sunbathing on it.

"I'd like to swim a bit on a hot day like this," we hear from below.

"But not for long, so you don't dissolve on me!"

"I'll just cool off a bit and I'll be right with you, darling. The sun is setting and another night of passion awaits us!"

Subsequently, there is a huge splash, and a wave washes over the beach, although it keeps its distance from the parchment man.

A little later, an inconceivable mass comes out of the water. Having absorbed a lot of water, the aspic has become translucent, even luminescent. It oozes onto the jetty.

"I love you."

The parchment rolls up and sighs, "Come to me. It's getting dark and I'm already trembling . . . The whole weekend is ours."

Indeed, the sun has dropped to the horizon. Waves can be heard. Waves of surf.

Thousands of stars twinkle over the beach. Some of the stars are blocked for a moment by a cigar-shaped object moving eastward. It's the Hindenburg airship on its regular route to South America. It circles the island and slowly descends. The aspic glitters intensely.

Sand, the warm stones of the jetty, the stars in the sky, a long weekend.

The jelly begins to ripple and blink, giving out a whole spectrum of light. The dolphins jump. I save my document in Microsoft Word.

2:20 A.M., Feb 15, 2002, La Aldea

TRANSLATED FROM SLOVAK BY MICHAELA FREEMAN

VESNA LEMAIĆ

The Pool

How can you explain yourself: You are human, and right now you must be standing by the pool, raking leaves off the surface. You're absorbed in your work, the shirt you're wearing is soaking wet, as is your tie. You are at the edge of the pool: you're holding a special pool net in your hands, which skims off everything, including the insects that keep falling in the water. The surface is completely smooth, but you go on skimming. Your progress is slow because you are meticulous, you go around the perimeter several times. A while ago, you would regard this as completely unnecessary, especially at this impossible hour. What's particularly surprising, for instance, is that you're not bothered by the scorching sun. Any other bareheaded person of normal body weight would suffer a sunstroke, if we consider that the sunbeams are not just blazing down upon the top of your head, but also reflect off the splashing water, glinting in your face. Then your phone rings, which you keep clipped to your belt. You hesitate, the people around you wave their hands dismissively, understandingly, it's not important, why answer it. But they've been here longer than you, they are more committed to the unusual situation you have found yourself in. Despite your reluctance, you therefore turn away from the splashing water, tensing up, your entire body trying to remember what your past life meant to you, and only then do you gather the strength to reach for the phone and press the green button. You hear your wife's voice sobbing in your ear: "Martin? Christ, Martin, is that you?" You hear the familiar beep—the battery will run out any moment now.

But before that, everything was different. You couldn't care less for pools; for a rich man, a pool is something that comes with a house and that's about it. Your brother has always been of a different opinion; he used to say, "Pools are more than just pools." Unfortunately, you understand your brother now, but back then, you and Dr. Vlah both agreed that your brother was nothing but a harmless eccentric. You let him be, until he dropped out of architecture school in his third year. He came back broke and mysterious. Dad took the middle path: He didn't ask questions, he gave him a job in his company; he appointed him to some junior but respected enough position, with a decent salary. Your brother didn't attend family gatherings, but, if nothing else, at least there wasn't anyone to start fights at those get-togethers. When you and Dad were alone, the old man would wave his hand dismissively and say, "Your brother is autistic. But you, my son, you too take the middle path."

Then, one day during the week, you receive the following phone call:

"Hi, son!"

"Dad, is something wrong?"

"No, of course not! Not at all. I'm doing very well, thank you—"

"Then I guess everything's in order . . . ? Dad, I'm in the middle of a meeting. I'll ca—"

"The thing is, your brother hasn't come to work for three weeks. No one had the guts to tell me, it was by pure coincidence that I—"

"I'll call him, Dad. I'll set him straight, I promise. Don't worry, take care."

You go back into the conference room and ask a colleague if you missed anything important.

Three days later, you remember your father's phone call, slapping your forehead. Your wife knows the gesture, she asks what you've forgotten this time.

"I really need to call my brother, honey."

"What for? You've heard something new about our peculiar little architect?"

You hate it that she has such a low opinion of him. Enough to resolve that you're not going to discuss this matter with her. You leave the room: You want to have a word with him in private. He doesn't pick up the phone and you get an unpleasant feeling, the kind you get every time you're about to make a bad deal. You're restless, walking up and down the room, thinking about your father; in half an hour, you try again—this time, your brother answers: his voice sounds unfamiliar—he's excited, he tells you that he's extremely happy you called. He takes you by surprise; your response is stiff and mechanical: "Where are you? What's going on? Dad's worried about you."

"Hey, I have a new pool."

You hang up: You can't keep up with these developments. Your brother hasn't been seen at the office for three weeks because he's got a new pool. Well. No plausible explanation comes to mind: You have no choice; you're going to have to go see him. You redial his phone number, he picks up again and asks if everything's okay. You don't answer him, simply announce your forthcoming visit in a somewhat cool tone. He tells you he's moved. You write down his new address on a scrap of paper and put it in your jacket's inner pocket.

You drive through the outskirts of the city for a long time

before you stop in front of a house. You check the address again. Nothing particular can be learned from its exterior, least of all omens of the fate that lies in store for you. The pool is nowhere to be seen. An uneasy feeling comes over you. A bad deal in the making.

Your brother appears at the door, unshaven and much thinner. He looks like a homeless person, so the first thing you ask is: "What's the matter? Do you need money?"

"Not at all, come in."

Once in the cool of the foyer, you regain your composure: Regretting your initial haughtiness, you put your hand upon your brother's shoulder almost spontaneously and hold him back: "Tell me, what's going on?"

Your brother's face is inscrutable: He's hiding something and it's driving you crazy. He wrenches himself from your grip and waves you to follow. Swimming goggles dangle from his hand. Stepping into the spacious living room, you stop again. The blinds are down but there's no doubt about it: There is definitely water sparkling outside.

"Wait," you tell him, a sudden rush of suspicion floods over you—you halt. Your entire body resists following him. "We need to talk." This time, you take a different approach. "You're in trouble. Dad found out that you haven't shown up for work for three weeks. You're going to have to explain yourself to him." Your words produce no effect whatsoever: He is watching you patiently. You think of Dr. Vlah, your family psychiatrist, who treats so-called female hysteria as well as male self-esteem problems in your family. "Listen, maybe it would be better if you set up an appointment with Dr. Vlah, I'm sure he would be able to offer you some advice."

"I talked to him earlier. Dr. Vlah feels fantastic."

Your brother's face is now expressionless, you can't figure out if he's joking; you try to find something definite close by, something to hang on to, and that's when you see the aquarium: Most of the fish are floating on the surface, riddled with bite marks, while the surviving ones swim up and down along the side of the aquarium closest to the drawn blinds. You close your eyes for a moment, praying that the fish died because of simple carelessness and not as a result of some new pathology of your brother's.

"How come you don't call me, we don't see enough of each other . . ." You don't know why, but at that moment, for the first time, you feel that your brother no longer belongs to your family. No longer belongs to anyone. You want to brush this aside now, so you go on talking animatedly: "We should spend some time together, throw a ball around. I mean, you know—we haven't seen each other in a long time—you have no idea what's been going on for me, or vice versa, I mean—"

"I have a new pool," he says. There's a glimmer of light from behind the blinds.

"A new pool?"

"Yes, it's magnificent."

"And that's all?" You're running out of patience.

"Sure. Do you want to go see it?"

"That's all you have to say to me?" you ask. Your voice quivers, its tone reserved and threatening. "After all this time?"

"Come."

Giving in is out of the question. "Look at yourself! You're a mess."

Your brother goes to the blinds and raises them, revealing a wall of glass; you shield your eyes, the pool glistens outside like a cave of gold, people are standing and sitting around it. You're bewildered: With all these friends around him, maybe your brother isn't doing so badly after all.

"I see you have a real pool party going on here. Looks like I'm intruding."

"Won't you join us?" he asks, looking at you as though you're the crazy one, not him.

"No, no. I don't want to impose."

"Well, too bad. Next time, then. You're always welcome here."

The sudden role reversal throws you completely off balance. Before you leave, you want to re-establish the position you had when you came in: "Listen—I came to see you because we've got to talk . . . it's serious. You haven't shown up for work in three weeks and here you are, throwing a party at your new pool. With all due respect," you try to preserve your brother's dignity, "this is completely irresponsible."

Your brother beckons you to follow. "Come, join us."

There's nothing more you can do here but accept the situation: As ever, you're cast as the middleman in this drama. "Okay. What should I tell Dad then?"

"Dad's by the pool," he says and leaves you alone.

First, you repeat your brother's last sentence several times. You hesitate for a moment or two, then run outside. Before you lies the pool, beautiful and frightening beyond description. There it is. You forget your father, the only thing that matters is getting as close to the pool as possible. Even though you were heading straight for Dad and couldn't have cared less about the damn pool before you got out of doors, now you head right towards its edge; if you could just stand by the water and look into it, see bottom.

But your brother stops you on the way. He takes you by the elbow. "Well, what do you think? Isn't it splendid?"

He gives you a tap on the shoulder and takes you to a chair next to Dad.

After some time, when your father stops staring at the surface before him, you whisper to him: "I didn't expect to find you here by the pool. What are you doing here?"

Slowly and with difficulty, he manages to turn around and gestures toward it: "I'm admiring it."

His answer makes sense, sort of, but something else unnerves you: A few meters away, you see Dr. Vlah talking—to himself, leaning over the water, visibly distressed.

You get up, restless. Your brother seizes you by the elbow as if to detain you. You break free from his grip, your advance is relentless, you move to the edge—and look in: It all slopes downward according to some unfathomable logic, the curves and angles antagonistic to each other, incorrect, cyclopean, as though simulating the rotation of something you have trouble naming. It's distantly reminiscent of an upside-down cathedral: When you stare into it, you lose your sense of direction—which way is up, which down; the bottom disappearing from sight under a murky arch. Your gaze slides along its inner walls glimmering in varying bluish shades, lost in the reflections of the underwater atmosphere. You're finally roused by the sound of your phone, releasing you abruptly from your rapture. Your wife's name flashes on the screen, and you don't answer it. You hear Dr. Vlah say, "Neurotics! God, how I hate them!" Dr. Vlah, a rational man by nature, keeps leaning over the water, bearing his soul to it. The sight of your family psychiatrist, talking about himself for the first time since you've known him, depresses you. Eventually, you feel a tap on your shoulder; your brother leads you back to Dad.

"How nice to have you all here!" he adds and moves away.

You sink helplessly into your chair, time is ticking away and the pool is right there in front of you. All around it, you recognize family friends, acquaintances, and, of course, your brother, who walks around the pool several times, swimming goggles dangling from his hand. Meanwhile, a minor incident: Your uncle is trying to pull his wife away from the edge; she breaks into piercing screams, struggling to tear herself loose;

seeing this, Dr. Vlah makes a face and says: "Well, what did I tell you! Now do you understand?" The wind whips up the water's surface, a wave washes over your uncle, who steps briskly away from the edge.

"What a beautiful pool!" sighs Dad dreamily. You can see three pool mattresses floating on the surface, a woman lying on each of them. They are all dipping their hands in the water. This would be a perfectly charming scene if they were showing any signs of life. Your brother comes up to you, swimming goggles still dangling from his hand. His smile is inscrutable.

"How nice to have you all here."

"Listen, shouldn't we wake those women? They'll get sunburned."

Your brother is momentarily confused, then replies mechanically, "Don't bother. Everyone is responsible for their own actions."

Night falls. You look at your watch; its hands have stopped at two thirty P.M.

When morning comes, all of you are still there; in the midday heat, a strong wind rises, blowing over the surface of the pool; the women whirl around on their pool mattresses; the sharp smell of burned skin tingles in your nostrils. Waves carry the floating mattresses gently toward your father and you. Dad looks away; you want the wind to blow in the opposite direction or abate immediately. But neither of these things happens: The blonde is the first one to get carried toward the pool wall, followed by her two friends at a respectful distance. The buzzing of flies accompanies the smell of burning human flesh. Dad shifts his position, turning to his side, away from the woman. The blonde lies stretched out on her back, dipping her hands in the water. The burns on her face, cleavage, and belly are much more conspicuous than her Hawaii-patterned bikini. She has big dark sunglasses on her nose, for which you are grateful. The sight of burnt eyelids or flies crawling from underneath them would be something you wouldn't be able to handle. Dad pants with effort, which makes you cover your nose with your tie and push the mattress away from the edge with your foot, hard. Too hard, as the woman, along with her big dark sunglasses, tips over and begins to sink deep down, getting smaller and smaller, until she disappears into the darkness. The pool must be very deep, as you're unable to make out the bottom, despite the clearness of the water. Your shoe feels soggy, you take it off nervously and hurl it into the pool, which responds by swallowing it without a sound. Only the beeping of your phone is heard, down from your waistband, letting you know that your battery is about to run out.

A few paces away, you see your brother and his swimming goggles, still dangling from his hand, swinging by his leg. He squats down at the edge of the pool and dips his hand in up to his wrist, as if he's checking the water temperature. He stays there squatting with his hand in the water: The temperature seems to suit him. More than it ought to. When he sees you watching him, he steps away. You've always felt what you considered a reasonable amount of love for your brother, but as you look at him now, standing between his guests and the water, it's clear to you that he belongs to the pool, not to the people. You can read from his lips that he's telling the people on the other side of the pool the same thing he's telling you and Dad: "How nice to have you all here!" And you realize it will eventually swallow all of you, you'll be stacked up on top of each other at the bottom of the pool, if there's such a thing as a bottom.

Thinking about the bottom distracts you, so you fail to notice that the pool women have been washed up dangerously close to you again. The one closest to you is wearing a string of giant faux pearl beads around her neck, reflecting the blinding rays of sun. With frantic strokes, you start kicking the water away from your side of the pool, but the women linger about, floating around in place. Dr. Vlah shouts to you in a feeble voice: "It's no use! You can't stop female neuroses!" He gasps for air. "It's the only weapon they have!" You give up—Dr. Vlah's words have always had a deterrent effect on you. Returning to your father, you see a wet stain around his crotch, and he says to you: "My son."

You tell him that you're going to get him away from there, but at the same time, you feel the pool looking at you over your shoulder. Dad leans in closer: "I know that what I'm about to tell you might sound crazy, but I really feel something bad is going to happen to me if I try to get away from it. Do you know what I mean?"

You look toward the pool; yes, it's unpredictable. The reflections in the water have a certain air of inevitability about them: Your eyes are transfixed. Is it possible that your brother could father something as horrible as this? When you look at his scrawny biceps, it's obvious that lifting more than a pencil would be beyond him. Would that puny little body of his be capable of such a horrendous conception?

Now you see your father's sweaty forehead and you simply snap. You feel ashamed, but you are unable to control yourself: Your teeth are chattering. Your father finally asks you to leave him alone for a while. You stand up straight as best you can and withdraw. The people in the beach chairs show definite signs of dehydration and the pool is getting more sinister and more beautiful by the minute; you wouldn't dream of leaving it: The pool becomes as intrinsic a part of you as your own subconscious.

The woman with the pearl necklace is getting dangerously close to Dr. Vlah now, stretched out languorously on her floating mattress, with one leg up to her knee in the water: even in death, she exudes complete confidence as she floats all the way to the psychiatrist, right when he's leaning over the water, his face close to the surface, as he says, "I know I'm fallible compared to you, but you have to admit—they are deadly." The woman's knee, sticking half out of the water, brushes against him, and this is the last you see of Dr. Vlah, as he jumps in after her, slipping off her pool mattress. Only his hand is seen as it drags the neurotic down with him into the depths of the pool. The empty mattress undulates innocently.

You lean over the edge and stare at the surface. How can you explain yourself? In no other way than in relation to the dreadful pool. It keeps looking over your shoulder, where are your hands, what are you looking at, listening to whatever you say. The pool has designated you a certain position next to itself; you are committed to it. Deserting it would be utterly irresponsible.

And now you're standing next to it: You're holding a special pool net in your hands, which skims off everything, including the insects that keep falling in the water. The surface is completely smooth, but you go on skimming. Your progress is slow because you are meticulous, you go around it several times. A while ago, you would regard this as completely unnecessary, especially at this impossible hour. What's particularly surprising, for instance, is that you are not bothered by the scorching sun. Any other bareheaded person of normal body weight would suffer a sunstroke, if we consider that the sunbeams are not just blazing down upon the top of your head, but also reflect off the splashing water, glinting in your face. Have you fallen into some psychological trap? You don't understand your own actions— you only know you have to perform them. You know you have to perform them properly, otherwise something terrible will happen to you. Then your phone rings, which you keep clipped to your belt. You hesitate, the people around you wave their hands dismissively, understandingly, it's not important, why answer it. But they've been here longer than you, they are more strongly committed to the unusual situation you have found yourself in. Despite your reluctance, you turn away from the splashing water, tensing up, your entire body trying to remember what your past life meant to you, and only then do you gather the strength to reach for the phone and press the green button. You hear your wife's voice sobbing in your ear: "Martin? Christ, Martin, is that you?" You hear the familiar beep again—the battery will run out any moment now. You have to decide whether or not to tell her the address of the hell you're in. Are you going to be selfish and tell her, where you'll all die together from sunburns and thirst, or keep the location of the horrible pool from her, out of love for her and the children? You take the middle path: "Whatever you do, don't come to 224 Richkill Street, honey." A pool mattress carrying a female cadaver comes floating by. You dip your net into the pool and continue serving it.

TRANSLATED FROM SLOVENIAN BY ŠPELA BIBIČ

SUSANA MEDINA

Oestrogen

April, orgasmic green, the intensity of the green was a visual massage and she had to pass by field upon field of green pasture, vivid green, on her way to the Sleep Research Institute. The laboratory was off junction 14 of the M1, down a track through a field just after the turning for the town center. The track was barely wide enough for one car, so you had to squeeze over to the side whenever one came the other way, destroying this or that patch of plant life and aggressively rearranging the molecules of the field. A white rectangular building of simple lines, the lab shone out in the darkness against the fir trees that surrounded it. The windows ran along the length of the building from floor to ceiling, letting you glimpse the surrounding vegetation from within, and there was also a skylight that ran from one side of the roof to the other so that, inside, if you looked up, you could see the clouds by day, and the lightly starred sky by night. The architect had designed the building to be conducive to sleep. In spite of its simplicity, the building retained a palpable air of mystery because of its location in the fields, the large windows that let in light from all sides, the rounded aluminum doorways, the unseen foxes, and all the sleepers between its walls.

Those were perfect days, perhaps too perfect. Eureka had reached a strange equilibrium in her life. For once, everything was going all right. She'd just finished her masters in clinical psychology and after months of filling in forms full of squares and rectangles, waiting for and receiving negative replies, she'd been invited to work part time at the Institute, under Doctor Mossman. Eureka was hoping her new employers wouldn't notice that her thoughts were always elsewhere, that they wouldn't read too easily into her erratic state of mind, or find out that when she was younger she'd committed pretty much every indiscretion in the book.

Eureka headed for the lab, cruising along in her Capri 2.8i. It was a silver '70s classic, a collector's item. It had been a gift from Toshi, her lifelong partner. Sometimes she went on foot, taking it easy, but never when she was on the night shift. She always took the car for the night shift. The roads were pretty empty then, and driving was a pleasure. She sped along with the windows down so the night air would help keep her sharp for the long hours of work to come. She didn't drink coffee to stay awake. She preferred guarana extract, which she found worked better. Passing by the airport, with its svelte, slight tower and palatial appearance, she allowed herself to be swept away by a dangerous fantasy, a sort of psychic recklessness. She imagined zigzagging from lane to lane, sometimes in control, sometimes letting the car veer wherever it wanted, maneuvering like a rally driver, overtaking cars on the motorway with aggressive sensuality, treating the drivers to a touch of danger, the little edge of fear their lives lacked. She liked giving in to her fantasies, letting those strange images reveal the mysterious lives that lay buried in her mind—in this case, a fantasy that was soothing and terrifying all at once. Eureka would never have hurt a fly, and she was a terrible driver anyway. But she didn't let this knowledge interfere with her fantasy life. All those other lives she could live were always there, latent, inside her; so long as she didn't act on them, they could be as violent or irresponsible as she liked. Now her psychic recklessness faded and she started to make out the leather of the steering wheel once more—the Capri's outdated suspension keeping her in inescapable contact with reality, with the tarmac, with the potholes.

At dusk the orgasmic green would disappear, but its smell became stronger. The cows, whose expressions wavered somewhere between placid and depressed, let the hypermarket of fluorescent lights burning unrelentingly into the night go by. The thought of the cows made her remember a paper she had read somewhere, a study carried out by a genetic engineer who had decided that cows didn't need heads, and so was working to alter their DNA so that they were born headless, with nothing but a tube with which to suck in nutrition.

The foxes dozed unseen around the laboratory. They were wild, urban foxes, and ever since the lab was built, they had loitered there, delighted by the chance to feed undisturbed. Eureka went inside and nodded a greeting to a triptych of photos. Three enormous images of brain scans during wakefulness, regular sleep, and REM sleep, respectively, presided over the entrance to the Institute. The active areas of the brain were shown in red, the less active areas in blue, and the background in yellow. She crossed the driving and drowsiness testing room, which housed the front end of a wrecked red car that had been sliced in half, a Volkswagen Scirocco that the lab had adopted as the emblem of their studies into the heightened incidence of sleep-related car accidents in recent years. She went into her office, put on her lab coat, and turned on one of the seemingly endless rows of equipment, which began to emit green, amber, and red light through little translucent rectangles. She thought about the Gin twins, who'd volunteered to take part in experiments recording instances of sexual arousal in sleep. They were attractive, the Gin brothers, attractive in a quirky way, with curiously blond hair and black eyelashes and eyebrows. She'd dreamed about them a few times, as if there was something about their waking presence that needed decoding. Surrounded by polygraphs, she primed herself for a hectic night and turned on her computer.

Cosmic orgasms, sexcapades, sex al fresco, sex in every room in the house, sex in the car, in garages, in lifts, sex at seventy, how to make your sex life last, start at the soles of his feet, heavenly sex, shampoos promising mind-blowing multiple orgasms, send him an anonymous erotic letter, all you ever wanted to know about sex and more, what he wants in bed, how to drive her wild, sexy alien abductions, aphrodisiac recipes, discover your submissive side, sex at ninety, turn up the heat, sex at regular intervals proven to raise life expectancy, tantric sex, amateur porn, how sex can save your relationship, tease him with a feather, what celebrities want in bed, sexual acrobatics, politicians and sex, how sex can keep you young, I often masturbate with an electric toothbrush, oysters and desire, don't forget to stop by a sex shop, sex is everything, sex at first sight, athletic sex, how to climax in an instant, why married men with children are easiest to seduce, undress him with your teeth, the most unusual positions, I'm in charge tonight, hot sex tips, discover your sexuality, say it with sex, it's good to talk about sex, journey to the center of sex, exploring unconventional sex, virtual sex, serial sex, quantum sex, kiss his toes one by one, the dark side of sex, everything you never dared to ask about sex, sex any time of the day, advanced sexology, sexercise, why we like sex so much, how to put the spark back into your relationship, erotic package holidays for wife-swapping in a relaxed and healthy setting, what men really think about sex, chocolate and sex, techniques that never fail to leave him begging, red-hot tricks, ice cubes and sex, try not to touch each other intimately for the first hour, fetish sex, keep at it afterward, sex and the big toe, transsexual sex, the tee-hee g-spot, put your finger in his anus and make him melt, wild Amazonian sex, how to be irresistibly sensual, how to cheat without your partner noticing, cybersex, sex, sex, sex, SEXO. Since the fifties we've witnessed the invasion of sex, sex filling all cavities, screens, doorways, degree courses, advertising; sex is all over the media, in the electromagnetic waves flying through the air, dissolved in tap water and enriching our breakfast cereals. No one is safe from the sexual onslaught. Sex infiltrates us by seeping into every one of our pores. It's enough to make us want to surrender to the luxury of frigidity, chastity, or platonic love.

The study to catalogue sexual arousal began that night. Under Doctor Mossman's orders, Eureka now found herself complicit in the incursion of sexuality into sleep science. She had been put in charge of experiments on erectile function, dilation, and oestrogen during sleep. Everything about sex had to be understood from a scientific basis. The experiments related to the physiology of sleep—it wasn't just dream content they were after. Even the sleeping body was riddled with sex.

The Gin brothers canceled at the last minute. Eureka felt herself slump a little, the crumpling of disappointment. It was raining, halfheartedly. Thankless drizzle. Tedium hung in the air like a virus. The penile tumescence experiments were dull, routine. Although female orgasms were still an almost virgin field of study, the topic of men's nocturnal emissions had been pretty much done to death. There were enchanting volunteers, but even so Eureka found them somewhat bland, unworldly. They did it for the money, convinced that the opportunity to get paid for having an ultra-uncomfortable plastic apparatus attached to their genitals while they slept was the greatest thing ever. She was surprised by her own irritation with the volunteers. When she was working the night shift, between one thing and another, she barely saw Toshi. His working hours meant their paths never crossed. This week they wouldn't see each other at all, for that matter. Toshi was away on a trip to Dublin.

The nights dragged on. Eureka dragged. The polygraphs dragged. It was as though some airborne tedium virus had snuck in through the vents—unless of course it was simply the absence of the Gin brothers alongside the monotony of the tumescence experiments that was putting Eureka to sleep. Or else, perhaps it was in fact she who was infecting everyone else with the virus . . .

This too would pass. Everything started to liven up when the volunteers arrived. This lively group was made up of single women who shared a real spirit of camaraderie, as if they were going to a ladies' sauna or some other girls-only get together. That was how she met Luciana, Doctor Mossman's strange friend. It was also how she discovered what sort of neural circuitry delivered her up to particular daydreams, after the third study with three groups of women. It all came down to oestrogen. That was the subject of the study, oestrogen levels. It was discovered that in both the preovulatory and premenstrual phases, the subjects' oestrogen levels rose, leading the women's dreams to contain a higher than normal amount of sexual imagery. Oestrogen being the primary female sex hormone—as testosterone is in males—studies were always being carried out into the hormone's relationship to libido, strength, and depression.

When she woke the participants from the three groups during different phases of REM sleep, both groups A and B described dreams full of highly attractive sexual partners, dreams that were explicitly pornographic, obscene, and unutterably exciting. Doctor Mossman dubbed group C, the one whose dreams lacked any explicit sexual content, "Group Chastity." From both groups A and B there was just one woman who maintained that she received nightly visitations from dazzling satyrs and succubae, and that night after night she awoke rejuvenated. She insisted that she didn't dream about the sex act in itself, but rather the act of seduction, limitless seduction. The woman was called Luciana, which wasn't her real name but a code name, to preserve her anonymity.

Even the steeliest celibates, the most devout, faithful, chaste, pure, monogamous, and prudish among us have an intensely erotic oneiric life, a dream life that is polymorphously reckless. Its intrusive pleasures catch us by surprise: Nature turns us all into nocturnal adulterers. To deny it is to deny our true selves, our boundless sexuality. Fidelity, monogamy, and celibacy are perversities inflicted upon our real natures by the lie of our waking lives. We all have wet dreams. We all have dirty dreams, though we rarely remember them. But Luciana always did. Eureka ended up going out for a few drinks with Luciana. Vodka and cranberry juice. And on the day the sexual arousal studies finished, they met up at El Chiquito and drank yet more vodka and cranberries. They talked about war, the corruption blighting the planet, and the versatility of Meryl Streep. Between giggles and embarrassed gestures, searching for affirmation or acknowledgement, fiddling all the while with her black, metal-studded purse, Luciana confided that she had nearly total recall of her dreams. And that the vast majority of them were dirty. She had come to understand, some time ago, that these dreams would be more common when her husband wasn't around, when they were apart for a few weeks. On her own, her dirty dreams became more regular and vivid. But these days they came all the time, who knew why: Her husband's permanent absence since their divorce; general loneliness; the sexual apathy that left her chronically listless; her rebellious biology . . . or perhaps something had simply broken inside her?

Dirty dreams, occasionally populated by strangers, occasionally by people she knew, sometimes women or beings endowed with science-fiction genitals. They were gratifying and orgasmic dreams, dreams that crept in to add spice to her waking life, revitalizing it. Luciana looked into Eureka's eyes, hoping for validation.

Eureka nodded and said she had recurring sexual dreams too, but usually about the same person. There were men who were hardwired into her neural circuitry, she said. About 8% of our dreams are known to be graphically erotic, she said. For men, 14% of these involved current or past lovers, whereas this was 20% for women. Generally speaking, our dream encounters are almost all with strangers, anonymous bodies conspiring with the honesty of our own. Men had a greater tendency for scenarios involving multiple partners or sex in public spaces, whereas women tended to pair off with celebrities, as from an evolutionary point of view, Eureka said, these would appear to be the best providers—at least, that was the theory. As if women could get pregnant from fucking oneiric men. All in all, our dreaming minds might be prone to make the occasional mistake, but there was no doubt that they wanted the body to have a good time.

Luciana listened, occasionally getting distracted looking at men in the bar, looking for something in her bag, playing with her black purse, or calling the waiter over. Her attention was intermittent, she needed breaks, pauses. Eureka had to get back to the lab. She could drop Luciana at home on the way back. It was no trouble. They got in the Capri and, once they had set off, Luciana told Eureka that every one of her dreams was about the same thing. That since her divorce, the number of her oneiric indiscretions had risen considerably, but so too had her waking sexual fantasies and now every night she found herself in an orgy of dreams that left her completely worn out. She added that if there was one thing she'd learned from her dreams, it was to laugh at herself. And she also told Eureka that when she'd finally divorced her husband, it was because her dreams had been crying out for it. Her marriage had been one of the most nefarious agents of habit in her life. A farce, she said.

They said good-bye with laughter and a hug. But Luciana had left a strange trace in her wake, a trace of doubt. Eureka returned to work. The traffic lights' insistent colors took on a strange intensity by night. Desire makes everything look sharper and Eureka had recently had a series of recurring dreams about a man from Colorado who'd published several papers on the alarming stateside epidemic of narcoleptic dogs, and whenever she dreamed about someone, she would spend some of the following day thinking about that person, considering them, what particular meaning they might have for her, and so they would come to take on even greater significance in her conscious mind, until finally they had won themselves a permanent and privileged spot in her memory. Emissaries of mystery, her dream gatecrashers sometimes ended up feeling more important to her than people she knew very well in daily life, but who had never made it into her dreams.

The grotesque moans of invisible foxes could be heard as they copulated around the Institute. Eureka went into the lab, passed by the wrecked red car belonging to the drowsiness and driving studies, and went into her office. She called Toshi and they spoke for an hour about Dublin and nothing in particular, groceries they needed to buy, the dinner with their friends they'd planned for the weekend. Then she turned to analyzing the correlation between oestrogen levels and erotic dreams by age, social status, and diurnal experience.

The man from Colorado. If her desire usually manifested itself in a fairly explicit way in her dreams, as far as strangers went, or even men she knew glancingly, when the man from Colorado was involved, things were always fairly veiled. She dreamed about work meetings, about talking shop with him. It was a very long series of dreams. An empty desk in an office. The man from Colorado dressed in casual clothes. She would wake up recalling scenarios so dull that they scarcely seemed worth the effort. But on one occasion, she woke up during a particularly dull dream and was surprised to find her body writhing, the intense smell of sex surrounding her, accusing her, her conscience giving her a wink and whispering: Ah, so this is the real subtext of these nightly conversations. And it occurred to her that if all those dull conversations about work were really about desire, it was more than likely that her graphic erotic dreams were themselves about something else—that they weren't about sex at all.

She thought about the man from Colorado, about the worrying trace of dirty dreams that couldn't help but make her wonder whether her sexual curiosity for strangers, acquaintances, or the man from Colorado had become more powerful than her desire for Toshi. It was another kind of intensity, the thrill and exhilaration of the unknown. Undoubtedly, she went through spells of varying lengths when the erotic charge in her dreams was something she no longer knew with Toshi. Her first taste of it had been with him, but it was rare that she felt it with him nowadays. Sometimes it wasn't there at all anymore, as if she were somehow dead. The desire she now experienced for Toshi was a washed out version of the desire she experienced in those early years. It had become pale. Diluted. Toshi equalled everyday tenderness, marital, paternal, fraternal, maternal love, kisses, caresses, nibbling, incredibly orgasmic sex, as well as normal, average, awful, and apathetic sex. He equalled attentive ears and words, shared flavours daily at the table, playfulness, joking, the same bed for so many years, a thousand intimations as well as the eternal struggle to get by . . . But, no, the proper lust she'd once experienced with Toshi, that deserted her at times. Sometimes it did come back, shooting through her like a spasm, but even then, it wasn't quite the same. Perhaps it was just a phase. She knew that desire is by nature a changeable beast, an effervescent liquid that sometimes bubbles over, and other times goes flat. Was she exaggerating things? Had that early desire of hers taken on an ideal and fictive quality in her memories? Perhaps it did still exist with Toshi, but just lacked the element of surprise, the novelty of those first encounters?

She tidied away some saliva test results from her desk as she thought about the men from her dreams. They didn't give her what Toshi gave her, she didn't share a whole experience with them. Their allure came down to the enigma of the unknown. They offered her the intrigue of a first encounter, but it was an excitement she'd only *truly* experienced with Toshi, as if her dreams were a way of disguising that spark as something new. The effervescence she had known with Toshi was abstracted now by familiarity. It had lost its zing but gained in tenderness, become something else. And yet, Toshi always managed to surprise her in some way or another. It wasn't quite that he'd lost his allure. It was just a different sort of allure, a different kind of enigma: the mystery of the inexhaustible familiar.

She went back to the wrecked red car from the drowsiness and driving studies. The bodywork on the left front panel was destroyed. The front windscreen had become a spider's web of cracked glass. Yet the interior was still like new. She sat down inside. A pair of fuzzy dice hung from the rearview mirror. She'd always told Toshi everything. But not about her dreams. She'd broken into laughter the one time she'd tried. She might as well have been living some secret life that she only shared with those mystery men. There was something about monogamy that never did sit right with her, anyway—it was an impossible concept, full of contradictions. Of course, she did understand the need to trust somebody, to have a lasting relationship, to comfort and be comforted—but she also understood her limitations, her weaknesses, her infinite capacity for obsession. That's why her dream life seemed a happy solution, a private territory in which she could indulge the promiscuity she would shrink from in waking life, then savor it when she was awake. But: solution? Solution implied that there was a problem, and maybe there wasn't a problem, unless it was precisely there that the problem lay, the fact that there wasn't a problem at all, *no hay problema*, the fact that she lived a contented domestic life by day, and a promiscuous erotic existence by night, free from the headaches that promiscuous behavior tended to cause in the real world. At least that's how it seemed to her: Promiscuity was a sort of trap; you're lured in thinking only of the reward, and then find yourself mired in paranoia and guilt. Sure, there were people who didn't seem to have much of a conscience about their affairs, but she couldn't be like that—or, at least, she wasn't there yet.

As she stared at the petrol gauge, she wondered if those unknown men, the intimate strangers and the man from Colorado, if those men dreamed about her too, and if it was at the same time as she dreamed about them, or on other nights. The man from Colorado probably dreamed about her all the time. Though she knew that it was likely that he didn't remember his dreams, that for him she existed only in the realm of sleep, never as a waking concern. Perhaps he might have remembered part of one dream, on some morning, but he wouldn't be aware of the whole series of them. His recurring dreams were, paradoxically, the most easily forgotten.

She became absorbed by the little icons on the dashboard. Icons. Symbols. People too can turn into symbols. The man from Colorado was very likely a symbol of the impossible, a symbol of what was, precisely, destined not to be. But she liked his company. She liked the fact that he was there, in her dreams, to remind her that it was worthwhile, on occasion, to settle for what one had already found, as opposed to dying still searching for the impossible. And she met this man only in dreams—their paths never crossed in waking life. Conditions were always unfavorable and hostile in reality, there was always a certain asymmetry in day-to-day existence. Whenever the American phoned the office, she was always on her way out and had to hang up straight away.

On those occasions he was in town, and visited the lab during the day, she would be on the night shift, and they would pass each other in the corridor heading in different directions with no time to talk. And this asymmetry no doubt extended to their dream lives as well: after all, when it was daytime for Eureka, it was nighttime in Colorado. It wasn't just that they lived in different locations and time zones, but perhaps the whole business relied on this very asymmetry—the unlikelihood of meeting each other by happenstance.

She put her foot on the clutch. It worked. And the gears did too. Maybe it was necessary to keep the boundaries between waking and dreaming in sight because they were forever leaking into one another, eroding each other, the two zones were always merging and cancelling each other out. Was the woman who dreamed about the same man again and again really Eureka? Or some sort of double? And were the men really themselves, or their own doppelgangers? It would certainly explain her fascination with those twins—each of us has a double, by night.

And yet, wasn't it all down to little more than a surge in her oestrogen levels? Observing those three groups of women in their different biological phases—group A in the preovulatory phase, group B in premenstrual phase, and group C in neither phase—Eureka had been surprised to see how closely erotic dreams were connected with biological cycles, with one's biorhythms; that hormonal fluctuations determined sex drive in sleep as well as when awake. Perhaps her secret, parallel erotic reality was just a chemical joke being played upon her by her body—a gag gift from her preovulatory and premenstrual phases, a gift from that word that sounds so much like an obscure insult in some forgotten language: oestrogen.

She went back into the office. Yes, her erotic parallel life was nothing but a strange conjunction of boredom, the unknown, and oestrogen. And she found herself doodling an oestrogen molecule on an unopened letter as if it were the emblem of this mystery that had been stamped onto her body:

Underneath it she wrote slowly and neatly: *The dreaming mind secretes the erotic body.*

One day, the man from Colorado had vanished from her dreams precisely as he'd arrived: gently. And while the brothers Gin were the latest to sing the song of Eros in her subconscious, they too would soon vanish, since these days even fantasies have a shelf life.

Eureka soon disappeared from the lab and reappeared in her bed. The bed was waiting for her, dutiful and empty, the sheets impregnated with the scent of her and Toshi. Sharing a bed with someone night after night is a blessing. But when that person goes away, or your sleeping times just don't line up, having the bed to yourself can be an orgasmic sort of experience. The only thing better than sharing a bed was not sharing it when you'd become used to never having it to yourself. For a few days at least, until you started to feel your partner's absence skulk around the room, and the double bed began to feel oversized.

She undressed quickly, pulled back the duvet, snuggled down into her soft bed, turned out the light, and it was then that the room became the nightly sanctuary that harbored the most orgasmic workings of the mind. To sleep for a million hours, that was what she needed. Her bed. So strange, and yet so familiar. There it was, indifferent in the middle of the room, with its mahogany headboard and its slats, co-conspirators in her erotic games, a fantasy of smooth and cottoned intimacy that was now the shelter for her tired, naked body. She usually collapsed into bed exhausted, took it for granted, didn't even give it the slightest thought, though that night she considered it an absurd piece of furniture and mused that while there was a chance we were conceived on a sofa, against a washing machine, in a wood, in an empty aisle at a twenty-four hour supermarket, or in a car parked in a deserted street, in all likelihood we were all conceived on a bed.

She got up, drew the curtains, slipped back into bed, and started to blend into that absurd item of furniture. She wondered what her dreams would bring. She might dream about the Gin twins, in keeping with her latest ongoing serial. Or maybe she'd dream about Toshi. Sometimes she dreamed about him when they hadn't seen each other for a week or two, although dreams with Toshi never formed part of a series. Her eyelids started to close and a host of chaotic images flashed quickly across her mind which lay resting on that absurd piece of furniture which has always been part of our existence, as if it were a nocturnal appendage, the limb closest to our unconscious, a limb that gathered in the most intimate parts of our selves, night by night, and when everything was still, kept these secrets safe in the amniotic fluid of the mattress. Sssssshhhh. Sssssshhhhh. Sssssshhhh. Silence. She was going deep into the unknown, into her horizontal existence, where she stopped being one Eureka and became many different Eurekas. Sssssshhhh. Sssshhh. Sssssshhhh.

TRANSLATED FROM SPANISH BY ROSIE MARTEAU

XURXO BORRAZÁS

Pena de Ancares

I came to A Pena because they told me there wouldn't be anyone here. I've always been solitary, without friends, or girlfriends. Since I was a kid, I've never cared about anything except books, books . . . and now the Internet. I rented this house on one condition, that it have a decent connection, no matter the price.

This village is made up of a couple dozen buildings. Besides mine, they're all basically uninhabited ruins taken over by vegetation. It seems that the guy who rented me the place is trying to buy the whole village off the owners, who have moved away to Barcelona. According to him, with the amount I'm paying him for the month, he can buy a corncrib and a shed off a guy named Liberto. At this rate, soon everything will be his, he'll have to figure out what to do next. Probably renovate with the help of government subsidies and fill the place with tourists in SUVs carrying shotguns. When that happens, I'm never coming back.

I want the Internet for porn. The rest is crap for people with too much time on their hands. I love books like I love life itself, which is why, beyond just reading them, I also wrote one. One, that is, as of now. I entered the novel in a contest, just to be mortified by defeat and the indifference of the public. But it turns out that I won, so I came here to write another one, to flee from the zealots who accuse me of writing in the language of the oppressor and who disappointed me by ignoring my provocations, talking like politicians instead of insulting and threatening me. I also came here to avoid the press, who, even before reading the novel, praised me for not writing in Galician. Maybe that's why they gave me the prize. In the end, I also came here because of the animals.

I brought some serious provisions along. If I need anything, I'd need to go up to Navia de Suarna, twenty-plus kilometers up the road from hell. I spent the first two days unpacking, checking out the rooms, the furniture, turning one of the rooms into an office, setting up my equipment, and getting the lay of the land by staring out the window. From there I can see chestnut trees, heath thickets, streambeds, hollows, sharp stone outcroppings. The way to A Pena is a trail along the bottom of the valley, all ruts and overgrown grass, which ends at the village. They had to bring me here in a Land Rover.

On the third day, I explored the rocks and paths strewn with rotten chestnuts. It was mid-September, and I picked blackberries along the stone walls that followed the road. I've always believed in ghosts, and I felt that a group of spirits was following me, stopping whenever I stopped, smiling innocently or in surprise with their rosy faces and their curly hair. As night was falling, I even thought I saw a thread of smoke rising from one of the farthest houses. I haven't written anything. I tried to read, but in the darkness, the village fills with the sounds of animals nudging at doors and scrambling among the crumbling walls.

The thing with the animals was cruel, it's the only thing like that I can ever remember doing. A Sunday magazine from Madrid wanted to interview me, the usual deal, the writer at home or whatever. What would they say if they saw the snails, the salamander, the shrew, the frogs and tadpoles in the murky water? I emptied two cans of peaches, trapped them inside with adhesive tape, and waited for them to die. When I finished eating the peaches, the creatures lay lifeless in their syrupy resting place. The next day, the paper called to say they were sorry but they were canceling the interview.

• • •

I can live without relationships. But not without animals. That's why I picked Ancares. On the fourth day I brought home a beetle and some snails; the next night, a weasel. That night I tore up all my writing paper and threw it in the fire, to avoid wasting my time scribbling my little stories. I could use the computer, but that's like writing on water. I'm writing this on the two sheets of paper that were left in the printer, cramming as much as I can onto each page. When there's no room left, the story will end. I'll have to keep it simple, no flourishes or tangents, so that the important parts will fit.

I said that I didn't have a girlfriend, and I'll add here that I never have. A sex life, yes. The reviews of my novel praised my sensitivity in the development of my female characters, especially the prostitute. My sexual relationships have all been with prostitutes, if you can call those relationships. I also jack off in front of the computer. And, look, just because my masturbation is inspired by pictures floating around on the Internet, don't assume it's just some sort of virtual reality thing, or a videogame. It's as real as everything else—and to each his own.

I didn't take any alcohol along. The idea was to detox a bit, but on the fifth day I had them bring up two liters of *augardente* in the Land Rover. I got drunk during the afternoon watching the animals, then I threw up in the toilet, washed my face, and headed outside as night was falling. Leaning against a stone pillar, I lit a cigarette, and then I saw her.

"Jesus fucking Christ!" I slipped on the loose gravel of the steep path. "Good evening."

"Good evening," the woman snapped, implying that the stranger here was me.

"I didn't think anyone lived in the village," I explained.

"No one does." In her left arm she was carrying a bundle of oak branches covered in lichen. "Just me."

I took a couple of drags off my cigarette, and she started back on her way. "I rented Xisto's house," I stopped her, "the one that's all fixed up."

She rearranged the branches and straightened her head scarf. "Rented," she said.

"If you like, you could stop by for coffee," I suggested, "I'm pretty much always there." She said nothing, but her silence pushed me to continue: "My name is Andrés and I'm a writer, from Vigo. A Pena is a beautiful place . . . So, which house is yours?" I couldn't imagine which of these ruins could possibly have someone living in it. The woman looked toward the pass and remained silent. "Do you want me to help you with your firewood?" I offered. She tightened her grip on the branches and set off walking.

"My name is Aurora," I thought I heard her say, her back already to me. That night I finished off one of the bottles of liquor, and I gave some drops of it to the animals. The ones who handle it the best are the beetle and the weasel, the snails can't handle it at all, worse than me. They flail around like ecstatic voodoo priestesses, these snails.

At three in the morning I saw smoke on the far side of the village. I ran over to get the fireplace going and I fell asleep there, inches from the coals, my head on the seat of the armchair and my body on the floor.

• • •

"So, Xisto's son fixed up the house?" She came up to the door and that was the first thing she said. It was noon and I hadn't even taken a shower or had breakfast, but I wanted to be friendly just the same.

"Come on in and have a look. I was just about to make coffee. This way you can join me."

"I'll leave the door open. There aren't any burglars around here."

"Right. Okay," I stammered. "It's just that I . . . it's a hard habit to break, I guess. But you're right."

Within half an hour, there were mice, sparrows, botflies, dragonflies in the house. She was interested in the computer, so we spent some time looking at sites about Ancares, music, women's fashion. She wanted to go pee, so I showed her to the bathroom. Before going in, she commented on its cleanliness, and confessed, "Years ago I promised that when I started collecting my pension, I would eat my fill of yogurt, one carton a day, no less. Well, that day came and I couldn't follow through because I didn't have a fridge." She smiled and went in.

I made the coffee and waited. I heard the animals below and went to shoo them away. When I came back up, I stopped by the bathroom and asked, "Are you all right, ma'am?" No response. "Do you need anything?"

"No, nothing. Thank you, son."

I thought I heard water in the bathtub. Moments later, she came out wearing my bathrobe. She was tiny and the robe swept the floor as she walked. She had even washed her hair.

"Xisto's father was always going around spouting this nonsense about how one should take baths more often," she said, "apparently that's what they do in Barcelona or somesuch. I see that his son has the same ideas."

Could anyone really be so ignorant, or was she fucking with me? As we drank our coffee, she kept looking at her hands and feet. Maybe because they were so clean.

"How old are you, Mr. . . . . What was your last name?" she asked.

"Thirty-three. Just call me Andrés."

"I'm seventy-four, if I haven't lost count. I could die anytime, and I have no one to bury me."

"Don't say that, ma'am. Don't you have family somewhere?"

She went back to talking about yogurt. And the fridge, she kept looking at the fridge. So many years to wait. It had become a sort of challenge, and she had lost.

"If I had eaten more yogurt as a girl, I'd have more teeth now, stronger bones," she lamented. "Tell me I'm wrong. I bet they gave you as much yogurt as you could eat when you were little."

I went to the fridge and brought her a vanilla yogurt. I opened it for her. She began to cry, soundlessly. I tried to comfort her, holding her hand, touching her hair.

"Go ahead, Aurora, try it."

The robe came undone and her naked body was visible. It was the first time I had seen an old lady naked, but the legs and belly didn't look bad, and some sixty year olds would have envied her bust. The wrinkles on her upper chest formed a sort of multi-strand necklace. Her skin was white, plain yogurt, but what surprised me most was the silver-white pubis, a polar bear.

She ate the yogurt like that, paying no attention to my presence. I looked out the window, nervous. Was anybody else going to crawl out from beneath the stones? When the old woman reached the bottom of the carton, scraping out the last bites, she was still crying.

"My husband also wanted to fix up the house," she said. "We had been married a week, he was fixing the roof and he slipped. I didn't even have a child to remind me of him, how he looked. It was the wrong time of the month."

"My God. That must have been a long time ago."

"I was about seventeen and he was on leave from the army."

There was a long silence, which I broke by mumbling, "It's a sad story." It was such a banal comment that the next silence was even longer. I swallowed and steadied my voice before speaking again. "Now that you've had a bath, why don't you go ahead and wash your clothes, if you like, Aurora." She licked the spoon and pulled the robe closed, without a word. "So, why didn't you ever buy a fridge?" I asked.

She breathed in deeply and let it out, like only old people know how. "If it were new . . ." I understood somehow that she meant life, not the fridge. I went to the bathroom to find her clothes, put them in the washing machine, added some detergent and fabric softener, and set the machine to a short cycle.

"You would have made a good girlfriend," she said at last. Five minutes later, the two of us embraced, who knows why. I was wearing pajamas and, embarrassed, I tried to hide the erection I got when I touched the old woman's face. I found that she had beautiful eyes.

• • •

I know I made a big deal about being antisocial, but this relationship was different, another thing entirely. The washing machine had finished; together we hung the clothes to dry and got into the bed. I didn't know what to do, what with a hard-on and that old woman in my arms.

"I also have banana and pineapple yogurt, Aurora. I'll take care of you."

She said that she couldn't give me a hand job because her arm would get tired, and I didn't dare suggest anything else. I held her against me, stroked her legs, and put a finger inside her. She reacted by pushing my hand away with a "Holy Mother of God!" During the night, the downstairs filled with animal sounds. But the desire to collect and keep bugs had deserted me. When my testicles began to hurt, I went to the bathroom and . . . relieved myself. Other things happened, too, but I'm running out of paper.

Aurora came to live at my house. Before making love, she always took a bath and ate a yogurt. After three days, she gave me a blowjob. I had gotten up to go take care of it by myself, but she called me over with her voice like a stream in summer, said a prayer to the Virgin, and it was divine. The effort wiped her out and she slept like a child. They always say that old age is like a second childhood, one needs a routine: bath, yogurt, fellatio. Never two yogurts, and always vanilla. Soon these all became habits. After a while she let me stroke her sex, and during the next session she guided and corrected my clumsy movements.

Eventually she began to stay in bed fifteen hours a day. I brought her yogurt in bed, and she asked me to be with her, to kiss her shoulders, her back, her toes, her calves, her thighs, her spine. She let me suck at her breasts, and she learned how to smoke like Marlene Dietrich.

"You shouldn't be alone, Andrés," she blurted out one day.

"What do you mean, alone? You're here. With you I can't be alone."

"Me?" she asked. "That's something else."

"What do you mean, something else? My whole life I felt alone until I met you. Now is the first time I've been not-alone."

"Life is long," she pronounced. "Your life isn't whole."

"With you it is. I don't need anything else. You've changed everything. My life before was a sham. Now I never even turn on the computer or open a book. The only thing we need is yogurt. Could there be anything more fantastic?"

"For me, no. I spend years calming my hunger for yogurt with carton after carton of milk, and now I get yogurt in bed.

But your situation is different."

"I was a miserable man before I came to A Pena, Aurora. I would be nothing without you."

"What nonsense. I'm the one who should be saying that."

"If it's a question of getting more yogurt, I can have them bring a couple dozen cartons up in the Land Rover. They have a cooler so that things don't spoil. Eat as many as you like; the people who live the longest are from the valleys of the Caucasus, and their diet is made up largely of yogurt. I read somewhere that they live one hundred and twenty years. Let's forget about time, Aurora."

• • •

That night, lying side by side, she took my erect penis and played with it in her hand. She came closer and led me to her pussy.

"Very slowly," she said. "We're not in a hurry. Lovingly."

I just repeated her name. A hundred times. That body was Aurora, heat, it was me. Outside the village slept in ruins, and the birds sang though morning was far off. The rocky peak surveyed the paths and trails, in the shadows the earth exhaled a moist breath through a blanket of fallen leaves, the rocks of the slope awaited the next slide, butterflies were dying by the hundreds, streams ran dry, the starved worms had already fled from A Pena's cemetery. In the bedroom, I could hear the hum of the fridge and I thought about the yogurt, about the creamy, sweet softness of cultured milk, about Aurora's skin. I thought that I was no longer myself, that she was the one doing all the moving. I lifted a leg above hers and moved around behind her, grabbing a breast in each hand.

"Do you like this?" I whispered. I felt her excitement and I began to move more vigorously. "Do you like it like this?" I stopped once and again to touch her clitoris, grab her back or her neck, play with her nipples. "Time doesn't exist, Aurora. There's no age, no death, no world. Can you hear the wind? Tomorrow will be beautiful."

Through our embrace, I thought I felt her come; I'd never felt anything like that before. It was soft, an orgasm without fanfare. Then she lay unmoving, relaxed, silent. I kept going for a few seconds and the feeling of her buttocks against my belly, of her upper thighs, quickly made me ejaculate with a euphoric squeak and a small, inaudible fart. Nothing in the world could have seemed more extravagant to me at that moment, and I thought: "Shit. This is how babies are made. This is how life starts."

I got up to wash myself. When I got back, Aurora was sleeping, but I decided not to wake her. There were wet spots on the sheets. Whether she died during the night or while we were making love, it must have been a peaceful death. And, indeed, the morning was a beautiful one; not until afternoon did the mist come down from the mountains. I sat down in front of the computer and searched the Internet for "sex and death." There were snuff pages, Nazi orgies, and oriental porn sites, all of them violent. The Net didn't understand.

I went for a walk through the village, trying to find her house. A cricket chirped somewhere in the lumpy ground along a stone wall, I plucked a long piece of grass and stuck it in the hole till I got it to come out. It was a male; I closed it in my hand and put it in the pocket of my shirt. In one house was a bed with the sheets still on it, all covered in dirt and grass. In another, a coffee pot sat atop an iron stove, the roofless kitchen open to the sky. In another there was a calendar from '63 with a picture of the Virgin. In yet another I startled some turtledoves that had nested in the rafters. To die in A Pena was a double negation; to be buried, a redundancy.

Even so, I would do it. As I walked, I decided that from then on I would never eat yogurt again. I would stop writing novels;

I would start keeping animals again in my parents' house. I was sure of all this until I found Aurora's house. The door, half open, had once been painted green. There was no kitchen, just an open hearth with a black pot suspended above the ashes. A cot, sunken with age, with a woolen mattress and a linen bedspread. A three-legged table, on top of it a bunch of cabbage leaves and a pile of chestnuts. A dresser full of old clothes and a fair bit of money in bills and coins. The rest of the house, all of the space in the two rooms, was filled with hundreds of empty milk cartons, whole milk, two percent, skim milk, different brands. Piled in a corner, below the bed, stacked against the walls, carpeting the floor. A convocation of milk cartons, all waiting for yogurt to come and turn them into garbage, bringing an end to memory. Aurora!

Today is the last day of my month here, and no one has called me, no one is waiting for me. I am writing between the lines I've already written, for lack of space. When I have paper, distance, energy, I will tell the rest of her life, I'll fill in some events that, I hope you'll excuse me, didn't happen exactly the way I've told you here. But nothing ever happens the way people tell it . . . never mind, that's another story.

TRANSLATED FROM GALICIAN BY NEIL ANDERSON

CHRISTOPH SIMON

Fairy Tales from
the World of Publishing

THE POETS AND THE READER

By now, the poets were living in Ireland for tax reasons, but there was no readership there. People knew only of one reader, and she was over in Scotland. In the end, a young poet set out for Scotland, where he found the reader and, ere long, became her husband.

One day, sitting out in the garden, he was pondering his imminent tax return. "But I have a reader," he reminded himself, "and my colleagues in Ireland have none." And privately, he felt very pleased with how good fate had been to him.

His colleagues back in Ireland, meanwhile, were keen to plagiarize the young poet's idea. They, too, set out for Scotland. Ere long, they took up position behind their young colleague's house, waited until everyone had fallen asleep, then crept in, got hold of the reader by the shoulders, and began to drag her away. Just as they reached the door, the young poet woke with a start and managed—just—to grab his reader and wife by the feet. A rough tussle followed, in the course of which the reader was ripped apart. The poet's colleagues took the top half of the body back to Ireland, while the young poet was left with the bottom half.

And so, ere long, they were sitting in Ireland and Scotland, carving the missing bits out of wood. They did this particularly badly, so the poets in Ireland ended up with a reader who was always falling over, and the young poet had one who couldn't turn the page.

The Poet And The Poem

A poet was travelling with his publisher. Passing through a forest, they came upon a poor proofreader who asked them to give her a little something. The poet handed her a franc, the publisher gave her nothing.

They'd hardly gone any further when an editor came toward them, also requesting that they give her something. The poet gave her his gloves, the publisher gave her nothing.

A while later, they came upon a translator—she'd have appreciated something too. The poet said to the publisher, "You give her something, you have several fortunes!" But the publisher refused, and the poet let the translator have his last rusk.

The first of the women, though, was the Virgin Mary; the second, Joan of Arc; the third the Lord God himself who rewarded the poet with two wishes.

"Just two?' the poet asked. "Why not three?"

"Two," said God.

The poet asked for a poem that would leave every audience that heard it rejoicing; and for a game bag with which he could catch everything and anything.

"You forgot to ask for the best thing of all," God admonished him.

"What's that?"

"Spiritual salvation!"

"I'd only go and lose it!" said the poet.

Ere long, the two wayfarers were passing some thorny bushes.

The poet recited the divine poem, and the publisher rejoiced, hopped and skipped until his garments and indeed his body were in wretched shreds—whereupon the poet banished him to the top of a very high tree.

The poet stopped off at an inn. Nearby was a bookshop that was under a spell, the innkeeper told him. Whoever broke the spell would receive the bookseller's hand in marriage.

"Is it worth the effort?" asked the poet.

"The bookseller is the most charming, companionable person around," said the innkeeper.

"Yeah, but is she beautiful?" asked the poet.

"Word has it she has small breasts, but she makes such skillful use of her brassiere that no man can guess, just by looking, where nature ends and art takes over."

Upon hearing this, the poet sent for the manager of the bookshop and told him he wanted to break the spell on the shop. The manager warned against it, but the poet showed no fear and asked to be taken there late that evening.

The bookshop that was under a spell looked as *triste* as the rest of the universe, but the poet took a Finnish novel down from a shelf and read until eleven. Not a single customer came by. Suddenly a critic entered, claiming he wanted to read too.

"Go ahead and try," said the poet, but the critic's nails were so long, they were soon tearing every page he touched.

"Stop! You mustn't do that!" the poet declared, grabbing the critic by the collar. "Put your fingers in the cash register! I need to cut your nails!"

He slammed the till shut, the poet, and the critic's nails broke off.

Hearing his moaning and groaning, scores of fellow critics rushed in. The poet reached straight for the divine poem and in an instant, whether they wanted to or not, the critics found themselves rejoicing and hopping and skipping. The poet caught one after another in his game bag. But first, the one caught in the till had to explain why the bookshop was under a spell.

"When readers dare to enter," he said, "we throw them all in a pit."

"But why?"

"Out of anger. Show me the reader, man or woman, who is interested in, never mind follows, the recommendations of critics. Now let me go! Beneath this register, you'll find a copper kettle. It's full of francs and gift cards."

Hearing this, the poet said his magic words and this critic, too, ended up in the game bag.

It was autumn now, and Book Fair time. The poet took the bag to Frankfurt and promised all his poet colleagues money and gift cards if they hit his bag hard. His colleagues beat the bag with evident relish, and the critics screamed. After a while, the poet said, "Now turn the bag round—to warm the behinds of the ones at the bottom too!"

Finally, he released the critics. "We'll never ever return!" they roared as they ran off.

The poet now visited the manager of the bookshop and announced he'd broken the spell. He was offered the position of bookkeeper in the shop, and was thus able to marry the bookseller as a man of means.

"Ivory-colored loveliness!" the poet exclaimed when he saw the bookseller for the first time.

"Savior of the bookshop!" the bookseller sighed.

On their wedding night, he saw that it was indeed the brassiere that helped the bookseller to make the best of what was there.

When, then, the former poet and his wife went for a walk in the forest, they saw the furious publisher high above them. The former poet knew what to do. He whisked out the divine poem and began to recite:

Beneath the almond, in the sun / his heart by her was surely won / with the books she was devouring / in the grass, among flowers flowering / There she lay and read, excited / of Finland and lives soon blighted / of heavy hearts and suns setting / girls dying, a blood-letting / Such a great time they had / he found no peace, our smitten lad / lost in the forest, deep in the night / two souls, now one, together, right.

"I'll be damned if I'll rejoice!" the publisher shouted down at the poet before shooting up from the treetop, right into the sky. The clouds were sent reeling, and he was never seen again.

THE BOOKSELLER AND THE MULE

A bookseller held a clearance sale in her bookshop, loaded her mule with the books that remained unsold, and betook herself to another land.

En route, she saw a group of critics who were throwing a poet into a river and pulling him back out again with a rope they'd tied round his neck. What the bookseller witnessed scalded her heart.

"Don't do that!" she called over. "Let the poet go!"

The critics said, "This is not your concern."

"What would I have to give you in exchange for the poet's freedom?"

"Essays! Unreadable essays! Whole deserts of letters!"

So she gave them a few of the unsold books, and they let the poet go.

The bookseller continued on her way and came upon a group of academics who were holding a poet in a half nelson.

"Fly, we said!" they shouted, kicking his behind. "Fly, *fly*, we said!"

The bookseller, again, was filled with pity. "What do I have to give you for the poet's freedom?"

"Old books, in Gothic print!"

And she gave the academics the last of her unsold books, so they'd let the poet go.

"Critics and academics," she thought, driving her mule on. "Think only the absolute worst of them and you'll not go far wrong."

Having given all her books away, the bookseller was now in no position to run a shop in her new homeland. She decided to "borrow" a basic selection of titles from the nearest distributor.

She tied up her mule at a thicket in the forest, then made her way to the largest national distributor, hefted a box of books up onto to her back, and made herself scarce.

Behind her, she could hear the cries: "Robbed—the distributor's being robbed!"

She was caught ere long and brought before the judge.

"For such an act of impudence," the judge said, "I order you to be put in a coffin, that it be hammered shut with an iron nail, and you be thrown into the river. The mule, however, should be turned into sausages."

The mule was slaughtered and hung up in the smokehouse. The coffin was thrown in the river but got stuck on a branch hanging down into the water. The coffin started to fill with water, and the bookseller came perilously close to drowning. "Whether old or young, a bookworm or a fool, a nomad or a stay-at-home—we all end up in a coffin!" she exclaimed with a sigh.

At that very moment, something started tugging at the nail, and the coffin opened. The bookseller could now see the two poets whose release she'd secured. She climbed out and lay down in a meadow.

Fine, she thought, just brassiere and panties will do the trick too. She undressed and laid her clothes out on the grass to dry.

The poets brought her berries and fruit and alcoholic drinks, and together they decided, from that moment on, to avoid the production and dissemination of versification, given the time-consuming and risk-ridden nature of said activity. It was easier, the poets reckoned, to do something more serious.

"More serious?" the bookseller asked. The juice of a berry was giving her lips a seductively red hue.

"Poets are sensitive," the poets said, "and tempting them, then acting dumb when things become too much for them, isn't a decent thing to do."

At that moment, the bookseller spotted something bright in the water and sent the poets to fetch it. They returned with the iron nail, and three wedding rings were fashioned from it.

Fast Forward:

The now married triad makes enquiries about entering a serious profession. Veterinary medicine is recommended to them. Ere long, they're known far and wide in the world of scholars for their successful reanimations of smoked mules.

The Rich Poet

Once, there was a rich poet. He started boozing and playing at dice and—ere long—was penniless.

Eternal Friendship

Once, a poet and his Swiss-French translator met in an alpine health resort. At daybreak, they left the closing-time-less Chinchilla Bar in Kirchgasse, each with a bottle of apricot schnapps. While the translator bathed his eyes with warm spring water from the fountain on the village square, the poet strove to make poetic sense of the various monstrous hotel constructions surrounding it. Early birds with venous circulatory disturbances were wobbling towards the Thermal Baths in their white bathrobes.

"Time to get our boots on!" the refreshed and cheerful translator urged. "Let's walk a bit! The broad valley is much to be preferred to the constant danger of falling rocks here at the foot of the mountains," he declared. "Let's go!—Off into the valley! *Regardons la rivière de plus près!*"

"On foot?" the poet asked.

"Why not?" said the translator. "*Allons-y!*"

The poet, however, did not wish to embark on such a foolhardy plan without first undertaking a wide range of preparations. Pringles needed to be transferred into good solid containers, headgear had to be procured, suntan lotion and topographical maps packed, the Agricultural Cooperative's weather report consulted, and bandages carefully counted, he cautioned. Preparing their hike was almost as elaborate as transferring an army to its new quarters.

"By the time we've finished packing," the translator sighed, "we'll have lost all inclination to walk."

On that point, the poet agreed, and so they headed—minus their rucksacks—for the end of the valley.

The translator stormed ahead, and the poet shuffled along behind, stopping every few steps to record some poetic inspiration or other. "Birdsong, chaffinches," he noted, for instance, in his notebook. "Wherever you turn, the ringtone of the great tit, the whispers of firecrests, and redbreasts warbling their little song."

The translator's favorite things were the letters making up the notices along the path—be these signposts, or information boards, or the names of houses. Carefully, he typed everything into the vocabulary app on his smartphone.

Leaving the bathrobes and flower boxes behind, they strode across a meadow contributing to the production of both animal fodder and human foodstuffs, passed the Larches (holiday apartments), then headed for the Weidstübli restaurant.

Their clothing may indeed have been light, and they were walking on the side of the valley that was in the shade, but the heat of the sun was already warming their blood.

The first bottle of apricot schnapps they emptied on the climb up to Wolf's Paw—a not entirely harmless ledge, which fact the plaque in memory of a certain "Edith" impressed upon the pair. But it was a perfect view, too.

They looked down onto the health resort, at the thermal baths and hotels that demonstrated both the imaginable and unimaginable in terms of structural engineering. Great savings had been achieved here with regard to architectural beauty, the two agreed. The translator handed the poet the bottle. "*Salam-Ati. Salud. Santé.*"

"Blue tits, jays, wrens," the poet noted.

"Waste disposal prohibited" and "No tipping," the translator typed in.

"Wrens, tracks of cloven-hoofed animals, alpenroses"—but they must have taken a wrong turn at the fork, as they didn't pass the restaurant, which annoyed them both, and they again found themselves at the top of an impassable rock face, into which wooden ladders had been secured that looked no less impassable. "Head for heights required!" the sign beside the first ladder warned—which frightened them both, well and truly.

The end of the valley seemed an endless number of performance miles away.

Below, the mountain river sounded like a motorway as it roared past and, from high above, the relentless sun was burning both their brows and writing hands. With a sigh, the poet sat down in an ecological compensation area and, using his fingers, measured the level of their liquid assets.

"The apricots are almost finished," he said, "our heat shield is insufficient, and our dehydration considerable. If one of us were to set out alone, he'd reach the next village, perhaps. If we both went, however, we'd be vaporized en route. Permit me, my friend, to tie my T-shirt round your head. I'd then ask you to make sole use of our supplies in order to fortify you for the remainder of the journey. I won't budge from this spot. I prefer to wait, at these ladders to heaven, until such time as my friend reaches a village. There, he will find reinforcements, and it won't be too late to return and bury me with full honors."

"How could such a plan ever be executed?" the translator replied. "We may not be descended from the same people, but preserving a friendship is a bigger deal than one's blood and background. How could I ever bring myself to continue alone?" And as a smuggler would his swag, he threw the poet over his shoulder. "*Allons-y!*" he said. "*Et que ça saute! Zut alors, merde.*"

At this, they climbed down the ladders. With each step, the rungs threatened to snap. On the other side of the earth, in a distant Mexican night, a vulture—resting in the shade of a cactus—woke from a visionary dream and opened its beak in expectation.

The poet voiced his observations, "Look, a plaque in memory of someone who crashed to his death here! Look, another memorial plaque!" and, increasingly breathless, the translator contributed a simple "Oh?" or a brave "*L'essentiel est que tu n'aies pas peur*" to the conversation.

They thus surmounted the challenge of the ladders and, in Mexico, the vulture took no pleasure in dozing off again.

Down below, they found a veritable forest of signs. One warned to watch out for monster scooters. A second insisted that the mountains still shouldn't be treated as waste disposal sites. A third advertised the sun terrace of Restaurant Flaschen.

Wine menus! Parasols! These visions gave the poet and the translator renewed energy. There was practically no stopping them as they rushed down the aisle through the forest that, in winter, would be a ski slope noted for causing only average injuries.

The restaurant was closed.

In the bottle deposit behind it, they found items that were still home to a drop or two of beer, kirsch, or wine, but the poet said, "Not even my mother would drink that"—which the translator translated ad hoc as "*Même mon chien n'en voudrait pas.*"

Disappointed, discouraged, and dropping into the mechanical trot of a Foreign Legionnaire in the stony Algerian desert, they followed a signpost to the next village that, an hour later, turned out to be so dead that neither God's Table, the inn that was closed, nor deserted apartment blocks such as Evening Star and Tschangaladonga—"A corruption of *champs à la dame!*"—could get them in any way excited.

"Not much happening here," the translator said.

"I don't doubt that, were one to stay longer, one would even come across interesting and good people," said the poet, quoting an illustrious predecessor. "But the sun and heat have become even fiercer, and our provisions more meager, and who will rush to our aid?"

They looked around for a place to rest and discovered a half-full fountain that would offer some respite, perhaps. The translator helped the poet in. Fresh water dripped only sparingly into the trough.

"I would ask my friend not to succumb to any form of self-deception," the poet said. "He should continue, immediately. I shall breathe my last here. In the mountains it is calm, there's no wind, the birds are silent—as I shall soon be too."

The translator burst into tears. "Continuing alone is, for sure, not how a just man would act. I can't do it."

"But who will tell anecdotes about me after my death if we both die?"

"The valley lies, horizontal, below us. We need only roly-poly our way down," said the translator. "In the cellars and grottos and cooperatives of the valley's inhabitants, we can purchase spirits on credit—so I would ask my friend not to linger any longer!" he went on, whereupon the poet climbed out of the fountain.

"I see our friendship has remained unchanged, which is of comfort to me," he said as they left the village.

The descent was lined by locked-up barns and boarded-up windows, and by unshorn sheep, gathered round the only tree offering any shade. When the trail reached the road, the poet—determined to throw himself in front of a mail bus delivering a new batch of rheumatics to the resort—raced onto the asphalt. The translator held him back, dragged him the final few yards into the village, and made him sit in the scant shade of the narrow street. As he fanned air towards him, he could hear and see the poet had fallen asleep.

At that, the translator knocked the last of the schnapps back and, glancing over his shoulder as he walked off, looked one last time at his *frère* and *ami*.

Since time immemorial, it has been said that translators are erratic types; that they have the same nature as fog and flowers: i.e., too little loyalty and too much concealment. The translator, having crossed the river and taken refuge in the air-conditioned kiosk at the station, didn't turn right back with fresh supplies. Instead, he dilly-dallied and chatted to the shop assistant. He tried on numerous pairs of sunglasses, and praised the range of souvenirs and cold drinks in a bid to win a smile from the mature beauty serving at the till.

"The station kiosk in Leuk," the translator raved. "For me, it's up there with Lafayette in Paris!"

For the poet, there was the happy coincidence that the local councilor responsible for the appearance of the village had chosen that very moment to carry out her duties. Coming across a heap of poet asleep at the foot of the postbox, she rolled him into the coolest place in the entire valley—the church's charnel house. There, surrounded by twenty thousand skulls and forty thousand thighbones, the poet thanked the councilor. "Had you not found me, it could easily have been the case that I'd have evaporated. And what's the point of dying like an animal or plant? I shall never forget your good deed!"

The councilor shrugged off his praise. What she'd done, she said, wasn't worth mentioning. Was the equivalent of dwelling on the fact that, in Argentina, they lack a word for *shoe rack*; and, in Persia, a word for *walker.*

"A translator yourself, are you?" the poet asked.

TRANSLATED FROM GERMAN BY DONAL MCLAUGHLIN

[UKRAINE]

YURIY TARNAWSKY

Dead Darling

"Imagination dead, imagine . . ."
SAMUEL BECKETT

A room in a hospital where bodies are kept or in a police morgue. Tall walls lined with white tiles that look gray and shine like viscera. Similar but not identical white tiles on the floor. In the back two huge stainless steel refrigerators for storing bodies, apparently three in each, closed. To the left and right stainless steel doors, also closed. In the center a stainless steel cart with black plastic wheels, for transporting bodies, covered with a green sheet that hangs down to the floor on the sides, empty. On the right, attached to the wall, a white ceramic sink that looks white for a change. A set of lights mounted in the ceiling cast a strong, vertical, white light that makes everything beneath it look worthless like a powerful analytical mind driven by a cynical personality.

A man, middle aged, of average height and build, dressed in a tan or gray suit (it is hard to tell which in the overly bright light) and a loose gray or khaki raincoat (also hard to tell which), open, paces nervously back and forth behind the cart, a cellular phone, like a tiny, severed hand, already black, pressed to his left ear. He speaks in an exasperated, desperate voice, as if hoping that the emotion he projects will change his situation.

MAN *(beside himself)*: ... yes ... a woman ... killed or died, we don't know which ... Was supposed to be in room number 13 ... *(A long pause.)* Yes ... yes. That's her. *(A pause.)* But she's not here ... The cart's empty. *(A long pause.)* No, I haven't ... Alright, I'll look. Wait, hold on. I want to have you on the line.

He goes up to the first refrigerator, the one on the left, and opens the door. The inside is in fact divided into three horizontal compartments, one close above the other like bunk beds in a concentration camp. They are stuffed full with articles of food, such as bags of flour, pasta, and sugar, cans of vegetables, meats, and soups, bottles of soda, vinegar, oil, soy sauce, boxes of cereals and crackers, bread in plastic bags, and so on, as well as household items of various kinds, among them, salt and pepper shakers, trivets, candlesticks, an electric coffee mill, a toaster, a tea kettle, a wire dish rack, what looks like two separate sets of dishes, a large stainless steel basin, pots and pans, kitchen utensils, loose and on a rack, a birdcage, empty, an aquarium, also empty, a butterfly net, a set of wine glasses, two electric fans, one a table model, another one freestanding, lying on its side, an electric iron, an ironing board, a plastic bucket, a mop, a broom, a dustpan, and a few throw rugs, neatly rolled up. The man runs his eyes over the things, but surprisingly isn't surprised by them, and speaks calmly into the phone.

MAN: There's no body here, just junk. Wait, I'll look in the other one.

He shuts the door, goes over to the second refrigerator, and opens its door. It is constructed exactly as the first one and is also stuffed full with household items, except these are mostly toilet and bedroom articles, such as a scale, a bathroom stool lying on its side, a rubber bath mat, neatly rolled up, bottles of shampoo, lotion, and toilet water, many bars of soap in a wicker basket, a plastic wastebasket, a long-handled brush for scrubbing one's back, two pillows without pillowcases, what looks like half a dozen sets of bed linen, blankets, towels, and two bathrobes, all haphazardly piled up . The man again runs his eyes over the things, again isn't surprised by them, and speaks calmly into the phone.

MAN: She's not here either, just junk. That's it . . . There're only two refrigerators.

As he speaks he turns around and walks toward the cart. Now he can see under it through its open end and apparently notices something unusual there, because he gets animated, runs up to the cart, kneels down, and lifts the edge of the sheet on his side. He speaks in an excited voice into the phone.

MAN: I think she's here . . . under the cart . . . Yes! . . . Oh, my God! She's dead!

He puts the phone on the floor face up without turning it off and pushes the cart to the right, exposing the body of a woman lying on her right side, in other words facing him, in the fetal position. She is dressed in a yellow bikini with white polka dots.

A tiny Lilliputian voice is heard coming out of the phone shouting something and sounding ludicrous in this situation. It does this a few times and then stops abruptly as if realizing its own inadequacy. The person has apparently hung up. After a few seconds the phone starts beeping out a busy signal. Lilliputian though it also is, it is annoying, like the dripping of a faucet. The man doesn't seem to hear it, however.

In the meantime he has covered the woman's body with his, embracing it. He rolls it over on its back in the process. The body, surprisingly, uncurls easily and naturally. It lies with its legs stretched out and the arms along the torso, appearing to be alive. The man unexpectedly straightens up and, holding the woman by the shoulders, shouts at her.

MAN: You're alive! But they told me you were dead!

The woman is in fact alive. She wears a pair of slanted, white-framed sunglasses which give her an exotic, oriental air. Her pubic region bulges unnaturally high under her bathing suit, as if padded with something. She tries to free herself from the man's hands, motioning with her arms for him to lean back. After the man has let go of her and straightens up she points at the ceiling indicating she wants him not to shade her from the light. It becomes apparent then that she is lying on a large white bath mat as if on a beach towel. She speaks in an aloof voice, as if physically far away.

WOMAN: You're keeping the light from me. I want to get tanned.

The man is clearly astounded at what he sees and hears. He looks at the woman in disbelief, unable to say a word. The sound of a melody being hummed comes from somewhere, most probably from the woman. From the snippets that can be heard it appears to be the song "Mary Ann" popularized by Harry Belafonte in the 1950s. The Lilliputian beeping sound coming from the phone once again becomes audible. For a few seconds the man continues disregarding it but in the end hears it, turns to the phone, picks it up, turns it off, and puts it in the breast pocket of his jacket. He is finally over his amazement and speaks to the woman.

MAN: Where have you been? What happened?

The woman lies still for a while and then answers reluctantly.

WOMAN: You always want to know everything ... too much ... I'm here now. Isn't it enough?

MAN *(exasperated)*: But they called me and said you were dead!

WOMAN *(with profound irony, scoffing)*: What do they know? They were wrong, as you can plainly see. I'm very much alive. *(After a pause she adds, clarifying her last statement:)* I answer to nobody. I do as I please.

She stirs finally, as if to make herself comfortable, moving her head from side to side, repositioning her arms, pulling up her left leg and keeping it bent at the knee, and giving a big sigh, indicating her impatience or displeasure with the situation. Then suddenly she sits up, almost hitting the man on the chin with her head in the process. He leans back just in time.

WOMAN *(annoyed in the extreme)*: What's the point? ... It's regular light, not ultraviolet. I can't get a tan here.

She looks around the room, breathing angrily, her nostrils flaring, as if looking for something, but apparently doesn't find it, stands up, goes up to the first refrigerator, opens it, takes out the stainless steel basin, not looking for it but locating it immediately, obviously knowing where it is, shuts the door, goes over to the second refrigerator, opens it, takes a hand towel out of one of the stacks of towels, which is white, shuts the door, goes over to the sink, hangs the towel over her left shoulder, fills the basin with water, waiting for it to get warm, and puts the basin on the floor. The man in the meantime has stood up, followed the woman with his eyes as she moved around, and is now looking at her with interest.

Facing the wall, the woman squats over the basin, hangs the towel over the edge of the sink, and with her left hand pulls aside the crotch of the bikini so as to expose her sex. As she does this, a large wad of money falls out of the bikini into the basin. It was this that made her pubic region bulge so high. The woman catches it immediately with her right hand, curses quietly, shakes the water off of it onto the floor, stuffs it in her bra, and starts washing herself off, using her right hand. The water makes a soft, melodious sound, splashing against the metal basin, like that of a harpsichord. The man continues watching the woman silently, again as if in disbelief. Crouching over the basin, the woman looks like a female dog urinating, squatting close to the ground. She takes a long time washing off, obviously wanting to make sure she has done a good job, but eventually she is done, stands up, still holding the crotch of the bikini to the side, her knees bent a little, reaches out with her right hand for the towel, takes it, and dries herself off. Having done it, she hangs the towel over the edge of the sink, takes the money out of her bra, holds it firmly in her right hand, walks to the door on the right, opens it, and walks out, leaving the door open.

There is total darkness behind the door, which falls into the room like a huge shaft of antilight. The woman disappears. A blast of cold air is blown into the room and with it a few snowflakes that dance wistfully in the air as if looking for a companion and being unable to find one. Eerie electronic music is heard at the same time, coming in through the door that seems black as the darkness and cold as the cold air, an apt accompaniment to the woman's disappearance and the dancing of snowflakes. The man stands looking at the empty door in amazement. His coat blows in the air that streams into the room. After a while his whole body starts swaying in the stream of air, as if he were just his clothes, empty on the inside. Then he too starts dancing, whirling through the room. At one point he collides with the cart and tries to use it as his dancing partner but has little luck with it. Then he is blown over to the second refrigerator and thrown against the door. Rebounding from it, he opens it and takes out of it the plastic wastebasket, which is white, shuts the door, dances over to the cart, places the wastebasket in the middle of it, dances over to the first refrigerator, opens its door, finds in the clutter inside it a long, dried-out lily stalk, shuts the door, dances over to the cart, and puts the lily stalk in it as in a vase. Then he dances over to the second refrigerator and takes a few items out of it, such as brushes with long handles or other long things, shuts the door, dances over to the cart, and puts the things in the wastebasket as he had done with the lily. After that he dances over to the first refrigerator again, opens it, takes a bunch of things out of it to complement what he has put in the wastebasket, shuts the door, dances over to the cart, and arranges the things there. He repeats this process a few times, alternating between the two refrigerators until he is satisfied with the arrangement he has created. It constitutes a pitiful ikebana of the memory of the woman who has gone away. While taking the things from the refrigerators to the cart the man sometimes presses them to his heart as if to indicate how dear they are to him or how much he values the purpose they will serve. While dancing over to the refrigerators he sometimes covers his face with his hands, hanging his head down or throwing it back, expressing through these gestures the sadness he feels at the woman's disappearance. His face grows more and more pale and blank with time and eventually streams with tears. It looks like a windowpane flowing with rain.

The wind has suddenly grown stronger. It whistles, drowning out the music. The door closes with a tremendous bang. The man continues dancing, however, as if not having noticed what has happened. Apparently he wasn't dancing to the music but to a tune in his mind that must have been very similar to the music. He covers his face with his hands, hangs his head down, throws it back, and cries as before.

As soon as the door closes, something red starts seeping into the room from under the doors on both sides, covering the floor. It is blood. The man dances in it, apparently not noticing what is happening. His feet make unpleasant smacking sounds on the bloody tiles like lips trying to say something but being unable to do it. The blood keeps rising. It reaches the man's ankles, then knees. He has a hard time dancing, but continues trying. He covers his face with his hands and cries less and less however devoting more and more of his energy and attention to the task of moving. The woman must have splashed a lot of water out of the basin because it floats easily in the blood. A black coffin and its lid now appear, floating in separately. Unlikely as it seems, they must have somehow floated into the room from under one of the doors. They bob up and down and sway from side to side as if making overtures to the basin, which blithely ignores them. The man also ignores the things. It's as if they don't exist. The blood has risen up to his waist. He can no longer pretend he is dancing but continues to move, turning around slowly. Now he has stopped showing his grief altogether and devotes all of his energy and attention to moving. The skirt of his coat has gathered like excrement around him. The excrement seems to be his. The blood keeps rising. The towel floats aimlessly through the room, not knowing what to do. The wastebasket that serves as a vase tries to float too, but tips over and its contents spill out. Some of these float in the blood, others sink to the bottom. Eventually the wastebasket does the same. The sheet that covered the cart has finally risen and floats in the blood as if looking for a place to sink.

The room now starts expanding. The walls grow wider and taller, as if fleeing, unable to stand each other. The ceiling also rises and disappears. The refrigerators detach themselves from the wall, grow tall, expand, and float in the blood. Blood has risen almost up to the man's chin. He has stopped moving and seems to be choked by his coat. Finally he apparently starts moving his legs, for he rises. Standing up, he takes off his coat, then his jacket, finally his tie, and starts swimming. The last glimpse of his face shows it to be completely empty—not like a blank sheet of paper but a sheet of paper virtually all of which has been cut out except for a thin rim around its perimeter. The room is now a sea of blood with the walls a white sky on the horizon on all sides. The refrigerators sway from side to side and bob up and down, tall like office towers made of stainless steel. The man swims with an expert crawl stroke, keeping his head above the blood, staring toward a spot on the horizon where his heart, huge as the sun, throbs laboriously, trying to rise into the sky.

TOM MCCARTHY

On Dodgem Jockeys

In one of his short pieces that hovers uncomfortably between being a novel, an essay and an exercise in clinical observation, Georges Perec muses that he's missed his true calling: Rather than a writer, he should have become a controller for the Paris City Transit Authority. The revelation comes at the end of a day spent sitting in the same spot noting down (among other things) the passage of pedestrians to and from the metro and the frequency with which the variously numbered busses pass by, some full, some empty. But, more subtly, his reasoning goes as follows: If the writer's task is to record events in time; to bring into sharp focus the trajectories of human lives, both singularly and in all their crowded multiplicity, the contingencies—be these of chance, or design—of a hundred, or a thousand, or a million comings-together, transfers and leave-takings; to intuit and communicate their overall rhythm; and, beyond even that, to peer beneath their surface and reveal the fabric holding the whole thing together, unpick and reconstruct its very weft and warp—well, the transit controller does exactly this.

By the same logic, I would suggest that the most noble and heroic thing to be in this life, or perhaps in any other, is the dodgem jockey. You know what I mean: those guys who work the bumper cars in fairgrounds. Not the fat, older one who sits in the control booth—Perec's fantasy—but the lithe, young things who cling onto the backs of moving cars, hopping from one to the next.

Considered structurally (and what is a fairground ride but a mechanical construction?), the dodgem ring is made up of three strata. At the top, the grid—that is, speaking Cartesianly, space itself, its sublimated essence and totality; and, speaking metaphysically, the heavens, electrified domain from which the gods cast out their bolts, zap life down to the realm below. That second realm, the floor, the stage across which human dramas play themselves out with a predictable, if frenzied and excited, regularity, is, despite its foot-stamping, wheel-grabbing aspirations to autonomy, powered by the first, which crackles from time to time with angry lightning to remind it where the charge lies in this set-up.

Dodgem jockeys, though, occupy the third stratum, the one lying between the other two: the realm of conductivity, of conveyance. This makes them angels: messengers, or mediators, who ensure that heaven's work is carried out uninterruptedly on earth, nudging things along, sorting out blockages.

In terms of volume, their zone is the biggest: where the ceiling, like the floor, is flat (even the gods are horizontal), it alone has a vertical dimension. While their nominal "patrons" are obliged to sit for the duration of the ride, they stand tall, towering, erect. Like erotic dancers swinging round their poles, these men are the stars of the show, and they know it. Each ride is a performance, a ballet whose choreography is made all the more exquisite by the casual way in which it's executed: *glissades* disguised as offhand sidesteps between moving vehicles, *coupés* as distracted shifts of weight from one foot to the other. They have mastered laws of motion not found elsewhere: Dodgem cars make no distinction between forward, neutral, and reverse, but submit rather to an endless coiling of the wheel through which every direction flows out of its opposite. A quantum field, vertiginous, abyssal, in whose depths these agents of relativity hover, paradoxically enabling movement to proceed along axes and vectors postulated by old, naïve laws of physics from which they themselves have long since been exempted.

The dodgem jockey, clinging uninvited to your car—*your* one, the one you've paid, downpayed for—represents the figure of the stranger lodged within the home. He's the *Unheimliche*, the Uncanny, stuck onto you like an incubus. What better image for the gypsy in the popular imagination, its fantasies and fears? Within the fairground, this rickety, nomadic mobile city brought to you on trucks, the bumper-car ride, mise-en-scène of rickety mobility, sits like a miniature reproduction of the whole. These men, then, restlessly moving between moving cars, replicate yet again the overall condition of nomadism: a regressiveness that partakes of infinity. Through such endless repetitions, they both multiply and merge with other quasi-folkloric characters who populate the margins of our consciousness: with cowboys, for example, hired hands exhorting mutinous, anarchic herds to follow a course that, if no two of its individual paths are identical, nonetheless amalgamates to a coherent whole; or logjammers, riding the very masses they prod and corral, skipping between these as they bump and roll, teasing equilibrium from the rim of chaos; or linesmen dangling from pylons as sparks leap into the air around their heads, whispering into their ears (and only theirs) the static, white-noise secrets of the firmament.

In Paul Klee's famous painting of (and here we loop back, like a dodgem, to an earlier motif) a hovering angel, Walter Benjamin discerns not just any angel: This one, he tells us, is the angel of history, who travels one way while facing the other, backward. Where mortals perceive a chain of separate events that amount to "progress," the angel sees one single, ongoing catastrophe that piles wreckage upon wreckage, hurling it before his feet. Are dodgem jockeys angels of history too? I would say: Yes, they are. They've seen it all before: these circuits blurring into one, these endless crashes, disasters playing out as pleasure, roar of the generator merging with screams of girls, bellows of boys who hope to get into their pants later that night when the ride's over, generate more generations, send more wreckage the angel's way . . . They've seen the entire tapestry, its pattern. Free-floating witnesses, they were there: at your conception, and the universe's, when circulating atoms deviated and collided.

ROBERT MINHINNICK

Scavenger

1.
A night of fat stars.
The sky full of blister packs.

2.
Just like the sea. There are times when the sea's as clean as I can remember. Others when it tries to spew everything out of itself. I could build a city from the plastic I kick through at the caves. A million sandwiches still in their packaging. Thousands of planks, six months, twenty years in the water, and yet I smell the forest. Those jewels of resin.

3.
Zigmas drowned. That's what they said. Even before the deluge and the biggest waves. He could have escaped like the rest but he ran to the ghost train and hid in a carriage on the rail. In the dark.

He was one of the Lits, we all knew, from somewhere in the south of that country. Not the Baltic, where people would have understood the ocean.

Someone said Zigmas had never seen the sea before he arrived at the fairground. He told people his father was a mushroom seller. It seems he thought he might have been safe. But in the ghost train? What can you say about people like that? There was also a girl drowned in the subway, under the school mural. You know, I think they get what they deserve. Why should I worry about those simple kids?

4.

Breathing. That's what I can hear. The stone, breathing. It's what I've always heard in Pink Bay. No, not the sea sighing, because sometimes the tide is far away. But in this place, where the limestone meets the sandstone, the red bleeds into the grey, I can hear the stone itself. Its ancient exhalation.

I didn't think like that as a child. It's something I've gradually learned I'm able to do. If I pay enough attention. Because that's something I'm good at. Paying attention. Yes, if I listen long enough I hear the sound of stone breathing.

But there are so many voices we never hear. Because we've forgotten how to listen. I mean really listen. Which is what I do when I come here.

Never alone now, are we? I mean, properly alone. That's vanished. Think about most people. They have no idea what it's like to be solitary. Or singular, a better word. What singularity can mean. Another reason to pity them.

5.

We used to bring cheese and bread. Packets of chocolate biscuits with milk for the morning. And booze, of course, that was the point. Dregs of sloe gin, the peppermint schnapps nobody ever drank, advocaat, grenadine. Anything we could filch unnoticed.

How bright those bottles were, our terrible cocktail. When I think of it now, they were the colours in the cave itself, yellows and purples, like bruised flesh. And the stone too, how alike it is to the human body, voluptuous and intricate.

In the candlelight we sang and played guitars, and I'd find my fingers straying to the stone. I'd stroke the stone as if it was alive. No matter the weather, that rock was always wet. And fissured like flesh, I discovered. Yes, one of my great discoveries.

6.

I think I've slept. I know I lay down and tried to make myself comfortable. The sandstone is hard. I had a sleeping bag with a blanket but it is so humid now I didn't need it. The weather again is strange. But the weather's always strange. These days. Neither was I sure of the tide, because the ocean doesn't behave as you think it should. As the sea once did. But I know I lay down and thought. And dreamed a shark in the fairground. The mall was flooded, and someone said the types of tides we have today have not been seen since Neolithic times. No, millions of years, they said. It was a voice in my head said that. Someone whispering to me. A lover, almost. Another of my voices. There are so many.

The shark was lost, misplaced from the deeps. Yet a shark still, a shark bewildered, that shark a victim too, but a shark all the same, a grey glimpse, a shadow that shark, out of the dark shoals, a shape in the ruins with all the storm debris, the archipelagos of shit, the new atolls. A shark in the shallows.

So I shivered into and then out of sleep.

When I woke for the last time I tried to open my eyes. But all I could make out was the blood colour of my own eyelids. Exactly what you see when you gaze into the sun. The red colour of sea anemones. Their raw flesh on the rock, shivering to the touch, like wet flowers. And I rubbed my eyes but the red colour remained the same. So I squeezed my eyes and licked my lips, tasting last night's supper, the wine crust around my lips, a ring of salt. Fierce that salt, its burn, its sting.

And a taste too of Lizzy's mouth where she had kissed me that time long ago, Lizzy's own wine-tasting tongue, the tang of her own salt, because all of us must taste the same now, wherever we are, though it's hard to think many remain. I'd say we taste of salt and sand and cheap whisky, of the smoke we suck into ourselves. Yes, we taste of the sunblock we have to use, even when it rains. We taste of sweat, dirty-sweet, as we tasted of the smoke from our driftwood fire that night, the wrack burning green as iodine. That time we lit the fire. The time Lizzy kissed me.

Once we tasted of the seawater that poured through the kitchen of the Blue Dolphin café. When the drains ruptured and the tide was huge. There used to be a picture of a shark on the wall there. Maybe that's why I dreamed. About the shark. No, there was no photo of a dolphin. And I tell you, it was real, that flood. Real in my dream. The arcades, the rides, all of it was underwater, and the shark grey in the black waters between the carousel horses and the characters from *Star Trek*, the horses with their names, Madeline and Myfanwy, painted on the golden poles. Someone said they were still going round, as the different currents pushed them one way and then pushed the other. Think of those dead children. Going round on the carousel.

And those *Star Trek* heroes? Each was drowned and swollen in the swell. I watched as the bears from the shies washed past, ruined of course, the pandas and koalas, the stuffing oozing out of the bad stitching. What they sold on those stalls was the cheapest gear possible. Sewn by slaves in Vietnam and Bangladesh. But imagine everything ruined and everything spoiled. All those prizes.

7.

I had expected the tide to wake me and was ready for that. But I was ahead of myself. Instead I awake to a crimson world, the sandstone redder than any stone I've ever seen, the sky pink, yes pink as that flower that grows in the dunes. Soapwort they call it. People long ago used to boil the roots to wash their clothes. I tell you, it's well known. That pink flower, almost as tall as a man. Or maybe its seeds, I can't remember, perhaps they boiled the seeds for soap. I'm still thinking about the shark, but finally my eyes are open. As I lie here astonished. By this crimson world.

Molten, this world. And I think, yes, I know this world. As it had been when it first formed. Volcanoes, their rivers of lava like the planet's blood. This new world is where I lie and have awoken. The shape of the shark is still dark in my dream and the prize bears are floating on the tide, and everywhere the smell of rot. Deep down, the stink of rottenness. And a child's shoe floating by.

8.

I lie where we always walked. It was a place famous amongst us. Others loved it, yes, generations had walked here, had been drawn to the red beach. There are patterns of white quartz that children always said was writing. I'd thought and said the same myself when I was young, when I looked at the quartz in the rock, a white language in the red sandstone, and tried to make sense of those hieroglyphics. As if it was an explanation. Yes, when I was eighteen I was certain the quartz said and meant something. If only I could decipher it. Which would be the challenge of a lifetime. And become my great work.

I've slept here once before, when I lay tracing with a wet forefinger the secret language. Who's to say it wasn't a warning? Who can be sure we haven't already been told what will happen? The white lettering, gleaming, like crystal milk, ignored all this time. And now it's too late.

That was the first flood. "The inundation" they called it on the news. These days the waves are higher and come further in. But the fairground reopened, as it always does. And the Blue Dolphin started up again, selling its cheap food. That food people around here were brought up to eat, the chips, the faggots, and peas. Twice to my knowledge it's been flooded out, and twice tried again.

When Zigmas died many other people drowned, but I remember only Zigmas. That strawberry birthmark on his cheek, his hair so blond it was almost white. Yes, it's only Zig I dream about, a boy running into the ghost train tunnel, thinking he'd be safe. People say the water rose to the roof, the hounds of hell floated away when their chains came loose. The hounds' eyes were yellow as the quartz in the cave.

Most days now I'm out on the peninsula. Yes, the tides can be huge, but when the water's low I explore the caves. Chilly places, even when it's hot. And dark as dungeons. Once I found a drowned porpoise, its beak a mattock of polished bone. But when the sun is in the right place the light shines directly into the cavemouths. That's when you see the starfish, the anemones.

Violet and red, those creatures. I listen to their breathing, the music they make.

Yes, since the inundation I've been relearning the old skills. Teaching myself what we should never have allowed ourselves to forget. That's the reason I've decided to live here. Because my father told me he was a beachcomber. Or that's what he said I'd become. Yes, he used to say, all of us will be beachcombers, one day. Almost a prophet, I might say. That was my father. And I am his prophecy.

But there's no food here. And all the world tastes of salt. The caves so smooth, so cold, taste of salt when I lick the crevices in the limestone. The rocks, the starfish, they all taste of salt. Have you ever eaten starfish? Or sea anemones? Boiled or fried I can't make them taste of anything but salt. Even with a samphire garnish, a side of coralweed.

So we're all scavengers. Yes, that's what they call me but that's merely another word for beachcomber. And if you know your history you'll be aware how people around here lived. They took whatever washed ashore, the brandies, the silks. Everything a stoven hold supplied. They were wreckers, I suppose. Old skills passed down the generations. How often was the riot act read to clear the beaches of men days drunk? In World War II a cargo of Guinness was lost and divvied up. And there is so much else afloat these days. The ocean's become a rubbish tip, burning, steaming. Yet still it teems with bizarre creatures. That shark gives me nightmares, but there are sunfish now, swollen like zeppelins. *Mola mola* they call the sunfish, fat and round and silver with blue tattoos. More like the moon.

I look at the moon from the cavemouth where I camp, sometimes from the red container where the lifeguards kept their gear. All those surfboards and paddles? I burned them on the beach. There are so many camps now in the dunes, or out on the sand, it takes time to learn the protocols of fire.

Last year I came upon a sunfish of monstrous size. Over a ton, it surely was, and stranded on rocks. When ripped open, its belly was full of plastic bags. I dined for three weeks off the creature, as long as I dared. Salty steaks, but that's how the world tastes now. I had to use my stick against the dogs. These days I carry a piece of lead piping. Perfect heft in my hand, that bludgeon. But there are so many dogs now. Even in the caves I hear them baying at night. Those Alsatians look and sound like wolves. Big as the hounds of hell. Of course I need a weapon.

Nights, I'm sometimes in the cave. The same place Lizzy kissed me, though maybe, look, maybe it was mutual. Or maybe I might have touched. Her. On the breast, perhaps. That's natural isn't it? No reason to run away. Was there? But it's a different world now. I don't have time to worry about that. The old laws don't apply.

9.
Zigmas loved the forest. The sawn wood that washed ashore? Those thousands of white planks? It might have been his home over there in Litland. He came to the fairground, beside a foreign sea, to a place where no trees grew and only salt thrived. A world of caves and a prophesy in quartz. Somewhere he could have never imagined. The frayed edge of a continent. Where the land is drowning.

Now look, twenty miles across the bay is the Meridian tower. A splinter, the colour of cuttlebone, built for those who thought they owned all they surveyed. I've been there once, a week's expedition. The dogs are bad but people are worse. There are places where the land's officially abandoned, but I ignore all that. I picked a way through the rubbish brought ashore by the new tides. Such adventures I've had. The faces of the drowned . . .

But I can't get Zigmas out of my mind. That's why I dream about him, he's one of my ghosts, a boy brought up in an ocean of trees who had never seen a beach. They said he couldn't swim for that reason, and I see the filthy water rising in the tunnel, Zigmas in the dark with all the glass cases smashing as they topple about him, the flood reaching his chin, his eyes. Zigmas in the tunnel with the worst things in the world . . .

10.

The stars have vanished. As they do. I'm awake now on a painted beach. Yes, the stone is breathing. I know the stone is alive. Under my body what's written in quartz spells out this world's fate. I feel the letters burning into my skin. Yes, it's agony, but I will lie here as they brand me, those words, and one day people will come to read the living prophesy.

I used to look at the sky and the jet trails there. I thought that was writing and it was written for me. The white lines were like quartz in the sky. But I was wrong. The prophecies have been here all along, given to me alone to understand. When I move I will be ready. And I am almost ready.

Author Biographies

Rui Manuel Amaral was born in Oporto in 1973, where he continues to live and work. He is the author of two books of short stories, *Caravana* (Caravan), published in 2008, and *Doutor Avalanche* (Doctor Avalanche), published in 2010. He is also the author of several books on the oral history and folk traditions of the city of Porto.

Kjell Askildsen was born in 1929 in Mandal, in southern Norway. At the age of twenty-four, he published his first collection of short stories, *Heretter følger jeg deg helt hjem* (From Now on I'll Walk You all the Way Home, 1953). In the '60s and '70s, Askildsen's output was restricted to short novels inspired by the works of such *nouveau roman* authors as Claude Simon and Alain Robbe-Grillet. In the '80s, he turned his back on the novel form for good after the publication in 1983 of his much-lauded story collection *Thomas F's siste nedtegnelser til almenheten* (*Thomas F's Last Notes to the General Public*, translated into English in the collection *A Sudden Liberating Thought* in 1994), for which he was awarded the Norwegian Critics' Prize for Literature. His later collections include *Hundene i Tessaloniki* (The Dogs in Thessaloniki, 1996), *Et stort øde landskap* (A Great Deserted Landscape, 1991), and *En plutselig frigjørende tanke* (1987; *A Sudden Liberating Thought*, 1994).

Askildsen has received numerous literary awards. Among them are The Critics' Prize (1983 and 1991), the Aschehoug Prize (1991), the Dobloug Prize (1996), the Brage Honorary Prize (1996), the Swedish Academy's Nordic Prize (2009) and the Sørlandet Honorary Prize (2010). In 1991, he was nominated to the Nordic Council's Prize for Literature. His books have been translated into more than twenty languages. He lives and works in Norway.

KATYA ATANASOVA was born in Sofia. She has an MA in Bulgarian Literature from Sofia University and an MA in Cultural and Literature Studies from New Bulgarian University. She has taught literature and has worked as a reviewer and editor for the weekly *Capital* as well as *Literature Newspaper*, and as producer of the urban culture show *Reflex* at Radio France International.

Katya has also worked in advertising, as creative director for Ideo Saatchi & Saatchi and Bright&Right, and as editor-in-chief for *EGO* and *Bulgaria Air Inflight Magazine*. Currently she is employed as a producer for Bulgarian National Television. She is the founder of the League of Storytellers (Bulgaria's only competition for oral storytelling, running since 2005), and has edited numerous books, including work by Radoslav Parushev, Jordan Petkov, and Nikola Miladinov. Her own first collection of short fiction, *Nespokoĭni istorii* (Restless Stories), was published in 2006. She is also the author of a play entitled *Eating the Apple*, now in performance.

XURXO BORRAZÁS was born in Carballo, Galicia, in 1963. He writes in Galician and has been called the enfant terrible of contemporary Galician literature. He has written novels, short stories, and essays, and has received many prizes, including the Spanish Critics Award and the Galician Critics Award. Some of his first novels helped to introduce postmodern narrative techniques into Galician letters. His fiction is often considered transgressive and he is particularly provocative in his essays, for example in his successful and controversial book *Arte e Parte: Dos Patriarcas á Arte Suicida* (Inside Writing: An Engaged Intruder's View, 2007), a challenging collection of essays on literature and politics.

Eric Chevillard was born in 1964 in La Roche-sur-Yon in the west of France. He published his first novel, *Mourir m'enrhume* (Dying Gives Me a Cold, 1987), at the age of twenty-three, and has since gone on to publish more than twenty works of fiction, including *La Nébuleuse du crabe* (1993; *The Crab Nebula*, 1997), *Au plafond* (1997; *On the Ceiling*, 2000), *Palafox* (1990; 2004), and *Démolir Nisard* (2006; *Demolishing Nisard*, 2011). He maintains a website at http://www.eric-chevillard.net.

Jens Dittmar was born in West Germany in 1950, and raised in Liechtenstein. After studying German language and literature in Zurich and Vienna, he worked as an editor for publishing houses in Munich and Stuttgart, and compiled the volume *Thomas Bernhard: Werkgeschichte* (Thomas Bernhard: Work History, 1981)—a comprehensive bibliography of writings, reviews, and translations by and of Thomas Bernhard. Back in Liechtenstein, he began publishing his own fiction in 2010 with the novel *Basils Welt* (Basil's World). This was followed by the story collection *Als wär's ein Stück Papier* (As If It's a Piece of Paper, 2011), and his second novel, *Sterben kann jeder* (Anyone can Die, 2010). Dittmar's forthcoming novel, *So kalt und schön*, from which "His Cryptologists" was excerpted, will appear in early 2014.

Guram Dochanashvili was born in Tbilisi in 1939. He graduated from Tbilisi State University and subsequently worked for the Institute of History, Archeology and Ethnography as an archeologist. His first work was published in 1966 and he has since published numerous short stories and novellas. From 1975 he spent ten years managing the prose section of the literary magazine *Mnatobi*, and since 1985 he has been the director of Georgian Film Studios. His most popular work is the 1975 novel *The First Garment*. His work has also appeared in Dalkey Archive Press's anthology *Contemporary Georgian Fiction*.

NINA GABRIELYAN, born in 1953, an Armenian living in Moscow, writes poetry and prose in Russian as well as being a successful painter and scholar writing on feminism. She has several collections of poetry to her name, two collections of short stories, and the short novel *Khozoain travy* (2001), which was translated and published by Glas along with a selection of her stories as *Master of the Grass* in 2004.

ELVIS HADZIC was born in 1971 in Gradačac, Bosnia and Herzegovina. After graduating from the School of Applied Arts in Sarajevo, he was a refugee in Austria and Germany, where he had art shows in Stuttgart, Aachen, and Mönchengladbach. He started writing columns for Bosnian websites in 2010, and published his initial short stories there. His first novel, *Beštije i Aveti* (Beasts and Ghosts) was published 2012. He currently lives in Salt Lake City.

VLADIMÍR HAVRILLA was born in 1943 in Bratislava, Slovakia. He studied sculpture at the Academy of Fine Arts and Design in Bratislava and later worked there as a professor in the sculpture department. In the '70s, he focused on experimental film as well as classic and conceptual sculpture, along with traditional media such as drawing, painting, and ceramics. From the end of the 1990s on, he devoted his time to computer graphics and 3D computer animation. In 2007, he published a book entitled *Filmové poviedky* (Film Short Stories). For more information, please visit www.havrilla.net.

Born in Montreal in 1965, THIERRY HORGUELIN has lived in Belgium since 1991. During the last twenty years, he has worked as a book reviewer and film critic for numerous magazines and newspapers in Canada, France, and Belgium. A former bookseller, he worked as a freelance translator, copyeditor, and proofreader for various publishers in France and Belgium. He is currently a member of the editorial board of the Montreal-based bilingual journal *Le Bathyscaphe*, copyeditor-in-chief at *Indications* (Brussels), editor and book designer for les éditions Le Cormier (Brussels) and assistant manager of Espace Livres & Création, a Belgian small-press network. His books include *Le Voyageur de la nuit* (The Night Voyager, 2005), *La Nuit sans fin* (Endless Night, 2009), and *Choses vues* (Lost and Found, 2012). *La Nuit sans fin* received the Franz de Wever Book Award in 2009. For more information, visit www.locus-solus-fr.net.

OLJA SAVIČEVIĆ IVANČEVIĆ was born in Split in 1974, and published her first collections of poetry when she was fourteen years old. She studied linguistics and literature at the University of Zadar, and works as a columnist for the newspaper *Slobodna Dalmacija*. Her first book of fiction, *Nasmijati psa* (Making a Dog Laugh) won the prize awarded by the prestigious magazine *Vijenac* for the best work of prose published in 2006, as well as the Ranko Marinković Prize for short-short stories. Her first novel, *Adio kauboju* won the *tportal* Prize for Literature as well as the Jure Kaštelan Award for Art in 2010, and will appear in an English translation by Celia Hawkesworth in 2015 as *Farewell, Cowboy*. Her poetry has been translated to English, French, Czech, Macedonian, Slovak, Slovenian, and Polish.

Born in 1972, VLADIMIR KOZLOV grew up in Mogilev, an industrial city in what was then the Belarussian Soviet Socialist Republic, now the country of Belarus. He has written more than a dozen books of fiction and nonfiction, many of which chronicle childhood, life, and popular culture during perestroika and the period following the Soviet Union's collapse. Several of his novels have been long-listed in Russia for honors such as the National Best-Seller Prize and Big Book Award. He was also nominated for *GQ Russia*'s Writer of the Year in 2011 and 2012. His most recent novel *Voina* (War) is due for release in the autumn of 2013, and he recently wrote, directed, and co-produced a feature-length independent film adaptation of his novella *Desyatka* (10). He currently lives in Moscow.

HERKUS KUNČIUS was born in Vilnius in 1965, and graduated from the Vilnius Academy of Art, majoring in art history and criticism. He is an essayist and playwright in addition to a renowned author of "grotesque" fiction, famous for satirizing the often absurd reality of life in Lithuania under Soviet rule and thereafter. Provocative and transgressive, Kunčius is as often accused of destroying Lithuanian literary traditions as he is praised for being its most radical exponent. His first novel, *Ir dugnas visada priglaus* (The Ground Will Always Give Shelter) was published in 1996. Since then he has published more than eight novels, eight plays, one book of fairy tales, and one book of short stories. He lives and works in Vilnius.

VESNA LEMAIĆ was born in 1981, and lives in Ljubljana, Slovenia. She has a degree in Comparative Literature, was the founder of the Anonymous Readers reading project, is a member of the informal Lesbian Feminist University initiative, and is actively involved in the program activities of a gay club in the Autonomous Cultural Zone Metelkova in Ljubljana. She was an activist in the Slovenian Occupy movement and continues to be involved in struggles against the European Crisis policies. She made her debut as a fiction writer in 2008 with her book of short stories entitled *Popularne zgodbe* (Popular Stories), which won the 2009 Zlata ptica Award, the 2009 Slovenian Book Fair Award, and the 2010 Fabula Award. Lemaić has also received the Radio Slovenia Award and the Lapis Histriae Award for two of her short stories, and thinks awards are especially good for filling up empty spaces in author biographies. Her novel *Odlagališče* (The Dumping Ground) was published in 2010, and she is also the author of a radio play. She believes in solidarity, grassroots movements, fighting power relations, and is always out hunting for new ideals.

Óskar Magnússon was born in Iceland in 1954. He holds law degrees from the University of Iceland, Reykjavik and George Washington University, Washington, DC. He has published two collections of short stories—*Borðaði ég kvöldmat í gær?* (Did I Eat Supper Last Night? 2006), and *Ég sé ekkert svona gleraugnalaus* (I Can't See a Thing Without My Glasses, 2010)—as well as a novel, *Látið síga piltar* (Lower it Down Guys, 2013). Magnússon is widely known in the Icelandic business world as a news editor, attorney-at-law, CEO of a number of prominent companies, as well as a newspaper and website publisher.

Mox Mäkelä was born in 1958. Based in Finland, she is a multidisciplinary artist and an avant-garde filmmaker as well as an author. She has been exhibiting her work in Finland and across Europe since the 1970s, and studied at the Turku Art Academy from 1980 to 1984. She works with sound, image, and text, and produces installations, assemblages, and short films, the latter being presented for free online at netmox.net. Her recent works include *idiot ibidem*, a combination installation, text, film diary, sound diary, and music performance, presented at the Rantakasarmin Gallery in Helsinki, Finland, in 2003, and the short film projects *meta matka*, published online in 2010, and

Story Ambient, a spoken word video project launched on the web in 2011.

Prose writer and children's author IOAN MÂNĂSCURTĂ was born in Popești de Sus in the Drochia *raion* of the Moldavian Soviet Socialist Republic in 1953. He studied journalism at the Universitatea de Stat din Moldova and went on to work as an editor for *Tinerimea Moldovei* and *Femeia Moldovei* magazines. In 1992 he was appointed director of the Union of Moldovan Writers Press and he is currently director of the Princeps publishing house. He made his literary debut in 1979, with a collection of essays entitled *Noi și gândurile noastre* (We and Our Thoughts). His other published works include *Bărbații Universului* (Men of the Universe, 1980), *Artefact* (a children's novel, 1989), *Mâine, când ne vom întâlni pe Pământ* (Tomorrow When We Meet on Earth, 1989), *Tăierea capului* (The Beheading, 1995), *Primul meu dicționar în șase limbi paralele cu cea română* (My First Dictionary in Six Languages Parallel with Romanian, 2004), *Vânătoarea cea mare* (The Great Hunt, 2004), and *Înnodarea lui ceva cu altceva* (The Conjoining of Something with Something Else, 2006).

TOM MCCARTHY was born in London in 1969. His first two novels, *Remainder* and *Men in Space*, have been published internationally to great acclaim. *Remainder* was the winner of the fourth annual Believer Book Award in 2008, while McCarthy's third novel, *C*, was shortlisted for the Booker Prize in 2010. McCarthy is also the author of two works of nonfiction, *Tintin and the Secret of Literature* (2008), and *Transmission and the Individual Remix* (2012). McCarthy also serves as General Secretary of the International Necronautical Society (INS), a semi-fictitious avant-garde network. He was awarded the Windham-Campbell Literature Prize for literary achievement in 2013.

Susana Medina was born in Hampshire, England, in 1966 to a German mother of Czech origin and a Spanish father. Her family moved to Spain (Valencia) in 1968, where she was raised. She writes both in Spanish, her native language, and English. In 2012, she published *Red Tales Cuentos rojos* to critical acclaim (in English and Spanish, co-translated with Rosie Marteau), and her novel *Philosophical Toys* is forthcoming in 2014, offshoots of which include the short films *Buñuel's Philosophical Toys* and *Leather-bound Stories* (co-directed with Derek Ogbourne), which have been screened internationally. Her other books include a collection of poetry and aphorisms entitled *Souvenirs del Accidente* (Souvenirs from the Accident, 2004); the "anti-novel" *Trozos de Una* (Chunks of One, 1991), written when Medina was twenty-five years old, and which won a Generalitat Writing Grant; and *Borgesland: A Voyage Through the Infinite, Imaginary Places, Labyrinths, Buenos Aires, and other Psychogeographies and Figments of Space* (2006), which explores imaginary spaces in the oeuvre of Jorge Luis Borges. She has been awarded several literary prizes, including the Max Aub International Short Story Prize, and a writing grant from Arts Council England for her novel *Spinning Days of Night*, now in progress. Medina has also published a number of essays on literature, art, cinema, and photography, curated various well-received international art shows in abandoned spaces (*Space International*), contributed texts to art catalogues, exhibited at the Tate Modern, and collaborated with numerous artists. Her mixed media work can be found scattered on the Internet, and she maintains a website at www. susanamedina.net.

Robert Minhinnick was born in 1952 in Neath, South Wales. He studied at the Universities of Aberystwyth and Cardiff, and is one of the founders of Friends of the Earth (Cymru), for which he served as joint coordinator for several years. He is an advisor to the charity Sustainable Wales, and edits the international quarterly, *Poetry Wales*. His debut novel, *Sea Holly*, was published in 2007, and shortlisted for the 2008 Ondaatje Prize. Minhinnick's other books of prose are *Watching the Fire Eater* (1992), winner of the 1993 Arts Council of Wales Book of the Year Award; *Badlands* (1996); and *To Babel and Back* (2005), which won the 2006 Wales Book of the Year Award. His poetry collections include *A Thread in the Maze* (1978), Native Ground (1979), *Life Sentences* (1983), *The Dinosaur Park* (1985), *The Looters* (1989), and *Hey Fatman* (1994). A *Selected Poems* was published in 1999, followed by *After the Hurricane* (2002). In 2003, his translations from Welsh were published as *The Adulterer's Tongue: An Anthology of Welsh Poetry in Translation*. His latest books are both poetry collections: *The Keys of Babylon* (2011), shortlisted for the 2012 Wales Book of the Year Award, and a *New Selected Poems* (2012). Minhinnick lives in Porthcawl, South Wales

Renowned Estonian author Tõnu Õnnepalu was born in 1962 in Tallinn. He studied biology at the University of Tartu, and worked as a teacher of biology and chemistry on Hiiumaa Island until 1987, after which he became a freelance writer, translator, and journalist. He has worked as an editor at the literary magazine *Vikerkaar*, and for Estonia's Ministry of Foreign affairs, as the director of the Estonian Institute in Paris. He began his writing career as a poet in 1985, with a collection entitled *Jõeäärne maja* (A Riverside House). His breakthrough came in 1993 when, under the name "Emil Tode," he published the novel *Piiririik* (*Border State*, 2000), for which he received the annual literary award given by the Baltic Assembly.

Another pseudonym, Anton Nigov, published an autobiographical novel entitled *Harjutused* (Practicing) in 2002, while Emil Tode published a semi-sequel to *Border State* that same

year: *Raadio* (Radio). Õnnepalu's other books include the journal *Flandria päevik* (Flanders Diary, 2008), the poetry collection
Kevad ja suvi ja (Spring and Summer and, 2009), and the novels
Paradiis (Paradise, 2009) and *Mandala* (Mandala, 2012). He has
translated numerous works from French into Estonian, including books by François Mauriac, Charles Baudelaire, and Marcel
Proust.

KRYSTIAN PIWOWARSKI was born in 1956 in Bytom, Upper
Silesia, Poland. He graduated from the Silesian University with
a master's degree in Polish Philology. Piwowarski has worked
as a teacher, businessman, manual laborer, security guard,
journalist, and clerk over the course of his life. His first novel,
Londyńczyk (Londoner) was published in 1988; subsequently, he
has published five further novels—*Marlowe, Mann i Superman*
(Marlowe, Mann and Superman, 1989), *Kochankowie Roku
Kota* (Lovers in the Year of the Cat, 1991), *Paryżanin* (Parisian,
1994), *Homo Polonicus* (2002), and *Klaun* (Clown, 2008)—as
well as two collections of short stories. Currently, Piwowarski
lives with his wife Halina in Częstochowa, and works at the
Muzeum Częstochowskie. His daughter Ewa lives in the United
Kingdom and is a teacher.

CHRISTOPH SIMON is an award-winning Swiss novelist. Born
in 1972, he travelled in the Middle East, Poland, South America, London and New York before settling in Berne. He has
published four novels: his cult-hit debut, *Franz, oder Warum
Antilopen nebeneinander laufen* (Franz, or Why Antelopes Run
in Herds, 2001); *Luna Llena* (2003), which focuses on an ice-
cream parlor of that name; *Planet Obrist* (2005), the sequel to
Franz, nominated for the Ingeborg Bachmann Prize; and the
much-loved *Spaziergänger Zbinden* (2010) which appeared
in English in 2012 as *Zbinden's Progress*, translated by Donal

McLaughlin. Simon's most recent book is a collection of his short work, *Viel Gutes zum kleinen Preis* (Lots of Good Things at a Low Price, 2011), which, among other things, includes a sequence of "Fairy Tales from the World of Publishing" and reflects the author's considerable skills as a cartoonist. Simon has also published one collection of his poetry, as well as a book for children. In 2012, he had a six-month residency in New York, as reflected in the stories written in English and included on the website he maintains at www.christophsimon.ch.

LENA RUTH STEFANOVIĆ was born in Belgrade in 1970. She has received master's degrees in Russian literature and diplomacy at Kliment Ohridski University, Sofia, and the University of Montenegro, respectively. She worked for many years as an interpreter and advisor for the government of Montenegro. Her first published book was a collection of essays entitled *Arhetip čuda* (Archetype of Miracles, 2006). A collection of short-short stories appeared in 2008 as *Io Triumpe*, while her most recent title, the poetry collection *Đavo, jedna neautorizovana biografija* (The Devil, an Unauthorized Biography) was published in 2011. Stefanović has been a member of Montenegrin PEN since 2010, served as president of the Montenegrin jury for the European Union Prize for Literature in 2011, and was elected to the executive board of the European Writers' Council in 2013.

YURIY TARNAWSKY was born in Western Ukraine. During World War II, he emigrated with his family to Germany and then to the US. An engineer and linguist by training, he worked as computer scientist at IBM Corporation, specializing in natural language processing, and then as Professor of Ukrainian literature and culture at Columbia University. He is a cofounder of the avant-garde group of Ukrainian émigré writers known as the New York Group, as well as a member of the Writers' Union of

VESNA LEMAIĆ
NINA GABRIELYAN

Dalkey Archive Press
& Rosie Goldsmith
welcome you to the launch of

Best European Fiction 2014

Herkus Kunčius
Lithuania
Belovezh

Óskar Magnússon
Iceland
Dr. Amplatz

Drago Jančar
Slovenia
Best European Fiction 2014 preface

Tõnu Õnnepalu
Estonia
Interpretations

Susana Medina
Spain
Oestrogen

Robert Minhinnick
Wales
Scavenger

Books on sale at a 20% discount!

EMBASSY OF ICELAND

EMBASSY OF ESTONIA
IN LONDON

MINISTRY OF CULTURE
OF THE REPUBLIC
OF LITHUANIA

JAVNA AGENCIJA ZA KNJIGO REPUBLIKE SLOVENIJE
SLOVENIAN BOOK AGENCY

Ukraine. For his contribution to Ukrainian literature, in 2008, he was awarded the Prince Yaroslav the Wise Order of Merit by the Ukrainian Government. He writes in Ukrainian and English. His works have been translated into French, German, Italian, Polish, Portuguese, Romanian, and Russian.

In Ukrainian, he has authored nineteen collections of poetry, collected in the volumes *Poeziji pro nishcho i inshi poeziji na cju samu temu* (Poems About Nothing and Other Poems on the Same Subject, 1970) and *Jikh nemaje* (They Don't Exist, 1999); six plays (collected as *6x0* in 1998); and selected prose (collected as *Ne znaju* [I don't know] in 2000), containing *Shljakhy* (Roads), *Sim sprob* (Seven Tries), and *Bosonizh dodomu i nazad* (Running Barefoot Home and Back); a story collection *Korotki khvosty* (2006; *Short Tails*, 2011); and selected essays *Kvity khvoromu* (Flowers for the Patient, 2012). His English-language works include the novels *Meningitis* (1979) and *Three Blondes and Death* (1993), the story collection *Short Tails*, and three collections of "mininovels": *Like Blood in Water* (2007), *The Future of Giraffes*, and *View of Delft*, published together as *The Placebo Effect Trilogy* in 2013, as well as a collection of poetry titled *Modus Tollens* (2013).

VLADA UROŠEVIĆ was born in 1934 in Skopje. He is a Macedonian poet, prose writer, critic, essayist, editor, and translator. He holds a PhD in literature and was a full professor at the Ss. Cyril and Methodius University, where he taught courses on the history of European poetry. In the 1950s and 60s, Urošević was a leading member of the "modernists," who gathered around the magazine *Razgledi* (Panoramas) and strove not only for the modernization of Macedonian literature but for a liberalization of the intellectual climate in Macedonia in general. Beginning with his first book *Eden drug grad* (A Different City, 1959), Urošević has published a dozen collections of poetry and is the only Macedonian poet to be a three-time winner of the Brakja Miladinovci Prize for the best book of poetry at the Struga Poetry Evenings. He also writes in several other genres and has published four books of short stories, five novels, seven books of critcism and essays, two of travel literature, two on the fine arts, and has edited a dozen anthologies. He has translated the poetry of Baudelaire, Rimbaud, Apollinaire, Michaux, Breton, and other modern French poets into Macedonian. For his significant contribution to the translation of French poetry he was made a Knight of the Ordre des Arts et des Lettres, and later raised to an Officer of the same Order. He lives in Skopje.

INGA ZHOLUDE was born in 1984, and received her master's in English from the University of Latvia. She also studied English literature at Southern Illinois University (Carbondale) through the Fulbright Program, and has worked as a project coordinator and manager in the field of culture and education. She is currently studying for her doctorate at the University of Latvia. Her prose has appeared in Latvian periodicals since 2002, and she has been a member of the Latvian Writers' Union since 2010. Zholude's first book was the novel *Silta zeme* (Warm Earth), published in 2008. This was followed in 2010 by her short-story collection *Mierinājums Ādama kokam* (Solace for Adam's Tree), and, in 2012, her second novel *Sarkanie bērni* (Red Children).

Zholude has received several literary awards of major importance. In 2011, she was awarded the European Union Prize for Literature for *Mierinājums Ādama kokam*, while *Sarkanie bērni* won the Raimonds Gerkens Prize awarded by the Latvian Writers' Union.

Her stories and excerpts from her novels have been translated and published in anthologies in English, German, French, Swedish, Polish, Lithuanian, Hungarian, Czech, and other languages.

Translator Biographies

NEIL ANDERSON is a graduate student at the University of North Carolina at Chapel Hill where he studies contemporary Galician fiction and the intersection between Cultural Geography and literary studies. He Holds an MA in Spanish from Middlebury College.

KHATUNA BERIDZE translates from English to Georgian, including works by Truman Capote and Oscar Wilde, as well as from Georgian to English. She obtained her doctorate in philology, with a specialization in translation, from Tbilisi State Technical University in 2009.

ŠPELA BIBIČ holds a degree in Translation studies (English-French) and works as a freelance translator. She has translated two novels into Slovenian thus far—Renée Vivien's *Une femme m'apparut* and Georges Eekhoud's *Escal-Vigor*. Her English translations of short Slovenian fiction have appeared in numerous anthologies and journals.

ALISTAIR IAN BLYTH was born in Sunderland, England, attended the universities of Cambridge and Durham, and now lives in the foothills of the Carpathians, near the village of Bughea de Jos. He translates fiction, poetry and philosophy by authors from the Republic of Moldova and Romania.

CHRISTOPHER BURAWA is a poet and translator. His awards include the 2010 Joy Harjo Poetry Award, a 2007 NEA Literature Fellowship for Translation, and a 2008 American-

Scandinavian Foundation Creative Writing Fellowship. He is the Director of the Center of Excellence for the Creative Arts at Austin Peay State University in Clarksville, Tennessee.

ADAM CULLEN originates from Minneapolis, Minnesota. He currently resides in Tallinn, Estonia, where he moved in 2007 to become fluent in Estonian through complete immersion. His complete translation of Emil Tode / Tõnu Õnnepalu's novel *Radio* will be published in 2014.

WILL FIRTH was born in 1965 in Newcastle, Australia. He studied German and Slavic languages in Canberra, Zagreb, and Moscow. Since 1991 he has been living in Berlin, Germany, where he works as a freelance translator of literature and the humanities. He translates from Russian, Macedonian, and all variants of Serbo-Croatian.

MICHAELA FREEMAN was born in 1975 in Prague. She is a freelance translator, writer, web designer, digital artist, and creativity coach. She focuses on specialty and creative translations from Czech to English. For this, she teams up with her husband, Jim Freeman, a writer, proofreader, and editor. She maintains a website at michaela-freeman.com.

MARGITA GAILITIS was born in Riga, Latvia, and grew up in Canada. In 1998 she returned to Latvia to work on a Canadian International Development Agency-sponsored project translating Latvian laws into English. Her poetry has been published in Canada and the US, and she is the recipient of Ontario Arts and Canada Council awards. In 2011, she was awarded the Order of the Three Stars by the President of Latvia.

Soren A. Gauger is a Canadian who has lived for over a decade in Krakow, Poland. He has published two books of short fiction (*Hymns to Millionaires* and *Quatre Regards sur l'Enfant Jesus*) and translations of numerous Polish writers (including Jerzy Ficowski, Bruno Jasienski, and Wojciech Jagielski).

Edward Gauvin has received fellowships and residencies from the NEA, the Fulbright Foundation, the Centre National du Livre, Ledig House, the Banff Centre, and ALTA. His work includes *A Life on Paper* by Georges-Olivier Châteaureynaud and publications in *Conjunctions*, *World Literature Today*, *Tin House*, and the *Harvard Review*, among others. The winner of the John Dryden Translation Prize, he is the contributing editor for Francophone comics at *Words Without Borders*. He maintains a website at edwardgauvin.com.

Andrea Gregovich is a writer and translator of Russian literature. Her translations of Kozlov and others have appeared in *Tin House*, *AGNI Review*, *Hayden's Ferry Review*, *3:AM Magazine*, *Cafe Irreal*, and two anthologies of Russian writing. She lives in Anchorage, Alaska.

Seán Kinsella is from Ireland. He holds an MPhil in Literary Translation from Trinity College, Dublin, and in addition to contributing translations to several years of *Best European Fiction*, he has translated two novels by Stig Sæterbakken, as well as a collection of Kjell Askildsen's short stories, which will appear in 2014. He currently lives in Norway with his wife and two small daughters.

Vija Kostoff is a linguist by education, and a language teacher, writer, and editor by profession. She has been collaborating with Margita Gailitis for more than ten years in translating the novels, short stories, plays, film scripts, and poetry of many of Latvia's major writers. Born in Latvia, she now resides in Niagara on the Lake, Ontario, Canada where she exercises her secondary passions for gardening and painting.

NATE LA MESHI is a freelance translator and language teacher, and lives in Boston.

ROSIE MARTEAU translates from Spanish, having lived and studied in Barcelona and travelled throughout Latin America. Her published work includes *Washing Dishes in Hotel Paradise* by Eduardo Belgrano Rawson, and a collaboration with Susana Medina and Anne McLean on Medina's short story collection *Red Tales Cuentos rojos*, published in a bilingual edition in 2012.

Irish Scot DONAL MCLAUGHLIN was featured in *BEF 2012* as both an author and a translator. Shortlisted for the Best Translated Book Award 2013 for his English edition of Urs Widmer's *My Father's Book*, he specializes in translating Swiss novels; in the case of Pedro Lenz, even from one dialect (Bernese) into another (Glaswegian). He maintains a website at donalmclaughlin.wordpress.com.

RHETT MCNEIL has translated work by João Almino, António Lobo Antunes, Machado de Assis, and Gonçalo M. Tavares into English.

MARCIN PIEKOSZEWSKI was born in Kluczbork, Poland. He studied at the English Departments of Opole University and Krakow's Jagiellonian University, graduating from the latter in American Literature. Having worked as a teacher, translator, journalist, and bookseller, he currently lives in Berlin where he runs a Polish-German bookshop.

KATINA ROGERS holds a PhD in Comparative Literature from the University of Colorado. In addition to translating contemporary francophone literature, she works on graduate education reform and emerging models of academic authoring and publishing at the Scholarly Communication Institute.

LOLA ROGERS is a Finnish to English literary translator living in Seattle. Lola's published translations include Riikka Pulkkinen's novels *True* and *The Limit*, and Sofi Oksanen's internationally acclaimed novel *Purge*. She is also a regular contributor to *Books from Finland*, *Words Without Borders*, and other publications.

NATHALIE ROY is a Russian-to-English translator based in Moscow.

BOGDAN RUSEV has an MA in English and American Literature from Sofia University. He is a published author and works in magazines, television, and advertising. He usually translates from English into Bulgarian, and has published translations of such different authors as F. Scott Fitzgerald, Charles Bukowski and China Miéville. He only translates from Bulgarian into English when he thinks a Bulgarian author is really worth it.

JAYDE WILL is a translator of Lithuanian, Estonian and Russian literature into English. He has contributed to a number of magazines and anthologies, including the forthcoming *Dedalus Book of Lithuanian Literature*. He has also translated the subtitles for a number of short and feature-length films, including *The Age of Milosz*, a documentary about Nobel Prize winner Czeslaw Milosz, as well as the award-winning Lithuanian film *Vanishing Waves*.

Liberté • Égalité • Fraternité
RÉPUBLIQUE FRANÇAISE
AMBASSADE DE FRANCE
AUX ETATS-UNIS

Service culturel

Republika
Hrvatska
Ministarstvo
kulture
Republic
of Croatia
Ministry
of Culture

Estonian
Literature
Centre

NORLA

MINISTRY OF CULTURE
AND MONUMENT PROTECTION
OF GEORGIA

POLISH CULTURAL INSTITUTE
www.PolishCulture.org.uk

DG LB
DIRECÇÃO-GERAL
DO LIVRO E DAS
BIBLIOTECAS

swiss arts council

pro helvetia

SPAIN
FOREIGN
CULTURAL
COOPERATION

FINNISH LITERATURE EXCHANGE

LITERÁRNE
INFORMAČNÉ
CENTRUM

Bókmenntasjóður
The Icelandic Literature Fund

PRINCIPALITY OF LIECHTENSTEIN

Elizabeth Kostova
FOUNDATION for
CREATIVE WRITING

Books
from
Lithuania

J A K JAVNA AGENCIJA ZA KNJIGO REPUBLIKE SLOVENIJE
SLOVENIAN BOOK AGENCY

Acknowledgments

Publication of *Best European Fiction 2014* was made possible by generous support from the following cultural agencies and embassies:

Books from Lithuania

Cultural Services of the French Embassy

DGLB—General Directorate for Books and Libraries / Portugal

Elizabeth Kostova Foundation

Embassy of the Principality of Liechtenstein
to the United States of America

Embassy of the Republic of Macedonia, Washington, D.C.

Embassy of Spain, Washington, D.C.

Estonian Literature Centre

Finnish Literature Exchange (FILI)

Icelandic Literature Fund

Literárne informačné centrum
(The Centre for Information on Literature),
Bratislava, Slovakia

The Ministry of Culture and Monument Protection of Georgia:
Program in Support of Georgian Books and Literature

NORLA: Norwegian Literature Abroad, Fiction & Nonfiction

The Polish Cultural Institute of London

Pro Helvetia, Swiss Arts Council

Republic of Croatia, Ministry of Culture,
Directorate for the Development of Culture and Art

The Slovenian Book Agency (JAK)

Rights and Permissions

SELECTED DALKEY ARCHIVE TITLES

FOR A FULL LIST OF PUBLICATIONS, VISIT:
www.dalkeyarchive.com

Janice Galloway, *Foreign Parts.*
The Trick Is to Keep Breathing.
William H. Gass, *Cartesian Sonata
and Other Novellas.*
Finding a Form.
A Temple of Texts.
The Tunnel.
Willie Masters' Lonesome Wife.
Gérard Gavarry, *Hoppla! 1 2 3.*
Etienne Gilson,
The Arts of the Beautiful.
Forms and Substances in the Arts.
C. S. Giscombe, *Giscome Road.*
Here.
Douglas Glover, *Bad News of the Heart.*
Witold Gombrowicz,
A Kind of Testament.
Paulo Emílio Sales Gomes, *P's Three
Women.*
Georgi Gospodinov, *Natural Novel.*
Juan Goytisolo, *Count Julian.*
Juan the Landless.
Makbara.
Marks of Identity.
Henry Green, *Back.*
Blindness.
Concluding.
Doting.
Nothing.
Jack Green, *Fire the Bastards!*
Jiří Gruša, *The Questionnaire.*
Mela Hartwig, *Am I a Redundant
Human Being?*
John Hawkes, *The Passion Artist.*
Whistlejacket.
Elizabeth Heighway, ed., *Contemporary
Georgian Fiction.*
Aleksandar Hemon, ed.,
Best European Fiction.
Aidan Higgins, *Balcony of Europe.*
Blind Man's Bluff
Bornholm Night-Ferry.
Flotsam and Jetsam.
Langrishe, Go Down.
Scenes from a Receding Past.
Keizo Hino, *Isle of Dreams.*
Kazushi Hosaka, *Plainsong.*
Aldous Huxley, *Antic Hay.*
Crome Yellow.
Point Counter Point.
Those Barren Leaves.
Time Must Have a Stop.
Naoyuki Ii, *The Shadow of a Blue Cat.*
Gert Jonke, *The Distant Sound.*
Geometric Regional Novel.
Homage to Czerny.
The System of Vienna.
Jacques Jouet, *Mountain R.*
Savage.
Upstaged.

Mieko Kanai, *The Word Book.*
Yoram Kaniuk, *Life on Sandpaper.*
Hugh Kenner, *Flaubert.*
Joyce and Beckett: The Stoic Comedians.
Joyce's Voices.
Danilo Kiš, *The Attic.*
Garden, Ashes.
The Lute and the Scars
Psalm 44.
A Tomb for Boris Davidovich.
Anita Konkka, *A Fool's Paradise.*
George Konrád, *The City Builder.*
Tadeusz Konwicki, *A Minor Apocalypse.*
The Polish Complex.
Menis Koumandareas, *Koula.*
Elaine Kraf, *The Princess of 72nd Street.*
Jim Krusoe, *Iceland.*
Ayşe Kulin, *Farewell: A Mansion in
Occupied Istanbul.*
Emilio Lascano Tegui, *On Elegance
While Sleeping.*
Eric Laurrent, *Do Not Touch.*
Violette Leduc, *La Bâtarde.*
Edouard Levé, *Autoportrait.*
Suicide.
Mario Levi, *Istanbul Was a Fairy Tale.*
Deborah Levy, *Billy and Girl.*
José Lezama Lima, *Paradiso.*
Rosa Liksom, *Dark Paradise.*
Osman Lins, *Avalovara.*
The Queen of the Prisons of Greece.
Alf Mac Lochlainn,
The Corpus in the Library.
Out of Focus.
Ron Loewinsohn, *Magnetic Field(s).*
Mina Loy, *Stories and Essays of Mina Loy.*
D. Keith Mano, *Take Five.*
Micheline Aharonian Marcom,
The Mirror in the Well.
Ben Marcus,
The Age of Wire and String.
Wallace Markfield,
Teitlebaum's Window.
To an Early Grave.
David Markson, *Reader's Block.*
Wittgenstein's Mistress.
Carole Maso, *AVA.*
Ladislav Matejka and Krystyna
Pomorska, eds.,
*Readings in Russian Poetics:
Formalist and Structuralist Views.*
Harry Mathews, *Cigarettes.*
The Conversions.
*The Human Country: New and
Collected Stories.*
The Journalist.
My Life in CIA.
Singular Pleasures.
*The Sinking of the Odradek
Stadium.*
Tlooth.

JOSEPH MCELROY,
  Night Soul and Other Stories.
ABDELWAHAB MEDDEB, Talismano.
GERHARD MEIER, Isle of the Dead.
HERMAN MELVILLE, The Confidence-Man.
AMANDA MICHALOPOULOU, I'd Like.
STEVEN MILLHAUSER, The Barnum Museum.
  In the Penny Arcade.
RALPH J. MILLS, JR., Essays on Poetry.
MOMUS, The Book of Jokes.
CHRISTINE MONTALBETTI, The Origin of Man.
  Western.
OLIVE MOORE, Spleen.
NICHOLAS MOSLEY, Accident.
  Assassins.
  Catastrophe Practice.
  Experience and Religion.
  A Garden of Trees.
  Hopeful Monsters.
  Imago Bird.
  Impossible Object.
  Inventing God.
  Judith.
  Look at the Dark.
  Natalie Natalia.
  Serpent.
  Time at War.
WARREN MOTTE,
  Fables of the Novel: French Fiction
    since 1990.
  Fiction Now: The French Novel in
    the 21st Century.
  Oulipo: A Primer of Potential
    Literature.
GERALD MURNANE, Barley Patch.
  Inland.
YVES NAVARRE, Our Share of Time.
  Sweet Tooth.
DOROTHY NELSON, In Night's City.
  Tar and Feathers.
ESHKOL NEVO, Homesick.
WILFRIDO D. NOLLEDO, But for the Lovers.
FLANN O'BRIEN, At Swim-Two-Birds.
  The Best of Myles.
  The Dalkey Archive.
  The Hard Life.
  The Poor Mouth.
  The Third Policeman.
CLAUDE OLLIER, The Mise-en-Scène.
  Wert and the Life Without End.
GIOVANNI ORELLI, Walaschek's Dream.
PATRIK OUŘEDNÍK, Europeana.
  The Opportune Moment, 1855.
BORIS PAHOR, Necropolis.
FERNANDO DEL PASO, News from the
  Empire.
  Palinuro of Mexico.
ROBERT PINGET, The Inquisitory.
  Mahu or The Material.
  Trio.
MANUEL PUIG, Betrayed by Rita Hayworth.

The Buenos Aires Affair.
  Heartbreak Tango.
RAYMOND QUENEAU, The Last Days.
  Odile.
  Pierrot Mon Ami.
  Saint Glinglin.
ANN QUIN, Berg.
  Passages.
  Three.
  Tripticks.
ISHMAEL REED, The Free-Lance Pallbearers.
  The Last Days of Louisiana Red.
  Ishmael Reed: The Plays.
  Juice!
  Reckless Eyeballing.
  The Terrible Threes.
  The Terrible Twos.
  Yellow Back Radio Broke-Down.
JASIA REICHARDT, 15 Journeys Warsaw
  to London.
NOËLLE REVAZ, With the Animals.
JOÃO UBALDO RIBEIRO, House of the
  Fortunate Buddhas.
JEAN RICARDOU, Place Names.
RAINER MARIA RILKE, The Notebooks of
  Malte Laurids Brigge.
JULIÁN RÍOS, The House of Ulysses.
  Larva: A Midsummer Night's Babel.
  Poundemonium.
  Procession of Shadows.
AUGUSTO ROA BASTOS, I the Supreme.
DANIËL ROBBERECHTS, Arriving in Avignon.
JEAN ROLIN, The Explosion of the
  Radiator Hose.
OLIVIER ROLIN, Hotel Crystal.
ALIX CLEO ROUBAUD, Alix's Journal.
JACQUES ROUBAUD, The Form of a
  City Changes Faster, Alas, Than
  the Human Heart.
  The Great Fire of London.
  Hortense in Exile.
  Hortense Is Abducted.
  The Loop.
  Mathematics:
  The Plurality of Worlds of Lewis.
  The Princess Hoppy.
  Some Thing Black.
RAYMOND ROUSSEL, Impressions of Africa.
VEDRANA RUDAN, Night.
STIG SÆTERBAKKEN, Siamese.
  Self Control.
LYDIE SALVAYRE, The Company of Ghosts.
  The Lecture.
  The Power of Flies.
LUIS RAFAEL SÁNCHEZ,
  Macho Camacho's Beat.
SEVERO SARDUY, Cobra & Maitreya.
NATHALIE SARRAUTE,
  Do You Hear Them?
  Martereau.
  The Planetarium.

FOR A FULL LIST OF PUBLICATIONS, VISIT:
www.dalkeyarchive.com